A West Tex

By H

MW01134365

Sweet Historical Western Romances

☆Estrella Publishing☆
October 2018

A West Texas Frontier Trilogy

Table of Contents

Ruth: The Rescued Bride

By Hebby Roman

Historical Western Romance

☆Estrella Publishing☆

Ruth: The Rescued Bride

Author's Note

In 1867 the United States Army established a permanent camp on the plateau where the North and Middle Concho rivers join, which is 210 miles northwest of San Antonio, Texas. For centuries, the high open plateau had remained barren except for passing expeditions or hunting parties.

With the opening of the Texas frontier after the war with México in 1849, American citizens began to cross into West Texas. They came seeking routes to the gold fields in California, to establish the short-lived Butterfield Overland Mail route in 1856, and to claim and settle the land, primarily as ranchers.

With the outbreak of the Civil War, the United States troops surrendered all the frontier posts in Texas to the Confederacy. The U.S. Army returned to Texas after the defeat of the Confederacy in 1865. By 1866, the famous Goodnight-Loving cattle trail followed the Middle Concho west. In 1867, a previous outpost, Fort Chadbourne, was relocated to a permanent outpost central to the area with a more reliable supply of water.

The soldiers, under the command of Major Hatch, chose the plateau at the junction of the rivers because of plentiful grass, an inexhaustible supply of limestone rock for building, and copious amounts of sweet water from the rivers.

The troopers were posted at what came to be known as Fort Concho to protect stage routes, supply lines, and settlers from Comanche and Kiowa raids. The town of San Angelo was founded as a result of the fort, primarily by Christian ministers and businessmen who brought civilization to the wild frontier area.

This book follows the general outline of the history of Fort Concho, but all the characters herein are fictional, with the occasional mention of well-known historical persons.

Ruth: The Rescued Bride

Chapter One

Near Fort Concho, Texas—1874

Eka Huutsuu bent her head and shifted the burden of firewood on her back. A twinge of pain pierced her abdomen, and she cradled her big belly. Her time was near, and she was filled with fear. Another sharper pain sliced through her.

She'd been having pains for the past few days. One would come and then maybe another. Then... nothing.

She stumbled forward, gritting her teeth, skirting the Chief's teepee. Her ankle hit something and suddenly, she was falling. She landed on her side and rolled to protect her unborn child.

She glimpsed a brown arm disappear under the teepee's edge and heard a burst of giggles. She wasn't surprised. *Wahaatu Mua,* the Chief's daughter, had made her life a misery since she'd been captured. And the other squaws had followed her lead.

In the beginning, she'd persevered, clinging to life, unable to shake the awful images of her family being slaughtered. Later, *Tasiwoo Pihi* had been kind, opening his heart and taking her to wife. He'd protected her and, as the foremost warrior of the tribe, he was powerful. But he was often away, hunting game. She'd learned to fend for herself, as best she could. And now she needed to endure for the sake of her unborn child.

But the Chief's daughter, *Wahaatu Mua,* Two Moons, hadn't forgiven her for taking the brave she wanted to marry. Not that her husband couldn't have more than one wife, Comanche fashion, but Two Moons would never consent to be a second wife.

Instead, Two Moons amused herself, making her life miserable.

The firewood lay scattered across the ground, and her body ached, particularly her right side. She'd have a dark bruise on her hip. Her husband would ask about it. She'd make some excuse, claiming she was clumsy, now that she was so big. It was simpler that way.

The Chief had lost both his sons to the soldiers. He was old and only had his daughter. And as much as he esteemed *Tasiwoo*

Pihi as a powerful warrior, *Eka Huutsuu* knew he grew tired of the simmering resentment over a captive, who should have been a slave, not an honored wife.

She stroked her belly and was rewarded with a strong kick. She smiled to herself.

The ground was hard and cold. It had been a bitter winter. She shivered and got to her knees. She levered herself to her feet. Then she bent over again to gather the scattered firewood.

"Deɪmdʒɚ, deɪmdʒɚ, taibo, soldiers coming! Danger, danger, white men, soldiers!" One of the youths who guarded the horse herd came running into camp.

At the mention of "soldiers," her heart leapt into her throat, and she longed to run toward the white men. But with the tribe surrounding her, boiling out of their teepees like a wasp nest that had been poked, she knew better than to try.

She dropped the firewood.

Tasiwoo Pihi, or Buffalo Heart, appeared as if from nowhere, fitted for battle with a carbine slung over his shoulder, a stolen soldier's sword lashed to his waist, and his hunting knife tied to his thigh. He was leading her docile paint pony, along with his powerful sorrel stallion.

He walked with a slight limp from an earlier battle. He'd been laid up for months with his wounded leg. When she'd first been brought to the camp, she'd been charged with caring for him. She'd used all the nursing skills her mother had taught her, even sewing up his wound so it could heal properly.

In some strange way, though he was the enemy, she'd felt sorry for him. He was a proud man, a warrior. He despised being wounded and lame. She'd taught him to hobble around, using a stout stick as a makeshift crutch, and he'd appreciated her. A bond had been formed.

"*Kʌm*. Come," her husband commanded, gesturing toward her horse. "We must go," he said in Comanche. "No time. Must run."

Obedient, she took the ends of the rope reins. Her husband, solicitous of their unborn child, helped to boost her onto the paint's back.

Ruth: The Rescued Bride

Her brothers had taught her to ride when she was a child. But riding with a bridle, saddle, and stirrups was different from how the Comanche rode. She had to make do with a simple rope hackamore looped around the horse's muzzle and a thin blanket covering its back.

Buffalo Heart rounded up the Comanches who were already mounted and herded them forward.

If the soldiers did come, they'd burn everything. The teepees, their hordes of food, buffalo robes, discarded bows and arrows. They'd smash pottery, wicker baskets, cooking pots, travois poles, and anything else they could find.

Not that she blamed the soldiers. They were her people, and this was war. Both sides were capable of vicious measures to terrorize and destroy the enemy.

But it was winter—there would be no way they could replace their meager possessions. They would need to take shelter with another tribe to survive.

The Chief had chosen a box canyon to spend the winter, whose entrance was hidden by a grove of live oak trees, hoping the soldiers wouldn't find them. But Buffalo Heart, ever cautious, had made certain there was another way out.

At the far end of the canyon, behind a jumble of giant boulders, there was a wild goat track, threading its way to the top of the canyon and onto the open plains above. That's where Buffalo Heart was leading them.

A smattering of snow fell from the dark, heavy-hanging clouds, dusting her face and shoulders. She shivered and clasped a thin blanket around her, pulling it tighter.

Her paint pony picked up speed, and she clutched his mane. Without guidance, her pony followed her husband's sorrel, dodging around a clump of purple-budded prickly pear, almost unseating her. She was thrown forward onto her horse's withers, and she thumped down against his hard backbone.

She winced and a gush of water coated her thighs, instantly chilling her. Alarmed, she looked down to see a dark stain spreading on the striped blanket.

No, no, no, not now!

Ruth: The Rescued Bride

She couldn't be giving birth. Not now, when all their lives depended on fleeing. But she knew the signs.

Hiʔopi, an older woman and her only friend in the tribe, had explained birthing to her, or as much as she was able to understand with her limited knowledge of the Comanche tongue.

She'd seen Comanche women giving birth. They would be scraping hides, butchering game, gathering firewood, erecting teepees, or working at any of the many unending tasks, only to stop, squat, and give birth. Then with the newborn child at their breast, they'd return to work, as if nothing had happened.

There were no midwives among the Comanche. If it was a difficult birth, the older women would help the pregnant mother—that was the exception.

But she wasn't Comanche. She was white. She was a captive, and her name wasn't *Eka Huutsuu*—her name was Ruth MacDonald.

She opened her mouth to tell her husband what was happening, but he'd sheared off and turned away to speak with the Chief.

She would endure—she had no choice.

Searing agony spiked through her. She panted and clung to her pony's mane. Then the cramp ebbed away, and she exhaled. It was only a brief respite, and more pains followed.

Her husband came beside her again, looked into her face, and frowned.

She looked away, not wanting him to see her weakness. He'd risked a lot, taking her to wife, against the wishes of the Chief and most of the tribe. She respected and admired him, knowing if he hadn't married her, she would have become the most wretched of beings, a camp slave.

As the leading warrior of the tribe, he needed to take them to safety. He leaned forward and touched her arm. Then he slapped her pony's rump and dug his heels into the sorrel, urging his mount forward.

Another pain pummeled her. Her heart raced and despite the snow falling on her, she was covered in foul-smelling sweat. The place between her thighs was sore and tender, bouncing on the back of the horse. With her thighs spread over his spiny back, the birthing pains made her feel as if she was splitting in two, like a deer spitted over a cooking fire.

She closed her eyes, ground her teeth, and prayed.

The two miles to the canyon wall stretched on and on. Seconds ticked by, slow and agonizing, her body racked by torment.

Finally, the boulders loomed before her, and her husband returned, taking hold of her pony's hackamore and leading her onto the almost-invisible track.

She swayed on the paint's back, unable to stay upright. Twisting and groaning, she wanted the pains to go away. She needed to stop and let the baby come.

Please, dear Lord, let the child come.

The contractions crested, coming closer and closer together. Leaving her panting and groaning, knowing the vicious torture would start again soon.

Buffalo Heart leaned close and in guttural Comanche, he asked, "The baby is coming. Yes?"

She panted, and her body spasmed. "*Haa*. Yes. The baby comes."

"Here. We stop here." He led her into a grove of mesquite trees huddled against the canyon walls. As another contraction ebbed, she glanced around. The trees were thick and low-hanging, a dense covering.

She looked over her shoulder, glimpsing a long line of braves, squaws, and children, some mounted and some on foot, climbing the canyon wall, half-hidden by the barrier of boulders. She couldn't follow. *Not now.*

Her husband led her into the thicket and threw his horse blanket onto the ground next to an ancient, gnarled mesquite tree. Then he lifted her off the paint and lowered her to the blanket.

Another contraction seized her, the agony unbearable, and she writhed and moaned, trying to escape the pain's vicious grasp. But there was no escape. She wanted to curl in on herself, anything to make the pain go away. And she prayed harder, wishing for the brief moment between contractions to gather her waning strength.

She needed to... needed to... Her body contorted and spasmed, and she opened her mouth to scream. But her husband thrust a stick into her mouth and put his finger to his lips.

"No cry out. Go and cover tracks." He stroked her cheek. "Come back soon."

The contraction passed, and she nodded.

"Good." He vaulted onto his sorrel and rode away.

Another spike of searing agony overtook her. She dug her fingernails into the dirt and gasped, panting, breathing in and out, as her friend, *Hiʔopi* or Sunflower, had taught her. Wave after wave of agony washed over her. Seconds ticked by, lengthening into minutes. She thrashed and struggled, and time stood still. The moments were torment, dipped in red-hot agony. How she wished Sunflower was with her.

A sharp spattering of gunshots shredded the silence. What if Buffalo Heart...? Then the agony gripped her again, and she bit down hard on the stick, almost crushing it in two.

Her body felt as if it was coming apart at the seams, and she wanted to push. The need was overwhelming. She grunted and lurched up, spreading her thighs wide and bearing down, pushing.

Covered in sweat and chewing on the stick, she pushed and pushed. Her insides were shredding. Buffalo Heart wasn't coming back. She and her baby were going to die with the soft snow drifting over them, covering them like the earth of their graves.

She shuddered, and pushed, and then there was a gush; a steaming stream rushed from her. Blood and more blood and water, too.

She glimpsed down and saw the wizened, miss-shaped head of her baby. She pushed once more, and his body slithered out.

The pain subsided, and she leaned forward, wanting to gather her child into her arms. Wanting to live, wanting her child to live. Wanting...

The sudden movement made her dizzy. Red and black dots danced before her eyes, like so many blow flies. But there were no blow flies in winter. She shook her head to clear it and tried to pick up her baby.

But her arms were weak. She couldn't lift them. Something was wrong. And her head was spinning. She tried to concentrate, tried to reach for her baby. A hollowness seized her, and her limbs turned to mush, liquified and useless.

She slumped back, hitting her head against the rough bark of the mesquite tree. She moaned and spit out the stick. Her eyes closed... and then there was nothing.

* * *

Jacob Wells dismounted from his pinto pony and kneeled down, studying the unshod hoofprints in the light dusting of snow. Snow, this far south in Texas, was unusual, but the winter had been a cold one. Despite the snow, tracking the Comanche wasn't easy.

The horsemen of the plains, his mother's people, were accomplished at hiding their tracks: splitting up, doubling back, and making use of rocky stretches of ground to camouflage their horses' prints.

He looked up at the looming walls of the box canyon. It should be easy to find the hostiles within the canyon, but he knew better. If the Comanche had settled here for the winter, there had to be another way out. He studied the cliffs around him, trying to find a track up the steep gorge's walls.

Company F of the Fourth Cavalry was a couple of miles behind him. They'd found the box canyon at mid-morning after two days of riding from Fort Concho. They were searching for the Comanches who'd raided the town of Paint Rock, taking cattle and horses, and setting fire to several of the settlers' cabins.

The Comanche village, at the head of the canyon, had been deserted, and his commander, Lieutenant Schultz, had ordered it fired and everything smashed that wouldn't burn, particularly weapons.

His mother's people were being exterminated or imprisoned on reservations. And he was helping. Sometimes, he wondered what he was doing.

He lowered his head and concentrated on the ground, noting a welter of tracks leading in all directions. He'd reached the end of the canyon where huge boulders had fallen. Maybe he should go back and ride closer to the canyon walls, looking for a trail out.

Ruth: The Rescued Bride

And then he heard a low moan—or was it just the winter wind—whipping between the tumbled boulders. But there was another sound, a distinct groan and then a thin wail. The sounds were human, and they were coming from a dense clump of mesquite trees.

Alert for a trap, he pulled his Spencer rifle from the saddle boot on *Paaka,* his black and white mustang. He cradled the rifle in his left arm while palming his Bowie knife.

Creeping along the ground, he moved cautiously to the copse of trees. But he wasn't prepared for what he found. Beneath a twisted mesquite tree, lying on a blanket, was a woman with her legs spread and a naked infant between them.

Good Lord, he couldn't believe his eyes.

Gazing upon the pair, a chill more bitter than the winter wind, crawled down his spine.

The infant was still tethered to his mother by a thin blue, pulsing cord. The woman had just given birth. The baby had his mouth wide open and his fists pumping. But his crying was weak and pitiful. Exposed, hungry and shivering, the newborn couldn't last much longer.

What of the child's mother?

The squaw moaned, and the front of her deerskin dress was covered in blood.

Making a quick decision, he squatted down and tied off the umbilical cord with a piece of rawhide from his jacket. Then he cut the cord with his knife.

He pulled down the woman's deerskin sheath to cover her and put the baby on her stomach. Then he folded the blanket around them. For extra protection, he removed his jacket and bundled the two tightly together.

Rocking back on his heels, he considered examining the woman to see how much she was bleeding. Comanche women didn't wear undergarments. He knew because his mother had hated conforming to the White Ones' ways. And he didn't like to look upon a woman's nakedness. But this was an emergency, and he needed to determine how much blood she was losing. When he lifted the woman's dress and saw her woman's mound, covered in light red hair, he gasped.

The squaw was a white woman!

He lowered her dress and looked over his shoulder. The soldiers of Company F were still a' ways off. He exhaled and gently lifted her head. Her eyes fluttered open, and they were a deep blue like the brightly-painted medicine bowl his mother had given him. But her gaze was unfocused, and her body limp. She closed her eyes again, slipping into unconsciousness.

Unable to believe what he'd found, he scooped up a handful of snow and scrubbed the ends of her greasy, braided hair. Flame-red curls emerged, and he knew he wasn't mistaken.

He used his knife to dig a shallow hole and buried the afterbirth. He took a clean bandana from his pocket and crushed some snow in it. Trying not to look too closely, he wiped her thighs clean and was grateful to find the bleeding had thinned to a trickle.

He tore up his shirt and fitted her infant into an improvised papoose. He pulled the tattered blanket and his jacket tighter around the red-haired woman and lifted her in his arms.

Trudging back to *Paaka* with his double burden, he barely realized their weight, trying not to tremble from the cold. But the woman needed his jacket more than he did, and he had an extra shirt in his saddlebags.

Paaka was waiting for him, munching on a clump of prairie grass. He lowered the woman to the ground and unstrapped the child. He dug out his extra shirt, pulling it over his chilled skin and strapped the baby to his back again. Then he considered waiting for the soldiers to help him get the woman onto his horse.

Not knowing how long Company F might ride in circles and sensing the child and woman couldn't last much longer, he decided to mount *Paaka* without help. He'd trained his pony and knew the mustang would stand still.

He inhaled, gathering his strength. Cradling the woman in his arms, he put his left foot in the stirrup. For the first time, he was grateful for Lieutenant Schultz's determination that he used an army regulation saddle and not ride bareback.

His arm and shoulder muscles strained with the effort as he lifted the dead-weight of the woman onto the front part of his saddle. She remained insensible, her head lolling to one side.

Holding her upright with both hands, he swung into the saddle behind her. The child had quieted, either soothed by the warmth of his body or... He didn't look back, as there was nothing he could do.

He pulled the woman close, holding her tightly around the waist. And despite his best intentions, fervent prayers, and her desperate condition, he couldn't help but respond to the soft roundness of her body, nestled between his thighs.

She smelled of the prairie and new blood, as well as the dried grease coating her braids. Those were familiar smells. His mother had often smelled the same.

A horse's whinny drew his attention, and he looked up to see his commanding officer, Lieutenant Schultz, approaching.

"What on earth, Wells?" The lieutenant asked. "I thought you were tracking the natives, not bringing them along for the ride."

"A woman and her newly-birthed baby, sir." Like him, a woman and a newborn were the last things the lieutenant would expect to find, tracking Comanche raiders.

But the Texas frontier was a land of captives and hostages. Two winters ago, Fort Concho had held over a hundred Comanche women and children, keeping them warm and fed.

The soldiers and their women's kindness to the captives had come at a crucial time. He'd followed his father to Fort Concho and been given a job as a hostler due to his skill with horses. After a few months, his father had approached their new commander, Major Gregor, and gotten him enlisted as an Army scout.

"What about the hostiles?" The lieutenant asked. "We need to catch them before they raid again."

Jacob nodded. "But the woman and child will die without shelter, especially the child."

The lieutenant exhaled. "I understand. Get them back to the fort at once."

Jacob saluted and added, "The woman is... was a captive. She's white."

The lieutenant moved his mount closer to gaze at the woman's face. His green eyes widened and then darkened.

Jacob stiffened and clenched his jaw, knowing that look—it was how the soldiers looked at the saloon women in San Angelo. And though the woman was a stranger, he felt protective of her.

"Good Lord, Wells, why didn't you tell me that from the first? The major will have both our hides should a rescued captive die." He craned his neck and gazed at the baby. "The child's lips are blue. I don't think he will make it." He shook his head. "Probably for the best. Then she won't be saddled with a half…" He stopped and turned his head.

Jacob knew what he'd been about to say—the white woman wouldn't be left with a half-breed child. *A breed like him.*

The lieutenant was a good soldier, but like most whites, he believed half-breeds were inferior. Useful for some tasks, like tracking, but not completely acceptable.

"Take them straight to the O'Connors. Mrs. O'Connor has a newborn. She'll know what to do. Probably better than Dr. Statler, who will most likely be drunk."

Jacob nodded, remembering how ineffective the post's doctor had been when his father was ill.

"Then report what happened to the major. I don't know when I'll be back to explain." The lieutenant gathered his reins and jerked his head toward the village. "We caught two of their braves, trying to muddy the tracks, and shot them. Which way do you think the rest of them went?"

Jacob raised his head and glanced at the lowering sun. He half-turned his mount, back from the way he'd come. When he'd brought the woman out, he'd seen the trail. It was faint but unmistakable, and though the Comanches had tried to cover their tracks, it was the only way out of the canyon.

"Back where I came from, behind those boulders. If you go to the end, you'll see a clump of mesquite trees. That's where I found the woman and baby. If you turn left before the mesquite trees, you'll see a faint trail leading up the side of the canyon. As far as I can tell, it's the only way out, Lieutenant." He saluted again.

"Good man, Wells." The lieutenant glanced at the woman in his arms again. "Carry on. I'll see you back at the fort."

Chapter Two

Jacob stopped *Paaka* in front of the O'Connor's limestone cabin. Captain O'Connor was an officer, and he had his own cabin with a covered porch.

He dismounted and gathered the woman into his arms. Despite the jolting ride, the red-haired woman had remained unconscious, and the child had been quiet, too.

Not good signs.

But the O'Connor home would be warm, and they were a kind couple. He remembered how generous they'd been with the Comanche hostages, sharing their food and blankets and other household items to help ease the captives' daily lives.

With the woman in his arms and the child strapped to his back, he managed to tap his knuckles against the door, calling out, "Captain O'Connor, Mrs. O'Connor, it's Jacob Wells. May I come in?"

The door opened and Captain O'Connor, a big, beefy-looking Irishman, stood in the doorway. His eyes widened. "What have we here, Wells? A squaw? Is she hurt? My wife might help, but I'm surprised ye didn't go to the doctor's surgery."

"May we come in and I'll explain?" Jacob asked. "It's cold out."

O'Connor nodded and opened the door wider, inviting them into the front room, which had a low-slung hearth at the end with a crackling fire. The cozy room welcomed him, its warmth enveloping his chilled body like the fleece of a snug blanket.

The captain cleared off the table. "Put 'er here, so my wife can take a look at 'er." He crossed to a door and opened it a crack, lowering his voice. "Nellie, are ye nursing the baby? There's an injured woman out here."

"Coming." A woman's voice replied.

Jacob sighed with relief and gently laid the woman on the table. Then he twisted around and loosened the papoose ties, cradling the blue-lipped baby in his arms.

Someone gasped, and he looked up. Nellie O'Connor, a short, stout, brown-haired woman stared at him. "And a wee babe, too?"

"Yes, ma'am," Jacob said.

"What happened here?" The captain asked, crossing his arms. "Why didn't ye go to Statler."

"Lieutenant Schultz said I should come to your wife first, as the woman has just given birth." He started to repeat what the lieutenant had said about Statler, but he didn't like to speak ill of anyone.

"I see." The captain turned to his wife. "Nell, I guess ye'd best look at the lass."

Mrs. O'Connor stretched out her arms. "The baby first, Ezekiel."

Jacob handed her the child. "I cut his birthing cord as best as I could, but it will need to be trimmed and—"

"Poor little mite," Nellie said, rocking the child in her arms. "He's not eaten?"

"No."

"Well, he needs to be fed first. The cord can wait. Luckily, I've enough for two." She turned toward the bedroom door. "If you'll excuse me."

"Thank you, Mrs. O'Connor. But I know the lieutenant was particularly concerned about the woman. She's white. I would guess a captive, and she's lost a lot of blood." Despite his misgivings about Statler, he asked, "Should I fetch the doctor to help out?"

This time, both of the O'Connors gasped and stared at the woman lying on the table.

"A white woman, ye say?" O'Connor rubbed the back of his neck and glanced at his wife. She nodded and turned again, obviously more concerned about the baby.

"Yes, with the two of 'em to care for, ye'd best fetch the Doc."

And if he hadn't told them the woman was white, would they have left her until the baby nursed? They were kind-hearted people, but a bloodied squaw hadn't prompted them to action. He gulped, wanting to swallow the sour taste on his tongue.

"I'm assuming the lieutenant wants ye to report to the major. Unless the troop is back?"

"Company F is still pursuing the hostiles, sir."

"Then ye best get on with it, Wells. We'll be expecting the Doc."

He saluted. "Yes, sir."

When he pulled open the front door, the icy wind penetrated his thin shirt. He'd forgotten his jacket, covering the woman. He closed the door and hugged himself. His jacket could wait; he'd fetch it later.

* * *

A thin wail pierced Nellie's sleep. She woke immediately; a nursing mother never sleeps deeply. *How well she knew.*

But her heart was filled with joy because she had two children to nurse. During the past two days, spent caring for the newborns and a rescued captive who slipped in and out of sensibility, she'd learned to discern her Johnny's cry from the nameless half-breed baby.

She got out of bed and pulled open the buttons of her nightshirt, hurrying to the bureau drawer, which held the rescued child. He usually cried first and wakened her baby. Thin as a scarecrow, it was as if the half-breed couldn't get enough to eat. He'd suck one teat dry while her Johnny, a rosy, chunky baby, took his time. Often, she had to encourage her son when he dozed off, tickling his feet and jostling him so he'd finish.

Scooping up the half-breed, she went to Johnny's cradle on the far side of the four-poster bed. Gazing down at her child, he appeared to be sleeping, despite loud squalls from the half-breed.

She didn't know if the captive woman would regain her senses; who knew what abuses she'd suffered at the hands of the savages. Poor woman. And she couldn't keep thinking of the baby as: "the half-breed." She should give the child a name. *Matthew.*

Her Matthew had been born strong and plucky, and he'd lived almost a year. When he'd died of consumption, she'd been plunged into despair for months.

Yes, she would call the half-breed baby Matthew.

Johnny slept on, oblivious to Matthew's fussing. That was odd. She shifted Matthew in her arms and offered him her breast. He latched on and suckled her with a desperation she'd not experienced with her children.

She usually sat down to nurse, but something, a strange feeling kept her rooted in place, standing over her son's cradle, watching him. He was quiet and unmoving. Swaddled as he was, she couldn't tell if he was breathing. Fear and dread gripped her, covering her in a cold sweat.

Gently, she turned her son over. His face was pinched and white, too white. She managed to pull her breast from Matthew's mouth. He let out a squawk in protest, but she ignored him.

She returned Matthew to the bureau dresser and snatched up her child, frantically peeling away his swaddling. His skin was cool to the touch, and his chest didn't move.

Blessed Mary, Mother of God, don't let this be happening again, she prayed. Don't let this... don't... don't...

A roaring in her ears filled her head, and a bottomless blackness beckoned. The room turned upside down, and she felt as if she was falling down a deep, deep well. She screamed and sank to the floor.

Her husband lurched up in bed. "Nell, what is it? What's happened?"

She opened her mouth, but no words came. She couldn't speak, couldn't tell him the unthinkable. And then the tears came, clogging her throat, spilling down her cheeks. Her mouth opened and huge, heavy sobs poured out, filled with all the anguish she'd lived through for the past twenty years.

Her husband got out of bed and came to her. *He knew, he knew.* It had happened too many times. She held up their son, half swaddled, to her husband, almost as an offering, a guilt offering. Shame scalded her. There was something wrong with her. As a mother, she was cursed.

Johnny had been their last chance.

Ezekiel took the baby in his arms, and his big, brown eyes filled with tears. Then he put one arm around her, too, holding her tightly, enfolding the three of them in his burly arms and rocking them back and forth.

* * *

Nellie didn't know how long she sat with Ezekiel on the floor, holding their dead baby between them. The half-breed infant,

Matthew, had stopped crying and gone back to sleep. And there was no sound from the other bedroom. The woman must have remained unconscious.

But why had her baby lived? A woman who'd lain with savages, and birthed her child outside in the bitter cold. Why was she so fortunate? It didn't seem fair. Nothing seemed fair.

The kernel of an idea formed in Nellie's mind.

Who knew if the girl would regain her senses? And even if she did, how would she care for her baby? The ways for a woman to make a living on the frontier were harsh. Having lain with a savage, there was only one path open to her. And her child would pay the consequences.

There was a glimmer of hope, though. Lieutenant Schultz had stopped by three times to see the woman. Nellie had turned him away. The woman wasn't in her right mind, unfit to receive visitors. But the lieutenant might be the key, if he could overlook her time with the Comanches.

Would he want to raise a half-breed child? Something told her the lieutenant was over proud and wouldn't want to be saddled with the evidence of her shame.

With each ticking second, Nellie knew what she must do—if she could convince her husband. She dried her eyes on her apron and got up, returning Johnny to his crib.

"I have an idea, Ezekiel." She licked her lips and swallowed. "Will you listen?"

He raised his bent head. "Of course, Nell."

"What if we adopt the half-breed child as our own?"

He gazed at her, the sadness clouding his eyes, making them opaque and hard.

She'd expected him to be shocked, but it was as if his grief had numbed him, wrung him dry of emotion.

He shook his head. "I don't know. I wanted *our* child—"

She clasped her hands and raised them, as if she was praying. "As did I. You know how much. And you know how I've suffered, but this would help the girl, as well."

"What do ye mean?"

"She's going to have a hard life because she's lived with the savages and birthed a half-breed child. What kind of future can she have? Where will she go, what will she do?"

"I thought ye said Lieutenant Schultz is interested—"

"Yes, in the woman, but I don't know if his designs are honorable, nor do I know if he would want to raise a half-savage child."

"I didn't think of that." He rubbed the back of his neck. "Ye may be right. A woman's lot on the frontier can be hard..."

"Harder yet if she has a child to support. And if she doesn't recover her wits, then—"

"Then, I would be overjoyed to adopt 'er child. It would be a mercy for us, the child, and for the mother."

"Exactly what I was thinking."

"Yes, but if she wakens and recovers, Nell, she has a right to 'er child. Not us. We could ask 'er, make it easier for 'er."

"And if she refuses?"

"Then we must abide by 'er decision."

"Even if both the child and mother will suffer?"

He took her into his arms again. "Oh, Nell, I know yer grief is talking. But we're both Christians—we can't play God with this woman's child."

She pulled away and gazed at him, pleading with her eyes. "Can't we? If we know it's the right thing to do?"

He hesitated, as if considering. "Normally, I would ask ye to tell 'er when she comes to her senses, but I understand how horrible this has been. I'll tell 'er and offer to adopt 'er child. It's the best we can do."

Invisible bands tightened around her chest. She couldn't let Ezekiel do as he wished. She wanted to tear her hair out, but she must appear calm and appeal to her husband.

She tugged on the sleeve of his nightshirt. "Please, don't tell her. It's our last chance. You know how old I am. We've lost how many children? Four, or is it six, if I count the ones who were stillborn? All of my babies weakened and died. None, except our Eliza, lived longer than a year. And this last pregnancy almost killed me. You know what the doctor said—"

"That drunken quack, Statler. Hummph. I wouldn't believe him if he said the sky was blue."

"But I'm a midwife, and I know my body. I know there won't be another child." She glanced at the woman's baby and lowered her voice. "He's strong, that one is. Look at what he's endured. He'll live. I just know it, and we'll have a son. A son to take care of us in our old age."

He got up and sat on the four-poster bed, cradling his head in his hands. She knew he was weakening.

"Won't the girl guess, if she recovers?" he asked.

"How will she know? We'll get a coffin for our Johnny tomorrow. It's only proper, and then we'll wait for the chaplain to return. He should be back in a few days. She's never seen the babies. How will she know?"

He lifted his head. "What about the way the child looks? Jacob saw the baby when he brought him and the girl. And as the child grows older, his Comanche heritage will be obvious. Just look at Jacob. No one could miss he's a breed. How will we pass off—?"

"You could ask for a transfer," she interrupted. "You're overdue. We've been here going on four years. The major would be hard-pressed to turn you down."

"Yes, but the District of Texas Commander will have to approve the orders."

"But you've fulfilled your duty and served bravely. When we came, most of the cabins weren't even finished. Remember the *jacale,* that pitiful wooden pen with a tarp for a roof, that we lived in for the first two years?"

He stroked his chin and glanced around. "I remember how pleased I was, due to my rank, when we got the second-best cabin. Only the major's is bigger." He shook his head. "I'd had such hopes for the other bedroom—wanted to fill it with children."

She held her breath.

He gazed at her, his mouth turned down, and his heavy jowls appearing to droop.

"How will ye keep the other women from suspecting the child isn't white until I can get a transfer? If I can get a transfer?"

"I'll keep him swaddled." She took his hands and pressed her lips to them. "Please, Ezekiel, please. It's for the best. I know it is, and I'll keep him inside and covered up. Surely by the time it's warm, if you ask right away, you'll get a transfer?"

"Maybe," he muttered. "But what reason will I give? The major has gotten used to me as his second-in-command."

"You could tell him I'm grieving because I nursed the half-breed child, and I grew to care for him. And with losing Eliza here, it's too hard for me. Tell him I need a fresh start."

"That's a lot to pull off, Nell. And what if the girl guesses he's 'er child?"

"I'll make certain she doesn't. Right now, he's just a dark-haired baby. We both have dark hair. Her hair is red, but the child probably takes after his father. And most new-born babies look alike.

"Please, husband, please. And if the worst happens and we're discovered, I'll tell the major I was going crazy. That I was the one who lied to her and—"

"Ye know that won't do any good, don't ye?"

She lowered her head and whispered, "Please, please, please."

He put his finger under her chin and lifted her head. "I can't tell ye no, Nell, not after what we've been through." He glanced at the child. "I do want a son. And yer right, he's a tough little boy, that one. Even so, I'll be praying every minute of every day until my transfer comes through."

He held up one finger. "But we must tell the major tonight."

"In the middle of the night?"

"Yes, the longer we wait, the more it looks as if we have something to hide. The sooner we do it, the better. Then it will appear as if we're acting on instinct, driven by grief."

She bowed her head. "You're right, Ezekiel, the sooner we embrace the child as our own, the quicker people will accept it. And I want to call him Matthew, after the son we lost to a fever before Eliza."

* * *

Major William Gregor came awake with a start. He'd done it again, gone to sleep at his desk. His oil lantern had sputtered out, and it was dark in his office. The fire in his stove had burned down, leaving a few gray-shrouded embers. He shivered.

He needed to get back to his cabin. Martha, his wife, might need him. Peggy, their eight-year-old daughter, sometimes woke in the night, frightened and anxious if he hadn't returned. Their one servant, a Mexican woman, Lupe, was a good nurse, but she needed to rest, too.

Someone knocked on his door, and he wondered if Martha had sent for him. He struck a match and lit the lamp. Then he fished out his pocket watch and consulted the time—past two in the morning—the middle of a long, winter night.

"Come in, Lupe." He scrubbed his eyes, yawned, and stretched. He got to his feet, grimacing at his stiff joints.

But when the door opened, it wasn't Lupe on the threshold. Captain O'Connor and his wife, who was carrying a baby in her arms, entered his office.

"Captain O'Connor." He inclined his head. "And Nellie." He observed the proprieties, but the couple's appearance in the middle of the night was most irregular, and his stomach clenched with dread.

The captain came to attention and saluted.

"Spit it out, Captain," he said. "It must be important for you to come at this time. Did you go to my home first?"

"No, sir, we didn't want to wake yer wife and daughter," O'Connor replied. "We hoped ye'd be here. Your orderly, Andrews, mentioned ye'd probably be working late tonight."

He grunted, not caring to admit the bald truth. Between his ailing wife and the failure of his command to bring the marauding hostiles to heel, he often worked late hours.

"Sir, we've come to ye on a personal matter. Ye know about the woman and child we've been caring for, the captive woman and 'er—"

"Yes, Scout Wells filled me in. When Lieutenant Schultz returned, he spoke to me, too. What's happened? I thought they were doing well."

"Not so good. The woman is still out of her head, and the doctor doesn't know if she'll regain 'er senses, savaged by those animals, Major."

"That's too bad. I'm sorry to hear it."

"And her baby—he was almost dead when Jacob brought him. My wife nursed him, and he seemed better. But when our little one, Johnny..." He hesitated and Nellie held out the child. "When Johnny awakened my wife to be fed, we found the half-breed child had died." He covered his eyes with his hand. "It brought back all our grief over losing Eliza. You remember, Major."

"Yes, I remember."

The captain bent his head, and the major realized he was hiding his sorrow. Tears rolled down his wife's cheeks, too.

The major looked down at the piles of paperwork on his desk but nothing registered. He didn't want to witness their grief. His chest constricted, the bands tightening, and he felt as if a boulder was pressing down on him.

He understood what they were feeling. After their daughter had been born in the first flush of their marriage, his Martha had suffered several pregnancies... and miscarriages.

This last time, even though she was older than most women to give birth, they'd hoped would be different. And it had, after a fashion. The little boy they'd christened Luke had lived for a week. Then one night, he'd slipped away.

Nellie had helped to birth his son, pregnant with her Johnny. After Luke had died, his wife, still weak from her pregnancy and hard labor, had remained in bed. Dr. Statler wasn't much help, trying one noxious nostrum after another and mumbling under his breath about "woman problems."

He'd applied for leave to the District of Texas commanding officer, Colonel Augur, wanting to take his wife to a specialist in Austin. But the necessary permission had been delayed, due to typical bureaucratic nonsense. He'd almost deserted his post, willing to face a court marital.

Lupe had intervened, bringing a *curandera*, a Mexican healer, with herbal remedies, and for a time his wife had rallied, giving him hope. But by the time his leave came through, winter had settled in, and he'd worried the long trip in the cold weather would be the death of Martha. Now, despite the best efforts of the *curandera*, his wife seemed to weaken, day-by-day. He cursed his decision—wishing he'd defied the army and taken his wife to Austin.

"Captain and Nellie, I'm sorry for your loss. And the girl's, too, if she lives to know it. More sorry than you can know."

"Thank you, sir," O'Connor said.

"I suppose you want to arrange for his burial. The chaplain should be back from Fort McKavett in a day or two. I'll send him to you at once." He shuffled through some papers on his desk. "In the meantime, Private Sims can build you a proper coffin—"

"We need to bury the child," Nellie cut him off, "'tis true. But that's not what brought us in the middle of the night." She sniffed and wiped at her eyes again. "We don't want the girl to think we didn't do right by her child, should she get well and ask."

He stiffened and stared at O'Connor's wife. "Why would she doubt you?"

"'Tis hard to lose a child, Major," she said. "I loved her little boy, and losing him brought back the memories of the children we've lost. I won't know what to say to her."

O'Connor's wife was right. Losing a child, even one that had been the spawn of a devil, could unhinge a woman, especially after what the girl had been through.

"The woman Jacob rescued, we don't know her name?"

"No," O'Connor replied. "She's not in her right mind."

"Will she live?"

"We hope so, sir," O'Connor said. "But the Doc isn't sure. She wakes and drinks some broth and then falls back asleep." The captain shook his head. "She's not asked after her babe."

He inhaled, saddened but not surprised. "If she's mending, she'll eventually remember, but I doubt she will blame you. Jacob told me the child was half dead when he found them." He turned his gaze to Nellie. "I'm afraid, though it will be difficult, you'll need to tell her." He scrubbed his chin. "I could speak with her, but it really should come from a woman. I'm sorry."

Then he had an idea.

"Major, *señor*," Lupe stood on the threshold of his office, behind the O'Connors. "My apologies for disturbing you." She frowned and glanced at the O'Connors. "Your wife, she is asking for you, *Señor*."

He wondered how much Lupe had overheard. Not that it mattered, except for the O'Connors' unreasonable fear they'd be blamed for the baby's death. Their concern was odd but probably prompted by guilt. Guilt their own child had survived.

He understood guilt, and how it could make you crazy.

"Lupe, tell my wife I'll be there in a few minutes. *Gracias*."

Lupe dipped her head and glanced at the O'Connors again. "*El capitán*, and *Señora* Nellie, *buenas noches*." She closed the door, shutting out the cold winter night.

He gazed at the O'Connors. "I'll send Private Sims, first thing in the morning." He grabbed his hat. "And the chaplain, as soon as he returns." He hesitated, turning the hat over and over in his hands, considering. "Does the woman's child have a name?"

"Nellie wants to call him Matthew after the boy we lost before Eliza."

"That's kind of you. Too bad the chaplain wasn't here to christen him before he..." He put on his hat. "I have to go now."

The captain snapped to and saluted. "One thing more, Major. This has been very trying. We'd like to start over... away from the grief and loss." He stood up straighter. "I'll be submitting the paperwork for a transfer tomorrow. I've been honored to serve under ye, sir, but given the circumstances..."

The major sighed and returned his salute. "I understand. You've served me well, Captain O'Connor, and suffered hardships. I'll do my best to expedite your transfer. But it will probably be spring before it comes through. Again, my condolences to you both."

He looked at the captain. "After your wife breaks the news, I'll send Jacob to the woman to explain how he found her and the baby. That might help."

"Yes, sir, we would appreciate it. And thank ye for understanding about my asking for a transfer."

The Major nodded. "Good night to you both."

* * *

Ruth MacDonald opened her heavy-lidded eyes. All of her body ached, as if she'd been beaten by the squaws when she'd first been taken captive. But when she looked around, she saw white-washed wooden walls, not the skin walls of a teepee.

What had happened?

Ruth: The Rescued Bride

Bits and pieces of her memory flitted through her mind, like bright butterflies on a spring day. She'd been heavy with child. The soldiers had found them, just as she'd started her birthing pains. They'd fled to the end of the box canyon, and her husband had left her to give birth in a mesquite grove. He'd promised to come back, but he hadn't. She'd had her child, a boy, and had wanted to hold him but then... something had happened.

She didn't know—couldn't remember if her child had lived or died—or what had happened to her husband.

A soft knock interrupted her tortured thoughts. She tried to raise herself and felt suddenly nauseous. "Come in."

A stout, brown-haired woman dressed in a white blouse and gray skirt entered her room. Now there was no doubt—she'd been rescued.

Being returned to her own kind was a blessing. But as thankful as she was, she'd trade her release a hundred times over to see her baby.

"Mistress, where is my child?" she blurted. "I gave birth and... What happened?"

The brown-haired woman looked startled for one moment and then she frowned, worrying her bottom lip with her teeth. She bowed her head.

"I know, Miss, and... and... I'm sorry. You were left by your Comanche captors... and gave birth. You were weak from losing blood, and the doctor said you hit the back of your head."

Ruth reached behind her head and found a lump there. She touched the egg-sized bump and winced, remembering how she'd fallen against the mesquite tree.

"Our scout found you," the woman said and lifted the pitcher beside the bed. She had her gaze trained on the wooden-planked floor, partially covered by a rag rug.

The woman shook her head. "I hate to tell you, Miss, but your little one died..." She raised her apron and wiped the corners of her eyes. "I'm so sorry. I nursed him along with my child, and he seemed to recover. But then one night, he fell asleep and didn't waken."

She kept her eyes on the floor. "We gave your child a Christian burial yesterday."

Ruth: The Rescued Bride

Ruth slumped against the pillow, and a black shroud descended, smothering her with hopelessness. At first, she was numb, but then the pain of her loss struck her. And her grief was like a living thing—a bird of prey with razor-sharp talons, tearing at her, pulling out her guts.

Tears filled her eyes and spilled over. She started to shake and couldn't stop. She clutched the quilt and wailed, screaming her sorrow, needing to expel her misery, just as she'd had to expel her child at the wrong time... the worst time. Giving birth on the hard ground in the middle of the coldest winter she could remember, was it any wonder her poor child hadn't lived? Regret and grief mingled within her, scalding her, dragging her down, making her want to sleep again.

She cupped her empty abdomen and sighed. More hot tears flowed, trailing stinging, salty tracks down her cheeks.

The woman finally lifted her head. "I'm Nellie O'Connor, wife of Captain Ezekiel O'Connor, and you're at Fort Concho. We've been caring for you and your child, that is... that is... until he—"

"He was a boy? That's what I remember?"

"Yes, Miss..."

Her Comanche husband had wanted a son. And as much as she'd respected Buffalo Heart and been grateful to him, she hadn't wanted to raise her child as a Comanche. In the dark nights, lying beside her husband, she'd plotted and planned, dreaming of a way to escape after she had her child. Now she was safe but at what price? Her poor baby never had a chance.

She wanted to curl into a ball and die, but this woman had taken care of her. The least she could do was remember the manners her folks had taught her.

Her parents... horrible, bloody images of that night, almost two years ago, flashed through her mind, delivering another devastating blow to her weakened body. She wanted to moan like a wounded animal, but somehow, she gathered her waning strength and lifted her gaze.

"My name is Ruth MacDonald. The Running Water Ranch was our spread about ten miles to the northwest, along the North Concho. My father raised cattle. We were raided by the Comanche almost two years ago. They killed my parents and my two brothers. They took me captive. I'd just turned sixteen."

"How terrible for you, Ruth. And how you must have suffered, but you're safe now."

"Yes, but I was wondering... not that I want to go back." She shook her head. Sorrow and a sense of futility crept over her, drawing her down again, exhaustion tugging at her. "I wish I could remember..."

Nellie raised her head. "Our commanding officer, Major Gregor, thought you might want to know what happened. I'm to send for Jacob, the scout who rescued you and—"

A baby's wail split the silence.

She lurched up, hope springing alive in her heart. "I thought you said my little boy had—"

"That's *my* boy, Johnny, and he must be hungry. He's always impatient." Nellie crossed her arms over her ample bosom. "That's why they brought you and your child here, so's I could nurse your little boy with mine."

"Oh, I see." Despair dropped over her again. "How long was I ill—?"

"I have to nurse my child, but Jacob will explain. He's a nice boy, even though he's a half-breed. I'll send for him, right away."

The baby's crying escalated, ending in a series of hiccups.

Ruth nodded, though, the child's cries cut through her like a too-sharp hunting knife. If her baby had lived, would he have cried like that?

She would never know.

Chapter Three

Jacob foraged the brown and gray meadow beyond the fort, dreading the meeting he'd been ordered to attend. He didn't want to face the captive woman he'd rescued—had been sorry to hear her baby had died.

What could he possibly say to the red-haired woman that would ease her grief?

The Major wanted him to explain how he'd found her and what had happened. Jacob wanted to give her some token—a silent offering for her sorrow. But he had nothing, so he'd gone to search for something.

The winter had been hard, and there wasn't much. He gathered some faded and half-brown yucca blooms, cut a handful of Possumhaw holly branches with their bright red berries, and added a few brown-tipped cattails from the riverbank.

He'd bought a blue ribbon to match her eyes and a white feather at the commissary. The sutler had said the feather was from a strange bird that lived thousands of miles away, called an ostrich, and it had come with a bonnet, which had fallen apart during shipment. He bought the feather because it was pretty and fluffy and soft to touch. He tied the bundle together with the ribbon. It wasn't much, but it was all he had.

He trudged back to the fort, wanting to get it over with. The short winter day was almost at an end, and he'd probably miss supper in the mess hall. But as sour as his stomach was, he didn't care.

Mrs. O'Connor answered his knock at once, as if she'd been waiting for him. He greeted the captain's wife and stepped inside, pulling the door closed and shutting out the winter chill.

She clasped his hand, startling him. "Thank you for coming, Jacob. I know it's not an easy task to explain what happened to Ruth—"

"Ruth?"

"Yes, that's her name." Mrs. O'Connor bowed her head. "She's very sad. Her baby, you know."

He doffed his hat and Mrs. O'Connor took it, hanging it on a peg in the wall.

"I don't know how I can help her," he said.

"Please, just talk to her. Explain how you found her and how her baby was—"

"I don't think—"

"Oh, I know it's hard, but she has questions only you can answer." Mrs. O'Connor patted his arm. "Now, there's a good boy. And after, you're welcome to supper. I've fresh venison with gravy, cornbread, and even some green beans I preserved from my garden. Peach pie, too, for dessert. It was my last can of peaches, but..."

He stared at the captain's wife. She was a nice lady but an officer's wife. He occasionally mingled with the non-commissioned officers, but the ranking officers and their wives seldom noticed him except for an obligatory greeting. Her sudden and unexpected hospitality almost embarrassed him. He couldn't say why—it was just a feeling he had.

"I thank you, Mrs. O'Connor. It's very kind of you, but I've already eaten in the mess hall." It was a lie, a small deception. He tried never to lie, but he knew of no other way to refuse. He didn't know if he could eat after he had to face the woman he'd rescued.

"Well, that's too bad. We would have enjoyed having you stay to supper."

He glanced around the front room. "Where do you want me to talk to her?"

"Oh, she's still abed, Jacob, too weak to dress and come out."

He frowned. His mother had taught him better than to intrude on a woman in her sick bed. He shook his head.

"Ah, Jacob, not to worry. I understand your discretion, and it does you credit. But you'll have to meet with Ruth in the bedroom." She put her hands on her hips. "I'll leave the door open. The proprieties will be maintained."

He exhaled. "Thank you, Mrs. O'Connor."

She took his arm and propelled him to one of the doors, opening off the main room. "It will be fine, lad." Then she opened the door.

Ruth: The Rescued Bride

The red-haired woman—Ruth—was propped against pillows, her long, fiery-colored hair spilling in waves over the white linen. He glimpsed the button-up collar of her high-necked nightdress above the brightly-patterned quilt tucked to her chin. Her eyes were lowered, and she appeared as embarrassed as he felt.

But her beauty hit him as if he'd been struck on the head with a tomahawk.

Cleaned up and with her hair washed, she was a sight to behold. Her red-hair was like a flame, and he was the moth. Her skin was a soft almond color, mellowed, no doubt by her time spent out of doors with her captors, and her cheeks were rosy tinted. She had a fine straight nose and full lips.

She raised her gaze to him, and the blush on her cheeks deepened. The look in her blue eyes held him. He remembered marveling at their pleasing color when he'd found her. He looked down at the blue ribbon and realized its color paled in contrast with her shining, sky-colored eyes.

He moved closer to the bed and offered his bundle. "This is for you... Ruth." He shook his head. "May I call you Ruth? Mrs. O'Connor said that was your name."

"Of course, you *must* call me Ruth. My name before I was taken was... is... Ruth MacDonald." She studied him, a frank appraisal in her eyes.

He knew what she was seeing for he had the look of his mother's people, especially when he left his long hair loose on his shoulders.

"My Comanche name was *Eka Huutsuu,"* she said. "It means—"

"Redbird. It's fitting. My mother's name was *Ebi Huutsu*, not because her hair was blue but because of her sunny nature."

Her lips quirked, a shadow of a smile. "I'd not have thought your mother would have blue hair." She hesitated and twisted the edge of the quilt in one hand. "Then your mother was Comanche?"

"Yes."

He wondered if she hated his mother's people, if her life as a captive had been sordid and hard. But he could detect no censure in her gaze, only frank curiosity.

She gestured toward a chair in the corner. “My apologies. My manners are sorely lacking. Please take the chair and be seated. Is that for me?” She held out her hand. “How nice of you.”

He surrendered his pathetic offering, and their fingers brushed. Even though he’d touched her intimately before, that had been different. He’d been determined to save her life. Now he had time to appreciate her long, slender fingers.

The tops of her fingers were soft, but the pads were calloused. He wasn’t surprised; Comanche women worked hard to gather and prepare food, scrape hides, and sew tough skins for clothing.

Ruth let her fingers linger on his hand, enjoying the feel of his rough, warm skin. He looked half-wild, but considering the past two years, he didn’t frighten her. On the contrary, there was something reassuring in his eyes and touch. Almost as if she was making contact with an old friend. It was an odd, fleeting feeling, but it left an impression.

She turned the bundle over, admiring the soft, white ostrich feather, the creamy yucca blossoms, and especially the blue ribbon. It had been a long time since she’d had a ribbon for her hair.

He fetched the cane-bottomed chair from the corner and set it a few feet from her bed.

“Thank you, Jacob... that’s your name, isn’t it? Nellie said it was.”

“Yes, ma’am, my name is Jacob Wells.”

“So, your father was...”

“A white man. Yes, ma’am. A soldier.”

“Oh, and you’re a soldier, too?” She gazed at his deerskin jacket, fringed along his forearms, wondering why he wasn’t in uniform.

“No, ma’am, I’m not a soldier. Just a scout. Half breeds are seldom allowed...” He stopped and cleared his throat. She thought she detected a hint of flush on his tanned face. “That is, ma’am, I’m not—”

“My apologies again. I wasn’t thinking. I know Nellie mentioned you’re a scout.” And she understood his half-spoken, bitter words and shame.

When she'd been carrying her child, she'd often wondered what would happen to him. If he'd stayed with his father's people, he would have been accepted. But she'd dreamed of escaping and taking her baby to safety.

The Comanche way of life was hard, and she doubted they could last much longer. Their numbers were dwindling, as they fought the onslaught of soldiers and settlers.

She'd often wondered, if she'd brought her child back to civilization, would he have been made to feel inferior?

Gazing at Jacob's strong face and seeing the wounded look in his eyes, her heart squeezed, knowing she had her answer. But even though her son would have been treated… "different" by her people, the knowing didn't lift her sorrow. She would have found a way to protect him, no matter what.

He crossed his legs. "Mrs. O'Connor said you had questions for me?"

"Yes, I do. Could you tell me what happened when you found me?"

He lowered his head, and his face flushed redder. That didn't surprise her. The last thing she remembered was pushing her baby out and not having the strength to lift him. If he'd found her like that, she hadn't been a pretty sight.

He lifted his head and gazed directly into her eyes. The slant and color of his eyes hinted at his Comanche heritage. His nose resembled a knife's blade, and his lips were fuller than most men's. Altogether, he had a nice face.

Inclining his head, he said, "All right. I will tell you what I know." He paused, as if gathering his thoughts. "I tracked your captors to the box canyon and brought the soldiers there. You left your camp, but the tracks were confusing. The Comanche do that, double back and cover their tracks and—"

"Yes, my Comanche husband…" Now it was her turn to blush because in her people's eyes, she hadn't been married. Not really.

"My husband, *Tasiwoo Pihi* or Buffalo Heart…" She glanced at him. "But you speak Comanche. Don't you? You knew what my name meant."

He smiled—his first smile—and she realized he was handsome. "Yes, I speak the People's tongue."

"I speak some, but my husband was always encouraging me to learn more." She sighed and plucked at the quilt. "I was very fortunate in my husband... though it was hard at first. His tribe attacked my family's ranch about two years ago. My husband wasn't there; he'd suffered a serious leg wound in a fight with some Kiowas. The Chief, though aged, led the raid. My father and brothers fought hard, but it was three against twenty."

"So, your husband didn't take part in the raid on your ranch?"

She knew what he was asking; the conclusion he'd drawn. "No, he wasn't there." She bit her lip. "It was fortunate that..." She stopped. Tears threatened again, not for her Comanche husband but for what she'd endured. For all the deaths and sorrow tugging at her heart. She swallowed hard and forced the tears back.

She put his improvised bouquet on the table beside her bed. "My mother was a good shot; she stood beside my father and fought, but she was killed, too. I hid in the root cellar, but they fired our home and smoked me out. They took me captive and made me take care of my husband, who was laid up with his leg.

"I nursed him as best I could, and he was fascinated by the color of my hair." She twined a strand around her finger. "I wasn't... that is..." She licked her lips and swallowed. "I wasn't *taken* against my will. Well, not exactly. Buffalo Heart appreciated me caring for him and he treated me kindly, wanting to win my regard."

"It is often the way with some captives," he said. "Buffalo Heart honored you."

"Yes, he did, and he tried to protect me from the hardest work and the other squaws who... who... wanted to be looked upon with favor by my husband."

"You were fortunate then, for the squaws can be brutal in their treatment of captives." He grimaced, and she knew it pained him to speak badly of his mother's people. "My mother was a kind soul and a devout Christian, but I know from talking to other hostages how they suffered."

"Yes." She licked her lips again. She wanted him to know she hadn't been ravished by all the braves. It was important to retain some shreds of dignity.

"I only *knew* my husband. He married me, Comanche fashion, very quickly. But the ill will of the rest of the tribe didn't stop. If anything, once I became with child..." She faltered and choked back a sob.

She stared out the one window, feeling as if she was vomiting her guts out, as if all the ugliness of being a captive was somehow her fault.

"The Chief... pardon me, but I never learned how to pronounce his name. The Chief honored my husband as his best warrior. It was his position with the tribe that made my life bearable."

"In that, you were also fortunate."

"Perhaps." She twisted her hands together. "My husband left me in the mesquite grove to cover our tracks. He never came back. I wondered if..." She couldn't finish, couldn't ask outright.

Buffalo Heart, in his own way, had been a good man. She hadn't loved him, and she'd wanted to escape. But the last thing she'd wanted was his death.

Jacob must have understood. "Most of the tribe got away. It took us too long to find the trail up the canyon wall. But two of the braves who stayed behind died." He frowned and looked down at his boots. "What kind of horse did your husband ride?"

"A sorrel stallion."

He nodded and turned his face away. "And what feathers did he favor for his hair? Did he wear beads?"

The commander of the fort had chosen wisely, sending Jacob. He knew how to identify individual Comanche braves. White soldiers wouldn't have any idea of how to single out the natives.

She shouldn't care, but Buffalo Heart had been good to her... in his way. "He wore two owl feathers in his braids and a necklace of amber beads."

Jacob's face darkened, and he shook his head. "I'm afraid Buffalo Heart was one of the braves who was killed. I'm sorry."

She bowed her head and took a deep breath. She wasn't surprised. Buffalo Heart was, like his name implied, courageous. It was only a matter of time before he was killed, trying to protect his tribe.

"Thank you for your kind words."

She had hoped her Comanche husband hadn't been killed, and his death was one more to add to her burden. But as much as she grieved for her family and her Comanche husband, what she really wanted to know was what had happened to her baby.

As if to punctuate her unspoken question, she heard baby Johnny cry out. Just hearing his cries, though Nellie quickly quieted him, tore her apart. Her arms ached, and her breasts filled with milk, hot and heavy.

She crossed her arms over her chest, worried about leaking through the bindings. "My baby, you saw him?" She looked at Jacob, and their gazes caught and snagged. "What did he look like? Was he hurt?"

"No, he wasn't hurt. He was alive when I found him. He was lying on the blanket under you, naked and exposed..." He rubbed his hand over his face and grimaced.

She couldn't keep the tears at bay any longer. She covered her face with her hands and sobbed, feeling as if her heart was being torn from her body.

He touched her shoulder—one gentle touch. "You weren't conscious. Don't blame yourself. You'd lost a lot of blood and the doctor said you hit your head, too."

How had he known she blamed herself?

She hadn't been able to cradle her child in her arms, to cover him, to keep him alive. She would live with that guilt for the rest of her life.

"He was still attached to you, Ruth," he said in a low voice. "I cut the cord, but his lips were already blue when I got there." He leaned forward and clasped his hands together. "I got you and your son to shelter as quickly as I could. Lieutenant Schultz had me bring you to the O'Connors because Mrs. O'Connor could act as a wet nurse if you couldn't..."

He lowered his head again. "I believe you know the rest."

She gulped again and nodded, reaching out her hand.

He surprised her by getting up and taking her hand.

"Yes, I know the rest. Nellie told me my baby... died in his sleep." She shut her eyes, but the tears leaked from the corners. "I didn't have time to name him. Poor little soul."

He squeezed her hand. "The O'Connors gave him a Christian burial, and they named him Matthew after one of the sons they'd lost. The burial couldn't wait, what with them not knowing if... not knowing when..." He squeezed her hand harder and sat beside her on the bed. "I hope they did what you would have wanted."

She shook her head. What did it matter? She was glad her child had been given a Christian burial, but it didn't bring him back. The only living thing she'd loved was gone. She'd lost everyone... everyone she cared about.

Jacob was being kind and, in his own way, he was trying to comfort her. She was grateful for his gentle understanding. She turned her head against his arm and sobbed, letting her pain pour out. He held her in his arms, not speaking. She was aware of the half-open door and how it must look to Nellie, but she didn't care.

Finally, her sobs eased and her eyes dried. She'd cried herself out. But she didn't want Jacob to go, not yet. She looked up at him. "Would you take supper with me? Here in my room?"

He pulled away and frowned. "I, ah, Mrs. O'Connor already asked and I..." His face cleared, and he nodded. "I'd be honored, Ruth."

* * *

Ruth cut a tiny piece of venison and chewed it slowly. She thought she'd be hungrier, living on broth for the past few days and meager rations with her captors. But the food tasted like dust in her mouth and all she could think about was her child, lying in the cold, dark earth. As soon as she was able, she would visit his grave and for as long as she stayed at the fort, she'd sit with him every day.

The room was so quiet, she could hear Jacob chewing. Nellie was in the front room, dishing up her husband's supper. The captain should be home soon. Their baby, Johnny, must be asleep in his cradle next door. She'd yet to see their child.

She sighed. Despite their kindness, did the O'Connors look down on her because she'd been wedded and bedded by a savage? It might explain why Nellie hadn't let her see their baby. But perhaps she was being unfair. Maybe Nellie didn't want to rub salt in her wounds by showing off her child.

When she'd been a captive, she'd dreamed of being rescued, thinking her problems would be solved. But returning to civilization, having been compromised by a native, wasn't as simple as she'd thought.

A scraping noise brought her back from her wandering thoughts, and she watched with pleasure as Jacob scoured his plate clean. He was of medium height but muscular. It probably took a lot to fill him. And she'd been remiss again, burying herself in her thoughts. She'd asked him to stay and then not paid him any attention. At least, he appeared to have enjoyed Nellie's cooking.

She held her plate out. "Here, take mine. I've only eaten a couple of bites. I must not be as hungry as I thought."

He got up and took the plate she offered. "Much obliged. It isn't often I get home cooked food." Then he frowned, and his brow creased. "But you need to eat to get your strength back. I shouldn't take your supper."

"Please, it will go to waste or be fed to the fort's dogs. If you're still hungry, you should eat. I'm accustomed to broth. It might take me awhile to get used to rich food again."

He took her plate and stacked it on top of his, digging in with his fork. "Since my mother passed, I try not to remember how good her cooking was." He wrinkled his nose. "You never know what you'll get in the mess hall. The cooks try, but there's nothing like home cooking."

Here was her opening—something they could talk about. Maybe it would take her mind off her baby... Matthew.

"How did your mother die?" she asked.

"From the measles." His voice sounded low and strained. "All the children at the fort got them one spring. My mother helped with the nursing, though she shouldn't have. The People have no strength against some illnesses. Measles is one of them."

"I'm so sorry. I didn't know that about measles."

"Most white man's diseases are deadly to the Comanche and other tribes."

"I can tell you loved her very much."

He grabbed a piece of cornbread and sopped up the remaining gravy. He kept his eyes on the plate.

"Tell me more about yourself, Jacob. You know almost everything about me."

"There's not much to tell. Though, you're right about my mother, I miss her." He picked up the thread of their conversation. "She was gentle and kind, always quick to help others, and a Christian. But life was hard because she was married to a white man, a soldier." He lifted his head and gazed at her. "She had to learn to fit into another world. Much as you did."

"Yes, I guess that's true." She was comforted by his understanding, by his ease at putting himself in her shoes. "How did your parents meet?"

He shook his head. "It isn't a pretty story. She'd been captured by some Mexicans and used... used... in a way a woman shouldn't be."

She sucked in her breath, and her heart turned over in her chest. It was exactly what she'd feared when she'd been captured. If it hadn't been for Buffalo Heart and his regard...

"How awful. I'm sorry. There are no words." Tears burned in her throat again. "I know I was lucky not to go through..." She couldn't finish. There really were no words. Her tears flowed once more. It was as if she couldn't get enough of crying.

This time, he either didn't notice or didn't feel right comforting her, unless she reached out to him.

"The Mexicans came to Fort Clark where my father was stationed. They'd tired of my mother. My father was tight-fisted. He didn't drink, gamble or frequent..." He frowned. "He'd managed to save most of his pay. He saw her and took pity." He put the empty plates on the floor. "Later, he said he'd fallen in love with her at first sight."

"How romantic."

"Not unlike you and Buffalo Heart."

"No, I guess you're right."

"And my mother fell in love with my father, too. She could never do enough for him. She worshipped the ground he walked on. Moved from fort to fort with him, but as hard as she tried, she didn't fit in. The other women would have nothing to do with her, unless they needed her nursing. She knew a lot about wild plants that could be used for sickness."

"My mother taught me about certain plants, and I learned more when I was with the Comanche. A lot of herbs work better than doctors." She managed to swallow her tears and dabbed at her eyes with the sleeve of her nightshift. "And your father? Is he here at the fort, too? You said he was a soldier."

"He was. An enlisted man, a corporal, a lifer. Not like some of these new recruits who join for the bonus and then..." He shrugged. "My father brought me with him to Fort Concho. He got me a job as a hostler because I'm good with horses. My mother's brother taught me how to tame and train wild mustangs. Handy, when the government seldom sends enough money to pay the soldiers, much less purchase good mounts."

"So, you were a hostler before you became a scout."

"Yes, and I still work with horses. I keep a herd of my own and sell them to the fort, if they can afford them, or to travelers passing through, or even to some ranchers, like your folks."

"You speak of your father as if he's..."

"He died a little over a year ago. Doc Statler wasn't much help. My father got sick one day, fainted while he was drilling on the parade ground, took to his bed, and never recovered. The Doc thought it might be typhoid, though, how he got it when none of the other soldiers sickened, I can only guess."

"What do you think?"

"I think he drank some dirty water while he was out on patrol. Just bad luck, I guess."

"Were you already a scout then?"

"Yes, as soon as Major Gregor was made our commander, my father went to him. He knew the major by reputation—that he was a good and fair man. I enlisted as a regular scout for the army. Scouting pays better than mucking out horse stalls, same as a private's pay."

"I guess that makes us both orphans."

He gazed at her, and she met his gaze. Staring into his black eyes, a shiver skittered over her skin. There was something about him that was compelling, as if he could see into her soul and liked what he saw.

Jacob retrieved the stacked dishes. "I'm going to get some of Mrs. O'Connor's peach pie for dessert. Do you want some?" he asked, wishing she'd eat something. "I know you said you weren't hungry, but peach pie, especially this time of year, is a treat."

She managed a small smile. "You're right about that, and I have an awful sweet tooth. Peach pie sounds wonderful. I would love a piece." She held out her tin cup. "And could you bring me some more coffee, please?"

"My pleasure."

He turned toward the half-opened door and could see Captain O'Connor and his wife, finishing their supper. The captain had come home while they'd talked. Jacob hadn't greeted him because he didn't feel comfortable, disturbing them.

Before he could ask for pie, there was a knock on the front door. Odd time to be calling—at supper time. He hoped there hadn't been another raid or someone hurt or...

Mrs. O'Connor got up and went to the door. She opened it and Lieutenant Schultz stood on the threshold, clutching what appeared to be a bouquet of wax flowers. What did his commanding officer want with the O'Connors at this time of night? The flowers gave away his true intention, and he remembered, all too well, how the lieutenant had looked at Ruth when he'd rescued her.

He stiffened, and his heart sank. A spurt of jealousy slithered through him, but he knew he had no right. Just because he'd rescued Ruth and enjoyed talking to her, he knew better than to have romantic feelings for a white woman.

He nodded to the captain and took the plates to the pump sink in the corner.

"How nice to see you, Lieutenant," Mrs. O'Connor said.

"Good evening, Mrs. O'Connor and Captain," Schultz said. He glanced at Jacob and nodded.

Jacob inclined his head.

"Miss MacDonald must be awake and talking if Jacob is here," the lieutenant said.

"Yes, she is. She and Jacob have been talking about her rescue," Mrs. O'Connor said. "Won't you step inside where it's warm? We've just finished supper, and I'm afraid there isn't any—"

"I wouldn't want to impose myself." He glared at Jacob, and Jacob knew exactly what he was thinking. A half-breed shouldn't have imposed himself, even though he'd come on direct orders from the major.

He hadn't planned on staying and eating, knowing the silent code of the fort and his place. But Ruth had needed him, had wanted him to stay.

"I made peach pie for dessert, and there's plenty to go around," Mrs. O'Connor said. "Won't you stay and have—"

"May I please speak with Ruth and give her these?"

Mrs. O'Connor twisted the edge of her apron into a knot and glanced at her husband.

The captain got out of his chair. "Let me ask her."

Jacob edged closer to the far corner, wondering how Ruth would respond.

The captain went to the half-open door of Ruth's bedroom. "Miss MacDonald, Lieutenant Schultz is here to see you. Are you ready to receive him? He wants to know how you're doing."

"Please, thank the lieutenant for his concern." Jacob could hear Ruth's voice. "Tell him I'm better, but talking with Scout Wells has exhausted me. I'd prefer if the lieutenant could wait until I'm feeling better."

Jacob wanted to smile but it would be unseemly, given the circumstances. He couldn't believe the lieutenant expected to start wooing a woman who was bedridden and grieving for her dead child. He knew what he should do, though, to honor Ruth's wishes. He needed to let her rest.

The captain turned around and said, "Lieutenant, she's tired. Jacob and Ruth have been going over her rescue and—"

"I understand," the lieutenant grated out between clenched teeth.

"Won't you stay for peach pie and coffee? It would be an honor," Mrs. O"Connor offered again.

The lieutenant stared at Jacob, as if he could skewer him with his gaze.

Chapter Four

Jacob ignored the lieutenant, turning his head to one side and pumping water over the dirty dishes. He knew it was a presumptuous thing to do in the O'Connors' home, but he didn't want to acknowledge the hostility emanating from his commanding officer.

He needed to work with the man, to take orders from him—no matter what happened with Ruth. There could never be anything between them. She was a white woman, and he was a half-breed. But if there was a way he could help her, once she got on her feet, he wouldn't hesitate.

"No, Mrs. O'Connor, thank you for your kind offer. But I'll not be staying." The lieutenant thumbed his flat-brimmed, regulation hat. Then he thrust the wax flowers at her. "Would you see Ruth gets these?"

"Of course." Mrs. O'Connor took the garish bouquet. "They're lovely—they'll brighten up Ruth's room. And I'm sure later, she will want to thank you personally."

Schultz nodded at the captain and bowed to Mrs. O'Connor. "I'll come another time."

Jacob didn't like leaving Ruth without a farewell, but he knew he should defer to the lieutenant. He wiped his damp hands on a dish towel, hanging next to the sink.

"Lieutenant Schultz, sir, I'll be going with you. I think I've told Miss MacDonald what she wanted to know." He turned to the O'Connors. "Thank you, Captain and Mrs. O'Connor, for your hospitality. Your supper was excellent, Mrs. O'Connor."

"How kind of you," Mrs. O'Connor said, and then she glanced at her husband.

He waited to see if she would offer him dessert, but she didn't. He wasn't surprised. He'd served his purpose, and he could see which way the wind was blowing. He followed the lieutenant out into the cold night.

The lieutenant turned to him. "How did it go, Wells?"

"It was hard, especially the part about her baby." He hesitated, wondering exactly what the lieutenant's intentions were. "She told me how she'd become a captive. Her family owned a ranch northwest of here. They were killed in a Comanche raid. She was the only survivor."

"That's too bad," the lieutenant said, but the tone of his voice told him something else. The lieutenant beat his gloved hands against his blue wool trousers. "Damnably cold this year."

"Yes, very cold. Two snowfalls already. Not common."

Schultz turned toward him and lowered his voice. "What else did she tell you? Was she, was she... you know. Did she tell you anything about what happened at the hands of the savages?"

Jacob recoiled as if he'd been struck. How dare the lieutenant ask such a question? Of course, it was what everyone at the fort was thinking. But the lieutenant had no right to put it into words. Ruth had been a captive, a victim. She'd had no say over what had or hadn't happened. How could this man judge her?

It was the way of most White Ones—judging and classifying others. He'd loved his father; basically, he was a good man. And he'd been a good husband to his Comanche wife. Yet, it was his mother's values that resonated with him. She'd been kind and accepting, turning the other cheek. Not thinking evil of anyone. She'd even forgiven her captors who'd enslaved her and done unspeakable acts to her. Her best friend, those last few months at Fort Clark, had been a Mexican laundress, Isabel.

Isabel had helped him and his father to nurse his mother before she died. According to the Scriptures, it was the way people should treat each other, with respect and caring.

Not scorn.

Though, to be fair, not all of the whites thought like the lieutenant. There were some, like his father and the major, who judged a person on their merits.

"Miss MacDonald was fortunate. The tribe's foremost warrior took a shine to her, and he married her. Her husband was trying to cover their tracks when we killed him."

"So, if it wasn't for this warrior, the other savages would have violated her without a thought." Schultz slammed his fist into his open palm. "They're a blight on the earth. The Comanche and all the hostiles need to be exterminated."

Jacob curled his fingers into a fist, too, and it took all his self-control not to strike the man. But the lieutenant held his life in his hands, could send him into danger or have him court-martialed.

He unfisted his hand. There was nothing to say, nothing he could do.

Schultz glanced at him. "I'm not including the tame hostiles, like your mother, of course. She chose to live with a white man and—"

"You seem interested in Miss MacDonald."

The lieutenant guffawed and slapped him on the back.

Jacob flinched away from his touch.

"Who wouldn't be interested? There aren't enough women on the frontier, and even if she's suffered a misfortune, I'd be a blind fool not to take an interest." He grinned, a wicked showing of his yellowed teeth. "You told me yourself, she has no family left. She'll need a man's protection."

Jacob knew he shouldn't ask, but his tongue got the better of him. "Then your intentions are honorable, sir?"

Schultz stared at him as if he was some strange species of animal. "Wells, you overstep yourself. I'm not beholden to you or any man to explain my intentions. Just because you rescued her, don't get any ideas."

He knew he shouldn't have crossed that invisible line. "Sir, pardon me. You're right, I shouldn't have asked." He bowed his head. "I need to report to the major. He was most insistent to know how Miss MacDonald is doing. I'm certain he'll be in his office. He often works late."

Schultz stroked his chin. "I hadn't realized the major would take such an interest. But with his wife ailing, maybe he..." He hesitated. "I better go slowly. Wouldn't want to overstep and get on the wrong side of our commander."

Jacob wanted to tell him the major was too honorable to take advantage of a woman. But perhaps he should let the lieutenant think of the major as a possible rival. It might give Ruth some breathing room.

"Yes, sir, you wouldn't want to get on the wrong side of the major." He half-turned and saluted. "Good night to you, sir." Then he hurried toward the fort's headquarters.

* * *

Nellie closed the door to Ruth's bedroom and opened the other bedroom door. Johnny slept peacefully in his cradle. At night, when no one else was around, she purposely kept his swaddling looser, so she could see, at a glance, if he was breathing.

Watching her son's chest move up and down, she sighed with relief and returned to the front room. The dishes had been washed, dried, and put away. The hearth fire had been banked for the night.

Her husband had fetched a bottle of whiskey from the cupboard, along with two mugs. "It's been a difficult night. Though, yer dinner, especially the pie, was delicious. I'm glad Jacob and Schultz didn't stay. I'm looking forward to finishing the pie meself." He poured out two draughts. "Won't ye join me in a tot of whiskey? I think we've earned it."

She sat next to her husband and sighed again. "You're right. We deserve it." She touched her mug to his and took a sip. It burned going down but coiled warmly in her stomach.

"So, ye told the girl this afternoon." His statement wasn't a question.

"She came to herself all of the sudden and asked for her baby. I had no choice."

"But did she try to question ye—"

"Yes, and I answered the least I could, as you told me. Then I sent to the major for Jacob."

He took a sip of the whiskey and placed his hand on hers, resting on the table. "Ye did the right thing, Nell. The less said about 'er baby, the better. She will have 'er plate full, adjusting to civilization." He glanced at the bunch of wax flowers. "And ye must encourage 'er to see the lieutenant. He could well be the answer to 'er prayers."

"I know. She's lucky he's interested. Not many men would..." She tucked her chin in and didn't elaborate.

A captive woman, birthing a savage's child, was often treated as a social pariah. Not that there wouldn't be plenty of sympathy for what she'd gone through. But she could never hope to be respectable again—not unless a white man chose to take her to wife.

She patted her husband's hand. "I'm thinking she'll be recovered enough to attend the St. Valentine's Day ball. Our ladies' auxiliary has already started making decorations. And the fort's band has agreed to play." She took another sip of whiskey. "I've begun to take in some of my dresses for her." She tapped her chin with one finger. "Though, I think for the ball, she will need something new. I saw a bolt of dark green velvet at the sutler's. Though, I warn you, husband, the fabric's cost is dear."

He exhaled and tipped his mug back, draining it. "I don't like spending the coin, but all things considered, I give ye permission to buy it. I want what we did to be..." He lowered his head. "I want the best for 'er. We need to make the sacrifice." He glanced at their bedroom door. "She's given us the greatest gift. I want 'er to be happy and have a new start. The lieutenant can give 'er that, but she must net the fish first. Aye?"

Nellie smiled and echoed his Irish brogue, "Aye, husband." But even as she agreed with him, a hollowness opened inside of her, realizing what they'd done.

* * *

Ruth woke up with a start. A baby was crying and her breasts ached, filled with milk. *Where was her baby?* Her thoughts were groggy, half-formed, and then reality struck, like the sharp sting of a serpent's tooth.

Her child was dead. The baby she heard crying belonged to the O'Connors. She sank back and wept, silent tears sliding down her face.

But her milk-heavy breasts had drenched the bindings from the day before. And she was tired of being in bed, tired of thinking too much...

She threw back the covers and put her feet over the side. She wanted to see the O'Connors' baby and get some fresh bindings. But when she stood, her legs were weak as water, and she had to grit her teeth to stay upright. Her hosts hadn't provided a wrapper, but she assumed the Captain would be at his duty.

She tottered to the door and grasped the latch. Gathering her strength, she clung to it and took several deep breaths. Then she opened the door.

Ruth: The Rescued Bride

Nellie O'Connor sat at the table, her breast in the baby's mouth. Loud sucking noises reverberated in the small room, and Ruth couldn't help but smile.

"Oh, Ruth, are you all right?" Nellie half-rose with the suckling baby in her arms. "You look peaked. Why don't you lie back down, and as soon as I finish, I'll come to you? I've got your breakfast on the back of the stove, keeping warm." She pulled up the baby's swaddling, covering him. "I'll bring it to you."

"No, please, Mrs. O'Connor, I know I'm weak, but I can't stay in bed any longer. I need to get my strength back." She inclined her head. "After he finishes, can I hold him?"

Nellie's eyes widened and a look of something odd darkened them. She bent her head and rocked the baby. "I guess so. But if you're still weak—"

"I won't drop him. I promise. I'll sit at the table, and you can stay close by."

"Shouldn't you have your breakfast first?"

"No, please." Ruth touched her chest. "My breasts are heavy with milk, and I thought—"

"I'm sorry. I should have known, but I didn't want to disturb you." Nellie lifted the baby's head and deftly changed him to her other breast. "Johnny has quite an appetite." She laughed. "Though, you don't want to hear that, I'm sure."

"I could help if he's too demanding. After all, you nursed my child."

"To be sure." Nellie lowered her head again. "But it's best we stop your milk. Otherwise, you'll be in pain."

"Oh, I didn't know."

"Yes, and I have fresh bindings for you and some sage to make a tea that will help to dry up your milk."

Ruth took a few faltering steps and dropped into the chair beside Nellie. "A tea to dry me up?" She'd never heard of such a thing, and she worried her soul would dry up, too, having lost the only living thing who might have loved her.

"Yes, after a few days you'll be like new. No more pain."

But she welcomed the pain. Didn't want to feel like new. She wasn't new nor would she ever be. She glanced at her milk-stained nightshift.

"I have nothing to wear, Mrs. O'Connor. My deerskin dress must have been..."

"Yes, dear, your deerskin was quite ruined. I... we... burnt it." Nellie patted her hand. "But not to worry. I've started taking in some of my dresses for you. They should suit. And I've an extra nightshirt and wrapper, too." She paused and lifted the baby from her breast, buttoning her shirtwaist. "I didn't know how soon you'd be out of bed."

Ruth held out her arms. "Can I hold him now?"

Nellie lifted the baby to her shoulder and gently patted his back. "He needs to be burped after eating."

"Oh, I see."

She dropped her arms and clasped her hands in her lap, twisting them. Her skin tingled, and her arms ached. She'd been the youngest of her family, and she had no idea what a baby needed. Nellie, despite there not being any other children in the house, seemed to know.

Johnny let out a huge belch, worthy of a mule-skinner after too many whiskies.

Ruth laughed and went soft all over. "He's a wonder, and you're such a good mother."

"Well, I, ah, try... That is, I've had a lot of experience," Nellie said.

"Do you have other children?"

Nellie bent her head and rearranged the child's swaddling. "Uh, yes. I've had several children, but unfortunately, like your little one, God called them to heaven. Though, my Eliza was over a year old when she took a fever and..."

Ruth put her hand on Nellie's arm. "I'm so sorry. That's terrible. It's awful to lose a child, isn't it?" Her throat clogged and tears seeped from the corners of her eyes. She couldn't quit crying. She'd turned into a waterspout.

She wiped her eyes and nose with the sleeve of her nightshift. "I'm sorry. I, ah, uh, it's just..."

Nellie thrust the baby at her. "Here, you want to hold him. Take him." She rose. "Let me get a clean nightshift and wrapper for you. And some fresh bindings for your breasts. I need to make your sage tea, too."

Ruth folded the baby into her arms. Feeling his sweet weight, her heart turned over and rose to her throat. Holding him and experiencing the warmth of his small body through his swaddling seemed so right, so very right. Her heart expanded and love flooded her. A perfect love. And for one brief moment, the first time since her family had been killed, she was at peace.

She gazed into the baby's face. He had dark hair, like Jacob said her child had. Her heart lurched, thinking about it.

Nellie bustled around the kitchen, laying out strips of clean cloths, a worn nightshift, and a quilted wrapper on the table. She heated a teakettle of water on the cooking stove and shredded some leaves into the bottom of a tin mug.

Ruth gazed at the child in her arms. He yawned and waved a fist. Then he opened his eyes, and she saw they were brown but with greenish-blue flecks. She had blue eyes, like her mother. But her father had had hazel or bluish-green eyes.

Her heart lurched again, and she wanted to cry out: *this is my child, look at his eyes*. But she controlled herself, knowing it was wishful thinking, though both Captain O'Connor and his wife had brown eyes. Why then, the flecks of blue-green?

She couldn't help but remark, "He has hazel tints in his brown eyes. My father had hazel eyes."

Nellie turned from the whistling teakettle and poured hot water over the crumpled leaves. "Most infants are born with lighter eyes, and they darken in the first year." She put the teakettle back on the stove. "Though, you never know. My husband's father had blue eyes, and my mother had hazel-colored ones." She shrugged. "Our Johnny might have lighter eyes than mine or my husband's. It's possible."

"Oh, I didn't know." And for some reason, she couldn't let go of the fantasy. If her child had lived, he would have looked so much like Nellie's Johnny.

"Yes, well, now," Nellie said. "You've held him, and he's been fed." She set the tin mug of tea on the table and stretched out her arms. "Let me put him to bed." She chucked her son's chin. "I think he's all done in."

Ruth offered the child up, wishing she could have held him longer. But he wasn't hers. Someday, she'd have another child, in a proper place, and it would live, but not now... not now.

She took a sip of the sage tea and grimaced. It was bitter, but if it helped her milk to stop, she'd need to endure. She hadn't eaten much last night, and her empty stomach roiled, wanting breakfast.

Nellie returned from her bedroom, hands on hips. "I'm glad to see you're drinking the tea." She waved her hand. "I know 'tis bitter, but it will help." She nodded. "Which will it be then? Breakfast or rebinding your breasts?"

"I think breakfast. I'm famished."

"Good, lass." Nellie grabbed a kitchen towel and took the plate off the back of the stove. "Here you are. And after, we'll get you some fresh clothes."

Ruth bent her head and scooped up a bite of scrambled eggs. "Thank you. You and Captain O'Connor have been so kind."

"Pish!" Nellie patted her arm. "Eat and get strong." Then the other woman leveled her gaze at her. "You'll be needing new clothes. As I said, I've started on some of my dresses. Have you any experience with a needle?"

Ruth swallowed a bite of egg and chewed on a piece of bacon. "Yes, I'm good with a needle. I was the youngest and the only girl in my family. My mother taught me how to sew."

Nellie beamed. "Then as soon as you feel strong enough, we'll start."

"I'd like that. To feel useful again."

Her gaze fastened on a gaudy bunch of wax flowers, lying on the sideboard. Why didn't Nellie have them displayed in a vase? It was odd to say the least.

"What are those flowers for?" she asked.

"Oh, me, I plumb forgot when you interrupted my nursing." Nellie picked up the bouquet and held it out to her. "They're for you, Ruth."

"But why... or should I ask... who?"

She had Jacob's unconventional bouquet on the table beside her bed. And she couldn't think of anyone else at the fort who would bring her anything. She accepted the wax flowers and grimaced at their garish colors.

"Those are a gift from Lieutenant Schultz," Nellie said with a big smile. "The lieutenant's a fine man, and he's been asking after you."

She glanced at Nellie. "I thought Jacob rescued me. Why would this Lieutenant Schultz be asking after me?"

"Oh, he's Jacob's commanding officer. It was his Company F that pursued the hostiles holding you captive."

"So, the lieutenant saw me bloody and unconscious, and he's been asking after me?"

"Yes, at least once a day since you were rescued." Nellie elbowed her gently. "Don't you remember, the captain asked if you wanted to receive him last night, sincc Jacob was already here."

She held her hand to her forehead. "Yes, now I remember. I guess I didn't pay much attention. I was so wrung out from talking with Jacob. From learning about my baby and..."

Nellie put her arm around her. "That's understandable. It's a lot to take in, lass. But things will be brighter from now on. And as soon as we have you something to wear, we'll have the lieutenant to dinner, so he can pay his proper respects."

"Oh, but, I'm not... that is... I don't want to be called upon."

"But lass, he's an officer and a gentleman. You said you've lost all your family. What will you do if you don't..."

She turned and stared at Nellie. "What will I do? I hadn't thought that far ahead. First, I'd like to get something warm to wear, so I can visit my child's grave... Matthew's grave."

"Of course." Nellie released her and bowed her head. "You'd want to do that first. I can understand why."

Then Nellie raised her head and their gazes caught and held. "I'll get a vase for your flowers, and I wish you'd think about receiving the lieutenant. It's the proper thing to do, seeing as how he's been so solicitous."

"I'll think about it." But it was the last thing she wanted, to be wooed by a man, wedded and bedded again.

Nellie clucked her tongue. "You miss your baby. I know exactly how that feels. But you can't have another child without a husband. Now can you?"

* * *

Four days later Ruth bundled herself in a wool suit that had belonged to Nellie and wrapped a thick shawl around her shoulders. She pulled upon the front door of the cabin and faced the world for the first time.

Nellie had wanted to come with her, but she'd talked the older woman out of it, explaining she wished to visit her baby's grave alone. She'd tried to pick the best time for visiting. It was mid-day and most of the soldiers were either out on patrol or in their barracks, resting between shifts of guard duty.

Being rescued was *not* all she'd expected it to be—not the joyous homecoming she'd dreamed about when she'd been lying beneath deerskins on the hard earth in a teepee. She had nothing of her own. No family or possessions. She was completely at the mercy of strangers.

And she'd spent the last few days, working almost as hard as she'd labored when she'd been a captive, wanting to repay the O'Connors' generosity. Despite some initial weakness and nausea, she'd sewed until her fingers were stiff and full of pin pricks, and she'd helped with the cooking. She'd dusted, mopped, and swept the two-bedroom cabin until it shined.

Even Captain O'Connor, who seldom spoke much at supper, had commended her efforts. She'd appreciated his compliment, but to her way of thinking, it was the least she could do.

The O'Connors were kind people, and she enjoyed helping them. But gratitude wasn't the only thing driving her. The busier she was, the less time she had to think.

Despite some initial reluctance on her part, Nellie let her hold Johnny and that was when she was happiest, when she almost forgot all the pain she'd endured, all the loss, all the sadness filling her with despair.

Gazing at Johnny's chubby face and dimpled arms, her heart had filled with a joy so complete, she wanted to break into song and dance around the room. But of course, she didn't dance around, knowing Nellie was over protective of her son.

While they'd sewed, and Johnny slept in his cradle, Nellie had confided in her about all the babies and children she'd lost. Just knowing the other woman understood what she was going through was a balm to her spirit, and she prayed each night Johnny would grow up strong and healthy.

Last night, she'd been holding Johnny when the captain had come home for supper, and he'd been obviously displeased, barely greeting her and asking Nellie to bring the child into their bedroom.

Surprised by his sudden change of attitude, she'd gone to her bedroom and shut the door. But the white-washed pine walls between their rooms weren't thick, and she could hear the sound of their voices, raised in argument.

The last thing she'd wanted was to cause problems. At the end of their meal, the captain had turned to her and told her the lieutenant would be coming to supper tonight. She'd put the man off long enough, and he'd run out of excuses.

She'd nodded, and her heart had sunk to her feet. But she had no say in the matter and knew she must accept the inevitable.

Nellie had been distant today. She'd burned the shriveled offering Jacob had given her, except for the ostrich feather and the blue ribbon.

She walked across the rutted track of the parade ground and headed for the western outskirts of the fort. Nellie had told her where to find the cemetery.

The cold wind, blowing from the north, pierced through the layers of her clothing, and she pulled the shawl over her head. Then she bent her head and walked as quickly as she could in an old pair of lace-ups that were at least one size too small.

Nellie was shorter, rounder and smaller than she was, and they'd had to be creative to alter the suit she wore, a couple of shirtwaist blouses, a plain brown skirt, and two calico day dresses. As for the shoes, she didn't have any choice. The sutler was out of women's shoes and wouldn't be getting any more until spring.

After what had happened last night and the strange way Nellie had acted today, she'd been forced to think about what she planned on doing with herself.

She owned a ranch of a thousand acres, and there was no one else to inherit the land. But the house and barn had been burnt, and the livestock had probably been stolen or killed by predators. Besides, she couldn't run a ranch by herself, even if she had a house to live in and the money to re-stock the ranch.

She had an aunt on her mother's side, her Aunt Alice, who lived in Arkansas. Her father had been an only child, and most of his people had passed, except for some remote cousins in Missouri.

Her Aunt Alice had married well, to a banker, but they'd not had any children. Perhaps her aunt would like to have some family close by as she grew older. Of course, she'd have to tell her aunt what had happened to her mother, Alice's sister, as well as the rest of her family, which would be painful.

Otherwise, she would need to marry quickly, most likely one of the soldiers at the fort, probably the lieutenant who was interested. The thought of another loveless marriage, made out of necessity, didn't appeal to her, even though, it would be a great deal different from being the captive bride of a Comanche.

She'd had her head down, bent against the wind, and so deep in thought she almost ran into the picket fence edging the cemetery. Looking up, she gazed at the barren, wind-blown patch of ground, punctuated with a variety of wooden crosses.

Nellie had told her Matthew was buried in the far north corner. She reached inside her skirt pocket, and her hand closed around the one thing she had to offer her child—she'd picked the least gaudy of the wax flowers to put on his grave.

She opened the gate and walked among the plots. Most of the wooden crosses were crudely made and inexpertly carved. The majority of graves held soldiers who'd lost their lives on the frontier. She wondered if Jacob's father was buried here, and then she saw his marker: Corporal James Wells, born in 1828 and died in 1872.

Her father's name had been James, too. If her child had lived, most likely she would have named him James—after her father.

She bowed her head and said a brief prayer. She often thought of Jacob and wondered if he would come and see her again.

There was something about him, maybe his understanding of what it meant to live with his mother's people, that drew her to him and made her feel safe.

She shook her head. She didn't know if she was a competent judge of character—not anymore. She'd thought the O'Connors liked having her.

She should have written her aunt sooner. After she suffered through supper with the lieutenant, she'd ask for a pen and paper and write her letter. Tomorrow, she'd walk to town and post it.

Chapter Five

Ruth saw the tiny mound in the corner, the hard, clay earth newly turned on it. The wooden cross was decently made and the lettering was still bold, done in black paint. No one had known her last name when she'd been brought to the fort, so the cross was plain, reading: Matthew, born and died, 1874.

Sinking to her knees on the stony earth, she wished the ground would swallow her up, too. What did she have to live for? What was the use? Everyone had been taken from her.

She pulled the yellow wax flower from her pocket and stuck it in the dirt. Then she bowed her head and talked to her son: nonsense words, syllables of love and affection, silly and childish cooing she'd learned, holding baby Johnny.

The sound of a footstep startled her, and she twisted around.

Jacob stood behind her, his hands clasped behind his back and a fake-looking smile on his face.

"Oh, I didn't see you come," she said. "I was just... it's my first time out of the house and..."

"I understand." He touched her shoulder. "I often come to visit my father's grave."

"Really?" She rose to her feet and stood almost eye-to-eye with him. She was tall for a woman. It was another reason Buffalo Heart had wanted her for his wife. He'd hoped to have tall sons.

"Yes." He ducked his head, and she saw the red stain creeping up his neck. "No, not so often. Not every day or anything. Every couple of weeks, I guess. But I was watching for you." He shrugged one shoulder. "There, you have the truth."

"You were watching for me to come to the graveyard?"

"Yes, you mentioned you wanted to come, that day when—"

"Why haven't you been back to the O'Connors'? I'd hoped you would come."

He lifted his head and stared at the dark, gray sky. "Uh, that wouldn't be seemly, Ruth."

"Why not?"

"Because that would be the same as... as..." He stiffened and shook his head. "I came the once, at the express orders of Major

Gregor to explain how you were rescued and what happened." He looked down again. "That's all."

"You didn't want to see me—you only came because you were ordered to?"

He rubbed the back of his neck. "Miss—"

"Please, call me Ruth. You said you would."

"I know. Out here, away from everyone else, I may. But not—"

"That's why you didn't come again because the people in the fort wouldn't think it seemly," she interrupted and looked him squarely in the face. "Am I right?"

He cleared his throat. "Yes, and Lieutenant Schultz wouldn't care for me to be seeing you... as if I was courting you..." He met her gaze. "He's taken a shine to you. And I understand he's to coming to supper tonight."

"Only because the O'Connors forced him on me. I don't want to be courted... by anyone. It's too soon. I'm too..."

He put out his hand as if to touch her again and then glanced over his shoulder. He pulled his hand back. "I understand. You need to make peace..." He glanced down at her baby's grave. "Grief takes a long time to see to its end... or to a place where we can go on living with it."

She took a deep breath and nodded. And she wished he would hold her hand.

"Your father's name was James," she said and inclined her head at the marker a few rows over. "My father's name was James, too. It's what I would have named my child, had he lived, not Matthew."

He swallowed visibly and this time, he reached out and took her hand. His gloved fingers were warm, and his grip firm. She liked having her hand nestled in his. He made her feel safe and other than holding baby Johnny, the feel of his hand, holding hers, fulfilled a need she hadn't even known she had.

"James is a fine name, as is Matthew," he said. "And Ruth and Jacob, too, all from the Good Book."

"Yes, they are... all good names."

He looked back at his father's grave. "I wanted him to be buried next to my mother, but there wasn't time to transport him to Fort Clark—it was the summertime and—"

"That must be hard, not having them together."

She covered her mouth, just now realizing, even though her parents had died together, there had been no one to see them properly buried.

"When you told me how you were taken captive, I asked the major. He wasn't stationed here yet, but he has the records. It happened when I first came to Fort Concho before I was a scout. My father was with the patrol who found your family." It was as if he'd read her thoughts.

"They were given Christian burials on your ranch." He hesitated and then added, "If you want to visit their graves and see to your ranch, the major said he'd be willing to send a patrol out with you."

"Oh, how kind of him." She shook her head and lowered her eyes. "I hadn't even... thought... that is until now. But then, I don't know how much longer I'll be at the fort."

"You're thinking of leaving?"

"Yes, I guess so." She lifted her head and gazed past his shoulder at the Stars and Stripes, displayed on a tall pole in the middle of the parade ground, whipping in the winter wind. "I mean, not right away, but probably by spring."

"Are you sure you don't want—"

"I thought the O'Connors didn't mind having me stay until I got stronger and knew what to do. But it seems they would have me marry the lieutenant and clear out as soon as possible."

"Oh, Ruth, I don't think so. Why do you say that?"

"The captain came home last night, and he seemed angry because I was holding their baby. Then they had an argument in their bedroom, and he told me the lieutenant must come tonight. Today, Mrs. O'Connor wouldn't let me hold the baby." She shrugged. "It's all so puzzling. I mean, I've worked hard, trying to help out and not be a burden."

She pulled her hand free and closed her eyes, biting her lips. "I will not cry. I will not cry. I've cried an ocean of tears, and it hasn't helped."

He took her hand again and squeezed it. "That's strange. I know the O'Connors to be kind people. Could be the lieutenant is giving the captain a lot of grief."

"But Captain O'Connor outranks the lieutenant. Right?"

"Lieutenant Schultz has his ways." He forced a chuckle. "I should know. He's my commander."

"Well, for their sakes, I'll suffer through supper tonight, but I know when I'm not wanted. I have an aunt who lives in Arkansas. I will be posting a letter tomorrow."

"You weren't raised near here, were you?"

"No, we came from Missouri. My father's father owned a dry goods store, but my father didn't like being closed in, working between four walls. He dreamed of living on the land; and when he inherited the store, he sold it. He moved our family here and bought land and livestock to start our ranch."

"I see." He glanced down. "I guess you're right, there's nothing to hold you. Sometimes, I think the same thing. My enlistment will be up soon." He released her hand again. "I hope you find peace and a new beginning in Arkansas."

She nodded and smiled. "Thank you, Jacob."

It was the proper response but, somewhere deep inside, she knew there was one person... no, two people, she would miss when she left—Jacob and her baby.

* * *

Ruth passed the bowl of green beans to Lieutenant Schultz. In mid-winter, the green beans were a luxury like the peach pie. Nellie had sacrificed her last jar of preserved green beans from the small garden she grew out back during the summer.

And Nellie had outdone herself with thick, fried steaks, mashed sweet potatoes, cornbread, pickled okra, and the green beans. The lieutenant appeared to be enjoying his supper, shoveling in food as if it was his last meal.

"So, you went to West Point for a year?" The captain asked.

"Yes, I was fortunate to get a small bequest from my grandmother, but when the money ran out, I had to finish at a place closer to home." He buttered another piece of cornbread and took a bite, talking with his mouth half full. "I'm ambitious. A 'lifer' like you, Captain. Finishing at West Point would have put me on the right path. But only rich boys can afford it. I finished at the Carson Long Military Institute and lived on my family's farm."

The captain shook his head. "That's too bad. Carson is in Pennsylvania. Right?"

"Yes, my family's Pennsylvania Dutch." The lieutenant snorted. "Another name for German. My grandfather and grandmother came from Germany with little but the shirts on their backs."

"And my family emigrated to Boston from Ireland when I was ten. They worked in the mills."

"Did you go to military school?" Lieutenant Schultz asked.

"No, I earned my commission in the War Between the States."

"That was the way to do it," the lieutenant said. "I was too young to go. It was a rare opportunity for lifers."

"Yes, it was," the captain agreed. He reached across the table and helped himself to another steak. "Men who were commissioned to begin with, some of them made General while in their twenties. Look at that Custer. He's a boy wonder."

"If I'd had Custer's advantages, I would have made general, too," the lieutenant bragged. "Nothing to it when you graduate from West Point and get assigned to the right places."

The men kept talking, their conversation swirling around Ruth. Nellie sat rapt, listening to them discuss military life. Ruth was bored beyond measure. If the lieutenant was interested in her, he certainly wasn't bothering to draw her into their discussion.

But then, her life wasn't exactly the subject of polite dinner conversation. She pushed the food around on her plate. She hadn't even tried the steak, which had left more for the men. When she'd managed to finish a piece of cornbread, and a few bites of the vegetables, she moved her plate to one side.

The men had scraped their plates clean, and Nellie cleared her throat, asking, "Would you care for dessert? I made some Brown Betty."

She knew Nellie was proud she could offer dessert. They'd scrounged some apple sauce from Corporal Harding's wife and used the last of Nellie's cracker crumbs and butter to make the special treat.

"Awww, Nellie, I'm disappointed, no peach pie," the lieutenant remarked.

Nellie ducked her head. "I've no more cans of peaches. The sutler says—"

"I was just funning with you, Nellie," the lieutenant retorted. He held out his dirty plate. "I'd love some Brown Betty, one of my favorites."

Ruth couldn't believe the effrontery of the man. To use Nellie's first name and to make her feel ashamed she couldn't produce peach pies all winter, was beyond impolite.

She leapt to her feet, took the dinner plate from the lieutenant, and started clearing the table.

"Thank you, Ruth," Nellie said. "If you'll clear, I'll serve up the dessert and coffee. Do you want some Brown Betty, dear?"

Her first inclination was to turn down the precious treat, but the lieutenant's rudeness had gotten under her skin. She hadn't had anything sweet in a long time, and she needed something to fortify her.

"Yes, please, Mrs. O'Connor, if I could have a spoonful or two."

"Of course." Turning to the lieutenant, Nellie said, "Ruth is quite handy in the kitchen. She helped with the dinner tonight, and she's a wizard with a needle and thread. I've enjoyed having her."

The lieutenant turned his gaze on her, his eyes tracking over her figure, as if he was undressing her, one garment at a time. "That's nice, Nellie. Glad your kind hospitality has been rewarded."

How dare he!

She turned away, her face flaming, and spent as long as she could, pumping water over the dirty dishes and putting them to soak.

A few minutes later with the skimpy dessert and coffee finished, the lieutenant got to his feet and bowed to the captain. "I thank you and your wife for having me to supper." He turned and inclined his head to Nellie. "It was delicious." He took her hand and kissed the top of it.

Nellie smiled and simpered.

The lieutenant turned back to Captain O'Connor. "With your permission, sir, I'd like to take Ruth for a walk. We won't be long; it's too cold out."

The captain wasn't her father. The lieutenant should have asked her. Could he be anymore insufferable? And the last thing she wanted was to walk out with him.

The captain speared her with his gaze, as if he was already expecting her to decline. "Get yer shawl, Ruth. A turn around the parade field will help yer digestion, lass."

So that was the way it was. She might as well be back among the Comanche. She still had no say—she was only good enough to order around. She lowered her head, tamping down her anger, and grabbed her hand-me-down shawl from a peg by the door.

The lieutenant took her arm and opened the front door. She sailed past him and was down the front porch steps, walking briskly toward the dark parade ground.

"Not so fast, Missy," the lieutenant grabbed her arm again and squeezed it... hard.

"I thought you said we were going to walk around the parade ground?"

"I didn't say that." He pulled her into the small space between the officers' houses. "The captain did. I've got other ideas."

He hauled her into his arms and lowered his head, capturing her mouth. His mouth was open, and his tongue pushed against the seam of her lips, demanding entrance.

She twisted and turned, trying to get away. She kept her mouth firmly shut and pushed against his chest with the palm of her hand.

He pinched her breast... hard.

She gasped, and he thrust his tongue into her mouth.

She raised her hand to slap him.

He caught her wrist and growled, "I wouldn't hit me if you know what's good for you. The captain wouldn't like it. Would he now?" He lowered his mouth again, spreading spittle across her lips.

Then he pulled away. "That's better, much better. It's not as if you don't know about men, Girlie. After all, you've been bedded by a savage, birthed his brat and—"

"Stop it!" She covered her ears with her hands. "You have no right!" Freed from his noxious embrace, she dropped her hands, picked up her skirts, and raced back to the O'Connors' cabin.

He guffawed. "I have every right. Every right," his words mocked her. "You'll come around, Girlie."

* * *

Ruth hurried along the rutted track to the fort. She'd visited her baby's grave and then gone to San Angelo and posted her letter. The fort had mail service, but the postmaster only came around once a week. And after last night, she couldn't get away from Lieutenant Schultz and Fort Concho fast enough.

She'd almost complained to the O'Connors after what the lieutenant had done. But when she'd gone back inside, Nellie had "surprised" her with a beautiful bolt of green velvet. The older woman had spent good money for the fabric to make her a gown for the St. Valentine's Day ball.

Ruth understood the gown was meant to entice the lieutenant to declare himself. Thinking about it, she shuddered. She was dependent on the O'Connors' charity until she heard from her aunt, which could take weeks. She had nowhere to go, so she bit her tongue and thanked Nellie and the captain.

As soon as she got home, Nellie wanted to cut out the pattern for her new gown. If it wasn't so cold, Ruth thought, she would stay out all day.

She heard the thunder of hoofbeats, spied a cloud of dust, and realized the commotion was coming from a corral behind the fort's stables. She left the track and cut across the prairie, wondering what was going on.

She climbed onto the bottom rail of the corral and hooked her arms over the top. Peering over, she glimpsed Jacob, standing in the middle of the pen, turning in a tight circle, with a pretty chestnut filly on a long lead rope, running along the inner wall of the corral.

Hanging over the top rail, she watched as he put the filly through her paces, making her turn and stop, start and turn again. About eight other horses, some of them looking half-broke, milled around in the corral, too.

After a time, he must have seen her on the fence, because he stopped for a minute and waved. Then he moved slowly toward the filly, his hand outstretched, a shriveled-looking carrot on the palm of his hand.

He untied the lead line and took the rope hackamore off the filly. Then he offered her the carrot. The filly backed up a few paces, snorted, and bobbed her head up and down, as if considering.

She must have made a decision, because as quick as a wink, she stretched out her neck and the carrot disappeared. The chestnut whirled around and mingled with the other horses, still crunching her treat.

Jacob took off his gloves and slapped them against his thigh, raising a small dust cloud. He smiled at her and walked over. He threw the lead line and hackamore over the fence.

"What brings you out here in the cold?" His smile faded. "Oh, I didn't think… you've been to see—"

"Yes, earlier. And you don't have to worry about being discreet, Jacob. You can speak of my baby. I'd rather you did." She touched her heart. "It makes him more real, since I barely glimpsed him when he was born."

"All right, I'll remember that."

"I just came from San Angelo, though. Posted that letter to my aunt."

"You didn't waste any time."

She was tempted to tell him about the lieutenant and what he'd done last night. But the lieutenant was his commanding officer, and she had a feeling Jacob might do something rash. Less said, the better.

"No, I didn't. I told you, I don't want to be a burden for the O'Connors."

"Yes, you did." He shook his head. "I could talk with the major. He might—"

"No, please." She reached down and touched his shoulder. "Let me take care of it."

"All right." He ducked his head. "If that's what you want."

"I didn't know you still worked with horses."

"Remember, I mentioned it the first day?"

"You did?" She smiled. "I was pretty groggy that day. I'm sorry I don't remember."

"No apology necessary." He half-turned and looked at the milling horses. "These are mine."

"Yours?"

"When I'm not on duty, I go out and catch mustangs on the prairie. Then I tame them, train them, and sell them to town folk, some ranchers, even the fort." He half-shrugged. "It brings in extra money. I want to save up enough to buy a ranch."

"Oh, I didn't know you wanted to be a rancher. I got the impression you wanted to be a soldier, like your father."

He nodded. "I'd like that. To follow in my father's footsteps." He shrugged again. "But that's a pipe dream."

"Because you're only half-white?" She probably shouldn't be so blunt, but with Jacob, she felt comfortable to speak her mind.

"Yes, the Army seldom lets half-breeds be more than scouts. They're afraid, I guess, we might turn on the soldiers."

"How silly and unfair."

"Life is seldom fair."

Truer words were never spoken.

"You're right. It's too bad, though. I have a feeling you'd make a good soldier."

That earned a guarded grin from him. "You do, do you?"

"Yes, I do. But ranching is good, too. My father loved ranching."

"Will you go home before you leave for Arkansas?"

She thought about it. Returning to her family's ranch and seeing their graves would be hard. Did she want to do that?

"I don't know. I'll have to wait and see."

The horses turned as a group and ran toward the far end of the corral. She heard a bleat and then a long drawn-out baaa.

"What's that?" She shifted on the fence and looked around Jacob. A black-and-white goat stood in the middle of the corral.

"Oh, that's Nanny, my goat. She helps me with the horses."

"How? I mean, what can a goat do?"

His grin returned, spread wider. "When I train them to stand in a stall, I put Nanny in with them. For some reason, she calms the horses down."

"Really?"

"Yeah, and she gives good milk, too. There's a Mexican lady in San Angelo who buys her milk and makes cheese." He grimaced. "It's a bit sharp for my taste, but the lady has no problem selling it in town."

"Ruth, Ruth, what are ye doing, girl?" She heard the captain's voice, calling to her from the stables.

"Captain O'Connor wants you," Jacob said. "You'd better go." He reached up and touched the tips of her fingers.

At his touch, a shudder ran through her. "Yes, I wonder what he wants. Mrs. O'Connor knew I was going to town." She stroked his cold fingers with hers. "Please, come by and see me."

"You know I can't."

"Ruth!"

"Coming!" She vaulted off the fence and waved to Jacob.

* * *

Ruth hurried to Captain O'Connor's side. "What's wrong? Why were you calling me?"

"I went home between shifts, and I found Nellie ailing, lass." He glanced over his shoulder at the corral and back at her, scowling. "What were ye doing out here?"

"Nell... uh, your wife was fine when I left. I went to see my baby's grave and to post a letter in town." She glanced at him and tried to match his long stride. "I wouldn't have gone if I knew she was sick."

"Hummph, and ye took the time to visit with Jacob." He shook his head. "Ye shouldn't be seen with him."

"Why not?" She knew she shouldn't confront the captain, but she couldn't help herself.

He grabbed her elbow, reminding her of the lieutenant's rough handling the night before. "I'll let my Nell tell ye. Better coming from 'er."

They hurried across the parade ground, the front porch, and into the cabin. Nellie was lying on the bed in her room, wrapped in an afghan. Little Johnny was in his cradle, but he was fussing.

Nellie raised herself onto her elbows and gazed at them with feverish-looking eyes. "Ruth, has your milk dried up?"

"Yes, ma'am, a couple of days ago."

The captain scowled and turned away. He sat down heavily in the ladder-back chair.

"Oh, dear," Nellie said. "I haven't been paying attention. I thought maybe you could nurse Johnny for me. I've taken a fever, and I'm afraid to nurse him. With my second child, Matilda, I took a fever and when I nursed her, she got sick, too." Nellie glanced at her husband. "None of the other women are nursing at the fort. I don't know what to do."

Baby Johnny let out an ear-piercing shriek, as if to punctuate his empty tummy. Ruth was torn between helping Nellie and seeing to the baby.

She made a quick decision and glanced at the captain. He sat with his head down, and his hands dangling between his knees.

"Captain, sir, could you please pick up your baby and walk him around. I want to check your wife and—"

"I could send for Dr. Statler." He got up and lifted the baby from his cradle.

"Please, let me see how your wife is first."

He jiggled the baby up and down to get his attention, and Johnny crowed with delight.

Ruth touched her open palm to Nellie's forehead. She was burning up. She rocked back on her heels, worried over what to solve first, how to feed Johnny or Nellie's fever.

She wondered if Nellie might have "milk fever." One of the Comanche squaws had had milk fever, and she knew the symptoms. But she'd have to look at the older woman's breasts.

"Nellie, there must be a milk cow in the fort."

"Yes, there are couple of them. But most babies as young as Johnny, don't do well on their milk, gives them spit-ups and colic."

She hadn't known that. Her family had kept milk cows, but they hadn't had any babies to feed. When she was ten years old, she'd found an orphaned lamb and fed him with a milk teat, which gave her an idea.

"What about goat's milk?"

Nellie reached up and clutched her arm. "Goat milk is good for babies. It's the best."

"Jacob has a goat. She's called Nanny, and she helps him with his horses, but she produces milk, too. I know he wouldn't mind loaning his goat."

Nellie closed her eyes, as if she was praying beneath her breath. "God Bless you, lass. Yes, a milk goat would be just the thing."

The captain lowered Johnny into his cradle. "I'll get the nanny goat right away." He glanced at her. "Will you see to my wife's fever or should I fetch the doctor?"

Knowing Dr. Statler's reputation all too well, she said, "Let me look over your wife while you bring the goat, and I'll ask her what kinds of medicinal herbs she has." She held up one hand. "I might be sending you back to town for some things when you return."

"I'm at your disposal, lass." He hurried out the door, closing it behind him.

"You're thinking it might be milk fever. Aren't you?" Nellie asked.

"Yes, have you checked your breasts?"

"No, I just thought of it when you said you needed to look at me."

Ruth poured water from the pitcher into the basin beside the bed. She took the wash cloth hanging there and wet it, swabbing Nellie's face. "A tepid bath is good for fevers."

Nellie bent her head and unbuttoned her shirtwaist. "But it's winter."

"I know, but cooler water can help bring down the fever. My Mama believed in it, even in winter." She didn't press, not wanting to add to the ailing woman's misery.

Nellie pulled down her chemise, exposing her distended, blue-veined breasts. "Here they are. I haven't noticed anything amiss."

"Let me look."

Ruth bent over Nellie's exposed bosom, gently lifting each breast and checking them. First, the nipples and then the undersides, too. But there was no hint of milk fever. Nellie's breasts were creamy-white without the characteristic red streaks.

"I don't think you have milk fever."

Nellie pulled up her chemise. "That's a relief." She started buttoning her shirtwaist.

"I think perhaps you have a bad cold," Ruth said.

"I'm still afraid to nurse the baby. Do you know how to make a milk teat from cheesecloth?"

"Yes, I do. It's what made me think of Jacob's goat."

"Oh, why?"

"When I was a girl, I raised an orphaned lamb with a milk teat, but he was able to take cow's milk."

"Ah, I see."

"Now, about your fever, Nellie. Do you know where you might get some fresh fruit? In town, maybe?"

"No, not in town. But the major has fresh fruit brought in for his wife, every month or so." Nellie glanced at her. "The major's wife has been ailing since she had her last child and lost him."

"I'm sorry."

"You could send my husband to ask for any fruit they might have."

"Do you have any honey, raisins, basil, saffron, turmeric, or..." She hesitated, trying to translate the name from Comanche into English, knowing the Comanche traded with other tribes to the east for it. What she was thinking of had great healing powers, remembering how it had drawn the infection out of Buffalo Heart's wounded leg. "I think you'd call it something like... ginger root?"

"Lordy, Ruth, that's quite a list."

"All are good for fevers. I learned some from my mother. The last one from the Comanche."

Nellie nodded. "We have some honey. I'll take it with a tot of whiskey. That's always good for colds. And I have a box of raisins in the back of the cupboard and some dried basil leaves. As to the other things... I've never heard of such."

Ruth dipped the cloth in the water again and bathed Nellie's face. "Is there a healer in town? Not Dr. Statler."

"There's a *curandera*, a Mexican healer in San Angelo. She might have some of those things you're asking for. She's been tending the major's wife. I know it put Dr. Statler's nose out of joint." Nellie chuckled and then her laughter turned into a deep, wracking cough.

"You need to lie back and rest." Ruth gently pushed Nellie down.

The baby started to cry again. She took the pitcher and basin to the kitchen. She emptied the basin and filled the pitcher. The water from the outside pipe was good and cold. Better and better.

She dipped the cloth in the cooler water and draped it across Nellie's brow. "Try to doze a little. I'll get the baby." She went to the cradle and picked up Johnny, savoring the feel of him in her arms, even if he was squirming and crying.

Nellie laid her head against the pillow and sighed. Ruth saw her look out the window. "It's getting toward dark. I know it's a lot to ask but can you fry some bacon and boil a pot of beans. There's some leftover cornbread in the cupboard. And ask Jacob to stay to supper, too. Will you? His nanny goat is a blessing."

"Of course." She shifted the crying baby to her shoulder. "And while I'm getting the bacon frying, I'll heat up some whiskey, honey and raisins for you."

Nellie sighed again and sank into the pillow. "Bless you, Ruth."

Chapter Six

Jacob watched as Ruth set aside the milk teat she'd fashioned and put Johnny across her shoulder, gently patting his back, waiting for him to burp.

He pushed aside his plate. Bacon, beans, and day-old cornbread had never tasted so good. They were standard fare in the mess hall, but then, he didn't get to look at a beautiful woman and a sweet baby while he ate.

He'd fashioned a makeshift lean-to for his nanny goat behind the captain's cabin. The baby had sucked the milk teat dry—he hadn't known goat's milk was good for babies. But now he knew.

Captain O'Connor had retrieved a couple of withered oranges from the major, and the Mexican healer in town had sent over some mysterious herbs. Ruth had made Mrs. O'Connor eat one of the oranges immediately, saving the other for later, and then she'd spent a while, dithering over how to prepare the other herbs. He'd almost suggested to send for the *curandera*, but he didn't want to hurt Ruth's feelings.

They'd eaten together, in peaceful isolation with the baby, while the captain had taken supper with his wife. He'd watched how Ruth held the baby. How she'd fed him, painstakingly getting him accustomed to the milk teat. How tender she was, how careful.

His heart had expanded in his chest, watching her.

He'd never envisioned living his life with another. Had thought, at best, he'd save enough money for a small ranch. Hire some half-breeds, like himself, who couldn't get work and maybe some Mexicans. Men who would be willing to take orders from a man who was only half-white. But that was as far as his dream had gone.

He'd never thought of himself with a wife. A Comanche wife would want to stay with her tribe, unless he took her by force or some other misfortune, like that which had befallen his mother. And a white woman wouldn't have him.

Given his circumstances, he had a hard time seeing how he could find a proper wife.

But watching Ruth and knowing her as he did, his hopes soared. She was such a good mother, and he knew, deep down, she'd be a loving wife. He couldn't ask for better.

Ruth changed the baby to her other shoulder and patted his back. Finally, Johnny gave out a huge burp, and Ruth laughed. He'd never heard her laugh before—and the sound was magical, like the tinkling of tiny bells.

She was one beautiful woman with her long, red hair curling around her shoulders and her blue eyes shining with love for the baby. He could understand why, as a Comanche captive, she'd been favored.

He leaned toward her, his gaze focused on her berry-red lips, wanting to kiss her. Wanting that and more...

The door to the O'Connor's bedroom burst open and the captain rushed out. "Her fever's down. I swear it! I've been bathing her temples with water, and she's almost like new."

The captain grabbed Ruth and the baby and swung them around in his arms. "Please, Ruth, go and see if what I say is true."

Ruth smiled and laughed again. She handed the baby to the older man and said, "That's wonderful, Captain. Let me take a look."

The captain held the baby and rocked back and forth, beaming at Jacob. He'd never felt so important or wanted in a White One's home. His heart was a warm spot in his chest, and he was happy. Happier than he'd been in a long time.

"Join me in a tot of whiskey, lad?" The captain asked. "'Tis reason enough to celebrate."

Ruth returned with a big smile, and her sky-blue eyes were alight with joy. "She's much better. I'll keep dosing her and if she'll rest for a few days, I think she will be fine."

"I've never seen my Nell recover so fast, Ruth. And thanks to you, the babe is happy and fed, too."

"Thank you, sir. I'm glad," she said.

Jacob smiled and rose, holding out his empty coffee cup. "I'm more than willing to celebrate. A sip of whiskey would be fine."

The captain handed the baby back to Ruth, and Jacob noted the look of joy on her face when she cuddled the infant.

Captain O'Connor fetched the bottle of whiskey from a cupboard and grabbed a tin cup for himself, pouring them each two fingers and touching his cup to Jacob's. "To my wife and our baby's health."

Jacob touched his cup. "To their health, sir, and long life."

They chugged the whiskey, and Jacob felt the liquor burn the back of his throat, and then it filled an empty place in his stomach, settling like a warm blanket.

"I'm going back to sit with Nell," the captain said. He held out his arms. "I'll take Johnny. She's been asking after him."

Ruth gave the baby a kiss on his forehead and handed him to the captain. He closed the door behind him, and Ruth had a half-sad, wistful look on her face.

Jacob opened his arms.

As if she'd been destined to find her way there, from the first time they'd met, she walked into his arms and laid her head on his shoulder. Her arms went around his waist, and she hugged him.

He breathed in the sweet wild-sage fragrance of her hair. Good Lord, how he loved this woman! It had come upon him like a thunderstorm, hot and fast, and without warning.

He wasn't good enough for her. He knew that. Knew it to the depths of his soul.

But if he was good and kind and patient and prayed, maybe God would smile upon him. For now, though, for now, he needed...

Lowering his head, he took his index finger and lifted her chin a notch. Then he covered her mouth with his, savoring the sweet, honeyed taste of her lips. Cherishing their kiss, he felt as if he was ascending to heaven on eagle's wings.

Their mouths fit like two joint-ends of a fence. Perfect. Too perfect and too sweet. He could go on kissing her forever and ever.

He pulled apart and gazed down at her. Her blue eyes twinkled like bright sapphires. He wished he could dress her in sapphires and diamonds. He wanted to give her the world and then some.

They hugged. And then he lowered his mouth again, taking her juicy red lips. She returned his kiss with a fierceness that matched his. Nothing had ever felt so glorious, so heart stopping, as holding and kissing her.

He lifted his mouth and rained tiny kisses over her throat.

She sighed and leaned closer, holding him tightly. He returned the favor, burying his face in her fiery hair and feeling as if he'd come home.

* * *

Nellie and Ruth sat at the kitchen table with a roaring fire in the hearth to keep the chill away, sewing. They had Johnny's cradle beside them, and he was sleeping like a little angel.

With Ruth's doctoring and four days of rest, Nellie almost felt herself again. Except for one thing, the fever had dried up her milk. Jacob had been kind enough to loan them his nanny goat indefinitely, until her baby could start eating solid foods and tolerate cow's milk.

Jacob was a good boy. And Ruth... She gazed at the other woman. Ruth was beginning to be like the daughter she'd never had. The girl had nursed her back to health with nary a complaint about doing all the household chores and getting the baby to drink from a milk teat.

Like the daughter she never had... With the fever overtaking her so suddenly, she'd forgotten about the letter Ruth had written and posted. Seemed the girl had family in Arkansas, but Ruth hadn't confided about her letter, and she'd been too sick to ask. Now the past couple of days had passed in a blur with them sewing as fast as they could to finish Ruth's gown in time for the St. Valentine's Day ball.

Ruth had her head bent, her burnished red hair gleaming against the lamp's light on this dark winter day. She was carefully sewing the hem of her green velvet ballgown.

The lass would be a sight to behold in her new gown. Now, more than ever, she wanted to see the girl happily married to the lieutenant. As an officer's wife, no one would be able to sneer at her as tainted. Nellie's heart filled, brimming over, thinking of it. And for good measure, as soon as the lieutenant declared himself, she'd ask her husband to urge Lieutenant Schultz to get a transfer.

Then Ruth could start over and have children of her own. Thinking of Ruth having her own baby, her heart stuttered, and she frowned, pushing away her nagging conscience.

Johnny started fussing in his cradle, and Ruth bent down to pick him up. Nellie started to ask for him, but she couldn't. Not when she glimpsed the look on the girl's face, how radiant she was when she held him. Another twinge of conscience assailed her, and she winced, saying a "Hail Mary" under her breath.

"I'll get his milk teat filled," Ruth said. "I've a bucket of milk from this morning, staying cool on the porch."

Nellie held out her arms. "Here, let me hold him while you do that."

Ruth kissed the baby's forehead and held him for a moment longer, gazing down at the child.

The bands around Nellie's heart tightened, and she swallowed hard, fighting back the tears that seemed to come too easy, since she'd been sick.

Ruth nodded and handed her the infant. Nellie gazed at his chubby face, covertly studying his features for any sign of his father's heritage. But Johnny, though a month old now, looked much the same as when Jacob had brought him home.

She exhaled and crooned, rocking him in her arms.

Ruth threw on her shawl and opened the front door. A cold blast of winter wind whirled into the cabin, making Nellie shiver. She cuddled Johnny closer.

Despite her cuddling, Johnny was waving his fists and crying. When he was hungry, he didn't like to wait. But the milk teat needed to be made fresh each time with new cheesecloth.

Nellie rose to her feet and paced with the baby, jiggling him in her arms to take his mind off his empty stomach. And then she heard voices outside. Come to think of it, she'd expected Ruth to step outside, fetch the pail, and return quickly.

What... or who could be keeping the girl? Jacob stopped by, at least every other day, to ensure his nanny goat was giving good milk. He even furnished the goat's hay from the stables. But Nellie had an idea his goat wasn't the real reason he came. Though she didn't deem him suitable for Ruth, after all his kindness, she didn't have the heart to turn him away.

Trying to ignore the voices outside, she told herself she didn't want to pry, figuring it was most likely Jacob. If it was, why hadn't Ruth invited him in, to warm himself against the cold?

She paced to the front window and looked out. But it wasn't Jacob who stood on the porch or rather on the steps to the porch with Ruth blocking his way. It was Lieutenant Schultz.

He'd been out on patrol for the past few days, since he'd taken supper with them, the night before she'd gotten sick. Ruth stood with her shoulders thrown back and her chin jutting out, holding the milk pail. And she was frowning at Lieutenant Schultz.

The lieutenant was arguing, loudly, but not so loud as Nellie could make out the words. He made a grab for Ruth's arm, and she jumped back, slopping some of the milk out of the pail.

What on earth was going on?

Nellie put her hand on the door latch, but before she could open the door, the door swung open and Ruth came storming in, pail in hand, and fury radiating from her.

Going back to the window, Nellie peered out to see the lieutenant striding across the parade ground, his back ramrod straight. And from the looks of him, he was none too happy, either.

Ruth put the pail on the counter, got out the cheesecloth, and tore off a swath. She fashioned it into a rough-cone-like shape. Nellie could see her hands trembling as she worked at the task.

Baby Johnny let out an earth-shattering squeal and started shrieking, his patience at an end. Nellie rocked the baby in her arms, and he quieted.

Surely, Ruth would say something. But the silence in the small cabin, broken only by the crackling mesquite logs in the hearth, was as thick as molasses.

When Ruth finally got the milk teat ready and held out her arms, she gave the baby to Ruth. The girl settled in a chair, offering the teat to him.

Loud sucking noises filled the cabin, and despite her concern about what had happened on the porch, Nellie couldn't help but smile. Ruth and Johnny... Johnny and Ruth... they looked so right together.

She grimaced and pushed aside the voice in her head. "Ruth, what happened out there? I could hear you arguing, and you didn't invite the lieutenant in for a cup of coffee. I'm sure he came straight from his patrol. Where are your manners, lass?"

Ruth raised her head and met her gaze. Moisture glistened at the corners of her eyes. Had the girl been crying? What had the lieutenant done?

Ruth lowered her head. "I know you and the captain want me to take Lieutenant Schultz's interest to heart." She bit her lip. "And I respect your opinion, but the lieutenant is not what he seems to be."

"What do you mean? He's an officer and a gentleman."

Ruth frowned. "He may be an officer, but he's no gentleman."

"Ruth! How can you say such a thing? You've barely spent time with him."

"One night was enough." She shook her head. "For one thing, he's an arrogant braggart."

Nellie chuckled. "Oh, you mean all that silliness he was spouting at dinner." She waved her hand. "He was just showing off for you. Typical man."

"Yes, perhaps, but that's not all." She shifted the baby in her arms, so he could drain the last drop of milk. "When he took me outside for a walk, we didn't walk. He grabbed me, kissed me, and pawed me, too." Her face turned a bright crimson.

"Oh, pish! He's a soldier, stationed on the frontier. He might be a bit over eager but—"

"More than over eager." Ruth's face grew darker. "He thinks since I was a squaw, he has the right to touch my breasts and..."

Nellie gasped. "You mean his intentions aren't honorable?"

Ruth cocked her head to one side, as if considering. "I don't know. I don't think so. We never got that far, to talk about anything. He just wanted to kiss and touch my—"

"Well, what were you arguing about on the porch?"

"He wants to escort me to the St. Valentine's Day ball."

"And you don't want that, I take it?"

"No, I don't, and when I told him, he threatened to go to the captain and complain about my wantonness and..." Ruth removed the empty milk teat and laid the baby across her shoulder, patting his back. "But I've not been wanton. He's the one with roaming hands. I can't help what happened to me when I was a captive." Tears streamed down her cheeks.

Nellie patted her shoulder. "I know you haven't been... a wanton. He better not say anything to my Ezekiel." She held out her arms. "Please, let me burp Johnny, and I'll put him down for his nap. And don't you worry. If you don't want to go to the ball with him, we'll take you."

But her heart sank. There were no other bachelor officers at the fort. What would Ruth do? Perhaps, when the girl had calmed down, she'd ask more about her aunt in Arkansas.

She burped Johnny and took him to her bedroom, tucking him into his cradle. He drifted off with one tiny hand fisted beside his head. Nellie fetched her shawl and rosary beads. When she returned to the kitchen, she saw Ruth had dried her eyes and was sewing again. That was a good sign.

She patted the girl's shoulder. "You don't have to go to the ball with the lieutenant, but I wish you'd give him another chance. Now you've stood up to him, maybe he will think twice before he disrespects you."

Ruth nodded. "Perhaps."

"Would you mind to watch Johnny while he naps? I need to go out."

Ruth raised her head. "Of course not. Is there anything I should start for supper? I can cook while he's napping."

"No, I haven't thought what we should make for tonight. You could check the provisions and see what might be likely."

With those words, she stepped out into the cold winter air, pulling her shawl tightly around her shoulders. She was headed for the plain timber building, serving as the fort's chapel.

The chaplain, Pastor Mapes, was a Protestant, and she and her husband were Catholic. But the pastor was an upright man, and she enjoyed his sermons. She'd learned, living on the frontier, to make the best of what there was.

She was looking forward to when the circuit priest, Father Francisco, would be stopping by. He came from San Antonio, and he made a circuit of towns and forts who didn't have a Catholic priest within a two-hundred-mile radius.

Pastor Mapes had christened both Johnny and Matthew, but she wanted Father Francisco to christen Johnny again in the Catholic faith.

She entered the dark church and pulled her shawl over her head. She missed the holy water and the flickering candles of her faith. But it was a peaceful place with simple white-washed benches, a small dais fenced off at one end, and a podium for the pastor.

Kneeling at the foot of the dais where communion was given, she crossed herself and got out her rosary. And then she began to pray, asking for God's guidance. Not certain if, in the first few hours of her grief, she'd made the right decision.

Her conscience had been bothering her, since she'd spent so much time in bed with her bad cold.

What if she hadn't done the right thing—taking the baby as her own?

* * *

Jacob stood behind the long trestle table, laden with refreshments. He ran a finger around the collar of his starched shirt. It was hot in the room. The weather had changed a couple of days ago and turned warm, a harbinger of spring on the southern plains.

He shrugged his shoulders in his store-bought jacket. His new matching trousers were a good fit, and he'd shined his best cowboy boots. He adjusted the clasp holding his string tie for the thirtieth time and dropped his hands. He'd never been dressed up in his life. He felt like a decked-out mule in a corral of thoroughbreds. And he'd never attended a ball before.

With the scarcity of women on the frontier, he couldn't help but wonder why this particular holiday was celebrated with such relish. Though it was true other women would come from miles around, from the neighboring towns and ranches, filling in some of the gaps for dancing, he couldn't understand the need for a celebration.

The other holidays, Christmas and Thanksgiving, and especially the Fourth of July celebration, complete with fireworks brought all the way from Galveston, made sense. Then everyone attended, children included. But a ball for grownups only, celebrating love, where there wasn't but a handful of available women, bordered on silly, to his way of thinking.

He glanced around, admitting the ladies had outdone themselves to transform the mess hall into a ballroom. Huge red and white paper hearts, some with arrows sketched through their centers, hung on the walls. And draped over the open rafters was red bunting leftover from the Fourth. There were even a few crudely cut-out cupids cavorting behind the dais where the band was. And the lamps were all decorated with red, heart-shaped paper cut-outs, giving them a soft glow.

The trestle table, where he'd decided to wait for Ruth, sported a red-and-white checkered tablecloth, a huge bowl of punch, and enough sweets to give all of Company F a toothache.

He shifted back and forth on the balls of his feet, but the waiting was hard. For the past couple of weeks, he and Ruth had been keeping company, stealing kisses and holding hands when no one was watching.

She'd told him about turning down the lieutenant's invitation to the ball. That had taken guts on her part. He knew the captain was partial to the lieutenant and wanted them to make a commitment.

He and Ruth hadn't spoken of commitment; they'd just taken pleasure in being with each other, talking and kissing. He'd wanted to ask her to the ball, but he knew it wouldn't be proper.

Finally, the outside door opened and Captain O'Connor ushered his wife, decked out in a blue taffeta gown, inside. Then he opened the door wider, and Jacob held his breath.

Ruth stepped over the threshold in the green velvet dress she'd sewn. Her shoulders were bare, the neckline dipped low, and her tiny waist was a mere hand span, accentuating the lush curve of her hips. The gown fell in a straight-line to the floor, with a small flare at the bottom to cover the only shoes she had, a worn, hand-me-down pair of lace-ups.

He inhaled, drinking in her natural beauty. Her long red hair was piled on top of her head in a complicated roll, with a few curls straying to her shoulders. Nestled amidst her hair was the ostrich feather he'd given her. Seeing it, his heart swelled, knowing she was honoring him.

A few women milled around the edge of the dance floor, looking tawdry and overdressed in comparison. She was truly a hawk amongst sparrows. Not a very feminine comparison, but he didn't know much about swans and such, like he'd read in books.

Every man, married or unmarried, who attended the ball would want her. All he could think about was the one dance they'd agreed upon and holding her in his arms. And for that singular honor, he'd persuaded Corporal Harding to teach him how to waltz, despite suffering some good-natured ribbing.

With his heart thundering in his chest, he turned away, got a cup of the too-sweet punch, and joined a group of privates who were discussing a high-stakes poker game at the Last Swallow Saloon in San Angelo last week.

One-by-one, he saw the men scrutinize Ruth. Their reactions ranged from jaw-dropping awe to undisguised lust. He didn't appreciate them looking at her that way. But the men knew better than to act on their base feelings. They looked and gawked but didn't say anything.

The seconds and minutes dragged by, as he waited for the improvised ballroom to fill. The major made a short, welcoming speech, followed by applause. The fort's military band started off with a foot-stomping Virginia reel.

Jacob edged over to another group of soldiers, including Corporal Harding, and listened to their conversation about a new band of Comanches who were reported to have come from México and were raiding south of the fort, near the town of Sonora.

Time passed, and dance followed dance. Ruth had started dancing with Captain O'Connor and then one partner after another appeared. As he'd expected, she didn't lack for partners. One more dance, and then he'd claim their waltz.

The converted mess hall was full to capacity, but one person, in particular, was missing—Lieutenant Schultz. Jacob was surprised. He knew Ruth had turned him down, but he'd not expected her rejection to stop his brash and arrogant commanding officer.

There was a pause between songs. He hoped he hadn't waited too long, and he prayed the next dance would be a waltz, the only dance he'd learned.

The familiar strains of a Strauss waltz filled the crowded room, and he breathed easier. He put down his empty punch cup and strode toward Ruth. Men thronged around her, but as tall as she was, he could see she was looking directly at him.

As if no one else existed in the room, he approached her and bowed. Then he held his arms out. She glided into his embrace. Remembering the corporal's instructions, he held her firmly but not too close; and somehow, his feet managed to stay in time with the music while he whirled her around the dance floor.

At first, they didn't talk. They didn't need to talk. For him, holding her was more than enough. But there was one thing he had to tell her.

"You're very beautiful tonight, Ruth."

She smiled and her cheeks tinged pink. "I'm glad you think so. I never knew a ballgown could make me feel so different." She winked at him. "This is my first ball, you know."

"Mine, too."

"Really? Are those new clothes you're wearing?"

He grinned. "Are they that obvious?"

"Couldn't be more obvious, unless you'd left the price tags on."

He laughed. "I resent that remark, but coming from you, I'll overlook—"

"May I cut in?" A familiar voice asked, and he felt a tap on his shoulder.

He stopped dancing and swung around. He saw the look on the lieutenant's face. Ruth tightened her hand on his shoulder. He smiled at her, what he hoped was a reassuring smile and stepped back, bowing slightly.

"Please, Lieutenant, be my guest," he said.

The lieutenant took her in his arms, and he could have sworn Ruth winced when he touched her. Jacob melted into the crowd and turned away. He grabbed another cup of punch.

The fort's band finished with a flourish and declared an intermission. He joined the soldiers again, refusing Harding's offer of whiskey. He wondered what Ruth would do during the intermission, but he forced himself to look away.

* * *

When the music stopped, Ruth tried to pull away from Lieutenant Schultz. But he grabbed her arm and said, "Not so fast. We've unfinished business. How about a breath of fresh air?"

"I don't want to go outside."

He tightened his grip. "You're going outside. Now. Don't make a scene."

She winced again and decided not to resist. The last thing she wanted was to draw more attention to herself.

When the evening had begun, she'd been happy to be attending her first ball and looking forward to dancing with Jacob. But as the dancing wore on, and some of her partners made unseemly suggestions and put their hands where they shouldn't, she wished the O'Connors had never bought the green velvet fabric.

The lieutenant pulled her outside onto a porch, overlooking the river. She glanced around, hoping there would be others on the porch, but they were alone.

She shivered and rubbed her hands over her arms.

"It's not that cold out tonight," he said, "Feels almost like spring." He took off his jacket and draped it around her shoulders. "Here, this should help."

It was his first kind gesture—other than bringing those awful wax flowers when they didn't know each other. But she wished he hadn't done it. His jacket was scratchy on her bare arms and smelled like him.

He grabbed her shoulders and pulled her toward him.

She bared her teeth.

He pulled back. "So, it's going to be like that. Is it?"

"I haven't given you leave to kiss me, not that night at the cabin or now. I don't want to be here with you."

"Living with the savages, you've forgotten your manners, Girlie. And maybe that's why you're so cozy with my breed scout. Can't get enough of those red Injuns, huh?" He lifted his hand and traced the ridge of her collarbone.

She cursed her pride in fashioning such a beguiling gown.

She stepped back. "He's not *your* scout, and Jacob rescued me. I don't see why you've singled him out. I danced with lots—"

"Don't bother with lying. I know you've been sneaking around with him. No one needs to check on a damned goat every day. I'm not stupid."

She gasped. "You've been spying on me."

He laughed. "No need. Plenty of people have noticed Jacob hanging around. The fort's a small place, and gossip is one of the few pleasures we have, besides killing savages."

She took his jacket off and held it out. "I'm going inside and if you try to stop me, I'll scream. I don't care if I make a scene."

He grabbed her wrist, and she glared at him, opening her mouth.

He raised his other hand and covered her mouth, holding her tightly and leaning in close, engulfing her in a cloud of his whiskey-laden breath. "You'll listen, and then I'll let you go." He kept his hand over her mouth. "You were a squaw. Your family is dead. Captain O'Connor has asked for a transfer, and the major has recommended it. What will you do?"

Her mind raced. Captain O'Connor had asked for a transfer? Neither one of the O'Connor's had mentioned it. They were biding their time, waiting to be rid of her. She'd thought things had changed since she'd nursed Nellie back to health.

A sob lodged in her throat, realizing she *was* a burden, and how the O'Connors couldn't wait to be shed of her.

The hurt part of her wanted to cry out that she did have family—an aunt in Arkansas. But what did it matter? The lieutenant was less than nothing and didn't deserve to be told. She'd make sure the O'Connors knew she planned on leaving as soon as she could find a transport to Arkansas, even before her aunt answered her letter.

"Listen to me, Girlie, you've got no one to turn to, and I'm willing to take care of you. So long as I'm stationed at Fort Concho. I'll find a room for you in town, keep you sheltered and fed, and you'll give me what you gave that Injun husband of yours."

Hearing his ugly words and realizing he wasn't the only man who felt that way filled her with anger and made her stomach churn with nausea. If she hadn't been so furious, she might have vomited on his shiny boots.

He shook her again. "You understand me? No one else wants you. You have no one but me. If you treat me right, I'll be good to you." He leered at her. "We could have some fun times together, Girlie. And if we get along, you can come with me should I be transferred."

Then he leaned in and tried to kiss her, but this time, she was ready. She'd learned some useful tricks while she was a captive. She kneed him in his nether parts... hard.

He yowled and clutched his groin.

She whirled around, dropping his jacket, and ran into the dark night.

Chapter Seven

Ruth stumbled, running across the rutted parade ground in her too-tight shoes and ruining the hem of her gown in the mud. Not that she cared. All she cared about was where she should go. She wished Jacob didn't live in the barracks with the other soldiers. If he had his own place, she knew he'd take her in and not ask for anything in return... unlike Lieutenant Schultz.

She should go back to the cabin, but first, she wanted to get baby Johnny from Lupe at the major's. At the same time, she hated to spend another night with the O'Connors. Or another day.

Would the major be home? His wife was ill, and she'd noticed he left after opening the ball. Would he help her? Would he believe her about the lieutenant or should she keep quiet?

Then she saw a light, shining in the window of the headquarters office. Was the major working late again? Nellie had mentioned he often worked late.

She sprinted to the office and knocked on the door.

"Enter," the major's voice commanded.

She threw back her shoulders and tilted her chin up. She needed to appear composed and in control. She opened the door and stepped inside.

The major looked up from a pile of papers on his desk. His eyes widened. He pushed back his chair and stood. "Miss MacDonald, why aren't you at the ball? What's wrong?"

She took several deep breaths, and then she forgot all her carefully-planned words. "Did Captain O'Connor ask for a transfer?"

The major lowered his head and cleared his throat. "It is highly irregular for you to ask. The captain's military postings are his business and confidential—"

"But he asked after they took me in. Didn't he?" She twisted her hands together until the joints hurt.

"Miss MacDonald, I don't know what someone has told you, but the captain asking for a transfer has nothing to do with you." He scrubbed his hand over his chin. "Not exactly." He grimaced. "That is, when your baby passed, it reminded the O'Connors of the children they've lost, especially their last child… Eliza. I believe they want to get away from sad memories. The captain has served on the frontier for four years. He and his wife are due for a better posting."

Relief rushed through her, knowing the O'Connors hadn't asked to be transferred because they were sorry to have taken her in. She could understand this posting was painful for them, losing their child and now, hers.

"I'm sorry to have caused them distress. I have an aunt in Arkansas who I'm sure would welcome me. I wonder how soon I might find transport there?"

He stroked his chin. "Well, come spring, you could go with the O'Connors and their military escort to Fort Sam Houston in San Antonio. From there, I'm sure you could take a stagecoach to Arkansas. What part of Arkansas?"

"Little Rock."

"That shouldn't be a problem. I know there's regular passenger travel between San Antonio and Little Rock on the Ficklin Line, and some say, the stagecoach has plans to come here, as far west as Fort Concho. But right now, you'll need to wait until we exchange troops in the spring for an escort."

She nodded, feeling a sinking sensation in the pit of her stomach. The captain and lieutenant were friends. Now she was trapped at the fort until the O'Connors left, and she wondered what awful story the lieutenant would tell the captain about tonight?

Then she had an idea. It wouldn't solve her problem, but it might give her and the O'Connors a respite.

"Major Gregor, sir, Jacob mentioned I could go and visit my folks' graves on their ranch. That you'd send me with an escort. Since the weather has turned nice, I was wondering if you could spare some of your soldiers to take me home?"

He smiled. "Of course, we can arrange for you to visit your ranch. I know Lieutenant Schultz would—"

"No, not Lieutenant Schultz. Please." She lowered her head, not wanting to say more. Not wanting to disclose what the lieutenant thought of her or his improper advances.

The major cleared his throat again. "Oh, I see. Uh, the captain thought you and the lieutenant—"

"No, please. The captain doesn't understand. The lieutenant, he..." She raised her head and met his gaze, hoping he'd understand her silent plea. "The lieutenant and I don't see eye-to-eye, Major Gregor." She lowered her eyes again. "It's awkward... explaining."

He nodded and averted his gaze. "I think I understand. I don't like what I *think* I'm hearing, but if you want to confide in Mrs. O'Connor and—"

"No, please, I don't want to cause any more trouble than I already have, sir," her voice was a husky whisper. She gulped, fighting the sobs crowding her throat.

"Very well, I'll have Corporal Harding—"

"And could Scout Wells go along?"

"The lieutenant is his..." He paused and didn't finish. "I'll look into it, Miss MacDonald. I want you to be reassured—"

A loud knock sounded on the door, interrupting him. He glanced up and frowned. "Enter."

As if her asking for Jacob had summoned him, he opened the door and strode into the room, coming to attention, and saluting. He glanced at her, taking in her muddied gown, and she glimpsed the flare of alarm in his eyes.

The major returned his salute. "At ease, Scout Wells." He inclined his head toward her. "You know Miss MacDonald, of course."

Jacob nodded and said, "Good evening, Miss MacDonald."

"Good evening."

"To what do I owe this late-night call. Is there no one left at the ball?"

Jacob glanced at her again.

"Is your message confidential, Scout Wells?" The major asked. "Should I send Miss MacDonald home?"

"No, sir, the ball has been cancelled, and everyone will know the news soon enough. Troopers arrived from Fort McKavett and went straight to the mess hall. I guess they saw the lights there."

"Spit it out, Wells. What are troopers from Fort McKavett doing here, and why is the ball over?"

"McKavett's soldiers are asking for back-up troops. There's a large uprising of Comanche out of México, and they've set fire to most of Sonora. They're raiding the surrounding ranches, too. We need to send reinforcements tonight."

Ruth gasped and covered her mouth with her hand. Her stomach rolled over and for the second time tonight, she gulped and swallowed, not wanting to be sick.

The major inhaled and stood up straighter. "Right. Thank you, Wells, for coming at once." He turned to her again. "Miss MacDonald, I'm asking you to return to the O'Connors' cabin for your safety."

He swung his attention back to Jacob. "Wells, go and find the captain and the lieutenant. They will need to muster out Company F, along with Company B. I will remain here with Company C to protect the Fort."

* * *

They left at first light. After covering only a few miles, a light rain began to fall. Jacob smiled to himself. The rain would muddy the ground, making it easier to track the hostiles.

The lieutenant hadn't spoken to him. Not that he was surprised. The man thought he'd stepped over that invisible line again when he'd attended the ball and danced with Ruth.

And what of Ruth?

There had been no time to speak with her privately, but he sensed the lieutenant had sent her running to the major for protection. He curled his hands into fists and couldn't help but wonder what the man had done.

About mid-day, they met up with the main body of soldiers from Fort McKavett. It was a smaller outpost than Fort Concho with fewer soldiers. Their men looked exhausted and some of them had make-shift bandages, covering fresh wounds.

A Captain Hawkins headed up their troops. He, along with Captain O'Connor and Lieutenant Schultz, had huddled together, discussing the situation. The lieutenant usually included him in such discussions, knowing his scout should be apprised of what they were up against.

But not this time.

After their discussion, the lieutenant and the captain, along with Hawkins, gathered their forces and prepared to leave.

As they moved off, Lieutenant Schultz wheeled his horse around and fell in beside Jacob. "I want you to scout ahead, several miles. According to Captain Hawkins, the hostiles are headed due north and are an hour or two ahead of us. And this is one of the largest raiding parties he's encountered, over one hundred braves." The lieutenant glanced at the columns of mounted men.

"Our Companies aren't at full strength, but we outnumber them two to one." He shot Jacob a piercing look. "But they have repeating rifles and will use all their tricks to ambush us and destroy our advantage. I expect you to avert such a disaster. Captain Hawkins lost his scout. You will be on your own. You know what to do."

Jacob didn't respond. There was no need. He understood what the lieutenant meant without him saying it. Schultz hoped he would meet his death, tracking the hostiles. He saluted.

The lieutenant returned his salute. "Carry on. Return by nightfall if you've not found anything."

* * *

Jacob urged *Paaka* forward. His horse was lathered and foundering. If he didn't find the hostiles soon, he'd be afoot, waiting for the cavalry to catch up. And he didn't like to think about the lieutenant's reaction.

He was closing in, though. The Comanche had lost time, splitting up, veering off, and redoubling on their tracks. But the earlier rain hadn't reached here, making their tracks harder to follow.

He entered a wide meadow. At the far end was an old, crumbling adobe wall. To its left was a deep ravine and to the right was a copse of trees, lining a meandering stream.

Pulling up his pinto, he stopped and considered. The tracks led in three different directions. The middle track to the adobe wall was churned and deep. Only a few tracks led to the ravine and trees.

Squinting his eyes, he tried to see beyond the old wall. If the hostiles had sheltered there, their ponies would be close by. But they weren't. Something wasn't right.

He wished he had a fresh mount. Then he would have circled back to make certain the cavalry was coming. But he didn't dare to force his horse. He decided to dismount and wait. He wished he could give *Paaka* a drink at the creek, but he knew it wasn't safe.

He squatted and ran his hands over the tracks. The meadow was strangely silent. No birdsong or insect chirping. The Comanche were there and keeping their mounts quiet. And he was a sitting duck, if one of them was a good enough shot.

The lowering sun was directly in his eyes when he heard the familiar hoofbeats and jangling equipment in the distance. The cavalry was coming.

He watched as they approached. The lieutenant spurred his mount and pulled up beside him. "What are you waiting for? You could have come back and given a report."

He saluted. "Sir, my horse is spent. We wouldn't have made it back and then—"

"All our horses are spent, Scout Wells." The lieutenant spat. "And the hostiles?"

Jacob glanced up, scanning the meadow. "They're here, waiting to attack."

"Are you sure? Most hostiles run when we come."

"This is different. They're confident in their strength," Jacob said.

"And hiding behind the adobe wall. That will be a challenge."

"No, sir. They want us to think that's where they are. But they don't fight on foot. And there are no horses behind the wall."

The lieutenant retrieved a spyglass from his saddle boot and put it to his eye. "You're right, no horses there. But what about the ravine? If it's wide and deep enough, they could be waiting there to ride out."

"It's a possibility. But I don't think so. They're in the trees, having rested their mounts and watered them."

The lieutenant frowned. "I disagree, Scout Wells. Those trees couldn't hide a hundred braves. I think some of them are behind the wall, and the others in the ravine. The ravine is close enough to the wall they could retrieve their horses."

Jacob lowered his head. "You're my commanding officer, sir. I respect your opinion."

The lieutenant gazed at him, and he smiled—a cat playing with a mouse kind of smile. "I'll have Hawkins lead the assault on the wall. My men and Captain O'Connor's men will ride on the ravine. And if you want to stick with your hunch, you may take ten of my men and lead a charge on the trees."

Jacob drew himself up and saluted again. "Very good, sir."

The lieutenant nodded and wheeled his horse around, joining O'Connor and Hawkins, eager to explain the assault.

Jacob waited and within a few minutes, ten of the soldiers from Company F joined him. He vaulted onto *Paaka* and pulled out his rifle.

Turning his pony around, he faced the men. The lieutenant hadn't given him command over the ten men. "You have your orders from Lieutenant Schultz. Correct?"

Sergeant Finley spoke up, "We're to follow you to the trees, guns blazing, as soon as we hear the call."

"Good, I'll be depending on you."

The bugler trumpeted their call to arms. The mass of cavalry surged forward, swords drawn, headed for the wall.

Jacob urged his tired pinto to a trot, riding for the trees with ten men at his back.

Gunfire erupted all around them, and the trees came alive with swarming Comanches, firing rapidly.

He and his men fired back. Bullets whizzed by, crack, crack, pop, pop, like a never-ending string of firecrackers from the Fourth of July.

He rode and he shot, killing several braves. He heard the grunts and moans of men falling behind him. And still he plunged on in the face of overwhelming numbers, knowing there was no going back. If he must die, he would die bravely, as a soldier should.

When his repeating rifle ran out of bullets, he pulled his sidearm from his holster and kept shooting.

The main body of the troops must have realized there weren't but a few hostiles behind the wall and in the ravine. Loud shouts and more bugle calls turned them around, and they rode toward the trees, returning a savage storm of gunfire.

Paaka stumbled and floundered beneath him. He looked down and glimpsed blood, gushing from a wound in his pinto's neck. He patted his pony one last time and flung himself to the side, wrenching free of the stirrups.

He tried to land soft, rolling, but then he felt a sharp crack against his head. He struggled to pull himself up, gasped at the searing pain, and blacked out.

* * *

Jacob stood at attention in his new store-bought suit. He felt out of place again, standing on the parade ground with the massed companies of soldiers at his back. And his head, where he'd hit the rock, still hurt like the devil.

The lieutenant stood off to one side in the forefront of Company F. Jacob glanced at him, and he could see the man's jaw clenched tightly. His fury was barely in check—that was plain to see—the lieutenant wouldn't want to have anything to do with him being recognized.

The major stood on the porch of headquarters. He saluted them and gave a signal to the band. They started up a rousing rendition of "The Star Spangled Banner." The major strode off the porch and approached him. They exchanged salutes again.

The band paused. The major pinned the Service Medal for Indian Wars to the lapel of Jacob's new suit.

Then Major Gregor raised his voice, "For courage above and beyond the call of duty." The major held out his hand. "Well done, Scout Wells, well done. You saved the lives of our officers by riding into the main group of hostiles." The major released his hand.

"And furthermore, after reports from both captains... and the lieutenant, I've decided to recommend you to the District Commander of Texas, for service in the U.S. Army as a full-fledged soldier. Private, first class. If you wish it."

A feeling of exhilaration swept him. If only his father had been here to see this. He gulped past the boulder lodged in his throat and took the major's hand again.

"I would like that very much, sir."

"Good. I should hear back in a few weeks' time. Again, my congratulations on your exceptional show of bravery." The major lifted his hand, and the band started up again, finishing "The Star Spangled Banner."

Jacob gazed up at the flag flapping overhead. He felt as light as thistledown, as if he could float on air. And though he tried to keep his demeanor serious, a secret smile tugged at his lips.

He was going to be a real soldier. It was a dream come true.

He glanced at the row of officers' cabins. Captain O'Connor, his left arm in a sling, stood with his other arm around his wife on their front porch. He'd been excused from standing at attention due to his wound. The captain had been nicked by a bullet, a flesh wound, in his upper arm during the fighting. Mrs. O'Connor held their baby in her arms. Off to one side, Ruth stood, watching the ceremony.

Now he was going to be a soldier with a solid career, would Ruth accept him as a suitor? They'd exchanged kisses and terms of endearment, but as a half-breed scout, he'd believed he had nothing to offer.

With his promotion to the regular army, even if he was a lowly private, would she consider him as worthy? He hadn't had a chance to talk to her since the night of the ball, having guessed the lieutenant was watching them. And he knew the lieutenant must have upset Ruth that night at the ball, too.

He pushed the worries aside, and his heart lifted again, thinking how he'd been honored while she looked on. But he wanted to get her alone and speak with her.

* * *

Ruth squatted beside the Comanche woman, *Tomoobi Nami*, Sky Sister, and placed a cool compress on her daughter's head. The squaw's little girl, *Tuaahtaki* or Cricket, was ill with a fever. Ruth had done everything she knew for the child—everything she'd done when Nellie had taken sick and then some.

Most of the Comanche squaws and children, twenty-one in all, who'd been hiding in the ravine the day Jacob had won his medal for bravery, were ill or starved. The large warband of braves had been either killed or chased away, leaving the remnants of their families behind.

A corner of the mess hall had been cordoned off and bed rolls had been provided. Dr. Statler had been through several times, but Ruth couldn't see how he'd helped much. Most of them were responding to having snug shelter and three warm meals in their bellies. But not Cricket.

The little girl had a fever when they'd arrived a week ago, and the fever hadn't broken. Ruth rocked back on her heels and met Sky's gaze. She shook her head.

Sky turned away and pulled the edge of a blanket over her face, silently weeping.

Ruth and Jacob had been pressed into helping with the Comanche captives because they understood the language. She'd hadn't hesitated, wanting to help beyond simple language skills. She'd used all her herbal knowledge to nurse the Comanche women and children to health. And they'd responded... except for Cricket.

She put her arm around Sky's shoulder and hugged her, murmuring low words of comfort in Comanche.

Someone pulled back the curtain, letting a shaft of pure sunlight pour into the shadowed corner. Ruth glanced up and saw Jacob standing there. So far, they hadn't been alone since the night of the ball. And she could understand why—they were being watched. The lieutenant had told her. And if she knew it, Jacob must know it, too.

She was so proud of him. She'd wanted to seek him out and talk to him, but there hadn't been a good time.

Jacob came over and squatted beside her and Sky. He gazed at the sick child. "How is little Cricket? Is she any better?"

Ruth shook her head. Now that he was near, she couldn't find her voice. *What was wrong with her?* She hadn't realized how much she'd missed him. Just being close to him made her skin tingle and her chest tighten.

She turned to him and whispered, “I haven’t had the chance to tell you. I’m so proud of you. How you risked your life. How brave you were.”

His gaze met hers. He shrugged. “Only following orders.”

“Oh, really?”

“The lieutenant didn’t take my counsel as to where the main body of hostiles were waiting in ambush.” He glanced around at the silent, patient Comanche women and children. “He sent me and ten men. I knew it was my fate.” He shrugged again. “I embraced it.”

She gasped and covered her mouth with her hand. “You mean, Lieutenant Schultz sent you and only ten men against the Comanche braves? Why didn’t you protest or tell the major or Captain O’Connor or—”

“Did you tell the major the truth about the lieutenant that night?”

She winced and lowered her head. “No, I didn’t know if he would believe me. Or how it would be with the O’Connors if I...” She bit her lip.

“Different circumstances, same result. I can’t criticize my commanding officer for his lack of judgment. He thought the hostiles were behind the adobe wall. I knew they were hiding in the trees, but he didn’t believe me.” He took her hand and squeezed it.

Cricket gasped and moaned.

Ruth pulled free and lifted the child up, appalled at how hot she was. She grabbed a mug and lifted it to the child’s lips. But Cricket’s mouth was tightly shut, and the water dribbled down her chin. Ruth wiped off the liquid with a corner of her apron.

“Jacob, can you fetch a big pail of cool water. I think I need to get her fever down again, and the only thing that has worked is bathing her in a tub of cool water. But not too cold. Can you?”

“Sure, I’ll be right back.” He stood up and pulled the curtain back.

Cricket groaned, and her head snapped back. Her arms jerked, and her legs twitched. Her body shuddered and spasmed, as if being pulled by an invisible puppeteer’s strings. She opened her eyes, looking up, but her gaze was unfocused, almost as if she was blind. Then her eyes rolled back in her head.

Ruth's heart stuttered with terror. She clasped the spasming child closer, curling her body around her. She didn't know what to do. She'd never seen anyone have fits during a fever, though Dr. Statler had mentioned something about it.

Sky started keening, a shrill, haunting plea to the Great Spirit.

Ruth held the little girl even tighter, praying under her breath. The child jerked and twitched for what seemed like hours. Ruth kept glancing at the curtain, hoping to see Jacob with a tub of cool water. And she prayed, curving her body around Cricket, holding her tightly.

Then the child went still in her arms.

Sky covered her eyes with her hands and keened louder. The other squaws joined in. And Ruth knew it was over. With tears streaming down her face, she laid Cricket down, straightened her limbs, and pulled the blanket over her face.

Her mother pulled hunks of hair out of her head and kept singing shrilly, a Comanche death song. If the captives had been allowed knives, Ruth knew Sky would have mutilated herself, honoring her child with the depths of her grief.

Feeling useless and despairing, Ruth sat there, reliving the loss of her baby and staring mindlessly at the outline of the child's body beneath the blanket.

The curtain was shoved aside and Ruth glanced up, hoping to find Jacob. But instead, she saw the lieutenant standing there, scowling.

"What is that damned caterwauling?" he asked.

She looked at him, wanting to pound his ugly face into a pulp. If only she was a man. "It's not caterwauling. The child just died. That's their death song—the way they honor their dead."

"I don't care what it is. Tell them to stop it."

"But—"

"I've got the tub of water, Ruth," Jacob interrupted.

"Get that thing out of here," the lieutenant barked. "Savages don't bathe. What the hell are you thinking, man?"

"Ruth says the cool water might bring down the child's fever."

"The child is dead. That's why they're all screaming."

Jacob glanced at Ruth. “I’m sorry. I didn’t realize—”

“It’s the breed kid.” The lieutenant pointed at the mounded blanket. “She and her mother should thank their lucky stars the kid won’t grow up.”

When the captives had been brought in, Sky had been desperate for help, worried they wouldn’t help her sick baby. She’d claimed Cricket’s father was a white man, who’d sheltered with the tribe in México, two winters back.

Ruth hadn’t realized the lieutenant knew Cricket was a half-breed. Her son, had he lived, would have been a half-breed. Jacob was a half-breed. She glanced between the two men, and then she knew. The lieutenant hadn’t doubted Jacob’s judgment. He’d wanted to send Jacob to his death.

Jacob set down one end of the tub. He turned to the other soldier. “Private Mahoney, thank you for your help, but we won’t be needing the tub after all.”

“Shouldn’t we take it back out then?” The private asked.

“In a minute, but you might want to step outside… or maybe not. I should have a proper witness.”

He stepped in front of the lieutenant. “Why should the mother be happy her half-breed child has died?” Jacob’s voice was a harsh whisper.

The lieutenant thrust his face into Jacob’s. “Because a breed is even worse than a red Injun. A breed is a nothing, neither red or—”

Crack! Jacob’s fist slammed into the lieutenant’s jaw.

Ruth gasped, and her stomach turned over, thinking about what the lieutenant had said. And what Jacob had done. Her heart pounded double-time, and she gulped, fighting to breathe. If the lieutenant had wanted Jacob dead, what kind of punishment would he inflict upon him now?

The lieutenant staggered back, rubbing his jaw and chuckling. “Now, you’ve done it, you filthy breed. You’ve shown your true colors.”

He fisted his hand, grimaced, and then dropped his hand. “I’m not going to waste my time, hitting slime like you. You aren’t worth a warm bucket of spit.” Then he ripped the medal Jacob had proudly pinned to his shirt collar and threw it down. "This will be the end of you!"

The lieutenant raised his fist again and shook it in Jacob's face. "I'll see you court-martialed. You'll never be a soldier now—you half-breed piece of garbage."

Turning around, the lieutenant shouted for the guard on duty. "Sergeant Krause, escort Scout Wells to the brig. I'll lodge a formal complaint immediately."

The Sergeant approached and drew himself up, saluting, "Lieutenant Schultz, Major Gregor doesn't allow any men to be incarcerated without his review." He stood stiffer, holding the salute. "Sir."

"Damn, I forgot. What a stupid order." He inclined his head. "Sergeant, return to your duty. Private Mahoney, escort Scout Wells to the major's office. I'll follow."

"I'm coming, too," Ruth declared.

Chapter Eight

Major Gregor scanned the orders from the District Commander and frowned. He'd need to send one of his officers with a squad of men to escort the Comanche women and children to their designated reservation in Oklahoma Territory.

He suspected some of the Comanches might return for their families, and he could ill afford to commit one of his officers and a squad of men from his undermanned troops.

He heard a knock on the door and called out, "Enter."

Private Mahoney, along with Scout Wells, came into the room, followed by Lieutenant Schultz and the MacDonald girl.

And they were all scowling, except for the scout, whose countenance was wiped clean of emotion.

The lieutenant stepped forward. "I want your permission to court martial Scout Wells." He rubbed his jaw. "He hit me, his commanding officer. And to incarcerate him until his trial, I need your approval."

Major Gregor's frown deepened. He'd been afraid that particular situation would eventually boil over. He remembered the MacDonald girl coming to him during the ball and what she'd said... or hadn't said. And he'd heard how Lieutenant Schultz had commanded Wells to ride into a nest of hostiles with only ten men.

Unwed women in a frontier fort, unless they were willing to sell their favors, were a distraction. It had been only a matter of time before Schultz and Wells had locked horns—like two stags fighting over the same doe.

He came to attention and saluted them. The men saluted him back.

He cleared his throat. "Wells, what do you have to say for yourself? Did you hit your commanding officer, Lieutenant Schultz?"

"Yes, sir, I did."

"And the provocation? There must have been a provocation."

Wells pressed his lips together and remained silent. Not good. Stubborn man, he was refusing to help in his own defense.

Private Mahoney stepped forward. “May I, sir?”

“Of course. I take it you were present when Wells struck the lieutenant.”

“Yes, sir. One of the Comanche women’s child died. A half-breed, and Lieutenant Schultz made a remark that it was a good thing, since breeds are…” He hesitated and glanced at the lieutenant. “The lieutenant said breeds were worthless, worse than Injuns.” The private stood up straighter. “I believe Scout Wells took offense because of his mother being… and him being…”

The major shook his head. Schultz was an empty windbag, and he had a mean streak a mile wide, especially when it came to the natives and anyone with native blood. Many soldiers on the frontier felt the same way, having seen what atrocities the hostiles were willing to inflict. But then, there had been plenty of brutality on both sides.

It was why he’d posted a guard, day and night, over the Comanche women and children—to protect them from some of the men in his command.

“Thank you, Private, for speaking up.” He turned to Wells. “You know I could have you court-martialed for striking your superior officer, no matter the provocation. Ugly words were said but that doesn’t give you the right—

“May I say something,” the MacDonald girl interjected.

He turned to her, not surprised she’d interrupted. She was a spunky girl; he’d realized it the night of the ball. But if she hadn’t been that way, she probably wouldn’t have survived.

He bowed. “Please, Miss MacDonald, go ahead.”

She twisted her hands together and bit her lip. “What the private said is true. And though it might not have given Scout Wells the right to hit the lieutenant, I think part of what he did wasn’t just about his Comanche blood. He knows how I’m grieving over the loss of my half-breed son… Matthew.”

The major raised one hand, palm out. “Point taken, Miss MacDonald, but still—”

“And furthermore, the lieutenant has repeatedly kissed and pawed me.” Her cheeks flushed with color. “Without my permission. He’s made lewd and indecent proposals to me, since I slept with... was married to a Comanche brave. For the lieutenant, I'm damaged goods, good for nothing but to be his whore."

Wells gasped and lunged for the lieutenant again, but the private stopped him, pinning his arms.

"Attention!" The major commanded.

All three of the men came to attention, but Wells bared his teeth at the lieutenant and mumbled something under his breath.

"Lieutenant, did you make indecent proposals and... touch or kiss...?"

"What if I did, sir? She's not under my command and considering she wed a savage and birthed his—"

"Lieutenant Schultz, that's enough! You've said more than enough."

He was glad the lieutenant had confirmed what Miss MacDonald claimed. If Schultz had denied his actions, it would be harder to come to a decision, since it would have been her word against his. Not that he hadn't already guessed the truth of the matter.

"Now I have two breaches of conduct worthy of a court martial." He swung his attention to the lieutenant. "Despite what you believe about Miss MacDonald, your conduct is offensive and unworthy, as an officer and a gentleman. You could be court-martialed for pushing yourself onto an unwilling woman while under my command. Do I make myself clear?"

The lieutenant's face turned a mottled red, but he held his tongue.

"Do you understand?" He wanted to drive his point home.

Schultz stiffened and saluted again. "Yes, sir."

"Good," he said. "Seems there's blame enough on both sides, but I can't afford to have soldiers languishing in the brig. No court martials, this time. But you won't get off without punishment."

He stared at Wells. "You will finish out the rest of your two-year enlistment as a scout..." He paused, noticing the torn collar of Well's shirt for the first time. "What happened to your medal?"

"The lieutenant tore it off, saying I wasn't worthy."

The major covered his eyes with one hand and counted to ten, trying to keep his temper in check. After a few moments, he'd decided what would be the appropriate punishment for each man, hoping it would teach them a lesson.

Raising his head, he stared directly at Wells.

"All right. You have a couple of months left of your enlistment. But you won't be scouting–you'll return, as punishment, to your former job as a hostler, caring for the horses and forego your pay." He spread his hands. "And I'll keep my recommendation for your enlistment as a soldier under consideration, pending the completion of your punishment. Understood?"

"Yes, sir." Wells replied. "Very good, sir."

"One thing more, Scout Wells, I believe you owe the lieutenant an apology for striking him, your commanding officer."

He watched Wells' face harden, and a muscle flinched in his jaw.

Wells didn't look at the lieutenant but stared straight ahead. Through gritted teeth, he managed, "My apologies, sir. I should haven't struck you. It was unfit conduct on my part."

The lieutenant didn't look at Wells, either. He nodded.

Then the major turned to Lieutenant Schultz, and he couldn't help but glare at the man. "Lieutenant Schultz, for conduct unbecoming an officer toward Miss MacDonald, who is under my personal protection, you will pick ten men from your troop and escort the Comanche women and children to their reservation in the Oklahoma Territory. You will leave as soon as the child has been properly buried." He pointed his index finger at the lieutenant. "And you'll make certain no one harms them. Understood?"

The lieutenant opened his mouth and looked him directly in the eye. Then he closed his mouth, frowned, and said, "Yes, sir. Understood, sir."

In the meantime, he needed to relieve some of the tension at the fort, if only momentarily. His gaze rested on the girl's bowed head. "Miss MacDonald, I believe you asked if you could visit your homestead and pay your respects at your family's graves. Correct?"

"Yes, please, if you would be so kind as to allow me an escort."

"Fine, then, I'll send you with Sergeant Krause and eight men from Company C. The chaplain will also accompany you to say prayers over your family. You'll leave as soon as Chaplain Mapes has performed the burial rites for the child."

"If I could ask a favor, sir." She hesitated. "Though, I know you've meted out the punishment."

He exhaled, knowing before she asked. "Of course, Miss MacDonald."

"Before he starts his punishment, could Scout Wells accompany us? I know it's a lot to ask, considering what happened today." She glanced at Jacob. "Under the circumstances, the only time I feel safe is with Scout Wells."

Her request would only feed fuel to the fire, especially the one burning in Schultz's gut. But the major couldn't help but think of his only living child, Peggy, and how she would feel if she'd gone through captivity, only to be brought to a place of safety, where she was treated like a debased woman.

He shook his head, not wanting to think about what Miss MacDonald had endured. "All right, Miss MacDonald, if you put it that way, Wells can accompany you. When he returns, his punishment will commence."

* * *

Ruth folded an extra set of clothes and stowed them in the saddlebags, which the captain had loaned her. Cricket had been buried yesterday, and her mother had tried to kill herself with a butter knife she'd found in the mess hall kitchen.

Sky had been stopped by the guard on duty. Her wound had been slight, a mere flesh wound. But Ruth understood the woman's grief and what had driven her.

She sighed and knew she'd miss baby Johnny, even if it was only for a few days. Sergeant Krause had said they would leave tomorrow at sunrise.

Outside her window, she heard the lieutenant shouting. He was pulling together his squad. Jacob had been kind enough to loan a dozen of his horses to the Comanche women and children. That way, they wouldn't have to walk all the way to the Oklahoma Territory, as the cavalry couldn't afford to give them horses.

And Jacob must have known he wouldn't see his horses again. Given what had happened between Jacob and Schultz, the lieutenant would probably sell the horses, pocket the money, and make up an excuse.

But it didn't matter. What was important was taking care of the women and children. She knew Jacob was more than willing to make the sacrifice.

She finished packing and sat on the foot of the bed, contemplating the journey ahead of her. She'd be visiting her family's ranch, and she had mixed feelings about going home.

She would be reliving the nightmare that had taken her family. But she'd escape the fort's confines, and the sticky situation she'd found herself in. The last two days had been tense. She knew the O'Connors weren't happy about what had happened. She was certain they would welcome time apart and so would she.

At least, she'd be alone with Jacob for a few days... or almost alone. She wanted to talk with him. It had been a long time since they'd had a private conversation. And too long since she'd felt his strong arms, holding and comforting her.

At a rap on her bedroom door, she lifted her head.

Nellie stuck her head in the door. "I've a letter for you, lass. It's postmarked from Little Rock, Arkansas." She smiled. "I believe it's the answer you've been waiting for."

She rose and took the envelope from Nellie's hand. "Thank you, I'm happy to get a response."

"Well, I'll leave you to read your letter." Nellie closed the door behind her.

Trembling with apprehension, she held the letter tightly in her hand and sank onto the foot of her bed again. She inhaled and tore the envelope open. Two pages of scented, fine linen stationery, along with a stamped, official-looking letter, spilled out.

> *Dearest Niece,*
>
> *I was both elated and disturbed to receive your letter. I had feared the worst for the past two years. Your mother and I had corresponded as regularly as possible, given the vagaries of frontier mail service. I've written a dozen letters to your mother*

since her last one to me, only to have more than half of them returned.

My heart is heavy with sadness for what happened to my sister, your blessed mother, and to all of your family. I can't even imagine what you've been through, dearest niece, at the hands of the savages.

I wish I could come to you, but my health is delicate. I can tell you, though, you have all my love and fondest wishes. Please, come to me and my husband as soon as you can. We will be waiting with open arms.

I've enclosed a note of credit for your traveling expenses. It's been drawn on a San Antonio bank and should be more than enough to cover your needs.

My blessings on you, dearest Ruth. We look forward to you becoming a part of our family.

Please, write back, and let us know when to expect you.

My Fondest Wishes and Love,

Your Aunt Alice

Ruth glanced at the amount of money on the letter of credit and gasped. Her aunt had sent a veritable fortune. More than enough to reach Arkansas and then some. Her heart squeezed, and tears threatened as she realized her aunt was doing all she could to help and let her know she was wanted and loved.

She folded the two pages of her aunt's letter and dabbed at her eyes with a corner of her apron.

Someone wanted her; she wasn't an orphan after all.

* * *

Nellie stood on the porch and waved goodbye to Ruth, wishing her a safe journey. The sun was a blazing, red ball on the horizon as the chaplain, Scout Wells, Ruth, and the escort of eight soldiers left the fort.

Nellie knew going home and seeing her family's graves would be hard for Ruth, but at least, the girl had an aunt who wanted her. And the aunt was a woman of means, too.

She and Ezekiel had stayed up late, long after Ruth was in bed, discussing how Ruth's situation had changed in the past few days.

Gossip was rife in the small fort, and they knew about the lieutenant's unsavory plans for Ruth. And Ruth had told them about her aunt's warm letter, as well as her financial help. The girl wanted to repay them for everything they'd spent when they reached San Antonio.

She shook her head and pulled the shawl tighter around her shoulders, though the air was barely chilly. Spring had finally come to the southern plains, and with the spring, her husband would be receiving his transfer.

Knowing what they knew now... she realized they'd made a terrible, immoral decision. And her husband's career would suffer for it.

She lifted her head to see her husband crossing the parade ground, having come from Dr. Statler's office. He joined her on the porch.

She touched his shoulder. "The doctor removed your sling."

Ezekiel lifted his wounded arm and winced. "It's as good as new... almost. It will still be a little sore and stiff for a couple of more weeks, the Doc said."

"Good, I'm glad you're on the mend." She smoothed her hands over the front of his blue wool uniform.

He bent his head and kissed her. Just like that, in the daylight, and in front of God and everybody.

She drew back. "Why, Ezekiel," she sputtered, "I'm surprised at you kissing your wife while on duty."

"All we have is each other, Nell." He tugged on his earlobe. "You're still set on going through with this?"

She gazed up at his kind face. She'd been the one who'd talked him into such a rash action when she'd found their baby had died. Now, her conscience troubled her night and day. But it would be her husband who would bear the brunt of the consequences, whose career might be ruined. Not that she wouldn't share his fate, but he was a lifer and she knew how important being a soldier was to him, along with his officer's commission.

Perhaps the major would be lenient, as he'd been with Scout Wells and the lieutenant. She could only hope and pray.

"Yes." She bowed her head. "I can't live like this, Ezekiel."

"Well, then, lass, we best be getting it over with. The sooner we face the music and know what lies ahead, the sooner we'll be able to go on living."

She laced her arm through his. "I'll do my best to defend you. It was my fault, my idea—"

He stopped her with another kiss. "We'll face this together, and together we'll overcome. Who's watching the babe?"

"Lupe said she'd watch him for an hour or so."

He nodded and together they crossed the parade ground to the major's office.

* * *

Ruth bowed her head, listening to Chaplain Mapes' words of comfort, spoken over her family's graves. And then he ended by reciting one of the most comforting verses from the Bible, the twenty-third Psalm:

> *"'The Lord is my shepherd, I shall not want. He maketh me to lie down in green pastures, he leadeth me...*
>
> *Surely goodness and love will follow me all the days of my life, and I will dwell in the house of the Lord forever.'"*

The chaplain closed his Bible, and one-by-one, the men from the squad drifted away, leaving her alone with her grief.

They'd arrived yesterday afternoon and pitched tents near the river. She remembered her mother's elation when her father had run a pipe from the river to a sink on the back porch of their ranch house. It had been a rare convenience and made life much easier than hauling buckets of water from the river every day.

More than the chaplain's words, thinking about her parents and the small pleasures they'd lived for, caused her eyes to tear up. Silent sobs shook her, and her tears tracked salty streaks down her face.

Turning away from the graves, she approached the burnt-out remains of their three-bedroom home. Another luxury, having that many bedrooms in a pioneer ranch house, but her father had wanted her mother to have the best he could provide. He'd wanted her to enjoy living on the land as much as he did.

She shook her head and walked through what had once been the front door. Grabbing a tree branch that had fallen into the main room, she poked and prodded the debris on the floor.

What was she looking for? She didn't know. Something that would remind her of her family—some small keepsake.

But between the fire and the weather, all she uncovered was sodden, misshapen lumps of things. There were a few pieces of crockery that had survived, blackened by fire, and her mother's big boiling pot stood rusting where the back porch had once been.

It wasn't until she crossed into what had been her parents' bedroom that she found a warped daguerreotype in a metal frame, which had somehow survived the flames. The picture showed her mother and father on their wedding day. She remembered the portrait well.

Her father looked so handsome in his stiff-necked shirt and dark suit. Her mother was a vision of loveliness, clad in a white gown and long, lacy veil, standing behind her new husband with her hand on his shoulder. She put the picture in her pocket.

She moved to the boys' room and was rewarded with one tin soldier that hadn't melted into an unrecognizable pulp. She stuffed the soldier away, took a deep breath, and stood on what had been the threshold of her room.

Everything was a charred mess. And then she remembered the tin box her father had given her for her twelfth birthday, where she kept her "treasures." She'd kept the box under her bed.

Bending over, she sifted through the charred remains. After moving the bits and pieces of her bed slats, along with some half-burned floorboards, she found it. Her little tin box.

She'd had a key for her box and had kept it locked at all times, else her nosey brothers would have... She gulped, wishing her brothers were still with her, to tease her and call her names and make her life miserable.

Miserable? Growing up, she didn't know the real meaning of the word miserable. But now she did. All too well.

Sobs lodged in the back of her throat. She swallowed and wiped her eyes with one blackened hand. Through her tears, she stared at the box. The fire had warped it and there was no need for a key now. The lid popped open.

Inside, she found the speckled-blue robin's egg, the marbles she'd won from her brothers, some melted wax crayons, and the little wooden horse her eldest brother, Ben, had carved for her. There was some other debris in the box, but she couldn't remember all the silly things she'd stowed away.

She took out the crudely-carved horse and turned it over and over in her hands, wondering how it had survived the heat from the fire.

Then she sank to the filthy floorboards and let the tears come... again.

* * *

Jacob, along with the others, had left Ruth to grieve at her family's gravesites. But all he could think of was how much she must be hurting.

He tried to busy himself with the horses. The major had been kind, to his way of reckoning, demoting him back to hostler when he could have just as easily had him court martialed. And though he knew the major to be a fair man, he couldn't discount how Ruth had stood up for him, which had deepened his regard and love for her.

He unloosed the horses' hobbles, one-by-one, and watered them at the river, and then re-hobbled their mounts and let them loose. After he'd finished, he looked up and stretched.

Spring had finally come. He'd turned their horses loose into a lush, green meadow, dotted with pink and white primroses. Soon, the bluebonnets and Indian paintbrush would follow with their vivid blues and orange-red flowers.

Ruth's father had chosen well when he'd bought this land. There were plenty of meadows with long, sweet grass for the cattle to graze on and get fat. And a huge swath of the pastures lay beside the branch of the North Concho, making it easy to water the herds without drilling for wells, putting in windmills, and digging out stock ponds.

He crouched beside the river and threw a few stones, trying to make them skip across the water. Most of them sank; he was out of practice. He tore off a long stem of Johnson grass and chewed on it for a while, watching the horses graze.

Who was he fooling?

He wanted to be with Ruth, to comfort her while she was sorrowing. And besides, there was no reason to hide his feelings any longer, at least, not from his fellow soldiers or the chaplain. All the fort had been gossiping about his run-in with the lieutenant and how it had been Ruth who had saved him from a much-worse punishment than a temporary demotion and a couple of months without pay.

He stood and brushed off the seat of his pants. He could see her on the rise above the river, poking among the ruins of her family's home.

He trudged up the hill and saw her standing, her back to him, gazing at something in her hands. She wore a blue-and-green calico dress that barely covered the tops of her lace-up boots. On her head was a straw-brimmed hat. She'd woven the blue ribbon around the crown and stuck the ostrich feather there.

It was as if the feather he'd given her was a talisman. And he could understand why; she had little enough that was hers. Even now, it appeared she was looking for fragments of her childhood in her family's burnt-out cabin.

Then he heard her sobs and saw her sink to the floor. His heart went out to her. She'd suffered so much—had to overcome so much grief and sadness.

He walked up behind her and put his hands on her shoulders. "Ruth, let me help you up. Your dress will be..." He didn't finish.

She grasped one of his arms and rose. Offering a warped, tin box to him, she said, "All that's left of me... before."

He gazed down at the fragile, speckled-blue robin's egg, some marbles, a mess of melted colors, and other unrecognizable lumps of things.

He shook his head. "Ruth, you shouldn't stay here. Going through your family's things will only hurt more..." He paused, wishing there was some way to take the hurt away. He cupped her face in his hands and gazed into her eyes. He wet his thumb in his mouth and gently rubbed away the streak of soot on her cheek.

"Let's walk by the river. It's beautiful there," he said.

She pulled away, sniffled, and wiped her nose on her sleeve. "I must look a mess." She tried to laugh and failed. "And I need to sew some handkerchiefs. I'm always crying, it seems."

He took a handkerchief from his pocket and handed it to her. He usually didn't bother with handkerchiefs, but being around Ruth had taught him how useful they were.

She wiped her eyes and blew her nose. Then she looked up at him and smiled a crooked smile. He knew she was trying to be brave and just watching her made his heart heavy.

He clasped her hand and pulled it through his arm. He concentrated on where they stepped among the charred remnants of her former home, not wanting her to trip and fall. Once they were outside of the house's blackened frame, he breathed a sigh of relief and looked toward the river.

He'd always liked rivers, enjoyed watching the rush of the water as it hurried along to the sea. He'd noticed a stand of weeping willows in a crook of the river. It was as private a place as he'd seen in the gently rolling landscape.

She walked with him, still clutching the tin box, until they'd reached the river. He used his free hand to part the long branches of the willow trees that brushed the ground.

After a few steps and when he couldn't see the soldiers and their tents, he pulled her around and lowered his head. He covered her mouth with his, gently kissing her while he stroked her back through the cotton of her dress.

She responded, kissing him back and then opening her mouth, inviting him closer. He'd never kissed a woman, using his tongue, though he'd heard enough of the raunchy talk in the barracks to know what to do... or so he hoped.

He deepened their kiss and slid his tongue into her mouth, exploring the warm softness of her. He clasped her tighter, and he could feel the hard buds of her nipples against his chest.

His groin tightened with wanting. And his blood was on fire, simmering, and threatening to boil over. But their kissing and touching was about lust... not love.

And he wanted her to know the feelings he carried in his heart. Since she'd stood up to the major and lieutenant for him, he'd become emboldened to declare himself. But there hadn't been a good time, not until now.

He broke their kiss and pulled apart from her. He took off his buckskin jacket and spread it on the ground. "Let's sit for a spell. All right?"

She blushed and lowered her head. "All right."

They sat down on the jacket together. He held her hand in his. "Did you find anything else in your home?"

She pulled out a carved wooden horse, a tin soldier, and a faded, warped daguerreotype of a bridal couple. "Are these your parents, Ruth?"

"Yes, on their wedding day."

"I can see where you get your good looks from." He smiled and glanced at her shyly. "Your mother was beautiful, and your father was handsome, too."

"Thank you."

"Let me guess, the tin soldier belonged to one of your brothers. And the horse was yours."

She nodded and then turned her face away. Her eyelashes glistened with moisture, and he knew she was crying again.

Tenderly, he took her chin in his hand and turned her to face him. "I'm sorry for all your losses, Ruth. So very, very sorry." He hesitated and cleared his throat. His emotions were like fragile eggshells, just waiting to be crushed.

He'd thought he wasn't good enough for her, but perhaps he'd been wrong. She'd let him kiss and hold her, and she'd championed him, too. Would she have him? He had to know.

He cleared his throat again and lowered his head until their foreheads touched. "I don't want you to be lonely and grieving. I love you, Ruth. Stay with me. Let's make a life together. Together, we'll never be lonely again."

Chapter Nine

Ruth heard his words of love and his offer. He hadn't said the word: marriage. But what else could he have meant? She knew he would never compromise her as the lieutenant had tried.

"Jacob, are you asking me to marry you?"

He took both her hands in his, raised them, and brushed his lips across her knuckles. And the touch of his mouth made her tremble with need.

She'd lain with her Comanche husband, but other than some discomfort, his touch hadn't roused her. She remembered the giggling conversations of the squaws who enjoyed bedding their husbands. Now she understood what those women had known.

Jacob's lightest touch set her on fire with yearning. And his kisses sent streams of pleasure pulsing through her.

He gazed at her and said, "Yes, Ruth, would you do me the honor of being my wife?"

And as much as she wanted to lie with him, heaven preserve her from sin, she didn't know if she wanted to be married again... not now... not to any man.

She pulled her hands free and turned her head away. Wanting him was easy, came naturally. But to be committed in marriage again would be hard. She didn't know if she would make any man a good wife, not after what she'd suffered. And no matter what she said or how she said it, her answer would hurt him.

He put his hand on her arm and turned her toward him. "Before, I had nothing to offer you. But now, I hope to be a regular soldier, and I've some money saved, too. We'd have a good life, Ruth."

She gazed at her ill-fitting shoes and tried to form an answer. But nothing came. Nothing that wouldn't hurt him.

"Or if you don't want to live as a soldier's wife, remember what I told you that day you watched me train the horses?"

"You said you wanted a ranch." She lifted her arm. "Like this. Like my father wanted. Didn't you?"

"Yes, I did. And that can be a good life, too."

"Or a death trap," she spat.

"The People wouldn't attack me or mine."

"Even though you've fought against them?" She touched the medal he always wore pinned to his lapel. "Even though you won a medal for killing as many braves as you could?"

He frowned and glanced away, as if considering. "I would make certain the Comanche wouldn't attack our ranch."

"What about the Kiowa or the Apache?"

He clenched his jaw, and she saw the muscle jump there. "There are dangers no matter what life we choose."

"Not if I go to Arkansas to live with my aunt. There are no hostiles there, no raids and killings... no burnings." She got to her feet and walked to the edge of the river.

Jacob joined her on the riverbank and threw another stone, trying to make it skip and failing. "You've heard from your aunt in Arkansas, and she wants you to come live with her."

"Yes, she does. She and her husband. They have no children. I could help them as they grow older."

"And that's what you want, to go to Arkansas and live with them?"

She moved a few paces down the river. "It's what I want for now." She buried her face in her hands. "I need to forget, to heal. I thought you understood. I need time, Jacob. So much has happened, so much grieving and being—"

"Do you have tender feelings for me, Ruth?"

She lifted her head. Their gazes caught and held. "You know I do. You know you're the only one who understands what I've been through and how hard it has been. Only you."

He shook his head. "You're talking about sympathy, not love. Do you love me?"

She looked at her feet again. Then she raised her hand and touched the feather on her hat. "I don't know what I feel for you. I know I loved my family. I know I loved my son, even if I only saw him for a moment." She pulled the feather from her hat and turned it over and over in her hands.

"I don't know what it means to love a man. I know I want to lie with you." She fisted one hand and stuffed it into her mouth. "There, I've said the worst. Now you know me for what I am, for what the lieutenant wanted to make me. But I don't want just any man's touch, only yours. Is that love?"

He scrubbed his face with his hand. "I don't know how it is for a woman. But I feel the same way. I only want to touch you, only want to hold you in my arms, to become 'one' as the Good Book says."

"You're a man, Jacob. Don't all men desire women whether they love them or not?"

"I don't know how other men feel." He shook his head. "But I know what you mean. I've watched the soldiers visit the saloon women in town, not only here, but at Fort Clark."

"And what about you? Don't you visit the women in San Angelo when—"

"I've never lain with a woman, Ruth. Never." He lowered his head and kicked at a rock with the toe of his boot.

"You've never been with a woman? Never? But—"

"When I was fourteen and heard the gossip about my mother, I went to my father and asked him if it was true."

"Did he admit the truth of it?"

"Yes, and even more, he explained how it was between a man and a woman." He leaned down and picked up another rock and threw it at the river. This time, it made two hops before sinking beneath the swift-moving, green water. "That was the day, six years ago, I made myself a solemn vow—I would never touch a woman unless I loved her." He shook his head again. "Never. And I've kept my vow."

"Then how do you know you love me? How do you know what you're feeling isn't what I'm feeling? That we both want the physical comfort we can give each other? Can't that be enough for now? All I want is your strong arms around me, protecting me."

"I don't just want you in my bed." He grimaced, and his face flushed. "I want you beside me, every day, come good or bad. I enjoy being with you, hearing you talk." He lifted his hand and tucked a strand of her hair behind her ear. "Just looking at you, knowing how beautiful you are, inside and out." He let his hand drop. "I want to share my life with you. Want us to have children—"

"No!" she hissed. "Not that, Jacob! Talking about having children, you remind me of what I've lost." She stared at him. "It's like you're plunging a hot knife into my chest."

He grimaced and exhaled. "Forgive me. We won't speak of a family then. I understand it's too soon. But I want you beside me, every day and every night."

She twirled the feather in her hands. "I don't know what I want. Or maybe I do know. I want peace, a life of peace. No more pain." Her heart constricted, clenching in her chest.

"No more hurting and suffering. Just peace, Jacob. And knowing that, I wouldn't be but half a wife." She dropped the feather and kept her head down. She didn't want to see the hurt she'd caused. It was a never-ending spiral, love, loss, and pain. She had to stop it now.

She inhaled and lifted her head, facing him. "Loving makes you vulnerable, Jacob. Loving hurts, especially when you lose the ones you love." She turned away and swept aside a willow branch.

She was leaving him, Jacob realized, going back to camp. But he couldn't let it end like this.

He stopped her, holding her by her shoulders and turning her to face him. "I understand what you've been through and how hard it's been. Your family, your baby... And your fear of staying on the frontier because of the hostile tribes."

He put his hand under her chin and lifted her face to his. "Is this about forgiveness? All the suffering you've been through is due to my mother's people. Have you forgiven them? Because if you haven't, then I must remind you of them, being a half-breed. Maybe this isn't about being in love or not being in love. Perhaps, this is about forgiveness?"

She twisted in his embrace, trying to pull away from him.

"You haven't forgiven, have you?" He had to know, couldn't help from driving his point home.

She turned on him and for the first time, he saw the fury within her, lurking just below the surface. It twisted her beautiful face into a hideous mask.

She lifted her arm and pointed over their heads, back to the ridge, back to the burnt-out husk of her family's home and the graves of her loved ones. "How can you expect me to forgive that?

"I don't despise you because of your Comanche blood, Jacob. There are good and bad people in all races. I know that." She pressed her lips together, thinning them. "But I don't know if I have enough goodness in me to forgive everything." She shook her head. "I don't know."

She lifted one hand and stroked his cheek. "You've been a good friend to me. You, more than anyone else, has understood what I've endured. But I don't want to remain on the frontier and be reminded of all I've lost." She lowered her hand and clasped her hands together. "I want to go someplace new, like Little Rock. I want to start my life over and see if I can... if I can..."

She gazed at him. "It's all too soon, Jacob. I've nothing left to give. I could give you my body, as I had to give it to my Comanche husband. But that's not love. And I don't know when I will be ready to love again... if ever."

He couldn't let her slip away—not for forever. Someday, she might change her mind. Someday, she might find forgiveness in her heart and be ready to love again. He could wait. He'd waited all his life to find her.

"Will you write to me?" he asked.

"Of course, but you need to let me know where you'll be posted."

"Or where I'll live."

"Still thinking of giving up the soldiering life?"

He shrugged. "Perhaps it's for the best. I've not enjoyed tracking and killing my mother's people."

"Now you understand some of my hurt that won't go away."

He crushed her to him again and captured her mouth, kissing her with all the pent-up love and yearning in his heart. Then he broke their kiss and gazed at her, wanting to memorize her face. Wishing he had a daguerreotype of her to keep.

"I understand, but I'm willing to walk away, to forgive and forget. Make a new life." He touched his forehead to hers. "You're not."

"No, I'm not." The tone of her voice was just this side of a sob. "I want to start over but far away from here."

She pulled away and plunged into the willow thicket. This time, he let her go, his heart sinking like one of the stones he'd thrown into the river.

Then he saw the ostrich feather where she'd dropped it on the ground. He bent and picked it up.

* * *

Ruth trotted her horse past the fort's watch tower and heaved a sigh of relief. The journey back to the fort had been miserable. She'd been miserable, unable to look Jacob in the eye. And to his credit, he'd avoided her, too. His silent understanding hurt her more than if he'd cursed her.

Sergeant Krause had roused them at sunrise, and they'd made good time, returning. Now, all she wanted was to know when the spring exchange of troops would take place. As soon as she knew, she'd write her aunt and give her an idea of when to expect her arrival in Little Rock.

They pulled up their mounts in front of the stables. Corporal Harding appeared and grabbed her bridle. He lifted his hand, as if he was going to salute her and then dropped it. Instead, he bowed and said, "Miss MacDonald, the major sent me to fetch you to his office. As soon as possible."

Her spirits lifted, hoping the major would tell her when she'd be leaving. What else could he want?

She dismounted, and Jacob took her horse away. She started to thank him but clamped her mouth shut. The less they interacted, the better. But still, just gazing at him, her heart turned over. She did care for him. She might never care for another, as she did for Jacob.

But she was broken inside, and he deserved better.

She dusted her hands on her improvised riding skirt and took off her straw-brimmed hat. Corporal Harding stood at attention, waiting. "I'm ready, Corporal. I'll fetch my saddlebags later."

"Private Sims," the corporal called out to a tall soldier, loitering by the horse trough and whittling on a stick. "Would you please take Miss McDonald's saddlebags to the O'Connors' cabin."

The private stood at attention and saluted. Jacob had already untied the bags and handed them to the private. Again, she had to bite her tongue to not thank him.

"Yes, sir." The private took the bags. "Right away, Corporal."

"Come with me, Miss MacDonald."

She trailed after the corporal. After she met with the major, she couldn't wait to hold baby Johnny in her arms. It had been only three days since she'd seen him, and she wondered if he'd changed while she was gone.

She would miss the baby... and Jacob. But at least, she'd be traveling as far as San Antonio with the O'Connors and their baby.

The corporal opened the door to the headquarters office and ushered her inside. He saluted the major and closed the door behind him. After the bright spring sunshine, her eyes took a moment to adjust to the darker office.

The major stood behind his desk, waiting for her. But what surprised her was to find the O'Connors there, too. Nellie held the baby. And without a word, she crossed the office and placed baby Johnny in her arms.

Nellie ducked her head, and her voice was barely a whisper, "He's yours, Ruth. Johnny... or Matthew... or whatever you want to call him." She wiped her eyes with her hand. "The baby is yours. Our baby died, not yours."

She raised her head and gazed directly into Ruth's eyes. "And may God forgive us for what I..." She glanced at her husband. "For what we did." Nellie choked back a sob. "I hope one day, you will forgive us, too, Ruth." She lifted her hand, as if to stroke Ruth's cheek.

It took a few moments for Nellie's words to sink in, but finally, she understood. And understanding, she flinched from the woman who'd deceived her. She looked down at the baby. He stared back at her, the green-blue flecks in the iris of his eyes, tugging at her heart strings.

A sense of pure joy poured through her, feeling the precious, warm bundle in her arms and knowing her child had lived.

He lived!

Then her head snapped up, and she stared at the O'Connors. They stood, huddled together, across the office. And the major hadn't said a word; he'd not even uttered a greeting.

Rage roiled through her, making her shake with the force of what she was feeling. Of what had been done to her. The grief and sorrow she'd suffered. The pain, the awful pain.

Her mouth worked, but no words came. She stared at Johnny again and then at the O'Connors. Slowly but surely, the enormity of what they'd done dawned on her.

"You, you, you!" She clutched the baby with one hand and pointed at Nellie with the other. "You stole my child! You did it! I should have known!" She turned to the major and demanded, "Lock her up! She's a thief!"

Her words rushed out, pouring over each other like water escaping a ruptured jug. "I demand you put her in the brig, Major. She took my child. Told me my baby had died. I cried and cried. I suffered and wanted to die, too. My heart was torn in two, I... I..."

She sputtered to a stop, inhaled, and closed her eyes.

The baby, upset by her spate of angry words, started to cry. She clasped him tighter, lowering her head and crooning to him. She jiggled him up and down and hummed a wordless tune under her breath.

After a few minutes, he quieted, made some sucking noises, and then closed his eyes.

Watching him, she'd always known, hadn't she? He was hers, her baby. She'd endured, and her child had lived. She'd never be lonely again.

The major cleared his throat.

But she didn't look up. Instead, she couldn't tear her gaze from her baby--couldn't get enough of looking at him—at his dark brown hair, chubby cheeks, rosy lips. He was beautiful, more beautiful than anything she'd ever seen.

"Miss MacDonald," the major called for her attention. "I understand how you must feel about the O'Connors and what they did. But I believe, as Captain O'Connor's commanding officer, you need to know all the facts."

"Why?" she asked.

"Because, Miss MacDonald, with the exception of the captain deceiving me, what has transpired, is primarily of a civilian nature."

"Does that mean they won't be punished?" She couldn't believe what she was hearing. She glared at the O'Connors. "They deserve to be punished, and I'll find a way if you—"

"Miss, please," the major held up one hand and lowered it slowly. "Please, calm yourself. Punishment will be forthcoming, but since the crime was primarily perpetrated against you, I feel you might want to hear all the facts and help me decide what to do."

She nodded numbly, but she didn't care about the facts. She just wanted to take her baby and retreat to her room... her room in the O'Connor's cabin. She closed her eyes again.

"May I sit down?" she asked.

"Of course." The major came from behind his desk and offered her a chair. "Please, sit and be comfortable. And I will try to make this as quick as possible."

He folded his hands behind his back and paced the length of the room. "One night, shortly after you were rescued with your baby, the captain and his wife came to me and told me your baby had died. They claimed your child was theirs—"

"They lied!"

"Yes, Miss, they did, but please, hear me out."

She gulped and rocked her baby, cuddling him close. "All right."

"You were still unconscious. No one, including Dr. Statler, knew if you would regain your senses. And you'd been a Comanche captive." He cleared his throat again. "A woman who has been held captive by the hostiles often finds it difficult to return to her people."

"Because our people judge them to be whores, as the lieutenant judged me, not fit to be accepted by our society?"

The major stiffened, and he grimaced. "Just so, what you say is true. That doesn't make it right and not all people feel that way. But—"

"The O'Connors felt they could give my child a better life than I could. And having lost their children, it was natural for them to want my baby."

"Yes, that is precisely what they thought. Even if you recovered, which you did, they knew you'd lost all your family. Without kinfolk to help—"

"And the lieutenant was showing interest in you," Nellie interrupted. "If his intentions had been honorable and he'd married you, you'd have been accepted. But I knew he wouldn't want a half-breed baby." She shook her head. "Somehow I knew."

Ruth stared at Nellie. The older woman had told herself what she needed to justify taking Ruth's child, and the captain had helped. Everything they said might be true, but it didn't absolve them of their guilt and the agony they'd caused her.

She turned and faced the major. "What do you want me to do?"

"I wanted to know your feelings, Miss MacDonald, to help me decide what punishment I should impose upon the captain. His wife, as a civilian, is not under my jurisdiction, though she admits she begged her husband to deceive you... and me." He spread his hands. "As a commander on the frontier, I have a great deal of latitude as to what punishment I can—"

"May I inquire what punishment you're considering?" she asked.

The major exhaled. "For deceiving me, I can have the captain court martialed, or I can relieve him of his commission, busting him back to Sergeant."

"And you want me to help you decide?"

He frowned. "Yes, since the preponderance of the crime was committed against you, I had wanted to give you a say in the matter." He lowered his voice and said, "I thought you and the O'Connors had formed a relationship, like you have with Scout Wells." He gazed at her. "You pled for mercy for Wells."

"But that was different. Scout Wells deserved mercy. He was defending the poor woman who'd lost her child. And the lieutenant wanted to make me his whore." She shook her head. "This isn't the same thing. Not at all."

"I understand, Miss MacDonald. You feel betrayed by the O'Connors. I can't say I blame you, but I wanted to give you a chance to let me know your feelings before I decide what to do."

She stared at the O'Connors. "Trying to steal another person's child is a hideous crime, no matter the circumstances."

"I understand," the major repeated himself. "Would you please think it over?" He held up his hand again, palm out. "If you would consider, for one night, what you want me to do, I would be satisfied."

"And his wife won't be punished?"

"I have no authority, though, I'm certain there are civilian remedies." He bowed to her. "Your aunt in Arkansas can assist you in that matter."

She gazed down at her baby. Just looking at him, filled her with awe. She wanted nothing more than to hold him forever.

She lifted her head and stared at the major. "For your kindness, I'll think about the captain's punishment tonight. But I might not have an answer for you, Major." She hugged her baby. "What I want to know, is where I will spend the night?" She shuddered. "Not with the O'Connors."

"I foresaw your awkwardness, and I had your belongings moved to my home. You'll be staying in Lupe's room tonight and until your transport to San Antonio arrives."

"What about Lupe?" she asked, not liking to displace their loyal servant.

"Lupe will stay with her sister in San Angelo and come to the fort every morning. She understood your inconvenience and is happy to help."

"That's kind of Lupe. She's a nice woman."

"Yes, she is."

"What about the transport?" Ruth asked. "I don't want to travel with the O'Connors to San Antonio."

"In that circumstance, we've been lucky. Fort McKavett has lost over half its force, fighting the hostiles. A new troop of soldiers will be needed to fill their empty ranks. Their escort will be returning to San Antonio. I'll send you and your child with them. The O'Connors will leave sooner, in about three days, when we exchange troops from the Texas headquarters at Fort Sam Houston to Fort Concho."

Knowing she wouldn't be forced to be around the O'Connors, made her sigh with relief. "Thank you, Major. I appreciate you taking me in and arranging a separate transport."

"My pleasure, Miss MacDonald." He bowed to her again. "I'm sincerely sorry for all the indignities and unpleasant issues your rescue has created."

The major turned to the O'Connors. "Captain, I will take your punishment under consideration. Be here at eight hundred hours for my decision." He saluted.

Captain O'Connor returned his salute, took his wife's arm, and left the office, closing the door.

The major turned to her. "May I escort you home, Miss MacDonald, and introduce you to my family?"

Chapter Ten

The major rested his hand on her elbow and guided her across the parade ground toward his home. Her baby wakened and started to fuss.

"I'm afraid he's hungry and wet. Has the nanny goat been moved, too? And I'll need some clean nappies for him." She ducked her head. "Having a baby is a lot of trouble, I'm sorry—"

"No apologies are necessary, Miss MacDonald. A baby is a joy to have. You will have everything you need." He shook his head. "Actually, I've been remiss, not introducing you to my family. But my wife has been ailing, and she's not been out of the house since the start of cold weather. Now, the weather has turned, I hope she will venture forth."

"Yes, I understand. Lupe explained when she helped me with Nellie."

"I appreciate you overlooking my breach of courtesy." He quickened his step, pulling her along. "I look forward to you meeting my family."

They climbed the steps to his front porch, and he pushed open the door. Unlike the O'Connors' cabin, the front room was larger. There was a kitchen table, like the O'Connors, but it was pushed into a corner of the kitchen. Facing the fireplace, there was room enough for a rocking chair, an overstuffed horsehair chair and a small couch.

A tiny lady, swathed in a shawl and an afghan sat on the couch. At the kitchen table, a young girl of about eight years old was scribbling on a paper tablet.

The girl jumped to her feet. She was tall for her age with long, lanky legs. Her blonde hair was braided, hanging in two lengths over her shoulders. "Papa, I'm glad you're home. And you've brought Miss MacDonald and her baby."

The blue-eyed girl peered at the fussy baby and glanced at Ruth. "May I hold him?"

"Missy, you've forgotten your manners." The major turned toward his daughter. "This is Miss MacDonald and her baby, Johnny."

Ruth moved her baby to the crook of her left arm and thrust out her right hand. "Please, call me Ruth. And I intend to rename my child. I want him to be called James."

The major nodded. "This is my daughter, Margaret."

The girl took her hand. "You can call me Peggy." Her eyes lit up, looking at the baby. "Can I come to his christening ceremony?"

"A christening—?"

"If you wish to rename your child, you'll probably want the chaplain to christen him again," the major said.

"Yes, I guess you're right. I hadn't thought."

The major took her elbow again, pulling her around. "May I introduce my wife, Martha Gregor." He crossed to his wife and tucked in a corner of the afghan. Then he leaned down and kissed her cheek.

The tiny woman, her blonde hair streaked with gray, reached up and touched her husband's cheek. Then he stepped away, and she gazed at Ruth.

"Welcome, Miss MacDonald, I'm happy to meet you. I've heard about you and your trials. You've been in my thoughts and prayers."

"How kind of you, Mrs. Gregor." She accommodated her baby again and thrust out her hand. Her baby, tired and hungry, started screaming at the top of his lungs.

Mrs. Gregor smiled and ignored her hand, pulling her down on the couch beside her. "I think a hug might be in order. And please, call me Martha."

Awkwardly, Ruth hugged the older woman, feeling how frail her frame was beneath the layers of swaddling. She felt like a bird whose bones were hollow.

They pulled apart and Martha looked down at her baby, a smile lightening the deep lines of suffering on her face. "A baby is such a blessing. New life starting." She chucked the baby's chin. "Are you hungry, little one? Of course, you are."

Martha Gregor raised her voice and called, "Lupe, has that goat been milked?"

Lupe, her young-old face wreathed in smiles, came from a back room. "*Sí, Señora* I've the milk teat ready for him."

Ruth got to her feet. "Lupe, thank you so much." She ducked her head. "And thank you for letting me stay in your room. I appreciate it."

"*Bienvenidos, Señora*, you're more than welcome. I'm happy you've been reunited with your baby."

Ruth understood Lupe was being kind without making reference to the O'Connors trying to keep her baby. Thinking about it again, she gritted her teeth, trying to stave off the wave of fury sweeping her.

Lupe approached with her arms outstretched. "*Con su permiso*, I will feed your little one while you visit with the major's family."

She gripped her squealing child tighter and looked around. The Gregor's were kind and loving; she could feel the warmth of their affection in the room. She wanted to get to know them better, but right now, she wanted her baby to herself.

"Do you mind, Major and Mrs. Gregor, if I retire to my room and feed my baby?" She exhaled. "It's been a long and tiring day and—"

"You poor sweet thing," Mrs. Gregor said. "Of course, we don't mind. I understand. We'll visit tomorrow when you're rested." She glanced at Lupe. "Please, show Ruth to her room and get her settled."

The major bowed and his daughter, Peggy, smiled.

"I'll have Lupe send you a tray for supper." Mrs. Gregor added. "I hope you will be comfortable. Have a good night."

* * *

Ruth heard a rattle of glass and turned on her side, groggy and half asleep. She had her baby tucked beside her in the bed. She cuddled him closer, taking comfort in his warm body next to hers.

There hadn't been a cradle in Lupe's room. She could have used a bureau drawer, but she wanted him close to her at all times.

Another rattle sounded, and she glanced up. It seemed as if something was hitting her bedroom window. It was spring on the southern plains. Perhaps it was hailing outside? She rose on her elbows and listened.

She remembered the frequent hail storms when she'd lived with her family on the ranch, but usually, the hail could be heard drumming on the roof.

She listened carefully, but there wasn't any sound above her. Then another scattering of pings hit her window. She leaned over and lit the kerosene lamp beside her bed. Moving James to one side, she threw her legs over the bed and pulled on the old quilted wrapper Nellie had given her.

Grimacing when the robe touched her body, she couldn't wait until she got to San Antonio where she would buy herself a new wardrobe and happily burn every stitch of clothing that had belonged to Nellie.

Lamp in hand, she moved to the window in time to see a spattering of small rocks hit her window. And then she knew... Jacob.

She lifted the window and stuck her head out. "What are you doing?" she whispered.

"I needed to get your attention," the sound of Jacob's voice reached her. She could see his shadowy form standing by the tethered nanny goat in the backyard.

"I hope you're not going to be so unkind as to take your goat back," she said.

"Of course not, but I need to talk to you."

She drew in a deep breath, wondering what he could possibly want. She hoped he wasn't going to press his attentions on her again. But thinking about him taking her in his arms, she trembled, knowing she was lying to herself.

"Jacob, what time is it?"

"Just past midnight."

"I'm tired, and the baby is sleeping. Can't this wait until morning?"

"No, morning will be too late. Can you come out for a few minutes? Bring your baby, it's warm out tonight."

"Oh, all right, I'm coming, but this isn't seemly. What if someone sees—?"

"That didn't bother you before. And besides, you'll be leaving for San Antonio soon. What do you care?"

"I don't want to abuse the major's hospitality."

"I'm waiting, Ruth."

"All right!" She lowered the window gently, resisting the urge to slam it and wake everyone in the cabin.

With baby James in the crook of her left arm and holding the lamp in her right hand, she found her way through the dark kitchen, into the storeroom, and let herself out the back door.

Jacob came forward. The lamp threw strange, sharp shadows onto his face. She set it on the ground and cradled her baby.

He touched the baby's cheek, stroking it softly. "You got your wish. Your child lives."

"How did you know?"

"Nothing is a secret in this fort. I thought you'd figured that out by now."

"You're right." The sound of her voice sharpened when she said, "I can't believe what the O'Connors tried to do—all the agony and pain they put me through. It's beyond hideous they thought they could steal my child."

"They didn't have to go to the major, you know?" he said.

She opened her mouth and then closed it. She hadn't considered how the deception had been uncovered. She'd been so hurt, so angry, and then so relieved to have her child, she'd not questioned the how or why.

"They turned themselves in?"

"Yes, they couldn't go through with it. Seems Nellie, who convinced the captain in the first place, started feeling guilty when you nursed her back to health."

"Oh, I see." She frowned. "And well she should. It was awful what they tried to—"

"Ruth, think how Nellie feels. She's probably past the time she can have her own child and when she realized her Johnny had died, she must have been ravaged by grief, crazy to have a baby. And you were unconscious—"

"I heard all of this in the major's office." She turned away. "I don't want to hear it again. It was a crime what they did, trying to take my child. When I came to my senses, the first thing I did was ask for my baby. Nellie lied to me and told me my child had died. I can't—"

"Forgive her," he finished for her and exhaled. "That word again, Ruth. Forgiveness. Now, you have your child because Nellie came to her senses, after she'd recovered from her grief and seen what was happening to you. I would think you could, at least, sympathize with how crazy she must have been when her child died that night."

"I won't. I can't forgive them. She should have come to her senses sooner. Should have told me, and the captain shouldn't have tried to foist me off on that awful Lieutenant Schultz, either. It wasn't their right. It wasn't right!"

"All right, Ruth, you can't forgive them." He touched her arm. "But could you ask the major for mercy when it comes to the captain's punishment? Like you did for me?"

"He doesn't deserve mercy. He backed up his wife and was willing to take my baby."

Jacob scrubbed his face with his hand.

There was nothing more to be said. She turned again to go back to her bedroom.

He reached out again and touched her arm. "Wait, I'm begging you to be merciful to the captain. He gave into his wife because she was—"

"Are you loco, Jacob?" She leaned in closer to smell his breath. "Or have you been drinking?" Instead, he smelled like he always did of leather, horses, and the half-wild scent of the prairie.

He took advantage of her closeness and lowered his head. Awkwardly, with the baby between them, he clasped her shoulders and pulled her closer.

His mouth covered hers, and his lips were warm and supple. He kissed her open-mouthed and with all the fierceness she knew he kept tightly wrapped inside.

And heaven help her, she welcomed his kiss, reveled in it. Loved the touch of his mouth on hers, the way he made her feel, as if every nerve in her body had suddenly awakened. As if the blood boiled in her veins, and her heart pounded double-time in her chest.

He broke the kiss and touched his forehead to hers. She wanted to stroke his face, to run her hands over his chest, to clutch him tighter. But she did none of those things, just stood shaking, like a newly-foaled colt, on unsteady legs.

"I thought a lot on the way back from your family's ranch about... forgiveness. And I realized why you couldn't forgive the Comanche or now the O'Connors." He ran his thumb over her lower lip, and she shuddered. "You must forgive yourself first, Ruth. Then you can forgive the others and start over."

She drew back. One moment, he had her enthralled, and the next minute, she'd like nothing better than to slap him. How could he be so wrong?

"Forgive myself?" she spat. "What on earth do I have to forgive myself for?"

"For living, Ruth, for surviving, when your family didn't. And for succumbing your virtue to a savage, whose people killed your family."

She recoiled another step, hating him for what he was saying. "You may not be drinking, but you're surely loco. I have nothing more to say to you, Jacob. Please, don't approach me again."

"All right." He lowered his head and pulled something from his pocket. He held it out to her. "You dropped it beside the river. I want you to have it. Something to remember me by. I doubt we'll be writing or—"

"You're right about that. I don't want to hear from you. As for that feather..." She wanted to push it away or throw it away. But something, she didn't know what, made her stretch out her hand.

He placed the ostrich feather in her hand. It was soft and smelled of the prairie... just like Jacob.

Then he turned and walked away.

* * *

Ruth awakened before sunrise. She yawned and stretched and gazed at her baby. He'd be stirring soon, wanting his breakfast. Better she got up early, as she didn't know when Lupe would arrive, and she might have to milk the nanny goat herself.

Her eyelids were heavy, but she needed to get busy...

Who was she fooling?

Since Jacob's midnight visit, she hadn't slept—not really. Hadn't been able to stop thinking about what he'd said. Hadn't been able to forget the magic of his touch and the warmth of his kiss. Good heavens, but she wanted the man. Wanted him more than anything else in this world, except for her child.

Her baby—he was awake now and waving his chubby arms. It wouldn't be long before he started squealing and woke up the entire household.

She got to her feet, washed her face and hands in the basin, and donned one of the calico dresses. Then she changed James' wet and dirty nappie, wondering where Lupe did the laundry. She should help, as her baby would be an additional burden. But first, she needed to get him fed.

She opened the door and stepped into the kitchen. Her room, or Lupe's room, opened off the kitchen. The other bedroom doors led from the sitting room. And she was surprised to find Lupe already at the sink with a pail of milk beside her.

"Good morning, Lupe. You must have come in the dark to milk the goat. I can help milk her, too, you know. But thank you," she said.

"*Buenos días, Señora*, the milking is simple. And I knew the little *muchacho* would be hungry." She gazed at baby James and touched his cheek. "He is beautiful. No?"

"Yes, very beautiful. Again, thank you."

"Good morning, Miss MacDonald." The major stepped into the room. "And Lupe." He bobbed his head.

"Good morning," Ruth said, and Lupe nodded.

"I'm putting the coffee on now, Major Gregor," Lupe said.

He pulled out one of the kitchen chairs and sat. "I'm not in a hurry, Lupe, but thank you." He glanced at the baby. "That young gentleman takes precedence over this grizzled soldier." He smiled. "Always."

"Would you like some coffee, too, *Señora* MacDonald?" Lupe asked.

"Please, if it's not too much trouble."

"No trouble." Lupe handed her a square of cheesecloth and the pail of milk. "Please, sit and feed your baby. I will bring the coffee."

Ten minutes later, baby James had sucked down the milk until his tummy was round as a drum. She put him over her shoulder and burped him. Then, settling him in the crook of her arm, she curled her hand around the warm mug of coffee.

Lupe was a whirlwind of activity, humming to herself, while she fried eggs and thick slabs of bacon on the cookstove. The major made polite conversation, and for the first time since she'd been rescued, she felt at home and truly welcome.

Now she understood the thread of tension she'd sensed with the O'Connors. Their deception had made her staying with them awkward. At the time, she'd thought they resented her as an extra burden. Now she understood their reticence and double-edged kindness.

But she couldn't stop thinking about what Jacob had said last night. Forgiveness was what a Christian should feel toward others. Turn the other cheek. The hardest thing was what he'd discovered and understood... she couldn't forgive herself.

Lying in her captors' teepees, she'd often despaired of living, wondering why she'd been spared and not the rest of her family. Thinking, as a Christian woman, she should have withheld herself from carnal relations with any savage who wanted to touch her, even Buffalo Heart. She hadn't welcomed his attentions, but she hadn't fought back, either. If she'd been courageous, she would have resisted and accepted her punishment or death.

But her will to survive had been too strong.

Could she forgive herself and the O'Connors, even the Comanches who'd slaughtered her family? She'd known kindness with Buffalo Heart and her friend, Sunflower. Though kindness wasn't the point, was it? She should love her enemies, as the Bible taught. But could she?

Thinking of how she'd been rescued and cared for and the miracle of having her child returned to her, she knew what she must do. Tears formed at the corners of her eyes, and she wiped them away. Tears of relief, of hope, and... mercy.

She raised her head and looked the major directly in his eyes. Her voice was scarcely a whisper when she said, "I don't want you to punish the captain. I understand why they did what they did... and I... and I... forgive them. Please, don't punish Captain

O'Connor. He only wanted to help his wife and comfort her. Please."

The major returned her gaze and nodded. "A very wise decision, Miss MacDonald, and more than kind of you, especially after all you've been through. I'll tell the captain this morning. I'm sure he'll appreciate your mercy, and Nellie, too."

He took a sip of coffee. "I saw what they went through when they lost their daughter, Eliza. I was having a difficult time, finding it in my heart to punish the captain, especially since he and his wife came and confessed to me."

* * *

Chaplain Mapes intoned the words of the christening ceremony, and sprinkled her son with water, saying, "I christen thee, James William MacDonald."

Baby James squealed when the water hit his face and waved his dimpled arms.

"Do you wish to name godparents for this child, Miss MacDonald?" The chaplain raised his head and glanced around the almost-empty chapel.

The major and his wife stood behind her. Ruth knew the effort it had cost Martha to come. The older woman was very sick, and she seldom stirred from her cabin. But she'd roused herself to come today. Her husband had his arm around her shoulder, and she leaned on him for support.

Ruth brushed a tear from her cheek with the white gloves Martha had given her. She'd given Ruth a lacy white bonnet to match, too. The ostrich feather Jacob had given her looked perfect, tucked into the frilly bonnet.

None of the older lady's clothes had fit, so she was wearing her best dress, the green velvet ballgown with a white scarf at her neck to make the neckline more acceptable for church. She'd never felt so elegant in her life, and it was all because of Martha Gregor's kindness.

In the back row of the chapel sat the O'Connors. At first, she'd been surprised to see them. But she should have known they'd want to come. She'd hoped Jacob would come to her baby's christening, but she hadn't seen him since the night he'd come to her window.

"Yes, Major Gregor and his wife, Martha, have been kind enough to stand as godparents for my child."

Chaplain Mapes finished the ceremony with, "Will you, William and Martha Gregor, do everything in your power to encourage and support James William MacDonald to be a good Christian?"

The Gregors answered in unison, "We will."

The chaplain held out his arms.

Ruth handed him her baby.

He dipped his fingers in the baptismal font again and made the sign of the cross on her baby's forehead. "I baptize you in the name of the Father and of the Son and of the Holy Ghost. We welcome you as a member of Christ's church. May all be well with you in your journey through life."

Chaplain Mapes smiled and returned baby James to her arms. "Go in peace and grace, Miss MacDonald."

She nodded, and a sense of deep peace descended upon her.

Hesitantly, the captain and Nellie edged to the front of the church and waited with bowed heads.

Ruth turned to the major and his wife, "Thank you. I appreciate you standing in as his godparents."

"It was our pleasure, Ruth," Martha said, and her eyes were especially bright today. "We wish you and your little boy all the best in the world. And we'll miss you when you leave." She squeezed her husband's arm. "Won't we, William?"

"Yes, we will. And I'm honored you named your son after me, Miss MacDonald. Very honored," his voice was gruff with emotion. "We have a christening present for you. The first wagon of supplies came in yesterday. It's not much, but we wanted to give you something to remember us by."

"How thoughtful," Ruth said and gulped down the lump that had risen to her throat. Their kindness and goodness surrounded her, and she would miss them.

Was that why she hadn't found the time to write her aunt to tell her when she'd be coming?

"And Lupe has made a cake, now we have sugar, and a special dinner. We'll have a small celebration tonight," Martha added.

"Oh, how nice. I'm sure Peggy will enjoy the cake, too."

"If she finishes her lessons," the major said. "Lately, that girl would try the patience of a saint." He shook his head. "She hates doing her lessons."

"Oh, William, it's probably just a phase," Martha said. "I'm sure she will grow out of it."

"Maybe." He glanced over his shoulder. "We'll leave you now, Miss MacDonald. I think the O'Connors would like to have a word with you."

"Yes, thank you. I'll be back in a few minutes, and I can help Lupe."

"No, you won't lift a finger," Martha interjected. "This party is our gift to you."

"All right." She nodded and lowered her head.

The major and his wife turned and walked past the O'Connors. They nodded again, and Martha said, "Good afternoon, Captain and Nellie."

"Good afternoon, Major Gregor and Martha. Nice to see you here," the captain replied.

Ruth waited, holding her fussy baby.

The O'Connors came forward and stopped. Captain O'Connor tugged on his earlobe, and Nellie said, "We want to wish you and baby James the best."

Seeing them for the first time, up close, sent strange sensations skittering through her. But uppermost in her mind was the feeling of goodness, of rightness, to be welcoming them and happy they'd come to her baby's christening.

Forgiveness was a balm to the spirit that just kept giving.

Ruth put her hand on Nellie's arm. "Thank you for coming. Lupe's baking a cake for supper. I'm sure there will be plenty—"

"Thank you, but our escort is ready to leave for Fort Sam Houston. We asked them to delay so we could see your baby christened," the captain said.

"Oh, how kind of you," Ruth replied.

Nellie shook her head. "Think nothing of it, lass. It was the least we could do." She glanced at her husband. "We wanted to thank you for forgiving us, and for asking the major to be merciful, too."

Ruth gulped again, and tears burned at the back of her throat. "Thank you for taking me in and helping me." Her eyes filled and spilled over. "Thank you both." She glanced at the captain and then she hugged Nellie.

Jostled, baby James squealed.

They clung to each other, and Ruth felt the warmth of forgiveness and mercy flow through her. She wished Jacob had come. She missed him. Maybe she would look for him and ask him to the christening celebration. She knew the Gregors wouldn't mind.

* * *

Jacob swung onto the back of his new horse, a gray gelding he called *Kiwihnai*. He missed *Paaka*, had raised the pinto from a colt, but the gelding was a good mount. He half-turned and secured the mule's lead rope to his saddle.

The mule was heavy laden, but he needed a lot of staples to spend the summer in the wild country north of the fort. He could always hunt for game, but there were precious few places where he could get coffee, salt, sugar, flour, ammunition, and the other basics.

He'd sold off his string of horses. He hadn't gotten top dollar, but he'd wanted to put Fort Concho behind him. And when the supply wagon had rolled in yesterday, he'd been the first in line at the sutler's store to buy what he needed.

Practically everyone else at the fort must have had the same idea and as soon as the supplies were sold out, the major had ordered his troops, who were transferring to Fort Sam Houston, to be ready to leave this afternoon.

Jacob had decided to ride along with them for aways before turning north. It might be the last time he saw these men and women who'd been a big part of his life, though, he knew he'd be back some day to visit his father's grave.

He watched as the O'Connors came from the small chapel and climbed into the buckboard, which was piled high with their furniture and other possessions. He'd wanted to see Ruth and her baby again. He'd considered going to the christening, but he didn't want to intrude.

The last time they'd spoken, she'd told him to stay away. She didn't even want to write him. But she must have taken some of his words to heart, as she'd shown mercy towards the captain and his wife.

That didn't mean she'd forgiven him. And just thinking about her and how much he loved her, made his heart hurt.

He shifted in his saddle, hoping the major would give the sign to ride out soon. A Captain Morse from Fort Sam Houston would be leading the group. He and the major were in the headquarters building, going over last-minute details, no doubt. In fact, the entire column had been held up by the christening of Ruth's baby.

The agony of leaving her behind, of never seeing her or baby James again, lanced through him. He doubled over in his saddle, as if he'd been gut shot.

And then he saw her, crossing the parade ground and coming straight for him. He took a deep breath, not knowing if he could stand another goodbye, and he almost kicked *Kiwihnai* into a gallop, leaving the others behind.

Ruth came up to him and took hold of his stirrup. He gazed at her, and she looked back at him, moisture sparkling on the tips of her long, red eyelashes.

"You're going without saying goodbye?" she asked.

"I thought that was what you wanted, Ruth."

She looked away. "I thought it was what I wanted, too. I was full of anger and hurt and..." She turned her head back and gazed at him. "You're not in uniform."

"No, I've cashiered out. I won't be joining the regular army, and my enlistment as a scout was almost up. The major let me go a couple of weeks early."

"I thought you wanted to be a regular soldier, like your father."

"I thought it was what I wanted, too," he echoed her and shook his head. "I've changed my mind."

"But you're going to Fort Sam Houston with the escort?"

"Only part way, then I'll head north."

"North?" She frowned. "Where are you going? To Oklahoma Territory?"

"No, not that far." He turned away and squinted at the sun, wondering what was taking the major and Captain Morse so long.

"Then where?"

"The Llano Estacado to catch wild mustangs. There are plenty of horses there. I should be able to have enough horses by the end of summer—"

"The Llano Estacado, but that's so dangerous! The Comanche and Kiowa roam free there, and there are no forts to protect you."

"I'll be fine. I speak some Kiowa, too."

"But you'll be taking the horses they believe belong to them. They won't take kindly to—"

"I thought you didn't care what happened to me."

"But I do, Jacob." She lowered her head and bit her lip. "I do. Why would you want to go to such a dangerous place?"

"To make money fast, so I can buy the ranch I've talked about."

"You decided to ranch, rather than be a soldier."

"Yes, I'm tired of the killing." He lowered his voice and spoke softly. "It was kind of you to show the O'Connors mercy. They deserved it."

She turned her face up to him again, and he could see the tears streaming from her eyes. Didn't she know she was tearing him into pieces? Facing hostiles, who were guarding their wild horse herds, was easier than facing her, knowing she didn't want him.

She gulped and swatted away the tears with the back of her hand. She never remembered to carry a handkerchief. He half-smiled to himself.

"Only because you showed me the error of my ways, Jacob," her voice was barely a whisper and she was staring at the toes of her ill-fitting shoes. "Only because you taught me about forgiveness." She touched her chest above her heart. "I've forgiven myself... finally. I had to... to go on... to be a good mother for James."

He lifted his hand, let it hover in the air for a moment, not knowing if she'd welcome his touch. But he couldn't resist. He leaned down and stroked the downy soft skin of her cheek.

She turned her face into his hand and kissed his palm. His breath caught, but he refused to let hope spring alive again. She'd always welcomed his touch but that was all.

"You did the right thing. Forgiveness brings healing. I hope my Comanche brothers can forgive me for fighting against them. And if not, if they need revenge, then—"

"Don't go! Don't go!" The sound of her voice bordered on hysteria. She'd stepped back but still clutched his stirrup. "I love you, Jacob. I love you as much as my child. I've never stopped loving you, it seems, from that first day."

She touched the feather on her bonnet. "I keep it with me to remind me of you." She shook her head. "But I don't want remembrances. I want you. Before, I was too broken, too hurt to open my heart again." She gazed up at him. "I'm ready now, Jacob. If you want a ranch, we can settle on mine."

"What about your aunt, what about Little Rock? I thought you couldn't stand to live on the frontier—"

"That was before, Jacob, before you made me understand why I feared to go on living. Before I had my baby back. Before I opened my heart and knew I didn't want to live without you."

He threw his leg over *Kiwihnai* and dismounted. He clasped her shoulders. "Ruth, do you know what you're saying? You love me? You want to marry me?"

She turned her face up to his and nodded. And then she smiled, a big smile, as wide and beautiful as a Texas sunset.

He pulled her to him. "My love, my sweet, we'll be married as soon as Chaplain Mapes can arrange it. Is that all right with you?"

"Yes, yes, I want to be with you, Jacob. I want you to be the father of my baby."

"Where is James?"

"I left him with Lupe." She stamped her foot. "And you missed his christening. I was disappointed."

Tears clogged his throat, and he didn't trust himself to speak. Instead, he kissed her with all the love filling his heart to bursting.

When they broke apart, he buried his face in her fiery hair. "I want to always be by your side." He cupped her chin in his hand and gazed into her eyes. "You don't mind living on a ranch on the frontier, where your family—?"

"'Where you go, I will go, and where you stay, I will stay.'"

"Like Ruth in the Good Book?"

"Yes."

He folded her into his arms and rested his chin on her head. "Amen to that."

* * *

Cristabelle: The Christmas Bride

By Hebby Roman

Historical Western Romance

☆Estrella Publishing☆

Author's Note

Fort Clark, Texas was established in June 1852, at *Las Moras* Springs by Companies C and E of the First Infantry, under the command of Major Joseph H. LaMotte. The name *Las Moras* means "the mulberries," and it was given to the site by Spanish explorers. In 1849, Lieutenant W. H. C. Whiting recognized the site's military potential and its prospect as a stop along a wagon route between San Antonio and El Paso.

The fort was named for Major John B. Clark, a deceased officer, who had served bravely during the Mexican-American War. A twenty-year lease was signed with Samuel A. Maverick, a wealthy rancher who owned the land.

Fort Clark was strategically located as an anchor to the cordon of army posts, which had been established along the southwest Texas-México border. Fort Clark's purpose was to guard the border, to protect the road to El Paso, and to defend against Indian depredations arising from either side of the Rio Grande.

With the establishment of Fort Clark, a neighboring settlement of *Las Moras* came into existence when Oscar Brackett established a supply village for the fort, and later, the town was named Brackettville for its founder. The stage from San Antonio to El Paso ran through the settlement, and for almost a century, the town and the fort remained closely identified.

At the outbreak of the Civil War, Captain W. H. T. Brooks surrendered Fort Clark to a small company of the Provisional Army of Texas. After the war the fort was re-garrisoned in December 1866 by Troop C, Fourth United States Cavalry. Between 1873 and 1875 most of the dilapidated log fort was re-built with quarried limestone, using immigrant Italian masons. A twenty-acre post was developed with the construction of barracks, officers' quarters, hospital, bakery, stables, and guardhouse. By 1875 the fort had quarters built of stone for more than 200 officers and men, along with four of the original log cabins to accommodate lower-ranked officers and their families. In 1884, the United States purchased the land from Mary A. Maverick.

Especially significant during the Indian campaigns were the Black-Seminole scouts (nicknamed the "Buffalo Soldiers" by indigenous hostile tribes). After the Civil War, attempts by federal troops to curtail Indian raiders coming from México met with little success until Colonel Ranald S. Mackenzie and the Fourth United States Cavalry, along with a contingent of Black-Seminole scouts, led a raid into México on a punitive expedition against the Kickapoos and Lipan Apaches, destroying three villages, killing nineteen warriors, and capturing forty prisoners, including the aged Lipan chief, *Costillitto*.

Despite México's protests the United States was violating its sovereignty, other sorties by Mackenzie followed, and as a result, Indian forays from México to Texas declined dramatically. Mackenzie was succeeded by Lieutenant Colonel William Shafter in 1876. Shafter took five companies of cavalry, along with the Buffalo soldiers, and established a base camp near the mouth of the Pecos River to pursue the Lipan Apaches across the border, earning the Lt. Colonel the nickname of "Pecos Bill."

This book follows the general outline of the history of Fort Clark, but all the characters herein are fictional, except for the occasional mention of well-known historical persons.

Cristabelle: The Christmas Bride

Chapter One

Fort Clark, Texas—1875

Cristabelle took the last wooden clothes pin from her mouth and fastened the sheet to the rope line. She bent and grabbed the straw basket, filled with dry clothes, and balanced it on her hip.

Dawn was breaking in the east, painting patches of gold and crimson across the flat expanse of mesquite and sagebrush. With the coming of daylight, she needed to hurry back to the laundry room.

The laundresses at Fort Clark were under strict orders to not mix with the soldiers. They stayed in the laundry area, affectionately known as "Sudsville," venturing out before dawn and at mid-afternoon when the soldiers were occupied with the daily changing of the guard.

Many of the laundresses were the wives of non-commissioned officers, but there were a few unmarried women, like herself, and the rules had been made for them. Last year, while the fort was under the command of Colonel Mackenzie, three of the unmarried women had gotten pregnant. Two of the offending soldiers had been found and forced marriages had taken place. The other girl had returned home, in shame, to give birth to her child.

Lieutenant Colonel Gregor, an upright and Christian man, had set up new rules when he'd taken over command. He didn't want any unsanctioned pregnancies on his watch.

Knowing she was late and breaking one of the rules, Cristabelle picked up her pace, trotting with the unwieldy basket bumping her hip.

Outside the Dawes' log cabin, she spied a long, thin shape stretched across the path. At first, she thought it was a stick but when she got closer, she realized it was a rattlesnake. She almost stepped on the deadly rattler before skidding to a stop.

Panic pummeled her, making her heart thunder in her chest. She screamed and dropped the basket. Picking up her skirts, she leapt over the snake and ran as fast as she could. A bush rattled to one side of the path, and a soldier stepped in front of her.

She collided with his broad chest. He caught her and held her shoulders. "You've ruined my surprise," he said, his voice low and gravely but with a lilting note to it.

Frightened out of her wits, she half-turned and pointed at the snake. But the snake hadn't moved. It lay still and in the same position.

"It's dead. Isn't it?" she asked.

"Dead and stuffed. Took me two days to get the look of it right."

"What... why?"

He still held her by the shoulders, and she gazed into his turquoise-colored eyes, eyes alight with mischief. His strong hands on her shoulders burned through the light cotton of her blouse. He smelled good—of leather and the starch they used in the laundry. He was a handsome man with a head of dark, curly hair, a wide smile, and a dimple in his left cheek.

She'd seen handsome men before, and most of them, were as low-down as that stuffed rattlesnake. Besides, the rule about laundresses staying out of sight was for a good reason. Most soldiers thought nothing of seducing young women.

She should know.

Her face was burning. She stepped back and shrugged him off. Not waiting for an answer, she fetched her abandoned basket and stuffed the spilled shirts and sheets into it. Most of them would need to be washed again.

He joined her and said, "Let me help you."

"I need to get back to the laundry. You know the rules."

"Stupid rules. I hate them."

"Not as stupid as putting a stuffed snake across the path."

He grinned and grabbed the basket from her, holding it away.

She huffed and planted her fists on her hips. "What are you doing?"

"Walk with me and I'll carry your basket." He glanced at the snake and then at the sky. "Doubt it will fool anyone now. I'm surprised your scream didn't bring Felix's wife running."

"She's sick with milk fever." Cristabelle twisted away. "I don't want to walk with you."

"Oh, I didn't know Felix's wife was sick." He looked over his shoulder. "Guess I'll have to wait until later to get my own back." He backed up a few steps, bent down and grabbed the snake, tossing it into the bushes.

"Give me the basket." She softened her tone and held out her hand, knowing men liked to be cajoled. She might have managed to avoid men most of her life, but she'd learned a thing or two, watching her mother.

"Please." She smiled and looked down, wanting to appear meek.

"No, I want to walk with you."

"That's not possible." Her patience and play-acting were at an end. "I could be let go for breaking the rules, and I need this job."

He laughed. "What are rules for—if not breaking them?" He pulled her off the path, leading her among a copse of live oaks trailing down to Las Moras Springs.

"My name is David Donovan, or Davie, to my friends." He still held her basket but managed to bow. "And your name is?"

"Cristabelle, er, Cristabelle Smith." It wasn't her real name, but he didn't need to know that. It was the name she'd used to get her job.

"Cristabelle, is it?" He tested her name on his tongue. "It's quite a mouthful. Good thing your last name is simple." He narrowed his eyes, as if considering.

She turned up her nose at his suspicion. "My friends call me Crissy. Not that you've leave to do it. You're a soldier, not a friend." She made a grab for the basket.

But he was quick, anticipating her, moving the basket away and holding it behind him.

She puffed out her cheeks and sighed with frustration. *Didn't he understand?*

She needed her job, and there weren't many respectable jobs for women on the frontier.

The daylight had sharpened, and she heard officers issuing orders. She had to sneak back to the laundry, but she couldn't leave the clothes behind. She crossed her arms over her chest and frowned.

"You asked me why I put the snake there," he said.

"I don't really care. You've compromised me. I could lose my job. My mother is ailing. We've no one else to..."

His smile crumpled. "I didn't know. I wouldn't want to be the cause of—"

"Give me the basket and let me go."

Still he hesitated, keeping a firm grasp on it. "Give me a kiss, and I'll show you a secret way back to the laundry. No one will know, except the other laundresses. Are you friends with them?"

"Yes... no." She didn't know what to say.

She'd never kissed a man before, and she wasn't going to start with this handsome soldier. Given what her mother had been through, she wanted nothing to do with men... ever.

"Please, please, don't do this." She folded her hands and considered getting on her knees.

"You're really something, Crissy Smith." He shook his head. "I've never known a woman so afraid of a simple kiss." He handed her the basket, and took her arm. "Let me show you the way. No one will know you've been out after daylight."

His touch stirred her, making her shivery all over and her knees weak. She was grateful for his help, even though, he'd caused the problem. She had to admit she liked him holding her arm and leading her. It was a strange, feel-good kind of sensation, being protected by someone stronger and more confident.

He escorted her through the brush and around prickly pear cactus, following a trail she couldn't see. Before too long, she glimpsed the white-washed, planked building, serving as the fort's laundry. As usual, a large cauldron of boiling water was simmering outside with one of the other girls, Constance, stirring the contents.

"There, you're back, all safe and sound," he said and handed her the basket. But he didn't release her arm.

"I put the snake out to scare Felix or one of his family. Felix got me in trouble with Commander Gregor over a piddling poker game."

"Soldiers are forbidden to gamble on the post."

"But we were using matchsticks, not real money." He shook his head and glanced down at his sleeve. "Felix is a line Sergeant under me with Company C. He wants to get me into trouble, so he can get my stripe."

"He has a family to support. You're a single man, aren't you?"

"Ah, now I've got your interest. You want to know if I'm available." He winked at her.

She clucked her tongue. "I could care less, Sergeant Donovan. I meant he needs the stripe and extra pay for his family."

"Well, you've a kind heart—I'll give you that, thinking of his family. But the differential in pay is hardly worth undercutting a fellow soldier."

"Your prank was to pay him back for turning you in?" She crossed her arms over her chest. "Why can't you leave well enough alone? Turn the other cheek?"

He gazed at her, his eyes boring into her, as if he could read her mind. "You're religious. I should have known." He grazed her cheek with his thumb. "You've the look of an angel about you."

She pushed his hand away. With a man, a simple touch always led to something else and then...

He pulled her closer, and his lips brushed hers. "There, what do you think of that, my Angel?"

She touched her lips. Now she was tainted like her mother. A flood of fear, mixed with anger at his effrontery, filled her. She'd vowed to never be kissed. And now, this smiling soldier with his beguiling dimple and sea-colored eyes had broken that vow—without her permission.

She drew her hand back and slapped him.

He cupped his red cheek.

With her basket safely tucked under her arm, she ran for the shelter of the laundry.

His laughter followed her, mocking her all the way.

* * *

Crissy opened the slatted door to the laundry, and found Isabel Garza waiting, fisted hands riding her hips. "Where have you been, young lady? Don't you know it's long past daylight? I was worried about you. I know how much this job means—"

"I'm fine, Isabel. But thank you for your concern."

"What happened?"

"A rattlesnake was on the path. I dodged him and went into the bushes, coming a roundabout way. It took longer than I thought." It was half of the truth. Crissy didn't like to lie, but she was still stunned by what had happened.

"Well," Isabel huffed. "I'm glad you avoided the snake, but in the future, you need to follow the rules. Lieutenant Colonel Gregor put those rules into place for a good reason. With a fort full of randy soldiers, none of us can be too careful."

Isabel might be her friend, but the older woman was also in charge of the laundry. "I know." Crissy dumped the basket's contents on the long table and began sorting out the soiled items.

"Looks like you had quite an upset," Isabel observed.

"Yes, I dropped my basket when I saw the snake, and some of the clean clothes got dirty."

"Here, let me help you." Isabel moved beside her, and they piled the items in two stacks.

Crissy shook her head and brushed her lips with her fingers again. How was it possible she could feel the imprint of the sergeant's mouth on hers? She'd never wanted to be kissed by a man. Had dreaded it and hoped it wouldn't happen.

But now, she couldn't stop thinking about the way his lips had felt. And how he'd made her body tingle all over. Was it those kinds of feelings that had driven her mother to be... to do... what she'd done? Her mother had always claimed she'd done what she needed to survive.

Now Crissy wasn't so sure.

Several of the other girls hovered nearby, dipping wet shirts into starch and arraying them for ironing. Ironing was the worst part of the laundry, to Crissy's way of thinking.

She didn't mind tending the pot in the yard with the strong lye soap making her eyes water; it was easier than ironing sheets or especially, the soldiers' shirts. Getting their collars ironed, without scorching them, was hard enough. Not to mention the cuffs and the crease along the sleeves. Ironing shirts was painstaking work.

She moved to the table with the soldiers' uniforms. For their blue, woolen uniforms, they had a special process, which used a solvent to clean the material. It dampened the wool but didn't soak it. They brushed out the half-damp uniforms and let them dry in the sun on racks out back.

Betsy McDuff elbowed her to one side and stood over the pile of dirty uniforms, as if protecting them.

With a flounce of her blonde curls, she said, "You know the rules. First one in, gets to choose, and then the next..." She shrugged. "You got here last today."

Crissy stared at the stack of shirts and mumbled a not-so-nice word under her breath.

"What's that, Miss?" Isabel demanded. "I thought you wanted to return to the Ursuline Convent. If true, you shouldn't be—"

"I know." She hung her head. "I'm sorry, but I had to iron shirts yesterday. Today should be my turn—"

"Not if you're late," Betsy piped up. "Last one in, gets what no one else wants."

Crissy crossed her eyes and stuck out her tongue. Betsy could be a big pain when she wanted, prissy and self-assured. And she was always hanging around, too, hoping to attract the single officers, which to Crissy's way of thinking, was a sure way of asking for trouble.

"Miss McDuff is right," Isabel confirmed. "You know the rule."

"But it wasn't my fault. If I hadn't seen the snake—"

"No exceptions. No excuses, young lady." Isabel hauled a flat-iron from the hearth fire and held it out. "Here, take this while it's hot."

Crissy took the heated iron. She laid a shirt on one of the ironing boards. Then she put the tip of the flat-iron down, testing how hot it was on the shirttail.

The hot iron hissed but it didn't mark the shirt. It was still a bit too hot, but not hot enough to scorch. She waited, counting under her breath, realizing she faced a long day of back-breaking labor.

And for the next hour and a half, she applied herself to ironing the pile of shirts, setting the lapels and cuffs, and the crease along the sleeves. She exchanged ten or more irons with Isabel, making certain each one was the right heat before she began, not wanting to scorch a shirt, knowing the cost would be deducted from her pay.

Her arms ached, and her back, from leaning over, spasmed. Perspiration, despite the coolness of the early spring morning, rolled down her face and slicked her body. The fire in the hearth kept the laundry room over-heated, and the steam from the outside cauldron rolled in through the spaces between the planks.

Her mother had applied for a laundress job at the fort, but she'd been turned down because the work was too hard, especially for an older woman. Crissy had met Isabel at church, and they'd struck up an acquaintance. It had been Isabel who'd given her the job. And though it was hard work, she was grateful.

She lifted her arm and wiped her brow with her sleeve. She hung up the ironed shirt and grabbed another. Glancing at the sun through the slats, she wondered if it was close to their mid-day break.

Why was woman's work so hard?

She longed for the cool quiet of the Ursuline Convent, where she'd spent her early days, learning her letters and praying to her Savior. Those days were long past—now she needed to take care of her mother. Being a laundress was one of the few ways, on the frontier, she could earn a decent living.

Sighing, she closed her eyes, only to find a mischievous pair of turquoise eyes, set in a too-handsome face, twinkling at her. She'd never thought about men before, but she'd never met a man she liked. Or such a handsome one. Much less been kissed. Dreaming, she touched her lips again.

The outside door swung open. "God help us, she's sick again."

Her eyes flew open to see Nora Phillips, the nurse who took care of the commander's wife, coming into the laundry room with a pile of towels and sheets. The linens reeked of blood and vomit.

Crissy set her iron down and went to take the soiled linens from Nurse Phillips.

Everyone knew the commander's wife was dying. She'd been in the hospital at Fort Sam Houston for several months. There had been nothing the doctors could do, and Martha Gregor had wanted to spend her remaining days with her husband and daughter.

When her husband had been transferred from Fort Concho to Fort Clark, the commander had honored his wife's wishes and brought her to Fort Clark, along with a nurse to care for her.

Crissy felt sorry for Mrs. Gregor. It was difficult being ill. She'd learned how hard it could be, taking care of her mother.

Nurse Phillips handed her the sheets and towels. "That's a good girl, thank you."

She squinted her eyes at Crissy and took out her spectacles, holding them up to her eyes and pointing. "You girl, I want you to come and help me with the Missus."

Crissy didn't know what to think about the abrupt command. She dumped the befouled linens in the dirty pile and turned to Isabel. "What do you want me to do?"

"If Miss Phillips has need of you, Crissy, you should go." Isabel gazed at the other laundresses and nodded at Betsy. "We'll find someone else to iron shirts."

"All right. I'll go." Crissy turned to Nurse Phillips.

The nurse opened the laundry door. "Get on with you, then."

* * *

First Sergeant David Donovan threw his shoulders back and held himself at attention for the trumpeter's call to the colors.

Corporal Livingstone hoisted the colors on the tall flagpole, and the stars and stripes waved in the breeze. Captain MacTavish shouted, "Attention!"

Davie and his fellow troops clicked their heels together, lifted their arms, and saluted the flag.

The trumpeter raised his horn again and tooted out the distinctive notes for their mess call. Captain MacTavish dismissed them, and the soldiers scurried toward the communal kitchen, eager to get their breakfast.

Davie held back, kicking a stone across the parade yard and gazing at the laundry. He felt as if he'd been struck by lightning, remembering the touch of the girl's lips on his.

He'd never met such a lass. She was bright as a new penny, her brown hair a glory, her tawny eyes sparkling, and her skin the color of an almond.

He touched his lips with his fingertips, tracing the lingering sensation. He'd kissed many a girl before, but none had knocked him off kilter, making his world spin and change course.

He was a bounder and for sure, he'd kissed girls and done more with some who'd been willing. But none of them had affected him as Miss Smith had. He snorted. *If that was her name.* She hadn't been too sure of it.

On the frontier, it was common enough to change your identity. Something about the wide expanse of land drew people who needed a second chance, who wanted to start over, despite the hardships and danger.

For Davie, the frontier gave him a sense of freedom—it was the reason he'd joined the Army. At the same time, being a soldier provided him with a purpose. He liked to think he was protecting his fellow citizens from the dangers of border raids and marauding hostiles.

He stood, staring at the laundry shack, wondering at the strange effect Cristabelle Smith had over him. He hoped to see her at mid-day when the laundresses left their steamy environs and went their separate ways home. He stroked his cheek where she'd slapped him. She was a feisty girl, that one. He liked women with spirit.

He felt a tap on his shoulder and someone hollered in his ear, "Atten, hup!"

Turning, he found Captain MacTavish beside him. The good captain nudged him with the butt of his carbine. "You've been commanded to spend the day in the brig, Sergeant Donovan, for gambling." The captain ripped a stripe from his shoulder. "And demoted."

Davie rolled his eyes and looked down at his torn sleeve. Another job for Miss Crissy and her fellow laundresses, to fix his stripes. He'd known punishment would be forthcoming, and he'd been waiting.

Well, the waiting was over. How many times had he been demoted and promoted again?

He'd lost count.

The guardhouse wasn't bad—a small, one-room building with a single window, set high up. The guardhouse was located behind the commissary and furnished with a cot, a table and chair. He'd been in worse places.

Still, he didn't like losing a stripe or spending the day cooped up. It would be a freezing day in hell before he forgot what Felix had done, turning him in, to pull ahead in rank and lord it over him. Some men couldn't be trusted, and Felix Dawes was one of them. A lifer and a lick-spittle.

He met the captain's gaze square on. "Gambling is it? Sure, and begorrah, a bit of playing at gambling with matchsticks. Not real money. How can a man be—?"

"No sweet talking me, laddie," the captain said, taking hold of his arm. "The commander said you're to stay a day in the brig, and a day, you'll stay. Gambling is gambling, no matter the coin."

"Oh, Sweet Jesus—"

"We'll have none of that, either. You know how the commander feels about swearing. He's an upstanding man."

Davie huffed. "All right. Take me to my doom without a say-and-so." He handed the captain his sidearm and sighed. The commander was a fair man, and everyone on the post knew his wife was dying, which must be hard for any man.

He glanced again at the laundry shack, wondering how he'd feel if he knew something bad might be happening to his Crissy?

His Crissy—where had that come from?

Chapter Two

Crissy followed Nurse Phillips into the largest of the limestone houses on Officer's Row. The commander's home, unlike the other officers' houses, didn't share a common wall between the row houses. His home stood in solitary splendor at the head of a dirt-rutted street and had a long, deep front porch.

She hesitated on the threshold, taking in the large but neat sitting room. There was a small couch, an overstuffed chair, and a rocker clustered around the hearth. Each of them had a lace doily covering the headrests and arms. A tall grandfather clock stood in one corner. And there was a refractory table with a large vase, holding a bouquet of spring wildflowers to lend color to the cozy room.

She'd heard of such opulence but had never, in her short life, seen a house like this. She was more accustomed to one room serving as both sitting room and bedroom, and sometimes, as a kitchen, too, if they'd been lucky enough to have a fireplace or pot-belly stove.

The wood on the furniture gleamed with oil and the lace doilies were pristine white, but in the corner by the hearth, a young girl sat, hunched over. Her head was in her hands, and Crissy could hear her softly sobbing.

The girl must be the commander's daughter, and Crissy's heart went out to her. She knew exactly how it felt to have a sick mother who could pass from this world to the next at any time. She took a step toward the girl, wanting to comfort her.

Nurse Phillips stopped her, yanking on her arm. "She's the daughter, Margaret. You've not been introduced." The older woman snorted. "And not likely to be. Leave the girl alone. Can't you see she's grieving?"

"Yes, but—"

"I need you to help *me, Miss Smith.* Not be bothering the commander's family." She tugged on her arm and led her down a short hallway to a door. The nurse opened the door, and they slipped inside.

The room was a complex mixture of the not-so-nice smells typical of a sickroom, overlaid with the stringent odors of lye and bleach. At least Nurse Phillips kept the room as clean and fresh as possible, given the circumstances.

Crissy struggled each day, working at the laundry, and making sure her mother was fed and cared for. Most nights, she was lucky to get a few hours of sleep.

The commander's wife, a small lump under a brightly-patterned quilt, lay on her side. Her pillow and the mattress were bare. Crissy realized the nurse had stripped the soiled sheets and brought them to the laundry.

"I need your help to move her, so we can make up the bed," Nurse Phillips said. "Before, she was strong enough to sit beside the bed for a few minutes, but now, she's seldom conscious." The nurse shook her head and sighed. "I can't lift her and make the bed at the same time. Lieutenant Colonel Gregor wouldn't be pleased to see his wife lying in an unmade bed, no matter the circumstances."

The older woman snorted again. "And their girl ain't no help. All she does is lolly-gag around and cry."

"I'll help, Miss Phillips. Please, tell me what to do," Crissy said.

The next hour passed in a flurry of orders issued by Nurse Phillips with Crissy doing her bidding. Half-way through getting a senseless Mrs. Gregor cleaned up and settled on freshly-laundered sheets, the fort's trumpeter bugled the second mess call of the day.

Crissy's stomach grumbled, and she glanced at the overhead sun through one of the large, glazed windows. Her fellow laundresses would be taking their mid-day break, and she was hungry enough to eat a bear. She hadn't eaten since supper last night.

But they weren't done. Nurse Phillips was a taskmaster, and she wasn't satisfied until Crissy had wiped down all the furniture and scrubbed the floor.

She almost balked at doing the nurse's housekeeping work but decided against it. Instead, she watched as the nurse cradled her frail patient's shoulders and tried to rouse her enough to dribble water into her mouth.

Mrs. Gregor woke for a moment and swallowed some water. But when the nurse tried to feed her broth, she turned her head away. Nurse Phillips hugged her patient and rocked her back and forth, as if she was a baby.

Crissy's eyes stung, and she had to swallow back tears. She looked away and finished the last patch of floor. She hefted the bucket of dirty water and trudged to the front door. Mrs. Gregor's daughter had quit the sitting room, and Crissy thought she smelled burnt bread, coming from the kitchen.

She walked a few yards from the house and dumped the water in a ditch on the other side of the dusty street. She returned, eager for her release, to eat the bacon and biscuits she'd packed. If she was late for the mid-day meal, she hoped Isabel would be kind enough to let her have a few minutes.

She entered the house and found the commander's daughter standing on the threshold of what must be the kitchen, twisting her hands in her apron.

"My name is Margaret," the girl greeted her. "Though most people call me Peggy." She held out her hand.

Crissy took her soft, child's hand and shook it. "My name is Cristabelle, though most people call me Crissy." She echoed the girl's introduction, while realizing Nurse Phillips wouldn't approve.

"Would you like some toast, butter, and tea? It's all I know to make. Nurse Phillips promised to teach me to cook, but my mother has been sick." She hung her head and gazed at the floor.

Crissy wanted to hug the half-grown child, but she settled for patting her shoulder. "How kind of you. I'd love some bread and butter and tea."

She'd had tea on rare occasions. It was an exotic luxury she saved for her mother. Mostly, she made do with black coffee, sweetened by an occasional sugar lump when they had a little extra money.

"It's thoughtful of you, Peggy, as I missed my break at the laundry—"

"And you'll not be taking your break here, girl." Nurse Phillips appeared and took her by the arm, tugging. "It's time you got back to the laundry." She pulled her out the front door and practically threw her off the porch.

The nurse shook her finger at her. "You'll not be befriending the commander's family." She sniffed. "Not the likes of *you*. But I'll need you to come every day to help with Mrs. Gregor."

"But I have to get permission from Mrs. Garza to—"

"See that you do." The nurse had joined her in the yard and stood towering over her. For a big woman, Nurse Phillips certainly could move fast and with the grace of a well-fed cat. "Be sure you get permission. I've no one else to help."

Crissy didn't mind helping, feeling sorry for the Gregors, but at the same time, Nurse Phillips had no right to order her around. "I'm sure some of the other girls could come, too. Knowing Mrs. Garza, I think it's what she'd want, to have us take turns."

Nurse Phillips grabbed her arm again, and her fingernails dug into Crissy's tender skin. "I don't want to be beholden to Mrs. Garza. Mexican woman, isn't she? Like those devils who raid across the border." She pushed her face into Crissy's. "You'll do my bidding and your job at the laundry, or I'll be telling the commander what your mother is, *Miss Shannon*."

Crissy gasped and lowered her head, her heart pounding in her ears.

She'd been careful to keep her mother a secret—only a few people knew she was taking care of her: Isabel, Father Fernández, and the fort's doctor, a kind man, Dr. Irving. And of course, Mr. Brackett and his wife, Maxine, who they rented their room from knew. And without thinking too hard, she could guess who had talked.

The commander was known as a fair man, but he was also puritanical in his beliefs, frowning on any kind of vice. Would Isabel be allowed to keep her on, if the commander knew her mother had been... a whore?

She looked up and found Nurse Phillips staring down at her, a smug smile on her face.

Crissy couldn't take the chance. Being a laundress at the fort was one of the few decent jobs for a woman in this frontier outpost. She knew because she'd tried everything when her father,

Renzo Martinelli, a stone mason, had fallen to his death when he was building the fort's headquarters.

With Nurse Phillips knowing her secret, her long, never-ending days had gotten longer.

"When do you want me to come?" she asked.

"I'll fetch you when you're needed. Peggy can sit with her mother for a few minutes."

"All right." Crissy screwed up her courage and stared the big, ugly woman down. "How long will you be needing my help?"

The nurse snorted, and her eyes filled with tears. She looked away. "Until Mrs. Gregor dies, Girl. What do you think?" She stared at her hands and sniffed. "Don't be worrying about the extra work." A tear slipped down her lined face. "It won't be long now. You'll be free and your secret safe."

Crissy gulped. Put that way, she was ashamed for dreading the extra work. It was obvious the nurse was a tough woman, accustomed to getting her way. And as a nurse, she must have seen a lot of sickness and death. Crissy was surprised at Nurse Phillips' genuine grief for her patient.

But Nurse Phillips obviously cared for Mrs. Gregor, and Crissy knew how precious that was—true and unselfish compassion.

She sighed, knowing it would be hard to keep Isabel happy, Nurse Phillips from spilling her secret, and her mother cared for.

Maxine often looked in on her mother during the day, but Crissy couldn't afford to pay her anything. She'd thought the woman was being kind, but now it seemed, Mrs. Brackett was gossiping behind their backs.

What would happen if her mother became as weak as Mrs. Gregor?

She mustn't dwell on it—praying daily her mother would get better. She had to meet each day as it came.

Thinking back to the morning, she knew she was being tested. She'd kissed a man, breaking her vow, and she'd dreamed about him, too. She was guilty, and this was her penance.

It couldn't have been more fitting.

* * *

Crissy opened the general store's front door, and the brass bell tinkled overhead. She glimpsed the beautiful, ice-blue moiré silk dress in the window. She'd often dreamed about the dress, wishing she could own one pretty thing in her life.

But for what?

To attract young men? Her longing was pure worldly avarice on her part. She needed to put those thoughts aside, especially now.

Staring at the floor, she wanted to go straight to her room in the back. It was long past mid-afternoon when she usually got off, and she was worried about her mother.

"You're late today, Crissy," Maxine Brackett greeted her from behind the store's long counter. "Everything all right at the fort?"

Crissy glanced up, but she was tempted not to answer, almost certain Maxine was the one who'd shared her mother's secret. Suspecting Mrs. Brackett of gossiping and compromising her position, she wished they could move.

There was the Sargent Hotel, but they couldn't afford it. And there were precious few other rooms to let in the small town. Again, she was trapped by circumstances, and for the sake of her mother, she had to overlook Mrs. Brackett's wagging tongue.

Not that their room was much. Originally, it had been a goat shed until Mr. Brackett had tired of keeping the animals, claiming they ate everything in sight, including his wife's laundry when it was hanging outside.

He'd upgraded the built-on shack when they'd moved in after her father's death, adding more planks to secure the walls, and loaning them a pot-belly stove for warmth and simple cooking.

She raised her head and gazed at Maxine. "Everything is fine. I've been given extra duties. I'm to help Miss Phillips, Mrs. Gregor's nurse, along with working in the laundry."

Maxine's eyes widened, and she must have realized what her gossiping had wrought because she had the good grace to look down and clear her throat. "You've been given extra duties?"

"Yes."

"I hope they've offered you extra pay."

"No."

"I see." Maxine gulped, glanced out the big front window and back again. "Well, um, I understand." She tried to smile, failed, and bobbed her head. "You best go on back. I looked in on your mother, and she's doing fine, but she's worried about you being late."

"Thank you," Crissy said.

Maxine came from behind the counter, grabbing up some items. "Here are a few extras for being such good tenants—a cone of sugar and a bag of coffee. I noticed y'all were almost out."

She turned to a slab of meat, hanging behind the counter. "And Wally brought in some fresh venison." She took a big hunting knife and carved off a few pieces of backstrap, wrapping them in brown paper. "Here's a little something for tonight's supper."

Crissy accepted the packets of food, knowing them for what they were, guilt gifts. "Thank you, Mrs. Brackett. It's kind of you," she said between gritted teeth. "I'll pay you when I get my wages."

"No, no." Maxine waved her hands. "You don't have to pay, and please call me Maxine, not Mrs. Brackett. They're gifts. Please?"

"All right, Maxine. It's kind of you, and I'll be sure to tell my mother."

At least, the woman appeared to regret her loose lips, but she'd made their life in Brackettville more precarious. If her mother hadn't been ailing, Crissy would pull up stakes and move to a place where no one knew their past.

It had been the original reason her father had brought them here—to start over. But he'd been killed in an accident after a few weeks on the job.

Not knowing what else to do, her mother had returned to her former profession, but discreetly, because the town was small. She'd entertained strangers, stagecoach passengers who were passing through, never any of the locals or soldiers.

But after a few weeks, her mother had taken sick. She was tired all the time and coughed a lot. Dr. Irving had said it was consumption but with rest, her mother might recover.

"Well, I won't keep you." Maxine wiped her hands on her apron.

Crissy bowed her head and walked down the long hallway connecting the former goat shed to the back of the house.

Her mother, Mary Shannon, was sitting in the windowless room, staring at a small fire in the pot belly stove. When she heard the door open, she jumped to her feet, and stood tottering, weak and off balance.

Crissy dumped the food on the table and embraced her mother.

Her mother reached up and patted her cheek. “Daughter, you’re so late. I was worried. I thought—”

“I’m sorry, Mama.” She bent and gave her mother a peck on the cheek. She took her mother’s hand and led her back to the bed. “Shouldn’t you lie down for a while? I’ll reheat the biscuits and fry up the venison Maxine gave us. Are you hungry?”

Her mother sank onto the bed, coughing and covering her mouth with a handkerchief. “I’m glad you’re home. I was worried.” She smiled. “Fried venison sounds good. I’m a bit hungry.”

Crissy nodded. “I’m glad.” She glanced at her mother, noticing she looked thinner.

Crissy got out a skillet and melted some bacon grease they’d saved. She sliced the backstrap and coated it in flour, seasoned with salt. Soon, the tantalizing odor of frying meat filled the tiny room. She reheated her skillet biscuits and stirred up some gravy with the venison juices.

With supper cooked, Crissy and her mother sat at the table, held hands, and said grace. Hungry from all the extra work today, Crissy dug in and ate quickly, sopping up the last drops of gravy with a biscuit.

Her mother, on the other hand, though she’d said she was hungry, ate a few bites of the venison and nibbled on one biscuit.

She started coughing again, and Crissy brewed some tea with honey and a dash of apple cider vinegar. She put her mother back to bed and brought the medicinal tea to her.

Her mother’s brown eyes were suspiciously bright, and Crissy checked her forehead for fever. She seemed a bit warm but not too feverish. She’d learned her mother often had fever with her condition, and Dr. Irving had said to bathe her temples with cool water.

Crissy left her mother drinking tea and stepped through the back door to the well to draw fresh water. When she returned, her mother had finished her tea and had her tattered deck of playing cards out, spread in a mysterious fashion across the plain quilt on the bed.

Her mother had learned how to tell fortunes from one of the other "girls" who'd worked at the Tin Star in San Antonio. The other lady had claimed to have gypsy blood and knew how to read the cards. To Crissy's way of thinking, it was a lot of superstitious nonsense, but it gave her mother something to do. For that, she was thankful.

Crissy made her mother lie back while she bathed her face with the cool water. She wrung out the washcloth and dampened it again, laying it across her mother's forehead. Her mother sighed and clasped her hand.

"You're such a comfort to me. I don't know what I would do without you." Her mother squeezed her hand.

"Oh, Mama, you know I would do anything for you. I want you to get well."

"I know, and I wish you could stay with me. I get lonely. I hope you won't be late again."

Crissy sucked in her breath. She didn't want to alarm her mother, but there was no help for it. She had to tell her, had to explain.

"I'm afraid I'll be coming home late for the next few weeks, Mama. I've been given extra duties."

Her mother sat up straight and removed the washcloth. "At the laundry? Will they pay you more? We can always use the money."

That was an understatement.

They barely got by on what she made with little enough to spare for things like clothes, or the tea and honey, which helped her mother's cough.

Crissy hated to tell her mother, but she had the right to know the gossip had started. They would need to face the ugly truth together. She didn't want to name Maxine, though, as her mother depended on their landlady's kindness.

It was odd Maxine hadn't said anything before, especially when her mother had been plying her trade in this very room and using the back door to let in her customers. But Nurse Phillips was a strong character. For all Crissy knew, the nurse had pressured Maxine into revealing her mother's past.

Why couldn't people mind their own business?

"Mama, I won't be paid extra." She took another deep breath. "Miss Phillips, who's the nurse for the commander's wife, needs my help, now Mrs. Gregor is worse—"

"Oh, no, God bless her. Poor Mrs. Gregor." Her mother bent her head. "I will pray for her."

Her mother was tender hearted, despite her own misfortunes and illness. Crissy had to turn her face away; she didn't want her mother to see her tears.

"But if the nurse for the commander's wife needs help, why shouldn't they pay you?" Her mother asked. "It's only fair if—"

"There's nothing fair about it." Crissy faced her mother and snagged her mother's gaze. "Somehow, Miss Phillips learned of your prior profession, and she's using it to make me work for her. Otherwise, she will go to the commander, and I'll lose my job." She shook her head. "I don't have any choice."

Her mother gasped and covered her mouth with her hand. "Oh, Crissy, and we were careful. How could it be—?"

"I know we were careful, but people talk." She shrugged.

And they'd tried to be cautious. Crissy had spent her nights, under the stars in the backyard, sleeping in a bedroll, while her mother earned them a living on her back. Some nights, she'd slept in one of the rockers on the porch of the general store.

Crissy bit the inside of her cheek and tried to blank out her thoughts. When her father had saved enough money to bring them to Fort Clark, her mother had hoped to put her past behind her.

But her mother and father couldn't marry because Mary Shannon was still married in the eyes of the Church, not knowing if her missing husband was alive or dead, though it had been years since she'd heard from him.

Of course, Mr. Brackett and his wife knew what went on behind their store. At the time, they'd passed no judgment, realizing earning a living in a frontier town for a single woman was difficult.

Her mother caught her hand again. "I'm sorry, so sorry, Crissy, to put you through this. I wish many things had been different in my life. That I'd been a better mother and an honest woman."

Her mother's eyes brimmed with unshed tears. "And now this." She blew her nose. "I didn't want you sullied by what I've had to do—"

"I know, Mama. I know you didn't want this kind of life." She gazed at her mother. "I know you couldn't help what happened. I don't blame you, Mama. Really."

Crissy knew the tragic story of her mother's past all too well. Her mother had been ill-used and left with few options. It was not a pretty story.

"I love you, Crissy."

"And I love you, Mama."

Crissy leaned forward, and they embraced.

Her mother drew back and glanced down at the cards. Her eyebrows arched, flying up like startled starlings and her mouth rounded into an "O." She bent her head and reshuffled the deck, laying them out again.

She frowned and closed her eyes, sinking against the pillow. "Do we have any more tea?" She pulled out her handkerchief and covered her mouth, going into spasms of coughing.

"Yes, we have more tea. I'll put the kettle on now," Crissy said.

"Good girl."

While she made the tea, her mother gathered up the cards, reshuffled them, closed her eyes, and mumbled under her breath.

She held the cards out to Crissy. "I know you don't believe in this, but humor me, please? I want you to cut the cards, and I'll read your fortune."

"Mama, you know it's not a question of me believing. It's forbidden in the Bible to tell fortunes."

"I don't do it for pay, just a bit of fun to take my mind off..." She lowered the cards and looked down. "I know how devoted you are to your faith, but I don't really believe... If you don't believe, it can't be a sin. Now can it?" She dabbed at her mouth with her handkerchief. "Besides, I'm feeling better now and after I've told your fortune, why don't we play some pinochle?"

Her mother loved card games and checkers, but lately, she'd been too tired to stay up. Crissy's heart lightened, hoping her mother was feeling better.

"All right, Mama." She put the tea on a stool beside her mother's bed. "It's a deal. I love playing cards with you, though, you always manage to win."

Her mother laughed and tossed her head. Like in the old days.

It gladdened Crissy's heart, seeing her mother happy again, despite what they were facing. She cut the cards.

Her mother shuffled and spread them out across the threadbare quilt.

Crissy gathered together the dirty dishes and placed them in the dry sink. After they finished playing cards, she'd use the remainder of the water to wash them.

Her mother gasped, and she cradled her face with both hands.

Startled, Crissy wondered what her mother saw. *Please, not more bad news.* Not for her sake, as she didn't believe in fortune telling, but she didn't want her Mama to be upset.

Her mother waved her hand, motioning her to the bed. "The cards have wonderful news! You'll be married by the end of this year to the man of your dreams. He's handsome and good and kind. And you'll be very happy together."

Crissy opened her mouth, but no words came. She didn't want a man in her life... any man. She'd seen what they could do to women; how they used and discarded them.

Her father had been a gentle man. An immigrant, he'd worked hard and tried to give them a better life but based on what she'd seen, he was the exception.

She didn't want a husband—any husband. All she wanted was to return to the convent as a lay sister and serve God. She didn't have the qualifications of a nun, not being of a good family, who could endow the convent. But she could serve the other nuns and lead a quiet and peaceful life. Away from the everyday world and all its ugliness.

Her mother's hazel eyes were wide and sparkling with joy. She was obviously happy, and they had precious few happy moments to share.

She put aside her qualms and said, "Thank you, Mama. It makes me glad to know I'll find someone to love and care for me."

"Yes, and you've already met him. You just don't realize he's the one."

Her heart turned over in her chest, and she felt the flush of heat spreading from her neck to her face.

Yes, she'd met a man, a Sergeant Donovan. And heaven help her, she'd be hard-pressed to withstand his charm. He was more than handsome, with his dark curly hair, turquoise eyes, mischievous smile, and a dimple in his left cheek.

It was uncanny, her mother seeing such a thing in the cards, especially after what had happened today. But it was probably a coincidence. She didn't believe in such stuff and nonsense.

Chapter Three

Davie pulled out a handkerchief from inside the vest of his dress uniform. He mopped his forehead and the back of his neck. When he entered the barracks, he found the building empty. Not too surprising, they had the day off, and most of his fellow soldiers had headed to town, using their free time to get drunk at the Spring Street Saloon.

He shucked out of his heavy wool uniform and folded it carefully, storing it in his locker. He changed into a white cotton shirt and a pair of patched dungaree trousers. He rummaged through his trunk, grabbing his sketch pad and some lead pencils.

He left the quiet building and crossed the parade grounds, heading for *Las Moras* Springs and the large pool of water it fed. He looked forward to the cool grove of live oaks rimming the pond and hoped, though it was the middle of the day, to glimpse some of the wild critters who came to the springs.

'Twas a sad day at Fort Clark—Lieutenant Colonel Gregor, the fort's commander—had lost his wife. All the fort had turned out for her funeral and burial, except the twenty men who'd been chosen by lot to stand guard duty.

After the funeral was over, the soldiers were given their leisure. Davie had glimpsed Crissy with her fellow laundresses. They had formed a row behind Mrs. Garza, wearing dark dresses and looking like a flock of blackbirds, lined up on a tree branch.

When the commander had dismissed them, he'd almost gone after Crissy. At the last minute, he'd changed his mind. For the past few weeks, he'd made certain to cross her path, more than once. He'd learned her habits and found she was helping Nurse Phillips take care of the commander's wife. And she and her mother lived behind the Brackett General Store.

Each time he'd approached her, she'd turned away and asked him not to bother her.

Bother her? Hell's bells, he worshipped her!

She was his angel; he'd taken to going to church on Sundays at the almost-finished St. Mary Magdalene's in town. He wanted her to know he was a Catholic and an honorable man.

He knew she saw him at Mass and sometimes, he caught her looking at him, as if she was studying him. But when he tried to meet her eyes, she invariably looked away.

He didn't understand it. He'd not forgotten their kiss, and he could have sworn she'd kissed him back. Now though, she wanted nothing to do with him. And he'd heard some ugly gossip about her mother at the saloon—something that was hard to believe—and one of the reasons he'd wanted to avoid the saloon today.

Sighing, he settled on a large flat stone, overhanging the spring-fed pond. Dragonflies skimmed the surface, the ever-present mosquitos hummed in his ears, and a bass leapt up and snapped at a fly. Across the pond, a spotted fawn broke from the underbrush and gracefully dipped its angular head to the water's surface.

Davie held his breath and, with the pad on his crossed legs, he sketched the fawn, getting down the deer's outline before it leapt away and disappeared into the thick undergrowth, probably to join its mother.

Bending over his pad, he filled in the lines and shadings, and slowly but surely, an image of the deer took shape. He stuck out his tongue and bit down on it, concentrating. His hand moved faster, wanting to capture the essence of the fawn before the image, etched on his brain, faded.

Once he had the young deer on paper, he relaxed and glanced up, taking in the quiet peace of the place, and noting the way the trees were formed and the tangled mass of underbrush, along with bright dots of wildflowers.

Sketching the background was easy and freeing. Slowly, tension flowed out of him, washing away in the low gurgle of the springs beneath the pond. He was glad he hadn't gone to town, happy for the tranquility and harmony of nature. And drawing was his secret pleasure.

Most of the time, he tried to make light of life, finding human nature humorous and silly. The wildness of this land and its natural beauty was a balm to his spirit, refreshing him, making all the foolishness of the fort fade away. Being able to capture the essence of his surroundings, albeit poorly, to his way of thinking, made him happy.

What would make him happier was if a certain shy girl with the prettiest, tawny eyes and the softest lips, would let him get to know her. No matter, though, she was still his angel. And no doubt, too good for him.

Being a soldier involved lots of hurrying up and waiting. As a boy, he'd enjoyed drawing things, though his industrious immigrant parents had frowned on the pursuit. And his fellow soldiers weren't above making fun of him, too, for liking to draw.

At least, the Army with its empty hours of being ready for a threat, which might or might not come, had given him more than ample time to pursue his drawing. And the more he sketched, the better he liked what he drew.

He held the picture at arm's length, studying it. He turned the sketch left and right, worrying about the perspective and his struggle to capture a three-dimensional world on a two-dimensional piece of paper.

Putting his pad to the side, he decided to come back to it later. Maybe he'd change the picture or maybe not, but he needed some distance before he studied it again.

He reached down and picked up a small round stone. Pulling back his arm, he sent the stone skittering across the pond's surface. As the stone splashed into the water, he heard a muffled sob coming from behind him.

Scrabbling to his feet, he realized how stupid he'd been, ignoring the ever-present danger of his frontier post—not thinking to bring his sidearm with him.

And then he saw her, a black-clad figure, huddled in a stand of willows with her head bent, quietly crying.

It was a wonder she hadn't seen him sitting there. But he had the advantage, perched on an overhanging rock and able to see around a bend in the pond. The thick underbrush must have hidden him.

He'd been desperate for weeks to get her alone. Now, she was here and no one else was around. *Would she run from him? Or slap his face again?* She was obviously distressed, crying as she was.

His heart leapt in his chest, an answering sympathy streaming through him. She needed comfort, and he wanted nothing more than to take her into his arms and shelter her.

He scrambled off the rock and strode toward her.

At the last moment, she must have heard him because she glanced up and frowned. Her face was scrunched and splotchy from crying, but each time he saw her, she was more beautiful than he remembered. He wished he could sketch her, capture her angelic beauty on paper.

Before she could run, he'd closed on her and gathered her into his arms, holding her tightly, and stroking her long, brown hair. She'd gathered it into a knot on the top of her head, but in her distress, most of the hairpins must have come loose because her sun-streaked, brown hair fell in long streamers down her back.

"Shhh," he said. "Everything will turn out all right. It can't be so bad. What can I do to help?"

She sighed and nestled in his arms, surprising him.

He caressed her back and hair. Her female curves fitted with his body like a tongue in groove joint, and he could feel his body responding. His groin tightened, and he grew hard.

Afraid she might react to his unseemly response, he kept hold of her shoulders while angling the lower part of his body away from her.

She gazed up at him, a flare of recognition, flooding her golden-brown eyes.

He half-cringed and stepped away, dramatically throwing his hands over his face. "Please, don't hit me. Don't hit me!"

She huffed and crossed her arms. "You can quit play-acting, Sergeant Donovan. And I'm not going to slap you." She turned her face away and sniffed. "I'm sorry I slapped you, but I'd never been kissed before and—"

"I'd already guessed, my Angel, but I'm glad I won't have to dodge your blows." His eyes twinkled, and he winked.

"Oh, you, you're ridiculous. You know?"

"Am I?" He leaned forward and kissed her. Lightly at first, his mouth touching hers, barely brushing the softness of her petal-pink lips. He drank in her clean and fresh scent, reminding him of the elusive smell of a newly-laundered shirt. “I’m glad to know you find me entertaining. Can I kiss you again?”

She sighed and said nothing. She turned her face up to him and closed her eyes.

He chuckled, glad he’d gotten past her obvious innocent naivete. With her silent acquiescence, he deepened the kiss, slanting his lips first one way and then the other, cherishing her mouth.

She sighed again, and his blood heated. He licked her lips with his tongue-tip, running his tongue along the sweet seam of her lips, hoping she would open to him. He didn’t know how she’d react, given how shy and evasive she was.

Slowly, she opened her lips and kissed him back, pressing her full, pliable mouth against his. He didn’t need any more encouragement, slipping his tongue between her lips and tasting her fully. Savoring the honey-sweet flavor of her, and the delicious heat of her mouth.

With their tongues tangled, she stepped closer to him, melding her body against his. She laced her arms around his neck and held on as if he was a kite that might sail away.

Sweet Jesus, she was tying him in knots and making him as hard as the stone he’d been sitting on.

She startled, like the fawn at the pond, and released a puff of her breath against his lips, while pulling back.

He refused to let her go. He held her in the circle of his arms and gazed into her face. He was an unchaste man and given his wishes, he’d tumble her to the mossy ground and bury himself in her.

She turned her face away, and he saw her blush, turning as red as the ripening mulberries on the trees, lining the pond. A snippet of the gossip about her mother flashed through his mind.

How could people be so cruel, as to start ugly rumors?

It was obvious she was pure and sweet—an angel. He wanted to pound Corporal Guerrin for spreading nasty gossip.

“Please, let me go. I’ve already broken my vow once... and now this,” she said.

“What vow? What have you broken?”

She shrugged one shoulder and looked down at the ground. "I shouldn't have mentioned... I spoke out of turn. I was schooled at the Ursuline Convent in San Antonio. I vowed to remain chaste and if I have the chance, I can return there."

"You want to be a nun?"

"No, I want to be a lay sister, to serve the nuns."

"Why on earth would you—?"

"Because it's peaceful and quiet and—"

"Yes, but being in your grave is peaceful and quiet, too."

"That's not funny."

He sighed and hunched his shoulders. "No, I guess not. But I can't begin to think of the waste, you burying yourself in a convent."

"It's none of your business. And I need to go home."

"Not so fast." He held her shoulders. "Tell me why you were crying. I'd like to help, if I could." He let go of her and ran his thumb over her cheek, wiping the fresh tears from her face.

She stepped to one side. "Oh, it's, ah, there's nothing anyone can do."

He wanted to reach out again and hold her, worried she was about to bolt. "Well, if there's nothing I can do, maybe talking about it would give you some comfort."

"I was grieving for the commander's wife. I've been helping Miss Phillips take care of her." She gulped and swallowed. "She was mostly out of her head, Mrs. Gregor, these past few weeks, but the few times she came to herself, I've never known a kinder lady." She sniffed. "My mother's been ailing, too. I'm afraid what would happen if—"

"Has your mother seen a doctor? The fort's doctor, Doc Irving, is very good at what he does."

Her mother was ill, and people spread vicious rumors. He wanted to shout and swear. Sometimes, people amazed him with their nastiness.

"I know. Dr. Irving has seen my mother, at least once a week, since she took sick. He seems hopeful, thinking rest and the clear, dry air will help. But he sent to Austin for some special medicine." She frowned. "He says it's the consumption."

Davie almost recoiled, but he held himself steady. He'd heard about consumption from his parents, and the toll it had taken on families in Ireland. Knowing what she was facing, he wanted to hug her again and never let go.

But he did none of those things. Instead, he wished he could divert her from thinking about her mother's condition. "I'm sure Doc Irving's medicine will get your mother well."

She looked at him, and slowly, her frown faded. Her eyes held a bright light, as if she was eager for hope, eager to believe the best.

"Yes, I'm sure the doctor can help," he said. "And I've seen you in church. Have you lit a candle for your mother and asked for Saint Mary Magdalene's blessing?"

"Oh, yes, I've lit a candle every day and prayed and prayed."

He put his hand over hers, and he could feel her hand trembling. "I'll pray for your mother, too, and light a candle, each time I go to Mass. What's her name?"

Her bottom lip quivered. "Oh, would you? It's kind of you, Sergeant. Her name is Mary." She tried to smile. "Mary, like the saint."

"All right, Mary it is, then." He nodded. "You can count on me." He hesitated, tracing his boot tip in the dirt. "But you have to promise me something."

"What?"

"Don't avoid me, please. Let me know how your mother is doing."

"Of course." She nodded. "I didn't know you would care."

"I care about you, Crissy. I won't lie to you."

"Oh." She lowered her head. "I should be getting back. I'm sure Mama is waiting for me. She would have come to the funeral but..."

"She's not feeling well?"

"No, she's not, and she keeps losing weight. Though, some days, she feels better than others."

"I know your mother needs you but could you stay for a bit?" He touched her cheek with his finger and slid it along her jaw. "It's peaceful here.'

Crissy shivered at his touch and gazed at him. He was being kind. His turquoise eyes gleamed with sparks of green, and he was smiling. She wanted to reach up and touch his dimple, but she didn't dare.

"I'd like to stay for a little while. It's seldom we get a holiday."

"Same for us," he said. "Being on duty all the time can be tiring."

"Don't you have certain hours and drills and such...?"

"Yes, but when you're on the frontier, you should be ready for anything." He grimaced. "When I first heard you, before I knew who it was, I realized how stupid of me, coming out here, alone and without my Colt."

She hadn't considered the area dangerous. For her, Fort Clark and Brackettville were safe but when he mentioned the danger, she realized she'd been foolish, too.

"What did you come out here for?" she asked.

"I could ask you the same thing."

She turned her head away and gazed at the slow ripples, spreading over the pond from where a fish had surfaced. "I thought I told you. I was... am grieving for Mrs. Gregor and worried about my mother."

He caught her hand in his, turned it over, palm up, and kissed it. "Yes, you did tell me. And I will pray for your mother... but..."

"Yes?"

"Crissy, when I'm around you, I forget about everything else." He widened his smile. "You've woven a special spell around me, like the fairies."

"Fairies?"

"Sure, and begorrah, you've heard of fairies. Haven't you?"

"Uh, maybe in books, but aren't they pagan and a lot of nonsense?"

He frowned. "Not to an Irish boy like me. Fairies are as real as..." He nodded toward the far shore. "As real as the fawn I saw right before you came."

"Really? But where are the fairies now? I've always loved Christmas, thought it was a magical time, especially in San Antonio. Wouldn't fairies be more likely to come out at Christmas?"

He let go of her hand and stroked his jaw. "I don't know—about Christmas and fairies, though, they are magical people, like old St. Nick." He rubbed his chin. "And I'm not sure if there are *American* fairies. All the ones I know of, live in the old country."

She couldn't help but smile. His silliness was catching. "No fairies here, only in... Ireland? Is that where you're from?"

He chuckled, and his dimple deepened. "Yes, I'm Irish, but I came to Texas as a wee lad. My parents were fleeing the potato famine."

"A potato famine... what on earth is that?"

He took her hand again and tugged on it. "Let's sit for a spell, overlooking the pond, and I'll tell you about it."

Realizing he wanted her to stay, she felt her face heat. She knew she should go home and see how her mother was doing. She'd avoided him before because he'd kissed her. But this time, their kissing had seemed right, like it was meant to be.

It had been a long time since anyone had shown an interest in her. Or wanted to spend time with her, except for the chores she could do.

Besides, wasn't this the man of her dreams—who her mother had seen in the cards?

She smiled to herself—card reading was stuff and nonsense, pure superstition. Still, she enjoyed being around Davie. And she'd love to know something of Ireland, particularly what he meant by a potato famine.

He pulled her along the pond's shore until they reached a large stone, jutting out over the water. He took both her hands and helped her to sit, with her skirts bunched beneath her.

She looked around and saw some lead pencils and a large pad of white paper with an image on it. "Is it yours? Is that what you were doing out here, all by yourself?"

He snatched up the paper and held it against his chest. "I thought you wanted to know what a potato famine is. Now, you want me to show you what I've been doing."

"It's only fair. I told you why I was here."

"Maybe." He lifted one shoulder in a half-shrug. "If you're a good lass, I'll show you my drawing. But first, you need to know about the Great Potato Famine."

A famine wasn't a nice thing—did she really want to know about it? She'd much rather see what he'd drawn on the paper. "Maybe I'd rather not."

"Ah, but it's important," he said. "It's why so many of us Irish came to America."

"What do you mean?"

He took a deep breath. "It's important to remember because in the Old Country, we Irish weren't free... not like in America. The Irish were tenant farmers and oppressed by English landlords and forced to live on smaller and smaller plots of land, feeding their families as best they could. For years, the safest crop to sow was potatoes. But a disease struck the potatoes, and when the farmers pulled them up, they were already rotted in the ground."

Crissy inhaled and said, "Oh, that's terrible."

"Yes, and because the potato was the main nourishment for the poor farmers, when they went bad, there was nothing to eat and no coin to pay the landlords."

"Why didn't the landlords help? I mean if their people were starving, you would think they'd want to help."

"Ah, politics, Angel mine." He stroked his thumb over the top of her hand, and she quivered. "Few can understand politics." He shrugged. "At first, the politicians in England tried to help, sending grain to be milled and made into bread to feed the starving tenants." He lowered his voice. "But then, another party took over the English Parliament, and they didn't send grain.

"Thousands of people starved, my parents told me, after being turned out of their homes, along the roads and in the hedgerows and—"

"No," she gasped. "How awful."

"Yes, it was, but no one could see the light of it."

"And your parents—"

"They were turned out by their landlord, but it was lucky they were. My father had a cousin in Texas at Galveston, who had come over a few years earlier and set up a carpentry shop. My father's cousin sent us the money for passage."

Then a smile lit his face. "It was a glorious time when we landed, my parents told me—plenty of work and more than plenty to eat."

Hearing his story, she realized how much it was like her own in some ways. When her mother's husband had run off to the gold fields, leaving her Mama in San Antonio, Crissy hadn't been born. But her mother had to survive, and she'd been forced to do the one ready job for a woman alone on the frontier. It was that or starve.

Somehow, knowing Davie's background, made her feel closer to him—as if he would understand about her mother. Not that she wanted to tell him, but if she did, maybe he wouldn't scorn her.

"Your family was lucky, having cousins to look after you," she said.

"More than lucky. My father is a fair carpenter. He's made a good life for our family with his cousin's help."

"You didn't want to help with the business?"

"No, I wanted something different—wide open spaces and adventure. The Army promised me those things." He lifted his arm and swept it across the horizon. "I would say the Army has fulfilled its promise. Wouldn't you?"

"Yes, but now it's my turn. I've listened to your story." She grabbed for the pad. "Now, it's time to show me—"

"Not so fast." He turned his body away, hugging the paper. "I want to know what brought you and your mother to this frontier town."

"Oh," she huffed. "Not fair. You told me I could see what you were doing after I listened to you about the famine."

He grinned. "Life isn't fair, Angel mine. How'd you come to Brackettville?"

It was the question she'd dreaded, lest anyone learn of her mother's past. The thing was to tell the truth, or as much of the truth, without confessing her mother's former profession.

"My father, Renzo Martinelli, was an immigrant, too."

"Italian?" He asked and lifted his hand, tucking a stray tendril of hair behind her ear. "You've the look of an Italian girl about you with your dark eyes and olive complexion." He traced his hand down her cheek. "But I thought you said your name was Smith—not Martinelli."

She sucked in her breath and looked down. Now she'd done it—she'd forgotten about the "false" name she used at the fort. But he was waiting—she'd have to come up with something.

She lifted her head and gazed into his eyes. She thought she saw the flicker of something there... Had Nurse Phillips told other people? The woman had promised, but now, with Crissy's part of the bargain fulfilled and the nurse leaving on the next stagecoach, there was nothing to keep her from talking. Was there?

"My father changed his last name to 'fit' in. No one knew how to pronounce Martinelli anyway. But he gave me my first name, Cristabelle. It's an Italian name." She crossed her arms and forced herself to chuckle, wanting to make light of anything he might have heard. "Besides, Davie Donovan, how would you know what an Italian girl looks like?"

He let what must be his sketchpad fall to the ground, face down, and grabbed both of her hands. "I know you're an angel. That's enough, isn't it?"

She laughed. "You can be a silly goose, you know?" She was plain to look at, but he made her feel special, and it was wonderful to have someone admire her with such longing in his eyes.

"But I've got your attention."

"Yes, and I think you're way too charming to be real." The words popped out of her mouth before she could stop them. She looked down and bit the inside of her mouth.

"Because I kiss you... like this?" He lowered his mouth to hers.

His mouth was warm, and his lips were soft, skimming hers. She sighed and closed her eyes, enjoying the intoxicating sensation of his firm lips against hers. But before he could deepen the kiss, she pulled away, laughing, realizing she was far from being immune to his charm.

"Enough kissing!"

"Is there ever enough kissing?" he asked.

"Maybe not for you, but..."

"All right. Finish your story."

"My father was a stonemason from Italy. He worked on many homes and store buildings in San Antonio. The Army offered him a lot of money if he would come to Fort Clark and help build the headquarters, the barracks, and..."

She lowered her head and fought back tears, remembering how sweet her father had been. “When the scaffolding broke on the headquarters’ building, he fell wrong, and broke his neck.”

There. She’d said it. And it still hurt—almost a year later.

“Ah, Crissy, I’m sorry. I wish your father hadn’t died.” He lifted her chin with one finger. “I should say my prayers, each night, because both my parents are alive and doing well. I can understand why you’re concerned for your mother.”

She nodded.

“I guess you’ve earned the right to see what I was doing. But if you make fun, I’ll extract a ransom from you.” He smiled and touched her lips with his index finger.

He picked up the sketchpad and showed her.

She gasped, seeing the picture of a spotted fawn at the pond, cleverly rendered on paper. “You did this?”

He turned his face away and gazed over her shoulder. “Yes, I love to draw, especially the wild things around the fort.”

“Oh, but, Davie, this is lovely and so life-like, too. Why would you want to hide it from me?”

“Because most people think my drawings are silly and a waste of time. My parents used to take me to task for whiling away the hours with sketching when I could be doing something more useful, like working in their carpentry shop. Which I did plenty of, anyway, after school.”

He shrugged. “And my fellow soldiers think it’s a sissy thing, too. Most like to whittle wood or play the fiddle or guitar or…” He grimaced. “When all you hear is criticism, it puts you on the defense.”

This was another side of Davie she would have never dreamed of—his vulnerability to other people’s criticism. She could easily put herself in his place, and it made her draw even closer to him.

“I know what you mean about people being mean or critical for no reason. Well, I don’t feel that way. I wish I had such talent.” She looked down at her raw and chapped hands. She shoved them in the pockets of her skirts and frowned. “Seems my only talent is for cleaning and washing stuff.” But her frown faded, and she couldn’t help but smile. “You should be proud. It’s a beautiful picture.”

He turned his head and pulled her hands free, raising them to his lips. “I knew you were an angel—didn’t I tell you? Thank you for your kind words.” He tore the sheet off the pad and folded it twice, handing it to her. “It’s yours. Please, take my drawing. I want you to have it.”

“Can I? Oh my, I’ll put it up in our room.” She gazed at the picture again, amazed at his gift. The drawing looked real, so like the deer she’d often glimpsed in the woods around the fort. She was in awe of his skill. “Thank you.” She put it into her skirt pocket. “I’ll cherish it.”

He faced her and grinned with his lips slightly open. She knew he wanted to kiss her again. And she was surprised she’d welcomed his kisses.

She’d changed. What had made her change?

After their first kiss, she’d been especially careful to avoid him. Somehow, today was different, though. The passing of Martha Gregor had made her sad and vulnerable, made her worry about her mother. The poison of the past had receded, buried by her need for comfort.

Having grown up in the shadow of her mother’s shame, she had trouble reconciling her fears with the way Davie made her feel. She’d never wanted a man to touch her... and then she’d met Davie.

She wanted him to kiss her again, but even more, she enjoyed learning about his life, getting to know him.

“Did you get your revenge on Sergeant Dawes? I noticed you lost a stripe.”

“Yes, and I lost a day in the brig, too.” He snorted. “Dawes is such a lick-spittle, he’ll do anything to get ahead. Now he’s the First Sergeant, and I’m demoted beneath him. Having to take his guff.”

He scratched his jaw. “No, I’ve not gotten him back... yet. I’m waiting for the right time.” He grinned, and his eyes twinkled. “Something will turn up. I want him to think I’ve forgotten and be taken by surprise when he least expects it.”

“Couldn’t you forgive him, as the Good Book says?”

"I could. And maybe I will." He touched her lips with his finger, gently brushing them. "Sure, and begorrah, you could make me forget my own name."

"Oh, Davie, you say the craziest things." She put her arms around him and closed her eyes, savoring the warmth of his body and the hard planes of his chest beneath his thin shirt.

She buried her head in the curve of his shoulder, but she knew it wouldn't deter him. If he wanted to kiss her, he would, and she'd more than welcome him.

He placed his hand under her jaw, his fingers lightly stroking her chin. He tilted her head up. He smiled at her again and slowly lowered his lips.

She heard the strident call of the bugle from the fort—a loud, trumpeting sound, shattering their kiss and the peace surrounding them.

Davie pulled back and frowned. He turned his head up, as if to listen.

"Sweet Jesus, it's the call to arms," he said. He got to his feet and helped her to stand. "Let me get you back to town. I might be called to muster out."

"No," she said, moving away from him, not wanting to make him late. "I can get back on my own."

"But you don't know who or what is causing the alarm. Let me take you back to your mother first."

She grasped her skirts and whirled around. The fairy-like atmosphere was gone—sweet dreams signifying nothing. They lived in a wilderness of wild animals, hostile natives, and Mexican bandits. How many times did her mother have to remind her?

And though Davie Donovan's kisses left her speechless and silently begging for more, she knew he was a kind of fairy... or a phantom. As much as they might enjoy being together, she must care for her mother... and Davie would answer the bugle call of his profession.

Beyond that—she didn't know what lay ahead.

Chapter Four

Crissy washed their supper dishes in the dry sink. She dried the last dish and put it away in the solitary cabinet beside the sink. Her mother was sitting on the bed; she was feeling better and had pulled out their homemade checker board.

Glad her mother was lively enough to play checkers, she reached down into the left-over suds and pulled the stopper from the sink, letting the water drain beneath the floorboards. Most of the buildings in town were built on cinder blocks, in case of flooding from the creek.

She touched her fingers to her lips, remembering this afternoon beside the pond and worrying about Davie. She'd run back to find her mother napping after leaving him. Not knowing if his squad would be called out, she'd returned to a copse of pecan trees at the front of the fort. Sure enough, Company C of the Fourth Cavalry had ridden out.

She'd watched from the protection of the trees and been proud of how good he looked on his chestnut horse. His back was ramrod straight, his shoulders broad, and his blue woolen trousers hugged his muscular legs. But as good as he looked, she knew he was riding into danger. She couldn't help but worry.

She still had the picture he'd drawn, tucked away in her skirt pocket. She wanted to bring it out and pin it to the drab walls of their little room, but if she did, her mother would have questions a mile long. And until she knew if he was back and safe, she didn't feel like telling her mother about Davie.

For her, it was like tempting fate. She knew it was pure superstition, on her part, which she abhorred, but somehow, she couldn't help herself.

Or maybe she didn't want to answer questions until she understood how she felt about him. Was he really the man for her? Were his intentions honorable? He'd called her his angel, but he'd said nothing of consequence, hadn't courted her properly, as a man should.

At least, how she thought someone should court her—not that she had any first-hand experience of such a thing.

If his intentions were honorable, could she forget what her mother had endured, including a lawfully-wedded husband who'd deserted her? Why would she deserve better? Other couples stayed together, until death parted them, like the commander and his wife. But would she be so lucky?

She glanced at her mother, saw she was busy lining up the checkers. She pulled out the picture and hid it in the top shelf of the cabinet.

Someone knocked on their door, and she started. Before she could cross to the door, Maxine Brackett cracked it open and stuck her head in.

"Can I come in? I've a piece of cake for your supper and some news," their landlady said.

Crissy folded her lips into a forced smile. She didn't appreciate Maxine acting as if the room belonged to her, and not allowing them any privacy. The room *did* belong to the Bracketts, but she worked long and hard, paying the rent.

"Oh, yes, Maxine, please, do come in," her mother spoke up. "What news do you have?"

Her mother didn't know Maxine had probably been spreading gossip. And if she had known, she wouldn't hold it against their landlady. Instead, she'd take the shame upon herself, feeling she wasn't worthy of having her secret kept.

Sometimes, her mother was too kind for her own good. Crissy often wondered if her sweet nature was a part of what had driven her to the life she'd led. Had her mother been too weak to withstand the beguilements of unworthy men? And if that was the case, was she fast becoming like her mother?

Maxine flounced into the room. "Good evening, Crissy." She held out a piece of cheesecloth-wrapped cake. "It's ginger cake. I know how you and your mother like it. I saved you a piece."

Crissy took the cake. Ginger cake reminded her of Christmas when she was growing up. Her mother had baked a lot during the holidays, and ginger cake was one of the treats of the season.

"Thank you, Mrs. Brackett. Please, have a seat and tell us the news."

Maxine crossed her arms. "Well, I wish you'd call me Maxine, but I guess your mother has raised you properly."

Crissy got out a plate and unwrapped the rich offering. A lot of eggs and butter had gone into the cake, not to mention the precious spice, ginger. She wondered why Maxine had bothered to give them only one piece of cake. Her mouth watered, thinking about its rich taste, but her Mama needed the treat more.

She fetched a fork and plate and gave the slice of cake to her mother.

Maxine sat down and folded her arms on the table.

"Crissy," her mother said, "don't we have some coffee left from supper? I'd like a cup to go with my cake, and we should offer Maxine a cup, too. Where are your manners?"

"Of course," Crissy said through gritted teeth. It went against her nature to wait on Maxine, especially after what the woman had done.

She grabbed the coffee pot from the back of the stove, added some water to the left-over grounds, stoked the fire, and put the coffee on to brew again. She set out two cups and teaspoons, and their small store of sugar on the table.

She put her hands on her hips. "We don't have any cream, Mrs. Brackett, er, Maxine."

"Oh, this is fine, Crissy, and I don't need sugar, either. Black coffee is all right."

Her mother joined Maxine at the table, took a bite of the cake and closed her eyes, obviously savoring the taste. "This is the best yet, Maxine. You've outdone yourself. Just the right amount of ginger, too."

Her mother half-turned in her chair and held out a forkful of the cake. "Here, Crissy, taste this."

Obediently, Crissy leaned forward and took the bite of cake. It melted in her mouth, filling her senses with its rich, spicy sweetness. She swallowed and said, "It's wonderful, Mrs. Brack..., er, Maxine. Sweet and savory at the same time."

The coffeepot started to rattle and pop, and she grabbed a dishtowel, pulling it off the stove and filling their cups. And she felt like her insides were rattling and popping, too. She was desperate to hear Maxine's news—knowing it must be about the soldiers.

Her mother took another bite of cake and smiled. She took a sip of coffee. Maxine cradled her cracked cup and sipped, too. Crissy stood to one side, ready to scream.

"Oh, I wanted to tell y'all the news." Maxine put her coffee cup down.

"Yes, please, do. We have so few diversions." Her mother licked the fork, polishing off the last crumbs of the cake.

"Well, Company C has returned, but the stagecoach line was attacked, about five miles from town. At first, it looked as if the Apache were to blame, but upon closer examination, Captain MacTavish realized it was Mexican bandits, made up to look like Apaches, to throw off our soldiers." Maxine quirked one eyebrow. "Who would have thought of such a ruse?"

"The founders of our country, if you remember the Boston Tea Party," Crissy interjected. The Ursulines had given her an excellent education, and she was proud of it.

Maxine glanced up and frowned. "Uh, yes, I suppose so."

"Did they get the bandits? What about the stagecoach passengers?" Her mother asked.

"All the bandits were killed." Maxine tossed her head. "And good riddance, I say." She shook her head again. "Sad to say, they'd killed everyone on the stagecoach, except the front rider, who'd managed to get away and alert the fort."

Crissy and her mother both gasped.

Maxine frowned. "Bloody business, living on the frontier. And there was a child, too, on the stagecoach, who either escaped or was taken by the bandits before the soldiers got there," Maxine added.

"Captain MacTavish wanted to search, but it was already getting dark. They'll bring out the Seminole scouts tomorrow to look for the child."

"What about the soldiers," her mother asked, "did we lose any?"

The coffeepot rattled and perked again, and she moved it to the back of the stove. She was glad her mother had asked before she blurted out the question. She held her breath.

Maxine sniffed and touched her handkerchief to dry eyes. "Unfortunately, two of the soldiers were killed." She put her hands together, as if she was praying. "It's sad and awful to lose good soldiers, fighting those murderous Mexicans."

Crissy's heart galloped and climbed into her throat. She'd heard enough. She doubted Maxine would know the names of the lost soldiers, but she had to know if Davie was safe.

"Mama, I need to go out. I feel like taking a walk—"

"But Crissy, it's dark and there could be other bandits out there—"

"I'll be careful, but I have to go." She tossed the dish towel onto the counter by the dry sink.

Both her mother and Maxine rose, as if to stop her. But she ignored them, lifting her skirts, and running for the door.

* * *

Davie rode back to the fort with his fellow soldiers. Today had been one of the longest days of his life. First, there had been the sorrow of the funeral for his commander's wife. Then, he'd known heaven on earth, spending time with Crissy. They'd talked and learned something of each other. And he'd kissed her until he was crazy with wanting.

But at the end of the day, he'd been mustered out to stop a group of Mexican bandits who'd attacked the bi-weekly stage from San Antonio. He rubbed the back of his neck and his shoulders slumped, remembering. He'd seen a lot of killing today. And he'd put a bullet through the forehead of one of the bandits.

A man didn't forget things like that—taking another man's life—even if the man deserved it for murdering innocent stagecoach passengers.

They'd shot down the eight Mexican bandits who'd attacked the stagecoach. The front runner, Jesse Thompkins, who had warned the fort about the attack, believed the bandits had thought they were carrying the fort's payroll.

Someone had obviously given the bandits the wrong route, which made him wonder where they'd gotten their information. And they'd taken pains to disguise themselves, too. If they'd been successful, the soldiers would be looking for a band of Apache, not Mexican bandits.

The fort's pay came overland, but by wagon, not on the stagecoach. Lieutenant Colonel Gregor had changed the way their wages were transported when he'd taken command, ordering the wagon to come by back trails through neighboring ranches. And they changed the route, each time, to ward off attacks like what had happened today.

It was sobering, to say the least, to see men who you knew die. Made you realize how short life was, especially guarding the frontier. Private Higgins was an acquaintance, a part of Company C. But Corporal Simmons was another story, they'd been friends, of a sort. They'd shared some good times together at the Spring Street Saloon.

Then there was Crissy.

If life was short, shouldn't he be getting on with it? She sparked feelings in him no other woman had. Was he ready to settle down and raise a passel of young'un's? If he was, what about her ailing mother? Was he ready to take on that responsibility, too?

If not, what *were* his intentions? Honorable, he hoped, but would she want to be an Army wife?

He'd never thought of marrying before, believing he'd remain single. His mother had scoffed, warning him the lightning bolt of true love would strike him, too. And she'd been right. He wanted his Angel, his Crissy, as his own. But should he drag her around from fort to fort?

He frowned, not certain what he wanted. It was all new to him. Could he be happy in Galveston, enclosed between four walls of a carpenter shop? Wasn't it the right thing to do, to give his wife and children a safe place to live?

Once they were inside the fort, he dismounted and handed off Rover, his chestnut gelding, to Private Bates, who took care of his mount. He took off his gloves and tucked them into his belt.

It was late, and he was tired.

The trumpeter stood beneath the lowered flag and belted out tattoo, the call to get ready to turn in. In another quarter of an hour, they'd hear taps, and the barracks' lamps would be extinguished.

Private O'Rourke ran up to him and saluted. "There's a lady at the front gate of the fort, asking for you, Sergeant."

Could it be Crissy? His heart warmed, thinking she might be concerned about him. "Thank you, Private O'Rourke. I'll go and see what the lady wants."

"Yes, sir." O'Rourke saluted again and whispered, "Remember, lights out in fifteen minutes, sir."

He wasn't surprised O'Rourke would be complicit in his meeting with a lady. The private was known as a godless womanizer, frequenting the saloon women every payday, and borrowing money from his fellow soldiers to finance his habits.

He returned the salute. "Yes, I know. I'll be all right. Thank you for finding me."

The private nodded and saluted again.

It was all he could do—not break into a run. But he restrained himself and strode to the gate of the fort.

Another line sergeant, Hickie Hayes, greeted him. "I think she's one of the laundresses." Hickie inclined his head. "You best be careful, man. The commander doesn't like us to mix with 'em." He grinned and winked. "I'll leave the gate open. You can lower the bar when you're through."

Davie clasped Hickie's shoulder. "Thank you. I appreciate your understanding."

"It's not my understanding you'll need. If you get caught, you'll lose your other stripe."

"I know, but she's worth it."

Hickie chuckled and turned away, heading back to the barracks.

Davie slipped out the gate, and he saw the dark outline of her, standing at the edge of the trees. She still wore the same black dress from earlier today. He crossed to her and took her hands.

She leaned up and pulled his head down, kissing him. It was the first time she'd taken the initiative, and his heart swelled with tender feelings. But she moved away too soon, and held him at arm's length, looking him up and down.

"I'm thankful you're all right," she said.

"Me, too. Though, I lost a good friend today."

"Oh, no. I'm sorry. I heard two soldiers were killed."

"Yes, one was an acquaintance, but Corporal Simmons was a friend." He sighed. "And all for nothing—the bandits had been misinformed—thinking the stagecoach carried the fort's wages. But it didn't."

She covered her mouth with her hand. "How horrible."

"Yes, makes a man think. But with you here, Angel, I don't want to think too much. Taps will be called soon, and I'll need to return to the barracks." He lowered his head and leaned forward.

She stepped back, and he almost fell on his face.

He frowned. "Why won't you kiss me? A good night kiss, at least. You kissed me first."

"Because I was happy to see you were safe." She lowered her head and bit her lip. "I need to know something, before we... before we..." She raised her face to him.

"What are your intentions, Sergeant? For us to keep hiding away and stealing kisses. Or... what?"

It was his turn to take a step back. He'd been wondering the same thing, too, but he was far from a conclusion. And he didn't like being crowded, either. Wasn't the man supposed to do the asking?

"What about returning to the Ursulines?" He was half-teasing, but he couldn't help but ask, wondering if she really wanted to marry. She was young and probably didn't know her mind. He wasn't much of a catch, why would she want him?

"You're right." She turned aside. "I shouldn't have forgotten what my plans are."

He grabbed her hand. "You're serious about going to a convent."

"Only if something happens to my mother."

He sighed and let go of her hand. "Then why did you ask me to commit—?"

"I don't know. I don't want to be compromised, I guess, and I feel like we're—"

"Moving too fast?" He stroked his chin. "I was wondering the same thing."

"Oh, I see." The tone of her voice sounded disappointed.

"I don't want to give you up, Crissy. Sure and begorrah, it's not that. But I hadn't thought to take a wife, and I'm wondering if you'd like Army life? And your mother—what if I'm transferred?"

"Yes, you're right, I don't know if my mother could travel. Some days she seems better, but..." She searched his face and gasped. "My mother? You're asking about my mother, cloaking your curiosity in concern for her health?"

"Crissy, we have to consider your mother, especially since you're taking care of her and she's ailing."

She stared at him. "But that's not what you're really asking, is it? You've heard the gossip. Haven't you? And you believed it and thought I would... Thought I was easy and..." She turned and grabbed her skirts.

He grasped her elbow, stopping her before she could bolt. What was she talking about? Then it came to him—that awful gossip about her mother. He didn't believe it, though it was odd about her father's name. But even if the gossip was true, what did it have to do with them?

Evidently, a lot, to her way of thinking. She thought he would take advantage of her? He might have been a bounder, but he'd never hurt his angel.

"Crissy, I... I don't know what to say. I'm thinking on it, wondering how best to provide for you and your mother." He paused. "As for the other, I don't care if it's true or not. I would never—"

"If you don't know what you want to do, I shouldn't be with you." She jerked her arm free. "Please, don't bother me again. I'll not be... not be easy and cheap."

"But I don't want to cause you any disgrace—"

"And I don't want to hear your lying words." She covered her ears with her hands and whirled away.

She ran toward town, and the night swallowed her.

Davie stared after her, wondering what he could do to reassure her of his love? He would never do anything dishonorable or hurt her. But it was late, and he'd be sneaking in, as it was. He'd better get back to the barracks.

He'd find Crissy tomorrow and straighten things out.

* * *

Crissy put her head down and ran as fast as she could.

He knew. He knew!

He thought she was like her mother—to be had for a few kisses. It was unbearable. Her heart felt like a piece of glass in her chest, a piece of glass that was shattering.

She rounded the porch of the Brackett General Store, thinking to use the back door to their room. At the corner, her foot hit something, and she heard a voice call out, "Ouch!"

Crissy caught the corner post to keep from pitching straight forward into the dirt. She looked around, but it was dark, and she didn't see anything. But she heard something, scrabbling in the dirt.

Leaning down, she let her eyes adjust to the dark and saw the thin legs of a child, sticking out from beneath the porch. It was obvious the child was frightened and hiding. She wondered who it could be?

She tried to make her voice soft and cajoling. "I'm sorry I tripped over your foot, but I didn't see you there. What are you hiding from? Won't you come out, please?"

No movement, but she thought she heard sniffling and crying. She squatted down, sitting back on her heels, and holding out her hand. "Please, come out. I want to help you, child."

She waited. Finally, she heard some scrabbling again, and a small girl stuck her head out. Her voice was a thin wail. "Is it safe?"

"Yes, of course, it's safe." Crissy took the little girl's hand. "Please, let me help you."

Slowly, the girl, who looked to be about ten years old, emerged and stood up. Her dress was dirty and shredded, torn with big holes in it. Her face was dirty and smudged, and her thin legs and arms were covered with scratches. Her lace-up boots were ruined, mere pieces of tattered leather, barely covering her feet.

Could this be the child who had been on the stagecoach?

She gathered the little girl into her arms. "Let me take you home, and you can explain where you came from. My mother and I live back here."

The girl said nothing, snuggling into her arms. Crissy's heart went out to her. *Poor thing, poor little thing.*

Holding the child, she couldn't get to the key in her pocket, but she managed to knock on the back door.

Her mother opened the door quickly, saying, "Crissy, I'm glad you're back. I was worried... Who is this?"

"I'm not certain, but I think it's the child from the stagecoach."

"The stagecoach!" The little girl cried out and squirmed in Crissy's arms. "No, no, no!" And then her teeth started chattering, though it was high summer and plenty warm.

"She's in shock," Crissy's mother said. "I've seen the signs before, when... when I worked at the Tin Star." Her mother pointed. "Put her on the bed and heap all of our blankets around her. I'll get some of the soup you made yesterday. And some iodine for her arms and legs."

Crissy did as her mother instructed and between the two of them, they got the little girl to stop shivering and swallow a few spoonfuls of soup. The child laid back against the pillow with Mary cuddling her.

"I'll sleep on the floor in my bedroll," Crissy offered.

"Yes, I think that would be best. She needs for me to hold her," her mother said.

"Shouldn't we ask her—?"

"If we can keep her awake long enough. We do need to know, though, it can wait until morning."

The girl's eyelids lowered, and her head nodded. But she must have heard them talking because she wiped her nose and said, "My name's Ellie Anderson. The Indians killed my parents."

Crissy knew they were Mexican bandits, dressed as Apaches, but what good would it do to correct the girl?

"I don't think they saw me at first, they were busy shooting... I ducked into some bushes. And I ran, and ran, and ran. I was scared." She sobbed. "I ran until I saw the town, and I hid under the general store." She squeezed her eyes shut. "I should have stayed with my parents." Tears streamed from her eyes. "I don't want to live. Don't want to live without my Ma and Pa."

She lowered her head, and her thin shoulders shook.

Crissy's mother held Ellie close, trying to soothe her, stroking her tangled hair, and rubbing her back. "There, there, Ellie. Shhh, child. You did the right thing. You saved yourself. I know your Ma and Pa would have wanted you to save yourself."

Ellie kept sobbing, and Crissy met her mother's gaze. "I'll get ready for bed," she said. "We'll have to go to Commander Gregor at the fort tomorrow."

"Yes, and I hope Maxine has some ready-made clothes to fit her. Poor thing."

Ellie's sobs slowly ebbed away. Her eyes closed, and Mary laid her gently against the pillow.

"I'll wash my face and change to a nightshirt," her mother said, gazing down at the little girl. "I don't want to leave her alone for too long. She might have nightmares and wake up crying."

Crissy gently stroked the little girl's hair back from her face. "You're the best with frightened children, Mama. I should know. I remember when I was scared of stuff or sick, you'd hold me until morning." She raised her head and snagged her mother's gaze. "You were always there for me."

"Oh, Crissy." Her mother hugged her. "I'm glad you feel that way. You don't know how much it means to me."

And Crissy did mean it—with all her heart.

She'd never be ashamed of her mother again. Never again, knowing her mother had done her best. Knowing her mother had always loved and taken care of her.

Her mother started coughing and had to pull away.

She got out her handkerchief, and Crissy couldn't help but notice a couple of red spots on the white cloth. Mary wiped her mouth and hid the handkerchief quickly.

Her mother had never coughed up blood before—what did it mean?

A sense of dread dragged at her. She'd been a fool to think her Mama was getting better. Tomorrow, she'd ask Dr. Irving when the medicine would arrive.

And she'd need to go to the fort at first light to stop the scouts from going out and searching for a child who'd already been found.

* * *

Lieutenant Colonel Gregor raised his head. He heard a tap on the headquarters' door and blinked his eyes, realizing he'd fallen asleep at his desk again. He hadn't meant to fall asleep in his office last night, especially after laying his sweet Martha to rest. He should have gone home to Peggy.

But he hadn't wanted to go home—not to the empty stillness of a house without his wife.

It wasn't fair to his daughter, though. She'd lost her mother. Good thing Miss Phillips hadn't departed yet. Or maybe it wasn't. The nurse was a reminder of what the past few weeks had been like. At least, someone had been at home to see to his daughter.

Miss Phillips already had another nursing job in San Antonio. He'd have to see about getting someone to take care of Peggy when the nurse left on the next stagecoach going east.

The stagecoach—he'd almost forgotten.

The knocking sounded again, harder this time. "Come in," he called out and smoothed his hair back with both hands.

Captain MacTavish of Company C entered the room and saluted. He approached the desk and held out a piece of paper. "The written report, sir, as you requested last night."

Gregor took the piece of paper and nodded. "Thank you."

"Lieutenant Bullis has requested twenty of our scouts to go and look for the missing child."

"Permission granted." Gregor peered out the window toward the horizon. Daylight was barely breaking; it must be between five-thirty and six o'clock. "See they're mustered out by seven hundred hours."

"Yes, sir." MacTavish said and hesitated. "There's one other thing. Something Sergeant Donovan—"

"What has Sergeant Donovan done this time?" Gregor huffed and scratched the overnight beard on his jaw. "Don't tell me—I have to demote him again?"

MacTavish averted his head. "He's a fine soldier, sir. Shot one of those bandits, right between the eyes, without appearing to take aim."

"I know he's a fine soldier. It's his other shenanigans that gets him into trouble."

This time, MacTavish didn't try to hide his smile. "Yes, he's one to test the limits, sir, but he hasn't done anything wrong. Thank the..." MacTavish caught himself. "Uh, thank heavens, sir. It's something he said to me last night after lights out."

"What were you doing jawing with a non-commissioned officer after taps, Captain MacTavish?"

"We weren't jawing, sir. He came to my cabin and asked politely to be excused for being out late because he wanted to ask me something. And he got me to thinking."

"What about, MacTavish?"

"Sergeant Donovan wanted to know who, other than the officers of Company C, knew about how you'd changed the pay transport. And who didn't know. Same thing in town, he asked, if anyone knew?"

Gregor straightened and gazed at MacTavish. David Donovan might be a prankster and full of mischief, but he was nobody's fool. "No one knows in town. And the officers of Company C knew, no one else."

MacTavish shook his head. "Doesn't narrow things much. Does it? Anyone but Company C officers could have given the Mexicans the wrong information."

"No, it doesn't narrow things at all." Gregor scratched his chin again. "But it makes me think of something else."

"What's that, sir?"

"The Fourth of July celebration is slated for..." He paused and pulled his calendar closer, peering at it. "For ten days from now. Correct?"

"Yes, sir. All the soldiers are looking forward to it," the tone of MacTavish's voice lightened and carried an edge of excitement. "The ladies' auxiliary has been planning the food, decorations, and dance for months. Now, if we can get that load of fireworks from San Antonio, we'll be—"

"I'm glad everyone is excited. But in the meantime, I want you to take twenty of your men into México and—"

"Oh, very good, sir, all the men have been asking to raid into México like Commander Mackenzie did. But I don't think twenty men will be—"

"Captain MacTavish, I applaud you and your men for their eagerness to storm into México, but for the time being, we will follow a policy of containment. The War Department is tired of getting Mexican complaints about our soldiers compromising the sovereignty of their country."

He cleared his throat. "No, what I want is for you and twenty men to go to every Mexican ranch and invite all their owners within a hundred-mile radius. Also, every *alcalde* of any town or village—"

"*Alcalde*, sir?"

He waved his hand. "Means mayor in Spanish. In other words, I want all the headmen here for our July Fourth celebration." He steepled the fingers of his hands. "Sergeant Donovan knows how to speak Spanish. Doesn't he?"

"Yes, sir, taught himself from a book when he was first stationed here. Takes every opportunity to practice on the locals."

"Take Donovan with you." He lowered his voice. "And I want you to keep the reason for these invitations strictly to yourself and, of course, Sergeant Donovan. It was his idea in the first place. Let him do the talking and have him keep his eyes open. Am I understood?"

MacTavish's eyes bulged out, but he managed to come to attention and salute. "Very good, sir. Can we leave tomorrow, or do you want us to leave today?"

"Tomorrow is time enough. Let's find the poor child first. One thing at a time, MacTavish."

Someone knocked on his door. "Could you get the door on your way out, Captain?"

"Yes, sir," Captain MacTavish said and saluted again.

"Thank you." Gregor wondered who else needed to see him this early in the morning. He really should get home to his daughter.

Chapter Five

Crissy found herself in the dark and the same copse of trees, outside the fort's front gate, waiting again. But not for the same reason. If she never saw Davie Donovan again, it would be too soon.

A corporal pulled back the heavy gates, as the sun was showing itself over the horizon. She would need to get an excuse for Isabel from the commander for being late, but the soldiers needed to know about Ellie before they sent scouts to search for her.

She sailed past the on-guard corporal with, "Good morning."

"Uh, good morning, Miss." The corporal tipped his flat-brimmed cavalry hat.

She looked neither right nor left, marching as fast as her legs would carry her to the headquarters' building and hoping the commander would be in his office. Yesterday morning, he'd mourned and buried his wife. To Crissy's way of thinking, yesterday morning seemed like a life-time ago.

A man in a long, white coat was crossing the deserted parade field. She recognized him as Dr. Irving. Offering thanks to the Blessed Virgin Mary, she ran up to him.

"Dr. Irving, sir, can I ask you something."

He peered at her over his spectacles. "Crissy, you're out and about early." He pushed his glasses with his index finger and nodded. "But I forgot, all you laundresses must be at it early. Commander's orders. Yes?"

"Yes, sir, and I'm on my way to the commander's office with a bit of news. But I'm glad I found you first."

"Oh, and what might you need, young lady?"

"It's about the medicine for my mother." She looked down and willed away the tears forming in her eyes.

"Oh, Crissy, I'm sorry." He touched her arm. "The medicine should have been on the stagecoach, but it was attacked and burned." He sighed. "I'm very sorry. I will send again, straight away, for the medicine."

"Please, sir, I want my mother to get better."

"Oh, well now, Crissy, your mother's condition is… delicate. The medicine will soothe her coughing, which is important because it stops her from hurting herself, internally. But she needs rest and lots of nourishing food."

He stroked his pointed, metal-gray goatee. "I've been sending for some medical journals, and there's a doctor in New York state who has had some success with rest, proper exercise, and three meals a day. His methods are new, but he claims to have cured himself, and now he's opening a place to take care of patients—calls it a sanatorium. And he believes clean, dry air also helps. We've plenty of that. I know you're worried about her—"

"More than worried, doctor. She's started to cough up blood."

He raised his head and stared at her. "When?"

"A few droplets, last night, sir."

"Well, hmmm, did you notice how red the blood was?"

"Sir?"

He put his hand on her arm and patted her. "Please, Crissy, don't worry. I'll go and examine her right away, and I'll telegraph for the medicine again. Should be here on the next west-bound stage."

"Thank you." She gulped, realizing her mother's condition might be more serious than she'd thought. How would she live without her mother?

She had a thought. "Is it the cost? I'll pay whatever it takes for my mother to get well. Anything, anything." She grabbed his sleeve and tugged on it.

He pursed his lips. "It can be costly, the medicine. Five dollars a bottle, but I—"

"I understand. I'll get you the money and more. You wait and see." She stiffened her back, knowing she must speak to the commander about the money owing her.

The doctor lowered his head. "Let's take one step at a time, Crissy. I'll examine her and send for the medicine again. All right?"

"Yes, sir. Please, Dr. Irving, help her." She hesitated, marshalling her thoughts. "There's something else, too. The child who escaped from the stagecoach attack—I found her last night. I think she's fine, except for some scratches and bruises. My mother said she was suffering from shock, but she took care of her. I think you should take a look at her and make certain she's all right."

"Why, Crissy, that is good news." The doctor looked up at the headquarters' building. "Have you told the commander?" He smiled, a gentle smile. "Of course, you haven't. It's where you are headed. Am I right?"

"Yes, Dr. Irving, I wanted to let the commander know as soon as possible."

"Good girl. And don't worry, I'll look at the child, too."

"Thank you, Dr. Irving, for everything." From the corner of her eyes, she saw a corporal with a trumpet, coming from the barracks. She nodded. "I best get to it."

"I understand." He bowed. "I will see you later, young lady."

Crissy turned away and found the headquarters' building in front of her. She ran up the front steps and raised her fist to knock on the stout wooden door. An officer, a captain, by the look of the bars on his uniform, opened the door as if he'd been waiting.

Nodding, she said, "Good morning, Captain. I've important news for the commander. Is he in?"

The captain stepped aside. "Right this way, Miss...?"

"Uh, Miss Smith. I work in the laundry, but I have something I need to tell the commander, straight away."

"Captain MacTavish, dismissed." A deep, gritty-sounding voice greeted her. "Miss Smith, is it? Please, come in and state your business."

The captain bowed to her and let himself out the door. She walked inside and stood before the commander's desk.

As a gentleman should, Lieutenant Colonel Gregor got to his feet and offered, "Please, Miss Smith, have a seat." He rocked back on his heels and looked her in the face. "Haven't I seen you before?"

"I work for Isabel Garza in the laundry." Her face heated at his intense scrutiny. She sat down in one of the two chairs. "And I will be needing an excuse for being late today, sir."

"No problem, Miss Smith." He leaned down with one outstretched arm propping him up, as he scratched out a note. "Here," he said, extending his hand with the scrap of paper. "Give this to Isabel." He straightened again and seated himself. "Now, Miss Smith, what can I do for you?"

The strident notes of the bugler broke the silence before she could answer. And she knew the call well—it was reveille, the official waking of the troops.

She knotted her hands together in her lap, waiting until the trumpeter finished. "I've come because we, my mother and I, found the child from the stagecoach raid."

The Commander stood up again. "Say what, Miss Smith?"

"The child, she's a little girl. We've found her. She must have run the whole five miles after seeing her Ma and Pa killed. She was hiding beneath the Brackett General Store's front porch. I found her and took her to my mother last night."

"Miss Smith, are you certain? Lieutenant Bullis is mustering out twenty of our best scouts to—"

"Oh, yes, sir. I know the child is who she says she is. Her name is Ellie Anderson. If you saw the way she looked and heard her sobbing all night, you'd believe me." She hesitated and twisted her hands in her skirts. "I would have brought her with me, but my mother wanted the doctor to see her first. Then she's going to get Ellie new clothes from Mrs. Brackett." She shook her head. "She tore her clothes, running through the brush to escape."

The commander narrowed his eyes. "Miss Smith, I know I've seen you before. And not at the laundry. I believe I've seen you at my home. Am I right?"

She'd made up her mind, after talking to the doctor. And after seeing how her mother was with Ellie. No more lying, no more subterfuge. Her mother deserved better. She'd see they had the best money could buy—at least, until it ran out.

"Uh, yes, sir. You're right. It's the other reason I wanted to see you. To confess and ask for the pay you... or Miss Phillips owes me."

"What are you talking about, Miss Smith?"

"I helped, these past six weeks, to take care of your wife without pay."

"Why on earth would you do such a thing, Miss?"

"Because my name isn't Miss Smith. I guess it's Miss Shannon, though, Renzo Martinelli owned me as my father."

"The Mr. Martinelli who was killed..." The commander looked up at the rafters of his office. "Building this headquarters building?"

"Yes, sir, he claimed he was my father. But I don't know for certain because my mother was a 'lady of the night' in San Antonio, where I was born. Mr. Martinelli couldn't marry my Mama because she was married before, to Ian Shannon. He ran off to the gold fields in California and left my mother to fend for herself."

"Really, Miss Smith, er, Shannon, what a story," he sputtered. "And why do you feel the need to confess now? Especially, as you must have obtained your employment with Mrs. Garza under false circumstances."

"Oh, please, sir, don't blame Isabel. We became acquainted, both being members of the Catholic Church in town, and she knew how desperate my mother and I were, after my father died. She said you wanted young ladies of blameless reputation, especially, if we're unmarried." She looked down. "I took the false name of 'Smith' so no one could trace me back to my mother."

"All right. I understand." He lowered himself into his chair again and wiped his forehead with a handkerchief. "What about this pay I owe you... or is it Miss Phillips who owes you?" He tried to smile and failed. "I'm afraid that part has escaped me."

"Miss Phillips found out my true identity..." She looked up. "Probably from Mrs. Brackett." Leaning forward, she placed one fisted hand on the edge of his desk. "Please, sir, don't mention it to Maxine, as we live behind her store, and there's no place else—"

"Yes, yes," he interrupted her, his voice sounding weary. "I get the gist of it. Your secrets are safe with me, Miss Shannon."

"Thank you, sir."

"Now the pay part, please. If I owe you money, I would like to know why or how or..."

"Oh, yes, well, Miss Phillips found out my true identity, and when your wife was... failing, she took me from the laundry and threatened to reveal my mother's past if I didn't help her take care of your wife." Crissy shook her head. "By then, it was too much for her to do alone, taking care of your wife and the house and all."

He snorted. “Miss Phillips did that, did she?” He covered his face with his hands and mumbled, “No wonder I never liked the woman.”

“Yes, sir, she’s not a nice person.” She softened her voice. “But your wife, sir, your wife, she was a wonderful and kind lady.” Her eyes filled with tears.

“A kind and sweet lady, Mrs. Gregor. And to be fair, too,” she gulped and admitted, “Miss Phillips loved your wife and took good care of her.”

The commander stood again and pointed at her.

Her heart stopped. Would he order her off the post? Would she and Mama be thrown out of their room at the general store without a cent to their names?

“You’re hired, Miss Smith, er, Shannon. Crissy, is it?” He nodded. “Starting today. I’ll have Miss Phillips removed to the hotel in town until the eastbound stage arrives. I want you to take care of my daughter, Peggy. She’s spoken of you, but she always called you ‘Crissy.’ I didn’t know.”

He scrubbed his hand across his face. “The last few weeks of Martha’s illness were a nightmare. I wish I’d paid more attention, but it hurt…” He sucked in his cheeks. “I wish Miss Phillips would have told me that she needed extra help.”

“Yes, sir. Given the circumstances, I don’t think she wanted to bother you.”

“Yes, I guess not.” He sat back down. “I guess not. But don’t worry, you’ll be paid, now I know.” He looked at her. “How does five dollars a week sound? Beginning back six weeks ago, I owe you thirty dollars.”

He opened a drawer in his desk and pulled out a pouch. He shook out some silver dollars and counted them. “Here, Miss, er, Crissy, this is for your back pay and for two more weeks. We’ll expect you an hour after reveille, and you can return home after supper is served. Or you can stay with us. We’ve an extra room. Which would you prefer?”

Crissy’s heart expanded in her chest. She opened her mouth, but no sound came out. She didn’t know what to say, how to feel, or what to do. If she listened to her heart, she’d get on her knees and kiss his hand. But no one did such a thing, these days. Did they?

"I'd prefer to stay with my mother. Can I tell my mother and Isabel, and start tomorrow?"

He made a shooing motion with his hands. "Of course, tomorrow is fine." He got to his feet again. "Let me see you out, Crissy. Oh, and can you bring the child to me, after the mid-day meal, with your mother, please."

"Yes, sir. Thank you, sir. You won't be sorry. I'll take good care of Peggy and your home."

He smiled. "I know you will, Crissy. You've already proven your devotion. Peggy will be over the moon. She's spoken very kindly of you."

She ducked her head, swallowing. "I'm glad, sir."

He stuck his head out the door and called, "Orderly, orderly... Corporal Livingstone, could you please fetch Lieutenant Bullis immediately, and tell him there's no need to muster out the scouts." He turned and smiled again. "This young lady has found our missing child."

* * *

Crissy plunked down several silver dollars on the long counter at the general store. "Here's what we owe you for the month, Mrs. Brackett, for our victuals and rent."

"Why, Missy, what did you do, strike buried treasure? It isn't payday at the fort." Maxine cocked her head and her eyes gleamed, as if she was savoring a particularly juicy tidbit of gossip.

"I got paid for helping Miss Phillips. My *back* pay."

It felt good, for once, not to have to scrimp and pinch every penny. It felt good to have money. And it felt marvelous to throw money at Mrs. Brackett's too curious, calculating countenance.

Maxine's mouth dropped open, and she crossed her arms over her chest. "Who paid you? I mean won't Miss Phillips be leaving—?"

"As soon as the eastbound stage comes, she'll be leaving. And the commander paid me."

"But, but, you didn't—?"

"Oh, yes, I did." She tossed her head back, proud of herself... for once. "I told the commander everything. And he hired me, at five whole dollars a week, to take care of his house and daughter for him."

"You told him everything?"

"Yes, Maxine, I told him everything." And she would have liked to tell Maxine to mind her own business because her mother's past couldn't harm them.

The older woman frowned. "Well, I never. I surely never."

"Good morning to you, Maxine. I need to tell Mama the good news."

"Dr. Irving is back there. I wouldn't—"

"Wouldn't interrupt?" She wheeled around and placed her fisted hands on her hips. "I sent the doctor to her. He needs to examine my mother and resend for some medicine. He'd ordered it from Austin, but it got burnt up with the stage. Besides, Ellie is there, too."

"Who's Ellie?"

"Never you mind. I'll tell you later."

"Well, if you're to have another boarder back there, you'll owe me..."

Crissy turned her back on Maxine and walked down the long hallway, letting the woman fuss without waiting to hear what she had to say. Besides, it would do Maxine good to not know the latest news until they were ready to tell her. She doubted Ellie would be staying with them for long, anyway.

She couldn't wait to tell her mother what had happened. How their lives had changed in such a short time.

She opened the door and called out, "Mama, I have the best news!"

She glimpsed her mother and Dr. Irving, huddled together at the table. The doctor had his arm around her mother, and her mother had laid her head on his shoulder.

Her heart stuttered in her chest, and she wanted to shout at them. Now she'd confessed and put their sordid past behind them, here was her mother, her *sick* mother, looking as if she wanted to take up her old profession again.

Her mother pushed away from the doctor, but he frowned and shook his head, keeping his arm around her. Ellie, poor little tuckered out thing, was still sleeping, curled up in bed by herself.

"Crissy, I'm glad you're here. I want to talk to you about your mother's condition," the doctor said.

"Seems y'all have been doing a bit more than talking."

Her mother gasped. "Crissy, you shouldn't—"

"Mary, let me handle this." Dr. Irving held up one hand. "It's true, I've a tender regard for your mother, but it's not what you think."

"No, Crissy, it's not," her mother interjected. "Dr. Irving has been nothing but kind." She caught his hand and nestled her cheek in it. "And he's a perfect gentleman, too—a refined and cultured gentleman."

He stroked her mother's cheek, and the look in his eyes was tender.

A frisson of something slithered down Crissy's spine. At first, she thought it was disgust, but she soon realized the truth. She was pea-green with envy. Davie had looked at her the same way... but now it was over. She'd demanded more than he could give, and he'd let her down.

"Does he know about everything?" She couldn't help but ask.

It was craven of her, she knew. But how, after having the courage to confess, was it fair for her mother to find happiness, while she was left with nothing?

"Yes, Crissy, he knows everything, and he's trying to help, by sending to Sacramento for records, to find out what happened to my husband."

"Couldn't you write to Calum, his brother, in North Carolina?" Crissy asked. "You told me about my uncle and how he kept the family farm. Wouldn't he know where his brother was?"

"Crissy, over the years, I've written Calum several letters, and he's never answered me but once." She slumped, curling her shoulders. "I didn't want to tell you how cold-hearted your uncle was, but he's a tight-fisted man. He knew I needed money to come home after Ian ran off."

"Oh, no, that's terrible," Crissy huffed. "But why do you care about what happened to your husband, Mama?"

"Doesn't your mother have a right to some kind of closure, Crissy?" Dr. Irving spoke up. "After all, she's a practicing Catholic and until your mother knows whether her husband is dead or alive, she's a prisoner to her past."

Crissy had never thought of it that way. The doctor and his big words, like "closure." She had to admit, he was a learned man, a gentleman, as her mother claimed. And her mother, by herself, wouldn't have known how to send for records or had the money to make inquiries. She worried, though he might be a gentleman, what the doctor wanted in return for helping Mama?

Please, not that.

She fished ten silver dollars out of her pocket and placed them on the table. "We can pay now, Dr. Irving. I want you to know. For medicine and records, anything my mother needs. Commander Gregor has hired me to take care of his house and daughter."

"Oh, Crissy!" Her mother got to her feet and came to her, throwing her arms around her and hugging her. "I'm so happy for you! What wonderful news."

"Yes, it is wonderful news. I'm glad the commander recognized your efforts, now Miss Phillips will be leaving us," Dr. Irving chimed in. "But I don't want your money." He glanced at her mother. "I told you, I've a tender regard for your mother, Crissy, and I want to help you take care of her."

He held up both hands, palms out. "And there's no need to pay me, either you or your mother. I won't be doing anything dishonorable—"

"What he's trying to say, is he cares for me, to sit and talk and be good friends, Crissy," her mother interrupted. "We've been seeing each other for several months, during the day, while you were working."

Her mother held her by the shoulders and gazed into her eyes. "Nothing dishonorable has gone on. Nothing. We play checkers or pinochle, sometimes, like you and I. Do you understand?"

Crissy wet her lips and tried to smile. She lowered her head and blushed, realizing how wrong and awful she'd been. "Of course, Mama, if you say so, I understand." She licked her lips again and raised her head. "And... and I'm glad for you, Mama. Very glad."

"Good. I'm pleased it's settled," her mother said, giving her another hug. "Now, you must listen to the doctor explain about my condition. All right?"

"Yes, please." She pulled out a chair and sat down.

The doctor glanced at Ellie, who was still sleeping. "I'll explain, and then I need to waken the girl and examine her for injuries."

"Of course, doctor," Crissy said.

She glanced at the pot-belly stove. It was cold-looking with the banked embers a dead gray color—there was no fire. Last night and this morning had been full of distractions; she'd forgotten to fetch wood and make coffee. She got to her feet.

Her mother reached out and touched her arm. "Sit, honey. We'll get the fire going and coffee brewing in a bit."

"Yes, Mama."

She took her seat again, and the three of them gathered at the table.

"All right, first, let me explain about the word, 'consumption' as a medical term. It is not the name for one particular disease," the doctor began. "Unfortunately, my profession, for lack of a better word or term, uses it to cover a range of lung diseases from a simple chill to bronchitis to... to... a deadly form of a disease some European doctors are trying to prove is contagious."

"Contagious?" Crissy asked. Another big word, but the Ursulines had taught her well. "You mean the disease can be given to another person, by being around them. Am I right?"

"Precisely, though, doctors and scientists are still researching how certain diseases are transmitted from one person to another." He inhaled and slowly released his breath. "Most doctors don't know how. At least, not yet, but science marches on.

"I believe when your mother first took ill, she had a severe bronchial infection with perhaps, the beginning of something worse," he continued. "But because you were willing to take care of her and let her rest, she's doing better. Coughing less and less with your simple home remedies."

He pulled out a large brown bottle and placed it on the table. "This is laudanum, a drug much used, but I wish it was used with more care. However, for now, it will control your mother's coughing. I've sent, again, to Austin, for a mixture of laudanum and an herb called bugleweed or Virginia horehound. The two, mixed together, are excellent for a bad cough, and the strength of the laudanum is less, which is always preferable.

"As I mentioned to you earlier, too much unrestrained coughing can damage other organs in the body—"

"What about the blood I saw on her handkerchief?" Crissy asked. "I could tell you were concerned when I mentioned it."

He pulled out her mother's handkerchief and laid it on the table, smoothing it with his hands. "See here." He pointed to the spots. "It's why I was asking you about the color, but I didn't want to alarm you until I could explain."

"Yes, I see the stains."

"They're a brownish red, not bright red, which in my experience, means your mother has irritated her throat from coughing. Bright red is another story... the killer disease of true consumption." He spread his long fingers on the table. His nails were close-clipped and perfectly clean. "Now, you understand my initial concern when you mentioned it at the fort."

"Oh, yes, I see."

She sat very still, her hands folded in her lap, trying to remember what Davie had said about consumption and all the people dying in Ireland. Though it had been yesterday, she guessed she'd not been paying proper attention, so taken with Davie, as she'd been.

Love... or what she knew of it... was a strange thing. Making you forget what was important, leading you on a wild goose chase, like Alice, the character in "*Alice's Adventures in Wonderland,*" one of her favorite books.

"I believe," the doctor continued, "with your care, rest, daily exercise, and nourishing food, your mother can get well." He nodded. "In fact, I'm very hopeful, indeed."

"Exercise? But I thought you said my mother should rest."

"Yes, but I mean gentle exercise, not working twelve-hour days... or nights." The good doctor blushed. "Simple walking, a little at first, then a bit more. But daily, around the town, working her way up to a mile or so."

"So much?" Crissy asked.

"In time."

"And you've mentioned nourishment. I cook as much as I can on our little stove, but..."

"Yes, three meals a day is what the New York doctor is advising. And he wants the patients to eat vegetables, fresh if possible, along with meat and staples, like bread."

"Oh, fresh vegetables, I don't know..." She pursed her lips, considering. Maxine carried canned vegetables in her store, but fresh vegetables were hard to find. Then a thought occurred to her. "Jubilee Jackson."

"Pardon me, who is Jubilee Jackson?" he asked.

"She's a wife of one of the Seminole scouts. She lives here in Brackettville, and she raises lots and lots of fresh vegetables. Lettuce, okra, cabbage, corn, collard greens, squash, string beans... Lots and lots of vegetables. Jubilee can grow anything.

"I have money now, and Jubilee sells her vegetables. I could buy my mother some."

The doctor reached across the table and touched her hand. "That's perfect. Your mother needs to regain her appetite; she's been losing weight." He turned and gazed at Mary. "I think the exercise will help, too."

Crissy's mother placed her hand on his arm and met his gaze. "I'll do anything you say, Isaiah. I want to get well."

Mama had used his given name, Isaiah, addressing him as friend or something more. Her heart squeezed, wanting what her mother had found.

* * *

Crissy and her mother walked from the commander's office, having delivered the orphaned girl, Ellie. Dr. Irving had examined her and found nothing serious. And Bless the Virgin Mary, Ellie Anderson had remembered where she came from, Nashville, Tennessee, and both her parents had relatives there.

Commander Gregor, good man that he was, had put her with Captain MacTavish and his four children until telegraphs could be sent and received, letting her kinfolk know of her plight and what they wanted to do about Ellie.

Crissy had initially wished the commander would have taken Ellie in, but she understood why hc didn't offer and had sought another solution. His home was in mourning, and it was difficult enough for the girl to have lost her parents. Better she be distracted by MacTavish's rowdy brood than sink into sadness at the commander's house, which Crissy expected to deal with starting tomorrow.

She had her head down, watching her feet, striding beside her mother and pleased her Mama wasn't coughing or out of breath, when she felt a light touch on her shoulder.

Whirling around, she confronted Sergeant Davie Donovan. "What do you want?"

"You found the child from the stagecoach massacre?" he asked.

"Yes." She glanced at her mother. Her mother turned to the side and walked away, a few paces.

Crissy crossed her arms over her chest. "Why do you want to know?"

He shrugged. "She's an orphan now. I wondered if she had kinfolk who would—"

"Don't concern yourself, Sergeant, she has kinfolk in Tennessee. The commander will be contacting them."

"That's good. I'm glad."

"But you must have had a reason for asking."

He looked up at the sky and down at his feet. "No one should be orphaned."

He pulled back his shoulders. "I know some of the ranchers around these parts—the Shahan's come to mind. They've lost three children. Their youngest was born at Christmas last year, but he didn't survive past a day or two."

She gasped, and tears gathered in her eyes. "Christmas is a special time, to lose your child then must have been..."

He grimaced and nodded. "I agree. They're due to have some happiness, and I know they're looking to adopt a child."

"Well, I wish I could help the Shahan's, and I will keep them in my prayers. But Ellie has kin she can go to." Gazing at him, and knowing his heart was in the right place, she couldn't help but soften her tone. "It was kind of you, thinking about the child."

He touched her sleeve and inclined his head. “Yesterday, you have to know I didn’t mean anything dishonorable. I don’t seem to know my own mind... or yours. Would you want to marry a soldier, shunted around from fort to fort? Not knowing if there would be decent housing for us and our children?”

What was he saying?

Was he asking her to marry him? And if he was, it was the most awful proposal she’d ever heard.

“Sergeant, I have no idea what you’re getting at. The gossip you heard about my mother is true.” She raised her head and faced him. “We’ve told everyone there is to tell. I’m not my mother. I thought you wanted to take me cheaply and—”

“Crissy,” he hissed. “You know that’s not true. I never meant to dishonor you, and I didn’t believe the rumors about your mother.” He glanced at Mama. “I don’t know how to take a wife, how to care for her, if I want to stay in the Army—”

“It’s obvious, you don’t care enough. Otherwise, you and I would talk it out and find a way. Wouldn’t we?”

He gazed at her and thrust his thumbs in his belt loops. “Yes, I suppose we would. But my enlistment isn’t up for two more years. And I’m to go to México tomorrow. I don’t know if we’ll be raiding or—”

“Don’t concern yourself, Davie.” She sniffed. “It’s a weak excuse. My mother’s husband told her the same thing, when he left in ’49, to go to the goldfields. He claimed he didn’t want to expose her to danger.” She looked down. “But he never sent word, never returned.”

“Crissy, I’m not like that.” He grabbed her arm. “I’m seriously trying to make this work between us. And if you want to sit down and talk, when I get back, we will.”

She pulled free. “We’ll see, Sergeant, when you return.”

He stood back. “All right. I hope you’ll be waiting for me.”

“We’ll see.” She held out her hand to her mother.

Her mother joined her, and they walked toward the fort’s gate.

“Crissy,” her mother whispered, “the young man I saw in your cards. He’s the one.”

"God Bless him then, Mama, because I don't know if I can count on him. He's a rogue, and I don't know if his intentions are honorable."

Her mother pulled apart a space and stared at her, catching her eye. "He's your Dr. Irving, Crissy, make no mistake about it." Her mother clucked her tongue. "He's a good and kind man, don't let him go."

Chapter Six

Davie laid the long fuse carefully on the ground. It started under Dawes' saddled horse and ended in a clump of bushes. Every few inches, he gathered some dirt and covered the fuse.

He and his fellow soldiers from Company C, headed by Captain MacTavish, had returned from México two days ago. The fort had been in an uproar, preparing for the July Fourth celebration, and the load of fireworks had arrived.

Davie had managed to buy a string of firecrackers and several long fuses from the ordinance officer. He'd experimented with the fuses, counting off the necessary length and the seconds it took for them to burn.

He'd waited and bided his time. In fulfilling his duty as the new First Sergeant, Dawes would be responsible for riding out with a dozen men from Company C to keep watch around the fort while the festivities were underway. They should be mounting up in a few minutes.

Davie dusted off his dress uniform and crouched in the bushes. He hoped he could time this right because the fuse would burn quickly. It was all a matter of timing.

Discordant notes of music from the mess hall assailed his ears. The orchestra, which would play tonight, some soldiers and some locals, was already tuning up.

Soon, the ladies would bring the food. Then, the celebrants, soldiers, citizens of Brackettville, neighboring ranchers, and all the Mexican citizens they'd invited, would arrive.

He'd been surprised when his few words with Captain MacTavish had been taken seriously by the commander. They'd been sent into México on a mission, and it had been clever of Lieutenant Colonel Gregor to invite the neighboring *hidalgos* and *alcaldes*, hoping to find a connection with the bandits who had attacked the stagecoach line.

Colonel Mackenzie was still revered on the border for having pursued hostiles and outlaws, of both Mexican or American origin, who made their livelihood by preying on local towns and ranches. His had been a heavy handed approach, raiding into

México and meting out "justice" to anyone who fell under suspicion.

But there had been objections by the Mexican government concerning Mackenzie's approach, and he'd been transferred to fight hostiles on the Llano Estacado, in what was known as the "Red River War."

The War Department must have chosen Lieutenant Colonel Gregor for his even-handed approach, hoping he could keep the fragile peace Mackenzie had wrought, while facing any new threats with discretion and a focus on proving who the real predators were.

Davie had used his Spanish while in México, kept his eyes opened, and tried to befriend the Mexicans. To his way of thinking, most of the *hidalgos* and *alcaldes*, had appeared blameless. There were two places which had given him pause, the largest ranches, south of the border: the Márquez spread and the de Los Santos operation.

At both these ranches, the men and their bosses had seemed secretive and guarded. Even so, their owners had been invited to the fort's July Fourth celebration. Javier Márquez had promised to attend, but Miguel de Los Santos had been ailing, and Davie didn't know if he would travel to Fort Clark.

He patted the pockets of his dress coat, checking to make certain the two bottles of expensive French brandy, from the commander's own stock, were still there and safely stoppered. Tonight, he would be approaching as many of the Mexican guests as possible to offer them brandy and to make small talk, trying to gather information. The commander hoped he might turn up some clue as to who had sent the bandits to steal the fort's payroll.

Two other west-bound stages had made it through safely while they were in México but that proved nothing. At some point in time, whoever was behind the earlier raid would probably try again, unless they learned of the new way the fort's wages were being transported.

Not only was Davie supposed to ferret out who was behind the raids, the commander hoped they could discover who was giving the Mexican outlaws their information. It was a tall order. There were four of them, counting himself, Captain MacTavish, First

Lieutenant Bullis, and Second Lieutenant Gordon, who had known how the commander had decided to move the payroll.

The line sergeants hadn't been privy to the change. In order to contain who was under suspicion and who wasn't, the commander had decided that Dawes, even though he'd been promoted to Davie's old position, wouldn't be given the new orders until they uncovered who was in collusion with the Mexicans.

No matter how little Davie liked Dawes, he doubted the man would stoop to a criminal act, but the commander had been adamant to keep the knowledge contained.

A door slammed shut, and First Sergeant Felix Dawes emerged from his cabin. He secured his sidearm and checked his carbine. The twelve men of his patrol had formed on the parade ground, waiting for him.

The front door slammed again, and his wife, a thin blonde, who was holding an infant, came out and kissed his cheek. Dawes stroked her cheek and leaned close, saying something to her. He bent forward and kissed the baby's forehead.

Davie's heart turned over in his chest. A mixture of strange emotions coursed through him: envy for the Dawes family life, something he might never have, along with a sudden sense of shame for what he was about to do.

But he'd come this far, and there was no turning back. He pulled out a match and struck it against a rock. It flared. He put the match to the end of the fuse and crossed his fingers, silently counting under his breath.

Dawes came down the front steps and put his carbine into the scabbard, tied to his McClellan Army-regulation saddle. He looked back at the mounted men, massed there, waiting for him. Luckily, he didn't look down.

Davie watched the seemingly-slow crawl of the flame along the fuse. He fisted his hands, fingers crossed, and waited. The fuse needed a few more seconds.

Dawes swung into the saddle and gathered his reins. He shifted his bulk and checked his stirrups. It was going to be close... very close. Davie knew it would be a matter of seconds between success and failure.

Bang! Pop! Crack!

The string of firecrackers sounded loud, despite the orchestra tuning up and a herd of women descending on the mess hall, carrying dishes, platters, and pans.

Dawes' dun gelding jerked his head up, and his wide-set, brown eyes rolled back in his head. The horse neighed and stomped his hooves. Then the gelding reared, pawing the air. Dawes stuck with him, but the firecrackers kept going off.

Terrorized, the dun flung himself into the air, twisting and sun-fishing, coming down into a series of crow-hops. He lifted off the ground again and bowed his back, bucking harder than a wild mustang, fresh off the prairie.

Dawes went sailing through the air, landing in a heap in front of Corporal Livingstone's mount.

The firecrackers were done—a hushed and appalled silence fell over the twelve men. The women's auxiliary halted to watch. They stood in a ring, gazing down at the crumpled form of the First Sergeant.

Private Bates dismounted and grabbed the dun's reins, hauling the horse close and talking low to him. The horse sidled and snorted, neighing and tossing his head. Bates hung on, and the gelding finally settled down.

A titter came from one of the women, and then a ripple of chuckles swept the crowd, and within a matter of seconds, everyone was laughing. The laughter rolled through the mob in waves.

Davie stood, showing himself. He threw his head back and slapped his thighs with both hands. He doubled over, laughing so hard tears rolled down his cheeks.

He'd gotten his own back!

Dawes groaned and scrabbled in the dirt. His left leg looked odd, bent behind him. His wife, still holding their baby, came hurtling down the front steps of the cabin and kneeled beside him, sobbing.

Dawes tried to lever himself off the ground. He sank back with a groan. He clutched his left leg and moaned.

Corporal Livingstone turned to Isabel Garza and barked an order, sending her scuttling for Dr. Irving.

Slowly, the seriousness of the situation settled in. The laughter died down.

Shame swamped Davie. His neck and face heated, and he knew he must be as red as a beet. And most likely, he'd lost his last stripe. He wouldn't complain—knowing he deserved it. He hadn't meant to hurt Dawes, just scare him a little. Who would have thought the dun could buck like a half-wild bronco?

When Davie lifted his head, he saw Crissy, standing in the crowd of women with her hand covering her mouth. She met his eye and glared at him. Shaking her head, she turned away.

Now he'd done it.

The small hope he'd had of getting back with Crissy shriveled. He'd gone by the commander's cabin to see her, as soon as he'd returned from México, but she'd refused to talk to him, saying she had work to do.

He'd hoped to dance with her tonight. Maybe talk some. Now that wasn't going to happen. But he couldn't stop thinking about her—being away from her had made him realize he wanted her more than anything. They needed to talk, to figure out what kind of life they could make together.

It would seem, though, she didn't want anything to do with him. And that hurt. He knew he'd hurt her, too, not knowing his own mind.

If he hadn't been ordered to speak with the Mexicans and watch for suspicious activity, he wouldn't have attended the celebration. With the way he was feeling, he'd prefer to creep off and dig himself a hole, hiding out like a hunted prairie dog. But he didn't have that option.

Losing Crissy's admiration and affection made his chest ache and tied his stomach into knots. He was miserable, and it was his own fault.

What did he have to celebrate?

* * *

Crissy placed the platter of cornbread on one of the long tables and dusted her hands. She arranged the red-and-white checkered napkins around the golden squares, hoping to keep them warm.

The ladies' auxiliary had tasked every woman who lived on or near the fort with cooking tonight. She and Peggy had offered to make cornbread, and the commander had allowed them to use the spacious oven in his kitchen. They'd cooked pans and pans of cornbread, and she still had another large platter to fetch.

She'd been surprised, at first, when Katie MacTavish, the president of the ladies' auxiliary, had approached her to help. She'd not expected to be welcomed by the officers' wives. But, so far, it would seem her being chosen by the commander to keep his house had conferred her a kind of special status.

The women of the fort treated her as one of their own, obviously prepared to forget and forgive, which made her feel like a part of a larger society for the first time in her life since she'd left the convent.

Her mother and Dr. Irving would not be attending the dancing tonight, due to her mother's delicate health. Or was it simply an excuse?

Crissy knew better. Her mother was proud of her daughter's new position and acceptance by the community. She didn't want to do anything to upset the situation.

On one hand, Crissy felt badly for her mother. On the other hand, she knew her Mama was, as always, prepared to make any sacrifice, wanting her daughter to have a better life than she had.

Peggy was staying with the other children who were too young to attend the dancing and adult celebration, which included the drinking of alcholic beverages. Katie MacTavish and four young girls, under the age of fifteen, were watching the children and keeping them busy, playing games.

Later, around ten o'clock, when the fireworks were set off, the children would be brought out to watch the sparkling displays over the parade ground. After the fireworks, it would be "lights out" for the children, while the adult dancing and revelry would continue into the wee hours of the morning.

Americans and Mexicans alike, from over one hundred miles away, had come for the celebration, some staying at the hotel in town, and others, camping out. No one was sure how many people would show up, but one thing was certain, the celebrating would go on most of the night.

The commander had said he'd make a brief appearance, but he wouldn't stay for long, being in mourning.

Dr. Irving trotted past her, black satchel in hand. He tipped his hat and headed to the Dawes' cabin. The soldiers had carried Sergeant Dawes, with his obviously broken leg, into the family's cabin.

Corporal Livingstone had been reassigned to head up the patrol, and the troop of men were leaving the fort now.

Davie was childish and vindictive. He'd done what he'd said he would do, get back at Dawes. He couldn't let well enough alone. Couldn't forget and forgive.

She'd been wise to break off with him. He wasn't the stuff of serious husband material. She should know from her mother's experience, and she didn't want to repeat the mistake of marrying a man who wasn't ready for the responsibilities of wedded life.

Her mother disagreed, saying Davie was the man for her based on those blasted cards. Crissy snorted. Stuff and nonsense.

She might never marry, fulfilling her dream of returning to the convent. Or she might use her new position to gain experience as a housekeeper and offer her services elsewhere when the commander was transferred.

Her life lay ahead of her—and good things were happening. Soon, she'd have enough money saved to move her mother to a small adobe house for rent beside Jubilee Jackson's place.

She couldn't wait to have their own place and move from under Maxine's gossipy grip. In a couple of more weeks, she'd have the money for a deposit and the first month's rent.

By the time she returned with the last platter of cornbread, the orchestra had started the music with a lively Virginia reel. Several couples were dancing, the tables were sagging with food, and a line for the food had already formed up.

Crissy untied the apron at her waist and tucked it beneath a table. She smoothed the skirt of her new ice-blue, moiré silk dress. As soon as she knew they had enough money for necessities, she'd purchased the gown.

She'd bought the dress as a balm to her spirit after she and Davie had argued. And... because she had the money. It was worldly conceit on her part, she knew, but she was tired of her worn-out, handmade cotton and wool dresses in drab grays and browns.

Her mother and Dr. Irving had both approved of her purchase, saying how lovely she looked. It had pleased her mother, seeing her daughter dressed up, which made Crissy happy.

She gazed at the mess hall, transformed as it was, by the ladies' auxiliary. The rafters were festooned with red, white, and blue bunting and behind the orchestra, was a huge American flag. Streamers of red, white, and blue hung from the rafters, too. And the serving tables were lined with cardboard depictions of the United States flag.

She loved holidays—holidays of all kind. Her parents had always made holidays special. The Fourth of July was fun, but her favorite holiday would always be Christmas.

It had been a magical time in San Antonio with *luminarias* lining the walkway beside the river, and the *Noche Buena Posada* on Christmas Eve, where the local town folk went from house to house, asking if there was room for the Holy Family. Her parents had always surprised her with a special gift on Christmas morning. They hadn't had much money to decorate, but she remembered her mother going to the market and getting greenery, along with red-berried holly branches.

The ladies of the auxiliary hadn't included her in the decorating, only asking her to help cook. But that was all right; she knew it would take time for them to accept her fully. At least, she was no longer living in the shadows.

She glanced at the crowd of Mexicans huddled on the opposite side of the hall. Most of them hadn't lined up for the food. She wondered if they'd already eaten or didn't like American cooking, having heard they preferred spicy food with lots of hot peppers.

It was strange, after the savage attack on the stagecoach, Commander Gregor had invited them to celebrate an American holiday at the fort. Being a good-hearted man, she knew he wanted to find a middle ground with their neighbors to the south, but she was surprised to find them included in the Fourth of July celebration.

The Mexicans were flamboyant dressers, even the men. Some wore wide-brimmed *sombreros*, others affected various versions of the cowboy hats worn on this side of the border.

The men sported white cotton shirts, partially covered by short, open vests, which were heavily braided and embroidered. Along the inseams of their close-fitting trousers, there was more braid and gold or silver ornamental buttons. Their trousers were slit at the bottom, some with lace-filled insets. And the tightness of their trousers made her face heat, leaving very little to the imagination.

The Mexican women, especially compared to their American counterparts, were dressed in a showy manner, like their men. They had tall, ornamental combs in their hair, covered with yards of the finest filigreed black lace, trailing down their backs. Their white cotton blouses were frilled and ruched and cut low in the front. And their multi-colored skirts were large and bell-shaped with a plethora of petticoats beneath and festooned with much gold and silver braid.

Gazing at the Mexicans and their colorful costumes, she smoothed her own skirt. She was pleased that large bell skirts were no longer the fashion in the States. Now a more svelte silhouette was preferred, conforming to a woman's natural figure. Still, she'd had to purchase and wear a corset for the gown to fit properly.

She wasn't accustomed to wearing a corset, being slender enough to wear her everyday work dresses without one. The whale-boned corset chafed and made her take short, quick breaths. But she was proud of her dress, knowing it was one of the prettiest gowns at the celebration.

The opening reel was followed by a square dance, and next, the orchestra played a lively polka. The Mexicans joined the polka, entering into the dancing for the first time.

Betsy McDuff elbowed her in the side and inclined her head. "Aren't you going to help with serving? Or will you just stand there, staring at those Mexican bucks?" She rolled her eyes. "I don't know what the commander was thinking, inviting all these foreigners to our Independence celebration."

Crissy jumped, startled from her thoughts. Betsy could be crude, but she *had* been staring at the Mexicans and thinking much the same thoughts. She glanced around and realized most of the ladies' auxiliary was helping people to fill their plates.

"Oh, I didn't know." She turned to Betsy and stared at her worn-thin yellow poplin dress. "What are you helping with?"

"Me? Nothing." Betsy fluffed her blonde hair. "I wasn't asked to contribute to the food. I'll not be serving." She smiled, a tight, smug smile. "You've been included because you're working for the commander. You'll need to fall into line."

Crissy bridled at Betsy's pointed comment. But she refused to let the other woman get under her skin. Instead, she nodded and fetched her apron, tying it around her waist again.

She approached Lieutenant Bullis' wife, Pattie, the vice-president of the ladies' auxiliary. Pattie was serving the line of people by ladling out pinto beans.

Tapping Pattie's shoulder, she asked, "What would you like for me to serve, Mrs. Bullis?" She wasn't comfortable with using the officers' wives first names. "I brought the cornbread."

"Oh, Crissy, thank you for asking, but I believe we've enough help." She inclined her head at the line of ladies serving. Then she hesitated and glanced at the end of the table.

"Though, I wonder if we'll have enough napkins for everyone." Pattie turned and looked at her. "You used to work for Isabel. Do you know if she's got more napkins laundered?"

"No, I don't, but I'll find out."

"Thank you," Pattie said. "Lordy, what a mob. Who would have thought?" She glanced at the Mexicans and arched her eyebrows. "Our commander is an unusual man, no doubt."

"Yes, he is."

She was singularly devoted to Lieutenant Colonel Gregor. He was a good and kind man—a fair man. He'd changed her life, and though she might question his decisions, as others did, he had her loyalty.

She had no idea where she would find Isabel, but the laundry, though the celebration was underway, was the obvious place to start.

Letting herself out the back door of the mess hall, she walked along the path to Sudsville. She didn't miss the hard, back-breaking days at the laundry. But with a couple of exceptions, like Betsy, she missed the easy camaraderie of her fellow laundresses.

She saw Isabel, hurrying along the path with a straw basket slung over her arm.

"Isabel, are those napkins in the basket? I hope so," Crissy said.

"Good evening to you, Miss."

"Oh, uh, good evening, Isabel." She hesitated, wondering at Isabel's sharp tone. "Mrs. Bullis asked for more napkins and since I worked in the laundry—"

"Something you've apparently forgotten until Lieutenant Bullis' wife reminded you."

Crissy stepped back; her feelings hurt. "I'm sorry. But I came to you, the first day I knew I'd be working for the commander and let you know."

Isabel pushed past her and stopped, shifting the basket to her other arm. "Of course, you did. You had to give me notice to replace you..." She nodded. "Though a day's notice was—"

"Isabel, I had no choice. Commander Gregor's wife had died, and his daughter needed someone to take care of her. He wanted me as soon as possible. I'm sorry I wasn't able to give you more notice."

Isabel sighed. "Oh, Crissy, you're right." She reached out and touched Crissy's arm. "Maybe, I'm a bit jealous." She shook her head. "I'm surprised you haven't been to Mass the last few Sundays. I've missed you, and I wanted to talk to you."

"Yes, Mass." Crissy bit her lip. "Sundays are a problem, and it's something I need to bring up with the commander. I need Sundays off. He goes to chapel with his daughter, but he expects Sunday dinner to be ready when they return."

She swallowed and licked her lips. "I hate to ask him, knowing how grief-stricken he and Peggy are. But as good and kind as he is, I'm surprised he hasn't thought about my needing time off. He expects me seven days a week." She tried to smile. "Not even in Sudsville, did we work seven days."

Isabel touched her arm again. "It's a delicate situation. I understand. But yes, I believe you need to bring him to his senses. He's not thinking, that's for certain. Typical man." She clucked her tongue. "I think I can help you. Several of the unmarried Misses would love the extra money so you could have some time off."

"Not Betsy, please."

Isabel's smile widened. "No, I won't send *her*. She'd make trouble. She's jealous of you."

"Really?"

Isabel laughed. "Of course, silly." She took Crissy's shoulders and held her at arm's length. "Look at you! You're a vision in your new gown." She pulled Crissy closer and hugged her. "I'm proud of you. You're beautiful, decent, and honest. What you did, confessing about your mother was..." She took a deep breath. "It was more than brave."

Crissy flushed at the compliment and returned the woman's embrace.

Isabel stepped back. "You did the right thing, Crissy." She shook her finger at her but smiled at the same time. "But don't go off and forget your old friends."

"No, I promise not to forget my old friends, especially you, Isabel."

"Good." Isabel took her arm. "Let's get these napkins to Mrs. Bullis, shall we?"

"Of course."

They walked back to the mess hall. Isabel took the napkins to Mrs. Bullis, who thanked her.

Crissy took up her place behind the serving tables, wanting to help if she was needed. This time, she didn't remove her apron.

The dance floor was crowded—the orchestra was playing a two-step and it looked like everyone was dancing, including the Mexicans.

But not all of the Mexicans were dancing, particularly the men, who outnumbered their women, two-to-one, like her fellow Americans. Crissy had often wondered, since there were fewer women on the frontier, why men didn't treat their women better, cherishing and taking care of them?

Unfortunately, the frontier was a place, which attracted rogues and bad men who'd fled the States to escape their sketchy or criminal pasts.

Speaking of rogues, she glanced up and saw Davie moving among the Mexican men, taking them to one side and speaking with them. Davie was Irish, and most of the Mexicans only spoke Spanish.

What on earth was he doing?

She saw him pull out a stoppered bottle and offer it to one of the Mexicans. Why was he offering them liquor? It was a recipe for disaster, to her way of thinking.

She crossed her arms over her chest and backed up a few paces.

As if he'd materialized by magic, one of the fancy-dressed Mexicans stood in front of her, bowing from the waist.

"*Me llamo es* Carlos de Los Santos," the man said. "*Por favor, perdóneme*, my English, she's not so good." He held out his arms. "I wish to dance with you."

She hesitated. She really didn't want to dance with anyone but Davie. Unfortunately, that wasn't going to happen, considering how he'd treated her and her determination to forget him.

"Of course," she said, offering her hand and nodding. "My name is Miss Shannon."

He bowed over her hand, murmuring something in Spanish. He gathered her into his arms and led her to the dance floor.

They joined the other couples, dancing the two-step. For the women, it meant two steps back and one step forward, a kind of dip and then repeat, moving around the dance floor in a box-like formation. She smiled at her partner and tried to relax, but it was hard.

Carlos' hand strayed below her waist, resting on the top of her buttock, and she felt her face heat. She angled her body away, making him accommodate her. He moved his hand back to her waist.

Their gazes caught and held. He was a handsome man with licorice black eyes and long, dark brown hair. And his dancing was as flamboyant as his clothes, with lots of dips and turns. She didn't know much about dancing. All she knew was to hang on and follow him as best she could.

After two dances, a corporal, whom she didn't know, cut in.

Carlos murmured, "*Hasta la vista*," and gazed into her eyes.

He surrendered her to the soldier. Next, she was assaulted by a number of privates and corporals, eager to dance. She'd never felt admired before or desired...

No, that wasn't true. She'd felt all those things in Davie's arms. But them being together was over.

She needed to take charge of her life. Davie was no longer a part of it. And she had new challenges, like getting time off from the commander. Though, to be fair, he had given her tomorrow off, knowing the new Catholic church was being consecrated.

Carlos came back, bowing low over her hand and asking her to dance again. She wanted to refuse him, looking around for another soldier, but they were all occupied, already dancing or standing on the sidelines, drinking from small metal flasks.

She sighed and nodded.

He took her hand and gripped her waist. This time, it was a fast polka, and he spun her around the floor. And this time, he was the perfect gentleman, keeping his hand on her waist.

He said, "*Muy bueno*, you dance very good, *Señorita* Shannon."

She smiled back. "Thank you. Uh, *gracias*," she remembered the simple Spanish word.

Then she saw Davie again, and his gaze followed her and Carlos around the room.

Chapter Seven

Davie watched Carlos de Los Santos swing Crissy around in a spirited polka. Of all the Mexicans, he wished de Los Santos hadn't asked her to dance. He'd been suspicious of Carlos' family in México.

He'd not expected Miguel, Carlos' father, who had been ailing, to accept his invitation and send his son, instead. When he saw Carlos, with his retinue at their fort's celebration, he'd been surprised. And he'd wondered why they'd come?

He was glad when a soldier cut in, taking Crissy away from de Los Santos, who, as far as he knew, was a snake.

But it didn't keep him from approaching Carlos and chatting him up. After some small talk, Davie invited Carlos outside for a drink.

He smiled at Carlos and offered one of the brandy bottles. "*Por favor*, take a sip. I bet you'll like it."

Carlos took the bottle and tipped it up, gulping down several swallows of the strong liquor. "*Gracias*." He wiped his mouth. "Excellent brandy, *Señor*." He bowed. "I'm appreciative."

The orchestra ended with a flourish, declaring an intermission, and they both looked up. Commander Gregor, in his dress uniform and with a black armband on his left arm, entered the mess hall.

A respectful hush fell over the crowd.

He climbed the dais and stood in front of the orchestra. Then he snapped to attention and saluted. All the soldiers, mostly in uniform, came to attention and returned his salute.

He cleared his throat. "I want to welcome everyone to our Fourth of July celebration tonight. I hope you enjoy the food." He inclined his head toward the tables, where there was still plenty to eat. "And the music from our orchestra." He turned around and clapped. The room joined him in clapping, and the orchestra members got to their feet and bowed.

"Later," the commander turned around and continued, "I hope you will watch our firework display. It's a Fourth of July tradition. The fireworks will be shot off over the parade ground, and my soldiers tell me it will be an excellent display.

"I want to thank everyone for coming to celebrate our country's birthday, and especially our neighbors from south of the border." He gazed at the Mexicans who had huddled together again. "I hope this is the beginning of a better understanding with our neighbors, along with working together in peace and harmony."

He smiled and bowed. "Please enjoy yourselves." He descended from the dais, shook a few of the Mexicans' hands, and quit the mess hall.

"A most singular commander," Carlos observed in Spanish. "He is the first of your Army, since the war between our countries, who wants to have peace between us." Carlos cocked his head, as if considering. "And he's lost his wife, too, I understand. How sad for him."

"Yes, I believe Commander Gregor misses his wife very sorely. But, as you say, he's always wanted to foster better relations, here along the border," Davie replied.

"Despite the attack on the stagecoach line?" Carlos asked.

Davie was surprised the man knew the attack involved Mexicans. Away from the fort and across the border, they'd been careful to claim the stagecoach had been raided by Apaches, as the Mexicans had wanted them to believe.

"Who told you that?" Davie asked.

Carlos reached for the flask again. Davie put it in his hand, and the Mexican took it, tilting it back and taking several long draughts. "Is it not common knowledge? The ruse was uncovered. Was it not?"

Davie hadn't been prepared for this. None of the other Mexicans had mentioned they knew the raiders hadn't been Apaches—but Carlos knew.

Was this what he'd been looking for?

But he needed the other part of the equation, and he'd yet to see any meetings between the soldiers and the Mexicans, beyond cutting in on each other to dance. In fact, the two groups took pains to stay separate.

"You're well informed, *Señor*. I'm impressed."

"My father makes certain he's knowledgeable about what happens on this side of the border. It is better to be prepared than surprised." Carlos smiled at him from beneath his bristly mustache. "Wouldn't you agree?"

"Yes, much better to be prepared," Davie said.

The orchestra started up again, playing another fast two-step.

Carlos bowed. "*Hasta luego.* I think I'll join the dance again, *amigo.*" He clapped Davie's shoulder. "I've enjoyed talking with you, *Señor*, and sharing your very fine brandy."

He swaggered across the floor and got to Crissy before anyone else. Davie gritted his teeth. He couldn't fault Carlos' taste—Crissy was far and away the loveliest woman at the dance tonight.

The blue dress complimented her dark eyes and hair and showed off her figure to perfection. Should he cut in? He didn't trust Carlos as far as he could throw him—and not just with his Crissy.

His Crissy.

There it was again. He couldn't let her go. She was his and if it took a lifetime, he vowed to win her back.

He saw another one of the single young women who had been a laundress with Crissy. She was a blonde, and she caught his eye and winked at him.

As jealous as he was feeling, seeing Carlos with his hands all over Crissy, it was high time to return the favor. He tucked the half-empty bottle of brandy inside his coat pocket. He'd already gone through the first bottle and learned nothing. To his way of thinking, Carlos was the one who seemed suspect. And he'd be more than happy to tell the commander of his suspicions.

He crossed the floor and executed a bow. "May I have this dance, Miss...?"

She giggled and held out her hand. "Miss Betsy McDuff, but you can call me Betsy."

He took her hand and put his arm around her waist, pulling her into the stream of fast-stepping dancers. He noticed, as he led Betsy around the dance floor, the celebration, fueled by lots of liquor, was getting louder and rowdier by the minute.

Betsy batted her eyelashes. "You're the Sergeant who keeps getting demoted and promoted again. Aren't you?"

Davie laughed. "You have the advantage."

"Well, I'm just saying. Everyone knows you for something of a prankster around the fort." She stuck out her lower lip and gazed into his eyes. "I like someone with a bit of mischief in them. Keeps things from getting boring and stuffy."

"I'm glad I could provide some amusement."

"The prank you pulled with Dawes was plain grand. He's such an old fuss bucket."

He'd never heard Dawes called a fuss bucket before. Silently, he had to agree. "I'm happy you enjoyed it, as I'll probably be busted down to corporal again." He exhaled. "I didn't mean for him to break his leg. That dun sure can buck."

She tittered and angled her body closer to his, brushing her very full bosom against his arm. He drew back but not before seeing Crissy watching them as she whirled by in Carlos' arms.

He couldn't help but notice Crissy scowling. Good. He hoped her baleful look meant she hadn't stopped caring about him. Still, he didn't dare to ask her to dance, dreading she would turn him down or worse, denounce him for hurting Dawes.

But he wanted to win her back and if he had to fight fire with fire, he'd do it.

The orchestra segued into another fast two-step, and Betsy seemed perfectly happy to remain his partner. Carlos and Crissy were still dancing together. A lot of the earlier dancers had retired to the sidelines to engage in some serious drinking. Two more polkas followed, and then the orchestra struck up another Virginia reel.

Davie watched as Carlos led Crissy to the edge of the dance floor, shaking his head. Obviously, the Mexican was unfamiliar with the steps of a reel.

But Betsy had no intention of letting Davie sit out the dance. She lined up with the other ladies, directly across from him, and they proceeded to swing and do-si-do through the intricate steps, crossing and re-crossing the lines to exchange partners.

When the reel ended with a flourish, the orchestra leader stepped forward, calling out in a booming voice, "Let's all take a break, ladies and gents." He pulled out a pocket watch and glanced at it. "I believe it's time for the fireworks to begin."

Betsy gasped and giggled, pulling a paper fan from her skirts and fanning herself. Davie half-turned and watched Carlos escort Crissy through the front door of the mess hall. The Mexican had attached himself to Crissy like a leech. And now Davie was stuck with Betsy.

She grabbed both his hands and tugged. "Let's go see the fireworks. I can't wait."

Davie held onto one of Betsy's hands, but he didn't take his eyes off Crissy and Carlos. The parade ground was full of people, waiting. Captain MacTavish's wife had brought the children out to watch, and some of his fellow soldiers had carried Felix Dawes onto his porch in a chair.

Dawes sat with his leg splinted and held bent at the knee with a sling-looking contraption holding it in place. Seeing the First Sergeant, he winced.

They didn't have long to wait. The fireworks started with a loud bang and huge blossoms of sparkling lights filling the sky.

The crowd ohhed and ahhed, exclaiming after each display. Betsy hung onto his arm, her face turned up. If he leaned forward but a few inches, he knew he could steal a kiss. Easy as pie.

But he didn't want to kiss Betsy, though her invitation was this side of blatant. Before he'd met Crissy, he wouldn't have hesitated.

Now, he kept his eye on Crissy and Carlos, and when the Mexican put his arm around her waist and pulled her close, he flinched and fisted his hands. It took all of his willpower to not confront Carlos and punch him in the face.

To his delight, Crissy pulled away from the Mexican and bowed her head. They spoke for a few minutes, and without waiting to see the end of the fireworks, she walked toward the front gate, as if she was intent upon going home.

He wanted to go after her, but Betsy brushed up against his arm again, a gentle reminder.

She sighed and pulled back. "You've got it bad. Don't you?"

Not understanding, he asked, "Pardon me?"

"For Miss Shannon. Anyone, even a one-eyed pirate, can see how you look at her." She huffed. "I'd heard she threw you over."

"You heard right."

"Well, then, Davie Donovan, what good will it do to pine after Miss Shannon when we can have some fun. The commander has given y'all tomorrow off. Hasn't he? We've plenty of time to slip away and..."

He turned to Betsy and squeezed her hand. "I thank you for the offer." He shook his head. "But it wouldn't be fair to you."

He saw, from the corner of his eye, Carlos walk toward the Dawes cabin, disappearing into the bushes he'd hid himself in earlier. The Mexican seemed intent upon going around to the back of the house, from the way he was angling through the underbrush.

That was interesting.

"Betsy, duty calls, and I can't explain." He needed to go after Carlos but stay hidden.

"Duty? You're going after her. Aren't you?"

"Shhh." He put his finger to his lips and glanced around to see if anyone had heard Betsy's outburst between the fireworks. No was watching them, but you never knew. "I'm not going after her, Betsy, but I do need to leave."

Feeling badly for how he'd encouraged her in the hope of making Crissy jealous, he leaned forward and kissed her cheek. "Enjoy the rest of the fireworks."

He glanced back over his shoulder to find Private O'Rourke sidling up next to Betsy. Not too surprising—considering the private's reputation and Betsy's willingness. They were meant for each other.

Davie followed after Carlos, careful to keep his distance, realizing the Mexican would be watching his back. Carlos retraced his steps to the mess hall and entered a copse of trees, which looped behind the Dawes' cabin.

Moving as quietly as possible among the dark trees, Davie circled behind the Dawes' place and drew up short. Felix had cleared a space behind his cabin for a garden. He could see the back door of the cabin, and he spotted Carlos, too, leaning against the house with his arms crossed, puffing on a thin cheroot.

Davie hunkered down to wait. The fireworks were reaching a dazzling finish with one bottle rocket after another slashing across the dark sky, resounding with loud pops and bangs. The children cheered, and everyone clapped.

He glimpsed a crowd of people pouring back into the mess hall. Soon after, the orchestra struck up again. This time, they played the first waltz of the night. He wished he was dancing with Crissy. He'd dreamed of taking her in his arms and waltzing her across the floor, winning her over again.

But it wasn't meant to be. She'd gone home early and here he was, crouched behind a tree, spying on de Los Santos to see what he was doing behind Dawes' cabin.

After a few minutes spent swatting mosquitos, a bright shaft of light cleaved the darkness. The back door of the Dawes' cabin opened, and Felix stood there, silhouetted against the light, standing on his right leg and leaning on a thick stick with his splinted left leg suspended in the sling.

It was awkward for him to move, but given the circumstances, Felix had no choice. And he hadn't brought any of his fellow soldiers with him.

The back door closed, cutting off the light.

Davie inched as close as he could to the edge of the trees, but the Dawes' garden was several yards long.

Carlos sauntered over to Felix, and they put their heads together.

Davie strained his ears, but he couldn't hear a word of what they said. But seeing them together, talking in the dark, was more than enough.

As much as he despised Felix and his low-down ways, he would have never, in a blue moon, dreamed he was the man who'd been selling information to the Mexicans.

Carlos slipped away, going the opposite direction from the mess hall, keeping behind the row of cabins, and glancing over his shoulder. Dawes hobbled to his back door and opened it, going inside. For all anyone knew, he'd been in his backyard, answering a call of nature.

Seeing the two men meet in secret wasn't proof positive because he'd not heard what they'd said, but it was enough to take to the commander. And the sooner, the better, especially after he'd broken Dawes' leg.

Trouble was, would Commander Gregor believe him? Or would the Lieutenant Colonel think the coincidence was too convenient?

* * *

Davie knocked on the commander's cabin door. The fireworks had ended about half an hour ago, and Crissy had gone home for the night. He was fairly certain the commander would be getting his daughter ready for bed.

He didn't like bothering the bereaved man at his home, but Gregor had told him to come, any hour of the day or night, as soon as he had something.

Gregor opened the door and glanced at him. "Oh, it's you. Come to take your punishment for your stupid stunt, *Corporal* Donovan?"

Davie winced. He'd been demoted again, but he'd been expecting it.

"I hope you found the time, Corporal, to follow my orders. Or did you drink the brandy and decide to light Dawes' horse on fire."

"I followed your orders, sir." He reached inside his coat pocket and pulled out the half-empty bottle. "I've this left and some news. It's why I'm here." He bobbed his head. "Sorry for disturbing you."

Gregor took the bottle of brandy. "News, is it? This better be good." He opened the door wider. "Come inside, Donovan, and have a seat in the kitchen. I don't want my daughter to hear, and her bedroom is closest to the sitting room. I need to see if she's tucked in."

Davie found the kitchen to the left of the sitting room, but he didn't sit down at the table. Instead, he remained standing, but at ease, with his arms crossed behind his back.

The commander came into the kitchen, mumbling under his breath about his daughter. He glanced at Davie and said, "You can stand if you want, but I need some coffee with maybe a tot of brandy. You can join me if you like or keep standing there." He rubbed the back of his neck. "Being a single man, you have no idea how trying children can be.

"Now Martha's gone, poor child cries herself to sleep every night. And she's afraid of the dark, too, since she lost her mother.

I have to leave a lamp burning." He grabbed the coffee pot and poured in a ladle of water. "I hope we don't burn the damned house down one night."

"I'm sorry about your daughter. I thought Crissy, er, Miss Shannon was of some comfort."

The commander stoked the fire in the stove and set the coffee pot on it. He turned and gazed at him. "Crissy, is it?" He pointed at him. "She's a good, kind girl. Pure, too." He waved his hand. "Bugger her mother's past. You'd best not lay a hand on her, Corporal."

"Yes, sir. Uh, I mean, no, sir." He bowed his head. "That is, my intentions are honorable, sir."

"Honorable, you say? Are you thinking of marrying Miss Shannon?"

"If I can convince her." He'd not wanted to drag Crissy into this, but now there seemed no help for it. "We've had a falling out, though, I plan on winning her back."

The commander fetched two china cups and a saucer with sugar lumps. It was odd, seeing his commanding officer, puttering around the kitchen.

"You'll get married, and I'll lose my housekeeper." Gregor shook his head. "I don't know as you'll have my blessing, if you manage to win her back."

Davie couldn't believe what he was hearing—the commander might stop his marriage? Then what would he do? His heart clenched, and he felt perspiration pour down his backbone.

"But sir, it doesn't mean Crissy can't be your housekeeper, if I'm not transferred." It would be a blessing if the commander could use his influence to keep him at Fort Clark, especially given Crissy's ailing mother. "Plenty of the officers' wives work."

"That's true." The commander poured two cups of coffee into the fragile china, sans saucers and added a shot of brandy to each. "Sit down, Corporal. I'll not be craning my neck, looking up at you."

Davie sat and cradled the fragile cup in his hands.

"You'd not keep Crissy from working if you married?"

How had they fallen into discussing his love life and possible marriage? He didn't know if he could win her back, though, he'd walk through hell and back, trying.

"No, but if she had a baby, she'd need a few weeks to recover. After that, she could come back. Wouldn't your daughter enjoy having a baby around?"

Gregor added two lumps of sugar to his coffee. He cocked his head, as if considering. "Yes, my Peggy loves babies. We had a situation at Fort Concho, rescued a young woman from the Comanche, and she had a baby. The young lady and her baby stayed with us for a time. Peggy and my wife..."

He hesitated and frowned, averting his face. "Yes." He nodded, having gotten his features under control again. "A new baby might be the tonic my daughter needs." He smiled and lifted his cup. "But I think we're getting ahead of ourselves. You need to marry the girl first."

"Yes, sir."

"And I need to know what you found out. Was it the Márquez clan or de Los Santos? I was surprised to learn his son came in his place."

"Me, too, sir. And it's the de Los Santos. I don't have irrefutable truth, but—"

"What have you got?"

"A meeting during the firework display, in the dark, between Carlos de Los Santos and First Sergeant Dawes."

Gregor slammed the fine china cup on the table.

Davie flinched, almost certain the cup must have cracked.

"The hell you say, Corporal! Or should I bust you back to private? You're expecting me to believe the same soldier who turned you in for gambling, and then you broke his leg by setting off firecrackers under his mount—he happens to be in cahoots with the Mexicans?"

Davie licked his lips and wished he had the brandy back and could chug it down. Under the circumstances, he thought it best to stay as calm as possible.

He met the commander's gaze, head on, not flinching. "Sir, that's what I thought when I saw them together. I wondered how it would seem to you?"

The commander wiped his face with his hand and muttered something under his breath. "All right, let's say I believe you—they were meeting in the dark behind Dawes' cabin. But the man is laid up with a broken leg, for Pete's sake."

"Yes, sir. He used a thick stick as a crutch and let himself out his back door. He didn't have to go far. Carlos was there, waiting for him."

"Did you hear what they said?"

"No, sir. Dawes has a long garden patch behind his cabin. I was in the trees. I got as close as I could, but I couldn't hear anything."

"Well, it's damned convenient. Isn't it?" The commander got up, poured himself another cup of coffee and added the last of the brandy.

"Drink up, Corporal. I'm considering what to do."

"Yes, sir." Davie raised his cup and drained it, welcoming the burn of the liquor.

The commander set down his cup and stared at him. "Here's what we're going to do. I know I've given the soldiers tomorrow off, but you need to find Sergeant Hayes and send him here. Tell him to keep it to himself."

"But he's with Company E, sir."

"I know. We can't use anyone in Company C, not now. We don't know who is loyal to Dawes and who isn't. Must be somebody outside your company. And Hayes can keep a secret."

"You're right. He's very close-lipped."

"I'm glad you approve, Corporal. You and Hayes will be working together, spelling each other, until you can bring me real evidence of what Dawes is up to." The commander sipped his coffee. "Since holding up the stagecoach didn't get them the money, de Los Santos might not have anything more to do with Dawes."

"But the Mexicans might not know who to believe, sir. Since we killed their men and took charge of the burnt-out stagecoach."

"Hmmm, you might have something there." He stroked the fine china cup. "I hope you're right because if Dawes is a traitor, I will court martial him." He stopped and considered. "Damn shame about his family, though. He has five children." He shook his head. "Damn shame."

"I think it might be why he did it, sir."

"Oh, for the money?"

"Well, he's always been ambitious and open about the fact he doesn't make enough to properly support his family."

"He has, has he?" The commander drummed his fingers on the table.

"Yes, sir," Davie said and added, "Will we be watching Dawes after the Mexicans leave—to what purpose?"

"They might have another way of signaling each other. We can't cross into México and watch de Los Santos. Must be Dawes."

"Yes, sir."

Gregor looked up and snagged his gaze. "You know I have to bust you, Donovan. Otherwise..."

"It won't look right."

"Correct. And you'll need to spend a day in the brig, too."

"Please, sir, can it wait until after tomorrow?"

"Why?"

"I want to go to the consecration of the new Catholic Church. I know Crissy will be there."

The commander stroked his chin. "All right. That's better, anyway, since I've given the soldiers their leisure. I won't need someone to guard you. Makes sense."

"Thank you, sir."

"MacTavish will carry out my orders at the call to colors, the day after tomorrow."

"Yes, sir. But what about spelling Hayes?"

"He can follow Dawes around during the day. You'll take the night shift, after you get out of the guardhouse." He held up one hand. "And no complaining."

"No, sir. I'm ready to take my punishment."

"You better be. Why on earth did you pull such a fool stunt, anyway?"

"Because Dawes snitched on me about playing cards for matchsticks, which to my way of thinking, isn't gambling."

"Maybe, but look what your revenge did. It got out of hand and you broke his leg. Now, everyone feels sorry for Sergeant Dawes."

Davie swallowed a bitter taste in his mouth. Unfortunately, the commander was right—he was a pariah, and now another demotion.

When it had happened, he'd been shamed by what he'd unwittingly done. But when he'd seen Dawes conspiring with Carlos, he'd almost felt vindicated. That wasn't the point. Two wrongs didn't make a right—he'd been brought up better.

Maybe Crissy was right—he should learn to forget and forgive.

* * *

Crissy stood and gazed at the newly-completed Mary Magdalene Catholic Church. She had her arm through her mother's.

The new medicine Dr. Irving had sent for had arrived a week ago, and it was helping. Her mother was coughing less and had more energy, which made Crissy hopeful.

They'd attended the consecration of the new church by Father Fernández. He'd blessed the church and held Mass on the day after the Fourth of July celebration. With most of the fort at their leisure and the church complete, it had seemed like the perfect time, though it was a Friday, and not a Sunday.

She'd noticed both Davie and Carlos in church, but she'd purposely avoided speaking to either one of them. If she had her way, she'd hurry back to their room, but her mother wanted to linger, feeling good to have attended Mass and being welcomed into the church.

As it was, both men stood on the street behind them, as if waiting for the noon stage, which was due from the west.

Father Fernández, with his arms folded into the loose sleeves of his cassock, came toward them, smiling. He stopped and joined them, gazing at the church. "She is beautiful, is she not?"

"Yes, such a lovely tall steeple," Mary said.

"I liked the carving inside," Crissy added, "especially on the altar rail and the pulpit."

The Father's smile faded. "Yes, but did you feel the lectern looked too... bare or plain. In comparison, of course."

Crissy tried to remember what the lectern looked like but failed.

Her mother said, "Yes, I thought it was rather... stark."

Father Fernández sighed. "I couldn't come up with a good design." He rubbed the back of his neck. "But the wood carver has been paid by the San Antonio Archdiocese until the end of the month, and I want to do something..."

The priest shook his head. "But I don't want anything too... elaborate. Something simple, natural, not necessarily religious. More of a lay nature to honor this beautiful country, as the lectern is dedicated to the lay members of the church."

"I will have to think on it before the wood carver leaves for San Antonio." He bowed to them and wandered off, his hands clasped behind his back, studying how the light struck the stained-glass windows.

Crissy smoothed her skirt, thinking about the area's nature and the picture Davie had done. She glanced back at him. He was still there, loitering on Spring Street. He could do with something to keep him busy and a bit of penance, too, after last night.

She cupped her hands around her mouth. "Davie, could you come here for a few minutes."

He started and pointed to himself, mouthing, "You want to see me?"

She almost giggled. Instead, she nodded and cocked her head.

Carlos narrowed his eyes, watching. She wondered what he was doing, hanging around. Most of the Mexicans had left for home this morning, but not the de Los Santos' bunch. It was odd.

Last night, before they'd parted at the firework display, Carlos had asked to escort her to the church's consecration. She'd been surprised he knew about such a thing, but she'd demurred, saying she would be going with her mother.

Still, he'd come anyway, and he looked like he was waiting for something... or someone.

She glanced up to find Davie standing before them. He bowed and gazed at her, catching her eye.

She lifted her hand. "Mama, this is Sergeant David Donovan."

"Soon to be Corporal Donovan," he interjected.

"Oh, I see," she said. "Tomorrow, when everyone is back on duty?"

"Yes, tomorrow."

"Well, it was a stupid stunt."

"Children, children, please." Her mother lifted her hands and looked at Crissy. "Since my daughter has forgotten to introduce me." She put out her hand. "I'm Mary Shannon, and I'm glad to meet you, Davie. Whether you're a sergeant or a corporal doesn't really matter. Does it?"

He took her hand and shook it. "No, ma'am, it doesn't." He bobbed his head. "Nice to meet you."

Crissy bit the inside of her cheek to keep from chuckling. "Sorry, Mama, I forgot myself."

"It seems you did." Her mother nodded. "And I doubt you invited Davie over to meet me. Seems you were thinking about the good Father's dilemma with his lectern."

"Yes, Mama, I was. Did you know Davie is an artist?"

"Hardly," he demurred. "I sketch a bit."

"But you like to draw natural things, like trees and wildflowers, like the picture you gave me," Crissy said.

He blushed. "Yes, I like to draw the wild things around the fort."

"Well, then, I suggest you go to the good Father and offer to come up with a 'natural' kind of design for his lectern."

"Me?" He pointed at himself again.

For the third time, she squelched a giggle. "Yes, you, Davie Donovan. I know you can help Father Fernández." She made a shooing motion with her hands. "Go and talk to him. Tell him you like to draw pictures of the plants and wildlife around here."

"Will it make you happy if I help the Father?" he asked.

"Very happy."

"Will you start talking to me again?"

This time she couldn't help but laugh. "Maybe."

She turned and took her mother's arm. "I've a day off, Mama, and I would love to take a nap. It was a late night, last night. Though, I didn't stay for the end of the fireworks."

"Yes, Crissy, let's go home. I'm feeling a bit tired myself."

Davie nodded and went after the priest. Then Carlos appeared, stopping their progress. He removed his hat and bowed low. "*Señorita* Shannon, may I be allowed to make the acquaintance of your mother?"

She noticed his English seemed to have improved dramatically, overnight. She was disconcerted, though, to have him approach them. She'd hoped he'd stay away, but her calling Davie over had obviously encouraged his forward behavior.

"Of course," she said, lifting her hand. "This is my mother, Mary Shannon."

"Mama, may I introduce Carlos de Los Santos. He and several of the neighboring *hidalgos* from across the border came to our celebration last night."

Her mother stiffened, and she didn't hold out her hand, as she had with Davie. Instead, she inclined her head and in her frostiest tone of voice, she said, "Pleased to meet you, Don Carlos."

For a moment, Crissy didn't know what to make of her mother's strange behavior, and she noticed Carlos was obviously offended, as he stepped to one side and bowed again. "*Señora* Shannon, I'm happy to meet you. I had hoped to ask if I could escort your daughter—"

"Please, Don Carlos, not now. I've been ill, and I'm feeling a bit faint. I think I need to lie down."

His plastered-on smile turned to a scowl, and he bowed once more. "Of course. I hope you feel better, *Señora* Shannon." He turned to Crissy. "We leave at first light tomorrow, and I see you're busy with your mother. But I will return to Brackettville, and I hope to find you again, *Crissy*."

Her mother tugged on her arm.

Crissy said, "Have a safe trip, Carlos." She followed her mother, not daring to reply to his rather pointed comment about seeing her again.

The westbound stage came into sight, throwing up a cloud of dust with its fast churning wheels and galloping team of horses. The stagecoach driver stood up and hauled back on the reins, setting the brake and yelling out, "Whoa, team! Steady up, there! Whoaaa!"

Chapter Eight

Crissy followed her mother into their room and once they were behind closed doors, she untied her bonnet and hung it on a peg. She planted her hands on her hips and turned to her mother.

"I know you think Davie is the man for me, but I've never known you to be rude to anyone—"

"That man, Don Carlos, is not just *anyone*," her mother said, and Crissy thought she heard a tremor in her Mama's voice. "He must be the son of Miguel de Los Santos, and I knew Miguel when he was going to St. Mary's Academy in San Antonio."

Crissy covered her mouth with her hand. "Do you mean—?"

"Yes, Crissy, he was one of my regulars. He was a young man and wild..." Her mother took off her bonnet, too, and threw it on the table. She faced Crissy.

"No, that's not right. Miguel was beyond wild." She shook her head and bit her lip. "I don't want to go into details, but he hurt me, once, and Madame Sally had to have her hired thug, Harvey, stop Miguel from beating me up." She frowned and clutched her hands together, sinking into a chair. "I've never forgotten the incident.

"Miguel was evil. He liked being mean for meanness sake. And his son... there was something about his son, which reminded me of his father." Her mother shuddered.

"Oh, Mama, I didn't know." She went to her mother and embraced her. "I'm sorry. I danced with him a few times last night to make Davie jealous. I don't much care for him, either. Though, I had no idea."

"No, why should you?" Her mother returned her hug. "It happened before you were born, before I met your father." She held Crissy at arm's length. "And if I hadn't met your father when I did, after what happened with Miguel, I believe I might have starved, rather than continuing to... to... sell myself.

"Then I met Renzo, and he became a regular. We fell in love, and he rented a room for us. We had you, and he was talented enough to help build the new mansions in the King William District. He got me piece-work from the rich families, embroidering handkerchiefs, towels, sheets, tablecloths and all manner of things." She took out her handkerchief and dabbed at her eyes. "I'd tried to find work, sewing, when Ian first left me. But I had no contacts, you see."

Crissy sat beside her mother. "I know you tried to make your way, but there was no work—"

"Oh, I found work." Her mother looked up and nodded. "Right enough, as a maid in a big house. But the owner, a wealthy banker, forced me..." She shredded the handkerchief in her hands. "I screamed and screamed, but the banker knew what he was about, dragging me off to the tiny room I had in the attic.

"When I tried to tell his wife... she refused to believe me. They threw me out on the street when I complained. Didn't pay me. I was huddled there..." Her mother tossed the ruined handkerchief aside and got up.

Crissy stood, too. "Mama, you never told me any of this. Why not?"

"Because, Daughter, it was ugly, and I was young and stupid. I should have never waited for Ian until my money ran out. Should have written immediately to my brothers and—"

"You had brothers? I have uncles? But you didn't tell me."

"No, I was too ashamed." She hunched her shoulders. "And now you've but one uncle, my younger brother was killed in the War Between the States." Her mother sighed. "I told you I grew up in a small farming community in the hills of North Carolina. It was mostly Scottish folk who lived there, like my family.

"When the typhoid fever struck, both my Ma and Pa died, along with my baby sister. My older brother, Niall, was already married. He took me in but begrudged me every mouthful of food. Treated me like a servant, he did.

"When Ian came along with his sweet talking and coaxing ways, I thought I'd been saved. We ran off and got married."

"Oh, Mama, I wish I'd known—"

"Why, Crissy? None of my kinfolk were willing to help me. Niall was glad Ian had taken me off his hands. Soon as the wedding night was over, Ian announced we were headed to California. He believed he'd get rich quick." She moved to the bureau and got another handkerchief and blew her nose. "He was always a flighty boy, Ian was, but I had little choice."

She reached into the cabinet and pulled out the coffee pot, filling it with ground beans and water from the bucket they kept in the dry sink. "I didn't think to write to Calum, Ian's brother, until after I'd started working at Sally's. Somehow, Calum found out and refused to send money.

"The Shannons had one of the best farms. It was close to the creek and had good, black soil. Ian sold his birthright, like Esau, for a mess of pottage. Niall bought him out, giving him a grub-stake to go to California, but then he washed his hands of us.

"Calum was tight-fisted, and he wrote back to say since I was a whore, I wasn't welcome at home." Her eyes filled with tears. She stoked the embers in the stove and added some wood. "My brothers were both dirt poor. Still..." She shrugged. "It was too late, anyway."

"But how did you... how did you become—"

"Become a whore? Sally found me, huddled on the street corner and crying, without a penny to my name." Her mother put the coffee pot on the stove. "I thought, despite what she wanted me to do, she was helping me because she was kind. Later, I found out she routinely walked the streets around the big houses, looking for women servants who'd been thrown out or gotten pregnant or...

"San Antonio was a wild frontier town. I should have gone home, as soon as Ian left me there."

"Oh, Mama, I had no idea, all you've suffered."

"And I didn't want you to know. It's why I did embroidery work until I thought my eyes would give out. Renzo's job made us a living, but I wanted to send you to convent school. I didn't want you to see the things I've seen. My embroidery paid for your tuition."

Crissy touched her mother's arm. "Why are you telling me all of this now?"

"Because you're old enough to know and because you have suitors." She took Crissy's hands. "I've been through a lot, but it taught me how to judge men." She squeezed her hands. "At least, I believe so, and Davie is a good man."

Her mother let go and touched the left side of her chest. "I feel it in here."

"After what he did last night? I told you about it, this morning, before church."

"I think he's learned his lesson." Her mother looked up. "You didn't tell me that he's an artist until today. Where's the picture you were talking about?"

Crissy got up and crossed to the cabinet beside the sink. She went on tip-toe and found the paper where she'd left it, wedged in the back of the upper cabinet.

She unfolded the sketch and handed it to her mother.

Her mother spread the drawing on the table and smoothed it with her hands. "Oh, Crissy, you're right. He is an artist! It's so life-like. Why did you hide it?"

Crissy hung her head. "I didn't want to talk about him, not at first, anyway."

"Well, I'm sure he will come up with something beautiful for the lectern."

The coffee pot rattled.

"Would you get us some coffee?" her mother asked.

"Of course, and we've got sugar."

Her mother smiled. "That's good." She gazed at the picture. "Your father was an artist, too, in some ways." She sniffed. "I still miss Renzo. He was such a good man."

She pointed her finger at Crissy. "And I forbid you to have anything to do with Carlos de Los Santos. Do you hear me? He's evil like his father. I know it. Promise me."

"I promise, Mama."

"You need to let Davie back in your heart."

"I don't know about that. I'm happy with my new job at the commander's house and—"

"Having a decent job is important, but it's not the same as finding a good man and marrying him."

"Why didn't you and my father marry? It had been a long time since your husband went away."

"When we moved here, your father and I decided to go ahead and marry, but we didn't want to marry in Brackettville. We'd acted as if we were already married when we came here. We needed to save money to go to Boerne, a small town outside of San Antonio, which had a Catholic church. Before we had the chance, your father had his accident."

Crissy set out two cups, two teaspoons, and the sugar. She grabbed a dish towel and lifted the coffee pot from the stove, pouring two cups. "I guess I won't be taking a nap." She glanced outside. "I need to think about what to cook for supper."

There was a knock on the back door. Crissy looked at her mother and asked, "Were you expecting someone?"

Her mother perked up. "I had hoped Isaiah might drop by. He always cheers me up."

"Oh, Mama, I think you're the one who's falling in love. Not me."

Her mother smiled. "Perhaps. Please, Crissy, open the door and see who it is."

Crissy crossed to the back door, and sure enough, Dr. Irving was standing on the stoop. He inclined his head. "Good afternoon, Crissy. May I come in?"

She opened the door wider. "Mama was hoping it was you."

The doctor smiled and held out an official looking envelope. "I've some news for your mother. It came on the stage."

"Isaiah," her mother said and got to her feet. "Is it what I think it is?"

"Yes, Mary, it's from Sacramento." He handed the letter to her. "I haven't opened it. It's your business; you must read it first."

Mary took the letter, but she lifted her head and glanced at the doctor. He gazed back at her and gave her an encouraging smile.

Mary sighed and seized her teaspoon, turning it around, and using the handle as a letter opener. She unfolded the letter and placed it on the table, scanning its contents. Pursing her lips, she nodded and pushed the letter away.

"Mama, what does it say?" Crissy was anxious to know.

"It was as I suspected. Ian died, shortly after staking a claim on the American River. He was murdered by claim jumpers. His partner survived and reported his death to the authorities." She sighed again and twisted her hands in her lap. "Ian hadn't bothered to tell his partner about his next of kin or where he was from." She shook her head and tears formed in her eyes. "All those wasted years for nothing."

Isaiah sat down beside her. "Not nothing, Mary. You were happy with Renzo, and you have Crissy. She's a good, kind girl and a devoted daughter. You did an excellent job raising her."

Her mother looked up, and he smiled at her. Embarrassed by the unusual praise, she ducked her head.

Mary leaned forward, putting her head on the doctor's shoulder. "You're right, of course, Isaiah, and wise." She held out her hand to Crissy. "I've been blessed by a daughter I can be proud of. It's my lasting legacy."

Crissy moved closer and took her mother's hand. The three of them gathered together around the table. Knowing all of her mother's sad story, she was glad Mama had the doctor in her life.

Mary sniffed and straightened, dabbing at her eyes with her handkerchief. "Thank you, Isaiah, for your help in settling this. It's good to know, one way or another. Though, I believe I knew, deep in my heart. Somehow. Otherwise..."

"Otherwise, Mr. Shannon would have returned to you. He couldn't have been so foolish," the doctor said.

"Perhaps," her mother agreed. She took the doctor's hands. "Won't you stay for coffee and if we've enough, for supper, too, Isaiah?"

"I'd be delighted to stay, Mary, but first, I must ask you something." He glanced at Crissy. "I'm glad your daughter is here."

"Yes?"

"Will you, Mary Shannon, do me the honor of being my wife?" Dr. Irving proposed.

Crissy gasped and covered her mouth with her hand.

* * *

Davie tucked his sketchpad beneath his arm and slipped his lead pencils into the pocket of his dungarees. If he was going to draw something for Father Fernández's lectern, he'd better get busy. He had this afternoon. Tomorrow, he'd be in the brig.

Hayes was on duty, watching Dawes, who had remained in his cabin all morning.

It was a long shot, winning back Crissy's esteem, but he was willing to do anything. He found his favorite rock, overlooking the pond, and settled down.

He glanced around, noticing how the leafy boughs of the trees were outlined against the sky, the way the wild mustang grapevines curled around the tree limbs, and the carpeted grandeur of the wildflowers.

He drew a simple lectern on his pad, wanting to set a frame for perspective, to help him to know what he needed to fill it in. He stared at the paper for a long time. A barn swallow flew overhead, and he had an inspiration.

He bent his head and sketched, his hand hovering over the paper, shapes and contours of the natural landscape filling his vision, dancing before his eyes, as he struggled to put them on paper.

The sun descended from overhead, hovering at the tops of the trees. He'd finished the outline of shapes. Now, he was shading and correcting them, rubbing out misplaced lines and re-drawing them.

He heard the galloping of horses on the slope above him, and he wondered who was coming to the springs. He put his sketchpad to one side and scrabbled to his feet. Through the gaps in the trees, he glimpsed men, most of them wearing wide-brimmed hats... *sombreros*?

De Los Santos and his five companions were the only Mexicans remaining in Brackettville. He'd thought it odd, they'd stayed this morning, when all the other Mexicans had departed. Jealousy being what it was, he'd believed Carlos had remained to see Crissy, and the man had been at the consecration. Carlos had approached Crissy and her mother after she'd sent him to talk to the priest.

But what was de Los Santos and his men doing here, by *Los Moras* Springs? Then he realized what was on the other side of the slope—the Dawes' cabin.

The Dawes' cabin, unlike the new handsome limestone homes, which had been built in the past few years, was one of four of the original log cabins, dating back from before the War Between the States.

Those four cabins had been kept for non-commissioned officers with families because they were the sturdiest and best maintained. Like all the original fort buildings, they clustered close to the springs and creek, making it easy to fetch water.

Realizing what was happening, he drew his Colt. At least, this time, he'd remembered to bring it. He scrutinized his surroundings for anyone else who might be around.

Where was Hayes? Was he close by, watching Dawes?

The copse of trees he'd hidden in last night were at the top of the slope. He made certain his sidearm was loaded. He bent over and ran in a zig-zag fashion, through the trees, climbing slowly and steadily, going as quietly as he could.

A twig snapped to his left, and his head came up. He grabbed his Colt and pointed. He noticed a patch of dark blue among the green leaves. Hayes stepped out with his finger to his lips and inclined his head toward the top of the slope.

Now, there were two of them. But could they get close enough to overhear what was happening? He lifted his hand and pointed, making a circular motion.

Hayes nodded and edged back to the left. Davie angled up the slope, going to the right. He saw Carlos and his men a few yards away. Carlos and one of his men had dismounted and stood beside their horses, waiting among the trees. The other four men remained mounted.

Dawes appeared on the edge of the trees, swinging awkwardly on one leg and with newly-carved, homemade crutches. His broken left leg was still bent at the knee, splinted, and heavily bandaged.

Davie edged closer, hoping Hayes knew to do the same. Finally, a few yards separated him from the secret gathering.

"I told you, I don't know how the next payroll will come," Dawes' voice drifted to him. "I nosed around and found out Commander Gregor no longer uses the stagecoach line."

"How does he transport the money?" Carlos demanded.

"By wagon, over ranch trails, but he changes the route each time." Dawes shook his head. "I couldn't find out which way the money will be coming next."

Carlos made a dismissive gesture with his hand. "You're of no use to us. We're done, Sergeant." He turned toward his mount and gathered the palomino stallion's reins.

Dawes hobbled forward, grunting. "Not so fast, you owe me money. I told you about the stagecoach. It was the way the former commander moved—"

"A useless piece of information." Carlos whirled around and placed his hand on the butt of his holstered pistol. He spat at Dawes' feet. "Why should I pay you for nothing?"

Davie saw the other Mexicans' hands move toward their guns.

It was now or never—and he hoped Hayes knew it, too.

He stood up with his Colt leveled on Carlos' chest and called out in Spanish, "Your guns, *caballeros*, throw them down. ¡*Ahora mismo*!"

Carlos went for his gun, and Davie shot. The bullet whizzed past the Mexican's shoulder and lodged in the silver-embossed saddle on the palomino. The horse neighed and reared. He came down and snorted, taking off down the hill.

Hayes emerged from the bushes and yelled in English, "Throw your guns down!"

He shot at the other Mexican who was standing beside Carlos, stopping him from reaching for his rifle in its scabbard. The bullet buried itself in his horse's neck, and the roan crumpled.

Carlos stared at Davie, and he drew his gun.

Davie shot him between the eyes.

By this time, Dawes was screaming, "Let up, let up! Quit shooting!" He tried to lift his hands into the air but couldn't, needing to hang onto his crutches.

Seeing their leader fall, the remaining four Mexicans threw down their guns and spurred their mounts, galloping away.

Davie took a bead on one and shot him off his horse. Hayes did the same. The other two men were out of range before they could get off more shots.

Dawes had dropped to the ground and was scrabbling in the dirt, sobbing over and over, "Don't shoot, don't shoot. I ain't no Mexican."

The Mexican beside the downed roan, like Dawes, had dropped to the ground and had his hands crossed behind the back of his head.

Davie and Hayes stood over Dawes and the Mexican.

"Search them," Davie croaked.

"Cover me," Hayes said.

Davie cocked his Colt and leveled it, sighting down the barrel, while Hayes checked the two men for hidden weapons. He found a long, wicked-looking knife tucked in the Mexican's boot and threw it away. He discovered a hidden derringer in Dawes' trouser pocket.

Looked like Dawes hadn't trusted the Mexicans.

Hayes glanced up. "That's it. No other weapons."

"Get up. We're taking you both in," Davie said.

"I can explain," Dawes sputtered, clambering to his feet, using the makeshift crutches to lever himself. "I was leading them on—"

"Save it, Dawes. We heard what you said." He punched him in the back with the barrel of his revolver, which still had two bullets in it. "You can explain—to Commander Gregor."

* * *

Crissy heard the knock on the commander's front door. She had a pretty good idea who would be calling at this early hour.

Peggy, who was sitting at the kitchen table, doing her lessons, jumped up. "I'll get it."

"Oh, no, you won't," Crissy said. "You need to keep after those lessons."

She pulled her hands from the sudsy water and wiped them on her apron. She'd been washing the breakfast dishes.

When she opened the commander's front door, it was who she'd suspected. Davie stood on the front porch, holding his wide-brimmed hat in his hands.

"May I come in?"

"No, I think not." She pulled the door closed behind her and joined him on the front porch. She crossed her arms over her chest. "Peggy is doing her lessons, and I've enough trouble, keeping her concentrated without a visitor, especially a visitor who's the big hero of the day."

"So, you've heard."

Of course, she'd heard. Quicker than any telegraph wire, Davie's killing of Carlos, along with his capture of Dawes, had been the first thing Maxine mentioned this morning. Besides, all the fort was buzzing with the news.

"Yes. I heard."

She bit her lip. She'd underestimated Davie, thinking he was too devil-may-care, but his actions told another story. "You're to be congratulated for stopping them." She shook her head. "We don't need any more orphaned Ellies because of men's greed."

Her mother had been right. Carlos had been an evil man, sending his thugs to kill innocent people so they could steal the Army's money. Not to mention what Dawes had done, throwing in his lot with the Mexicans.

"Thank you, I'm glad you approve." She thought she detected the slightest trace of sarcasm in his tone.

"Oh, Davie." She uncrossed her arms. "You're a hero! Do I need to say it out loud?"

He dropped his head. "No, I'm glad I could stop them. I was afraid they'd try again and more people would be..."

"Hurt or killed." She nodded. "You did the right thing."

"Well, I'm glad then."

"Yes." She didn't know what more to say.

Though she might have changed her mind about Davie's frivolous nature—where did that leave *them*? He'd appeared to be trying to make amends yesterday at the consecration, but he still hadn't declared himself or courted her properly.

He rubbed his chin. "I'm to leave within the hour."

"Back to México? But why?"

"No, I need to take Dawes to Fort Sam Houston to be court martialed, along with the Mexican we captured. The Army will have to get with the Mexican authorities to decide what to do with him."

"Oh, I didn't know."

"That's why I wanted to come by and tell you." He shook his head. "And the commander has warned me; these legal things have a way of dragging out. I could be gone for a month or more."

"So long?"

"Yes." He reached inside his jacket and pulled out a folded paper. "I wanted you to have this—for Father Fernández. It's the sketch for the lectern. I hope you like it, and the Father approves."

She took his sketch and unfolded it. She exhaled. "Oh, Davie, it's lovely, truly lovely." She looked up and smiled. "I'm sure the good Father will like it."

He returned her smile. "Sure, and begorrah, it brought me luck—you asking for that sketch. I was drawing when I heard Dawes meeting with the Mexicans. They met behind his cabin, right above the pond, where I was sketching."

"What a stroke of luck!"

"Yes." He stood there, twirling his hat in his hands, and looking decidedly unsure of himself. "Crissy, since I'll be gone for so long, could I kiss you goodbye?"

She thought about his request. He had done her sketch, but he still hadn't addressed their future. *If they had a future? Who knew?*

He might be away for a long time. Just yesterday, she'd learned the true extent of her mother's suffering. She was still having trouble dealing with what her mother had told her.

Besides, every time she let Davie touch her, she turned to water. Better to wait and see if he came back to Fort Clark and what he intended to do.

She shook her head. "I don't think so."

"But..." He looked down again and nodded. "All right. I understand. I'll write you, though. All right?" He lifted his head and gazed into her eyes.

"Yes, I would like that."

* * *

Crissy unpinned Davie's picture from above their bed. Mama had encouraged her to hang it there, saying such a beautiful sketch shouldn't be hidden away. And her mother had been right, despite her ups and downs with Davie, she studied it every night before she went to bed, marveling at his talent. She folded the drawing and tucked it into her apron pocket.

Then she turned and surveyed the room. All their belongings had been sorted and packed, placed in wooden crates. Dr. Irving—

Isaiah—had found the crates for them. There were three crates and her carpetbag left. Those were her things. She was moving in with Commander Gregor and his daughter.

Mama and Isaiah had married yesterday, at the Kinney County Justice of the Peace's home. Her mother was free to marry in the Catholic Church, but Isaiah wasn't a Catholic. It had been a small and quiet ceremony with Crissy and the Justice's wife as witnesses.

They'd spent their wedding night at the doctor's home on the fort. Crissy had been lonely without her mother.

She couldn't help but remember how happy her mother had looked on her wedding day, wearing a plain brown muslin dress, and clutching a bunch of wildflowers Isaiah had gathered for her.

First thing in the morning, Isaiah had sent two privates to haul her mother's things to his home. And the good doctor had offered to have them take her belongings to the commander's cabin, but she hadn't finished packing. She looked around at the shabby room—she'd be glad to leave this place and gossipy Maxine behind.

She sighed and sat down, folding her hands together, wishing she knew what to pray for. Unfortunately, she didn't know what she wanted. She was keeping her job as housekeeper, for now, but with her mother safely married, she was free to return to the Ursuline Convent... to live her life in peace... away from all the ugliness of the world.

Was it what she wanted?

Davie had already been gone over a month. He'd warned her court proceedings could drag out. But he had written her, as he said he would. In his letter, he'd declared his love and asked her to marry him again. It seemed he was more eloquent on paper than in person, about serious things, at least.

Perhaps, if she'd allowed him to kiss her that day, he would have declared himself. But it wouldn't have mattered. Would it?

She didn't know if she wanted to marry anyone—not now. Though, sometimes, when she was lonely, despite the hustle and bustle of the fort, she wished she possessed her mother's resilience and trust.

Someone knocked on the back door. She got up, thinking Isaiah had probably sent back the privates to help. She still needed to roll up the bare mattress to keep it from getting dusty and leave the key with Maxine.

She didn't have any furniture to move, nor had her mother. When her father had died, they'd sold off the few pieces of furniture they'd brought from San Antonio, hoping they could live on the proceeds until her mother found a job.

She sighed again, wondering what was pulling at her in this awful room. All the furniture belonged to the Brackett's.

Slowly, she got to her feet, moving as if she was old and lame. She wasn't, but her spirits were low. Mulling over what she wanted to do with her life, made her feel as if she was walking underwater, moving against a strong current.

She opened the door.

Davie stood on the stoop in his full-dress uniform, twirling his flat-brimmed hat in his white-gloved hands. And he'd won back one of his stripes, too.

Oh, my, he looked good enough to eat—with his turquoise eyes shining and his dimple deepening when he smiled.

She gasped and fell into his arms.

He held her, burying his face in her hair, and kissing the top of her head. "I guess this means you've forgiven me?"

"I guess so."

"And you missed me?"

She snuggled her head into his shoulder, not wanting to let go. Realizing this was what she'd been missing. Now she understood how her mother had overcome her fears and learned to love again.

His touch brought her back to herself, filling her heart with joy. How could she have doubted the strength of what they felt for each other? She reached up and stroked his jaw, reveling in the bristly feel of his chin.

"Of course, I missed you, silly."

He smiled. And then she did something she'd thought about for months—she caressed the deep dimple on the left side of his mouth. He laughed and lowered his head.

She knew he wanted to kiss her. And heaven help her, she wanted him to kiss her, too. But not here, not on the open stoop.

She pulled him inside. The mattress was bare, but it would suffice. Would knowing Davie, in the most intimate sense, put her fears to rest and help her make up her mind? But would she appear wanton, offering herself?

Would he think, as he might have in the beginning, like mother, like daughter? It wasn't quite fair, though, because he had no way of knowing everything her mother had been through.

He followed her inside the room and glanced around. His eyes widened, and she saw a flicker of alarm in the depths of them. "You're moving? Where are you going? Where's your mother?"

She smiled, realizing he'd come straight to her, not stopping to talk to anyone. *He must love her.*

"I guess you haven't heard." She tugged on his hands, pulling him closer to the bed, wanting to feel his skin against hers. Needing the reassuring thump of his heart in her ears. Longing for him to take her and make them one.

"Mama and Dr. Irving, Isaiah, were married yesterday. They've moved into his cabin on the fort behind the surgery. I'm moving to the commander's house." She kissed his cheek. "Hold me, please, Davie, and don't let me go."

"I never want to let you go. I hope you got my letter and—"

"Yes, I received it. Thank you." She stroked his cheek again. "I've missed you so much and so much has happened."

"I'm amazed your mother married," he said. "Is she feeling better?"

"She's much better. Thank you for asking. Isaiah knew how to make her well."

He took both her hands and kissed them. "Oh, Crissy, I'm happy for you and your mother."

She reached up and put her arms around his neck.

His lips captured hers and the touch of him was beyond anything she'd remembered. She kissed him back and drew him forward. When she felt the bed with the back of her legs, she sank into the mattress, pulling him with her.

Davie fell on top of her, and his mouth ravaged hers.

She could feel his male hardness, pressed against her bunched-up skirts. She wanted him, all of him, inside of her. She kissed him with all of the pent-up passion she'd kept locked inside, thesc past weeks.

Davie stroked his tongue inside of her mouth, making her crazy with longing. He put his hand on her thigh and caressed her leg through her petticoats. He lifted her skirts and stroked her calf.

She shuddered, every nerve in her body coming alive. She held him closer, kissing him deeper, twining her tongue with his, encouraging him.

He slid his hand beneath her petticoats and up her thigh.

She trembled, waiting for him to touch her in that most secret of places.

He stopped suddenly and pulled his hand from beneath her skirts. He put both his arms beside her head and pushed himself up, gazing down at her.

"Crissy, it's not supposed to be like this." He shook his head. "I'm over the moon, knowing you want me... but I want you for... forever. Not just for now. Do you understand?"

He nuzzled her neck with his lips, and she caught her breath.

Davie was a good man, an upright man. Not like her mother's first husband or the men who'd used her. Was today about her passion and missing him... or had she, without knowing it, fashioned a kind of test?

She wasn't certain of her motives, except she knew she loved and wanted him.

He kissed her on the mouth and got up. He held out his hands and pulled her to her feet. "There," he said, "let's talk about us and getting married."

She gazed into his eyes. He was asking her outright, to her face, not just in the pages of a letter. Her eyes burned and she struggled to swallow, stifling a sob. "Oh, Davie, you really mean it?"

"Of course, I mean it. Why would you—?"

"My mother... all that my mother has been through." She dabbed at her eyes with the corner of her apron. "I thought you wanted to take advantage of me like my mother had been—"

"Crissy, my Angel." He grabbed her hands. "I heard the gossip about your mother a long time ago." He shook his head. "It meant nothing to me, except for wondering how cruel people could be with your mother ailing.

"I've not been a perfect man, but I never wanted to take advantage of *you*." He wiped his hand over his face. "Being almost thirty and thinking I would stay single and in the Army for life, I'd not thought much about marriage or what it would take."

He squeezed her hands. "I know it made me seem confused or uncertain or... And I know, too, because of what you and your mother have been through, trusting men is probably not—"

"No, you're right, it's been difficult. I remember the day of my sixth birthday. My mother tried to give me a party." She looked down. "But none of my friends came. I was so hurt, I cried myself to sleep. Later, most of the neighborhood girls and my new friends at the convent shunned me. They talked about my mother, saying horrid things. It was then I learned..."

"Oh, Crissy, I'm sorry—"

"And the day of the consecration," she continued, "Mama told me more about her past. How, before I was born, she *knew* Carlos' father and he hurt her, Davie. He hurt her." She gulped and sobbed.

He pulled her into his arms. "Oh, my Angel, I'm so sorry, so very sorry." He kissed her forehead. "I wish I'd known. I'd have killed Carlos' father, too, when we were in México."

She pulled apart a pace. "You would?"

"No man should ever hurt a woman. No matter the circumstances."

"Oh, Davie, you're so sweet." She hugged him.

"Then you'll think about marrying me?"

"Of course, I will." She swiped at her wet face and managed to smile.

"Good." He exhaled. "I'm glad you know my intentions are honorable." He bent his head and kissed her tears away. "Now I want to show you something. I think you'll like it."

He glanced at the packed crates. "Did Commander Gregor give you the day off to move?"

"Yes, he did."

"Let me show you my surprise, and then I'll get these crates moved for you."

She placed her hand in his. "I'm ready. Show me."

He nodded, grinning when he took her arm. He walked briskly, exiting the room, and directing them toward Ann Street where the Catholic Church stood. He stopped in front of the church.

"I know you gave my sketch to Father Fernández, but I was wondering, have you checked on the woodcarver's progress."

"No, I wanted to wait and see the carving when it was finished. Father Fernández promised he would send for me."

"Well, he sent me to fetch you."

"Really?"

"Yes, the good Father saw Hayes and me when we rode into town," he said. "Father Fernández was excited and happy with the lectern, and he knew you wanted to see it. Now, we'll see it, for the first time, together." He paused and grinned. "But I want you to do something for me."

"What?"

"Close your eyes, and I'll lead you inside."

"Oh, really, Davie, don't you think it's a bit silly—"

"No, humor me."

"All right." She closed her eyes and felt his hand covering the upper part of her face. She welcomed his strong arms guiding her and savored the all-male smell of him: of leather and horses, of wool and starched linen.

They walked in tandem for a few moments, and he lifted his hand, saying, "Look!"

She gazed at the gleaming wood of the lectern, admiring Davie's drawing of leaves, vines, and tree branches, alive with birds. And the clever carving showed the rough outlines of a raccoon and a fawn, half-hiding in the curlicues.

She took it all in, how marvelous the lectern looked, and how well the woodcarver had captured Davie's sketch. She turned to him and threw her arms around his neck, tears welling in her eyes. "Oh, Davie, it's beautiful, so very beautiful."

"Yes," he agreed. "I think it turned out rather fine."

Chapter Nine

Davie held her close, returning her hug. He wondered about himself, why he'd turned her down when she'd wished to be... intimate. But he hadn't wanted to take advantage. It was obvious she was especially vulnerable today. And he'd never had a virgin nor an unwilling woman. Not that she was unwilling... but he knew his Angel.

He didn't know what had possessed her to act with such passion—it wasn't like her. He believed she would have regretted it, the minute they'd laid together. The last thing he wanted was to cause her regret or... *fear*.

Given her past reticence, he believed she secretly feared the physical demands of marriage because of her mother's experiences. But now that her mother was married to a good man, maybe it would help Crissy to feel more secure.

Grasping her shoulder, he drew her to his side. "I'm pleased you like it. I tried to draw what you wanted. And the woodcarver has done an admirable job, though, Father Fernández told me it took him an extra week to carve it."

She turned to him and snuggled closer. "Yes, I thought he would never finish." She pulled away and gazed at the carvings again. "But it was worth the wait. It's beautiful beyond measure, and I'm glad."

"Good. I'm happy, if you're happy."

"Really?" She stroked his jaw and turned her face up to be kissed.

He kissed her on the cheek.

She pulled apart and glanced at the lectern again, her eyes going wide. "Oh, Davie, do you know what this reminds me of?"

"Uh, no, I can't say."

"Of Christmas."

"Of Christmas? But it's not quite the end of August." He swatted at a fly. "And still hot as... Uh, very hot outside. How on earth can you think of Christmas?"

She closed her eyes and went very still. "Remember, I asked about Christmas and fairies—the first day we met?"

"I remember everything about the first day. Vividly."

She opened her eyes and regarded him. And he almost lost himself, glimpsing the golden flecks in her tawny eyes.

"Christmas is my most favorite time of year. I guess I never told you."

"No, you haven't mentioned it."

"Well, Christmas was a special time in San Antonio with the decorations, the *luminarias*, and the *Noche Buena Posadas*."

"I've heard of the *posadas*, where people go, with lit candles to their neighbors' homes, asking if there's room for the Holy Family." He rubbed his jaw. "I know some Spanish but what are *luminarias*?"

"They're candles, usually secured in a holder with sand and covered with oil cloths. The Mexicans light the candles at night, and the light shines through the oil cloths. They're enchanting-looking, lining the river in the old part of town."

She grasped his arm and turned toward him. "And there are decorations, especially in churches: wreaths, boughs of greenery, and Christmas trees."

He glanced around. "You're wanting to decorate the church for Christmas?"

"Yes, if you'll help me."

"Of course, I'll help you." And he would, if he'd returned in time.

The commander should be giving him specific orders soon; he hoped they didn't need to be apart for too long.

"What kind of decorations are you thinking of?" he asked.

"I'd like to put wreaths above the pulpit and the lectern. I would drape the altar rail and the pulpit with greenery, mixed with red berries like holly." She bit her lip and tapped one finger against her chin. "For the greenery, we could use *piñon* or cedar.

"Though, I'm not certain what to use for the red berries. I haven't seen holly bushes around here. The wealthy people in San Antonio used to grow holly in their yards. My father would get us a few branches at Christmastime, while working on their mansions."

"You're right. I remember holly bushes. It was the same in Galveston, some of the rich folk had them in front of their porches."

"I don't guess holly grows wild around here. Does it?" she asked.

"I haven't seen any..." Then he had a thought. "Have you heard of a tree called Possumhaw Holly?"

"Possum... what?"

He smiled. "I know it's a silly name, but it's what the locals call it—Possumhaw Holly." He scratched the back of his neck. "I'm not sure how it got the name, and it's definitely a tree, not a bush. You'll find them growing beside cedar breaks, and in the winter, they lose all their leaves, but the branches are chock full of bright red berries."

She clapped her hands together. "That's perfect, Davie, perfect. I can weave the branches in the greenery for the garlands and wreaths. And I can get some velvet fabric and make big, red bows for the wreaths, too."

Her enthusiasm was infectious. "We could line the pathway to the church with the *luminarias*. Father Fernández could light them each night. I can get candles from the sutler," he said. "Or maybe Maxine would like to donate some." His eyes twinkled with mischief, knowing what Crissy thought of Maxine. "We could organize some of the townsfolk to put on a *posada* for Christmas Eve."

"Oh, Davie," she squealed, bouncing up and down. "It would be wonderful. So very wonderful!" She went on tip-toe and kissed his cheek. "I can hardly wait until Christmas."

He smiled at her, wishing Christmas was at hand, and he was safely returned to the fort.

She shook her head. "But I don't know about the Christmas tree. I would love to put one, right here, in front of the lectern."

He stroked her cheek and said, "I don't know much about Christmas trees, either. Where did you get the idea?"

"I had a friend at the convent, Agatha, or Aggie, as I called her. She wasn't Catholic, but her parents sent her to the Ursulines because it was the best primary school in San Antonio."

Crissy widened her big, brown eyes, as if remembering. "One day, before Christmas, she took me to her Episcopalian Church. And right in front of the lectern, do you know what they had?"

"A Christmas tree?"

"Yes, a Christmas tree, decorated with wondrous things." She closed her eyes again. "I can still see it in my head, it was tall and green, and it smelled heavenly. They'd put the tree in front of the lectern, all decorated and bright and shimmering."

"Sure, and begorrah, it's a grand idea." He'd hesitated, uncertain at first, but the happier she appeared, the more he realized he wanted to make her Christmas dreams come true... and more. If everything worked out.

Maybe, if he helped her plan for Christmas in the next few days, she'd not be too sad when he had to leave again.

He tried to remember if he'd seen a Christmas tree, and he finally recalled, when he was a young lad, one of the finer shops in Galveston had a Christmas tree in their store window. He remembered candles, some kind of garland, and the most beautiful, glittering decorations, fashioned like balls and pendants.

He nodded. "Now I remember seeing a Christmas tree once."

"The tree I saw had tiny lit candles, at the end of the branches, in some kind of tin holder," she said.

"I bet the fort's blacksmith could make us some candle holders, if we explain what we want."

"Oh, thank you. How clever."

"What else do you need for the tree?" he asked.

"More garlands, but Mama is a good seamstress. I'm sure she'd be happy to fashion yards and yards of multi-colored garlands. We could ask around town and the fort for rags."

"Sounds like a good idea, but what about the ornaments?"

She bit her lip again. "That's the hardest part—the ornaments—they were quite glorious. They looked like metal, all covered in bright paint and glitter, but Aggie let me touch one of them, and they were light and fragile, made out of glass or something."

It was what he'd remembered, too, when he'd asked the storekeeper about the glittering ornaments. They were glass and painted or dipped. And they came all the way from somewhere in Europe. He couldn't exactly remember where, maybe from Italy.

Galveston was the premier port city in Texas. All kinds of goods passed through his hometown, including lots of luxury items for wealthy customers.

He had planned to write his parents about Crissy tonight, hoping they could come for the holidays to meet her. In the same letter, he'd ask about the glass Christmas tree ornaments and see if they could order them—as long as they arrived in time for the holidays.

He knew the imported ornaments would be expensive, but they'd make Crissy happy. It would be his special Christmas surprise for her. Realizing how much she loved Christmas had given him another idea, too.

"There must be other things you could hang on a Christmas tree to decorate it," he said.

"Yes, I suppose so." She turned to him and half-shrugged. "But I want the tree to be beautiful."

"I'll ask around the fort and see if anyone has ideas."

"And I'll ask the commander. He might have seen a Christmas tree and know what we could use."

She turned away and gazed around thc church, as if she was envisioning it decorated for Christmas.

"I want the decorations to look magical, Davie."

"Like fairy dust?" He winked.

She smiled and turned her face up, begging for his kisses—right here in church. He glanced around, but they were alone.

What would the good Father think?

She returned his wink and puckered her lips, closing her eyes again. "Yes, like fairy dust."

* * *

Davie walked along the rutted road leading to the commander's house. The past two weeks had been as magical as any Christmas Crissy might envision. Each night after supper, they'd walked out together, enjoying the waning summer evenings.

She had her mother's approval, and he had the commander's backing to court her. He was careful to return Crissy before dark, but they'd had plenty of time to kiss, talk, and get to know each other better.

Despite his honorable intentions, there had been many a time he wished he hadn't turned down Crissy's offer in her old room. Sometimes, he wanted her so badly, his whole body ached. In the old days, he would have found a willing saloon girl in town but not now. The thought of betraying Crissy, along with her telling him what her mother had been through, was more than enough to discourage him from touching another woman.

And he knew their marriage had to wait. The commander had sent him a dispatch at Fort Sam Houston, explaining his next mission. It would take several months' time away from the fort. If they laid together, he might get her with child, and she would have to face everyone's condemnation all over again.

She'd managed to overcome her mother's past and put it behind her. The last thing he wanted was to make her a social pariah once more.

Today, he'd finally gotten the orders he knew were coming. It had taken a while for the commander to pull together the necessary men and supplies. And today's stagecoach had brought an answer to the letter he'd written to his parents.

It was long past time to tell Crissy, but he dreaded doing it, knowing how upset she might get. He couldn't help but feel insecure, too, asking her to wait. She was a beautiful woman and could have her pick of single men, now she'd come out from the shadows.

He climbed the cabin's front steps and knocked on the commander's door.

Crissy opened the door at once, as if she'd been waiting for him. She frowned, pulled on a bonnet, and grabbed his hand.

"Shouldn't I greet the commander and Peggy before we go walking out?"

"I've no time for pleasantries, Davie Donovan. I need to talk to you."

She knew.

Not that he was surprised. The fort's gossip grapevine was fast and efficient, relaying news, almost as soon as it happened.

"Where are we going?" he asked.

"I thought, the usual place."

"All right."

She picked up the pace, and he trotted after her. In no time, they arrived at the spring-fed pond.

Crissy let go of his hand and climbed onto the large rock overhanging the water. She sat down and tucked her skirts around her, covering her legs.

He sat across from her and reached for her hands.

She scowled and leaned back, crossing her arms over her chest.

Uh, oh, it was as he'd feared.

Maybe he should have told her sooner. He knew she had trouble trusting men and, by not telling her, had he lost her trust? He hoped not. He hadn't told her because he'd wanted to enjoy their time together, these past few weeks.

They'd spent a lot of time at the pond, kissing and doing what lovers did. He'd made her sit for a drawing—hers was the first portrait he'd attempted. The sketch hadn't done her justice, to his way of thinking, but she'd loved it. He hoped to have more chances to work on his portrait skills, especially drawing Crissy.

"Why didn't you tell me?" she asked without preamble.

"I was waiting for my orders, so I would know more."

"I'm not talking about your orders." She shrugged one shoulder and bit her lip. "Though, I'll miss you, heaven knows. I was talking about the commander and his transfer."

"Oh, that's it," he said.

"Yes, I wish you or the commander would have told me I won't have a job after the end of the year. My job is important to me."

He knew she was proud of her job as the commander's housekeeper. And the job made her feel independent. They'd talked about her continuing to work after they married, and as he'd told the commander, he didn't mind if she did.

Realizing she was more concerned about her job than their being separated, he couldn't help feeling hurt and a strange kind of jealousy, too. Would she be content as his wife and trust him to take care of her for the rest of their lives?

He shrugged. "Commander Gregor's transfer was inevitable, after I killed Carlos."

"Why? He was a bad man, and you were doing your duty."

"Yes, you're right, and the Army recognizes the commander's part in bringing the men to justice." He spread his hands, fingers wide, wishing she'd let him hold her hand. "But the Mexicans don't see it that way. Killing Carlos and two of his men, along with imprisoning the Mexican we caught, has caused a great deal of fervor in México. They're angry and have used the incident as an excuse to raid along the border again. They're targeting remote farms and ranches to exact their revenge.

"They're murdering everyone, even women and children, burning their homes, and driving off their livestock."

She gasped. "But that's horrible and unfair. They're the ones who started this, by killing the passengers on the stagecoach."

He shook his head. "They don't believe one of their rich *hidalgos* would do such a thing. They think we made the story up, to justify Carlos' killing."

"Well, they're wrong. If they'd seen that poor, orphaned child, Ellie—"

"Crissy, people are going to believe what they want to, no matter the circumstances. It's the way of the world."

She sniffed. "I know, but I wish it wasn't so."

He nodded.

"What do these new raids have to do with transferring Lieutenant Colonel Gregor? Someone needs to guard the border and put a stop to the raids."

"The Army and politics, that's what this is about." He exhaled and bent his head. "When Mackenzie, the former commander, put an end to the border raiding by crossing into México and pursuing the bandits and hanging them, the Mexican government lodged numerous complaints about their sovereignty being breached. Our government replaced Mackenzie with Gregor.

"Lieutenant Colonel Gregor is known for his adept handling of the Comanches when he was at Fort Concho. The District Commander had hoped he would bring a lighter touch to our relations with the Mexicans. And in some ways, he did, until Carlos de Los Santos decided to attack the stagecoach."

"I still don't see—"

"They're replacing Gregor with Lieutenant Colonel Shafter. He's a hard-liner and ham-fisted. He won't have any compunctions about pursuing the Mexicans across the border."

"But won't it cause the Mexicans to complain again?"

"Probably, but we can't let our citizens live in fear of being murdered in their own beds. Something has to be done."

She huffed. "I guess you're right."

"Besides, the move for Gregor comes with a promotion and a chance to put sad memories behind him."

She nodded. "I can understand why he'd like to leave Fort Clark, where his wife died. But a promotion?"

"Yes, he's to take over Fort Davis, as a full Colonel, to pursue and contain the Apache in west Texas."

"I see. It's a long way off and a wild place. I hope he can find a new housekeeper."

He leaned forward and tugged on her arms. She sighed again, uncrossing her arms, and letting him take her hands.

"He won't find one as good as you. I know for certain."

She smiled. "That's kind of you to say." She threw her arms around his neck and tilted her face up, obviously wanting him to kiss her. And he didn't mind. He lowered his head, but she interrupted him with, "Why do *you* have to go? What are your orders?"

"I'm to take a squad of soldiers and build an armed camp at the mouth of the Pecos River where it flows into the Rio Grande. The Army hopes our presence might discourage some of the raiders. And it will serve as a base camp for Shafter if he decides to go into México to apprehend the bandits."

"But why *you*?"

"Because I speak Spanish and was able to unmask the stagecoach conspiracy. In a way, it's an honor. And if I get the camp set up, the commander promised me a promotion, too. I'd earn my other stripe back and be a First Sergeant again."

She kissed him on the cheek. "Oh, Davie, I know you'll be successful. You're clever and dedicated and brave." She exhaled and frowned. "But isn't the commander offering you a promotion because of the danger?"

He didn't answer. What good would it do? Instead, he put his finger beneath her chin and tilted her head up. And then he kissed her, long and deep, hoping he could show her all the love he felt, welling in his heart.

She broke their kiss and gazed at him. "I don't want you to go away again."

He thought he saw tears, forming in the corners of her eyes. "It's only for a couple of months. I should be back by late November or early December."

"It's still a long time, Davie."

"I can write to you, though. The commander said I can send you letters with the dispatches the Seminole scouts will bring to the fort. And you can send me notes, too, with the return dispatches. It's kind of Commander Gregor, especially since it's against Army regulations."

He paused and lightened the tone of his voice, trying to tease her. "I thought you didn't care about my going, only the commander being transferred."

She turned her face away. "You know that's not right. You know I love you."

He grasped her chin again and made her face him. "Do you?"

"Yes, you know I do."

"Enough to marry me when I get back? I know how much you love Christmas. I thought being a Christmas bride might make you happy."

"A Christmas bride?" She smiled, and her brown eyes shown. "It would be wonderful, magical. Getting married on Christmas Day—I would love it."

"I wrote to my parents, and they will be coming for the holidays. They want to meet you and are excited I'm getting married."

She lowered her head and blushed. "I hope they like me. I hope they approve."

"They will. Don't worry." He took her hands and turned them over, kissing the soft, tender skin of her wrists.

She shuddered and nestled closer to him. "I wish Christmas was tomorrow."

He inhaled the homey scent of her, of soap and flour and bacon frying. And he couldn't wait to set up house with her and start a family, too. "I wish Christmas was already here, but then I wouldn't have the pleasure of helping you decorate the church."

"That's true…" She hesitated. "After the wedding, they won't send you back to the Pecos. Will they?"

"No, I've the commander's word on it. Don't worry."

"Well, I hope the new commander honors Gregor's word." She clasped his arms and held him closer. "It's hard not to worry, being a soldier means you face danger all the time." She hugged him. "I don't want to lose you."

He leaned back and gazed into her eyes. "That's something else I wanted to talk to you about. I'll need to finish my enlistment, but after, I'll let you decide what you want me to do.

"I can re-enlist or my father would be happy to have me work in his shop. They're building more and more mansions in Galveston. I wrote him about my drawing and the church lectern. He said he could use my skills to draw designs for mantels, staircases, paneling, lots of things."

"Oh, that's marvelous, Davie! I knew your talent was something special, not a worthless pastime."

He grinned. "I never thought my father would approve of my 'useless' sketching, as he used to call it. Guess he's changed, too."

"What will you do?"

"Whatever you want me to do, Angel. Do you want to be an Army wife or settle in Galveston? As long as I have you, I'm content, either way."

"Oh, Davie," she said, her voice almost a sob. "To let me decide…" She gulped and wiped her face. "It's kind of you to take my feelings into account. Most men don't."

She looked him in the eyes, and her lower lip trembled. "Do you know you're very special, Davie Donovan? And I'm blessed to have your love."

He gathered her into his arms, settled her on his lap, and kissed each one of her tears away. "Not as blessed as me, my Angel. I love you more than life itself."

He captured her lips and lost himself in the joy of holding her close and kissing her until they both had to gasp for air.

* * *

Davie strode toward the barracks, whistling the catchy tune, "Old Susannah," under his breath." His heart was full, brimming over, and he was happier than he'd ever been. Now, all he had to do was get the base camp built and return to Crissy, making her his bride.

It was already dark out and taps had been played a few minutes ago. Gregor had chided him for being late, but it was the first time. And he and Crissy had had a lot to talk about—their wedding and the rest of their lives.

Since Dawes' arrest, there hadn't been a first Sergeant for Company C. Davie was unofficially acting as the top non-commissioned officer. Gregor had written a note for his immediate superior, Lieutenant Bullis, saying he'd been out late on Army business.

He turned at the commissary toward the parade ground. From the corner of his eye, he saw a movement in the shadows of the trees to his left. Though the fort had a front gate with a dirt road for wagons and horses, only a small portion of Fort Clark was fenced in. It was the way of most western forts.

He drew his Colt and crouched down. The dark shape moved again.

"You, there! Halt! Put your hands in the air or I'll shoot."

The dark silhouette shifted and changed. Maybe, whoever it was, had put their hands into the air. Or maybe not; they could be going for their gun. It was too dark to see, but none of the soldiers should be out after taps.

"Come forward slowly. I want to see you. Keep your hands up or I'll shoot."

The shadow shuffled forward, out of the gloom of the trees. The man's hands were in the air.

"Don't shoot, Sergeant, don't shoot."

Davie lowered his sidearm. The man was Private O'Rourke, and he was part of Company C. In fact, he was one of the men who'd been hand-picked for his squad to build the base camp on the Pecos.

O'Rourke hailed from Kentucky, and he was an expert shot, as well as an accomplished hunter. They'd be taking rations with them by mule because the terrain around the Pecos was rugged and without proper roads. If their rations ran low, it would be O'Rourke's job to keep them in fresh meat.

Tonight, the private was dressed in civilian's clothes: a dirty shirt, corduroy trousers, a scruffy-looking vest, and a wide-brimmed cowboy hat.

A horse neighed—the sound coming from the trees.

If he had to guess, he'd caught the private, trying to desert. Was O'Rourke in some kind of trouble? Had he been giving the Mexicans information, like Dawes had?

Davie hoped not.

"Unbuckle your holster and let it slide to the ground."

O'Rourke did as he asked, and Davie took his arm. He towed the man toward the sound of the horse's neighing. They found O'Rourke's brown mare tied to a tree.

He jerked the private around to face him. "You were trying to desert. Why?"

O'Rourke gulped and ducked his head.

Davie shook him. "Why, Private? Why were you deserting? If you tell me now, I can try to intervene with the commander for you. If not..."

O'Rourke kept his head down, as if considering.

"I can have you court martialed," Davie warned.

The private raised his head and grimaced. "I don't want to go to the Pecos with you. It's too dangerous. We'll be sitting ducks for the Mexicans."

"Maybe, but it doesn't mean you can desert."

"I know."

"I can turn you into Bullis, and he'll throw you into the brig. Then Fort Sam Houston and—"

"No, please, sir, Sergeant Donovan, don't turn me in." He clasped his hands together, as if begging. "Have pity."

The past few months had taught Davie an important lesson—everyone deserved a second chance. He was prepared to give

O'Rourke another chance, but he also wanted him where he could keep an eye on him, while they set up the camp.

It was a risk, though, because if O'Rourke was in league with the Mexicans, he might bring them howling down on their heads. Davie found it hard to believe the Mexicans would rely on a private for information.

Another thought niggled him: O'Rourke's excuse for wanting to run. The man had never shown a trace of cowardice before. It was strange, the private saying he was frightened. Few men, even those who were cowards, would admit such a thing.

"All right, Private. I won't turn you in, but you'll be going to the Pecos. And if you attempt to desert again, I'll turn you in faster than you can say 'skedaddle.'" Davie held the man's gaze. "Understood?"

The man bobbed his head.

"I'll be watching you. Don't doubt it." He hesitated, considering. "I hope you can get your mount stabled and sneak back into the barracks because I won't help you."

O'Rourke opened his mouth, as if to protest, but thought better of it. Instead, he drew himself up, saluting, "Thank you, Sergeant."

"Get your gun and get on with you."

He turned his back on O'Rourke, realizing he was taking a chance, but he had to know what he was up against. O'Rourke's reason for deserting hadn't convinced him.

* * *

Crissy knocked on the door to the laundry, and Isabel opened the door. It was after hours for the laundry, and she hoped the other women had gone home.

"*Buenas tardes*, won't you come in, Crissy?"

"Aren't you about done? It's getting toward supper time."

Isabel glanced at the setting sun. The days were short now.

"You're right. I was trying to catch up on some of my accounts, but I should get home for my children."

Isabel was a widow with two sons and a daughter.

Crissy stepped inside the quiet room, remembering the long, back-breaking hours she'd spent in Sudsville. She didn't miss the work, but sometimes, she yearned for the easy camaraderie of her fellow workers.

Isabel closed a large ledger book, put it into a drawer, and took a key from the bunch dangling at her waist, locking the drawer.

"You can walk me home, *mi amiga*. I enjoy your visits, whenever you can get away."

Crissy linked her arm with Isabel's. Since their confrontation on the Fourth of July, she'd made certain to visit Isabel at least once a week. They shared lunch or went to church together. Occasionally, Crissy saw Isabel after work and walked home with her.

And Isabel had been as good as her word, sending over one young woman after another. Now Crissy had Sundays off, to attend Mass. But today, she needed to ask another favor.

"Isabel, Mama wants me to have Thanksgiving dinner with her and the doctor. I'll cook the meal for the commander and his daughter, but I'd like to spend the holiday with my mother. Are there any of your girls who would be willing to serve Thanksgiving dinner for the commander?"

"Hmmm, let me think."

Crissy wasn't surprised Isabel needed to consider. Most young women wanted the holiday off—to spend with their families—or have a day to rest.

"I think Sylvie Pedersen might do," Isabel said. "She's doesn't have family, and she could use the extra money."

"She sounds perfect. Thank you. I don't know Sylvie. Is she new?"

"Yes, I hired her last week to take Irma's place."

"Irma left the laundry? I'm surprised. Is she getting married or—"

"Yes, that fiancé of hers finally got enough money together. They're to be married after the new year."

"Oh, I'm happy for her. Please, give her my congratulations when you see her." She had to bite her tongue to not blurt out her news, but until Davie returned safely, no one knew about their engagement, except their families and the commander.

She lifted her chin and said, "You know, I've been meaning to mention it, but I didn't want to stir up anything. It's been weeks since I've seen Betsy around. I know I told you I didn't want her to work at the commander's, but—"

"You're just noticing? Where have you had your head, *amiga mía*? In the clouds? Betsy has been gone since..." Isabel frowned, as if trying to remember. "Since right around the time your sergeant left for the Pecos."

"Oh, I hadn't noticed." She flushed. "I guess I haven't been paying attention."

Isabel tilted her head to one side. "What I don't know, is why Betsy left so suddenly." She frowned. "Said she was going back to those relatives who have a ranch near Fredricksburg. But I don't know... she came here to get away from them."

Isabel pursed her lips. "I hope she's not in trouble."

"Trouble?" Crissy inhaled. "As in, the family way?"

"I wouldn't be surprised. She loves men and likes to flirt. But if the man was a soldier, she refused to turn him in." Isabel shrugged. "Maybe it was someone from town. Otherwise, I don't know why she wouldn't name the father."

"Oh, my, I'm sorry to hear it."

"Well, I don't know for certain. Just guessing."

Despite her run-ins with Betsy, if she was in the family way, Crissy felt a spurt of sympathy, and at the same time, a sense of relief.

After all, she could be facing the same shame, if Davie hadn't possessed the self-control to turn her down, the day she was moving. Not to mention all the time they'd spent together at the pond.

"Well, I hope you're not right about Betsy," Crissy said. "Perhaps she went to her cousins because they needed her."

"Yes, I hope so, too." Isabel nodded. "Let's hope and pray for the best." She pulled on Crissy's arm, saying, "*Ven conmigo*, I want you to see my children. How they've grown! You'll see," Isabel said. "Can you stay for supper?

"Yes, I already made the commander's supper, and Peggy can heat it up."

"*Bueno*." Isabel nodded. "We'll have a real visit."

Crissy smiled and thought about Davie. A visit with Isabel would be a welcome diversion. She'd known she'd miss Davie, but once he was gone, she'd counted every day, missing him more than she'd dreamed was possible.

And this time of the day, at twilight, was the worst.

He'd kept his word and written her, sending the notes with the official dispatches. Commander Gregor had given her the letters.

She'd written him back—but it wasn't enough. It was already late November, and she wanted him home. Home and in her arms. Home and kissing her. Home and getting ready for their wedding.

Chapter Ten

Crissy gazed at Davie's sketch, which she'd pinned above her bed when she'd moved into the commander's house. But today, she couldn't stay still for long. She hurried down the hallway, checked on Peggy, who was working on her school lessons at the kitchen table, and went into the parlor.

She paced the commander's sitting room, barely able to contain her excitement. The forward scout had arrived this morning, telling Commander Gregor the squad was on their way back. And she couldn't wait to see Davie again.

It was early December, and it had been three months since they'd parted. She'd tried not to show it, especially around the commander, but she'd been scared out of her wits the whole time, worrying about him.

If something were to happen to Davie, she didn't know what she'd do. How could she survive without him? Now, she understood why her mother had remarried and what she'd told Crissy about her job.

She should have never worried about her job. The commander had told her, one night over supper, if she hadn't been engaged to marry, he would have asked her to come with them to Fort Davis and continue as their housekeeper.

The offer hadn't appealed. All she wanted was Davie. A job was a job, she'd learned, working for the commander. Not all jobs were the same, of course, and she'd been singularly blessed to become his housekeeper.

But nothing took the place of being with the person you loved, heart and soul.

She twisted her hands together and glanced at the grandfather clock. The scout had said the troop would arrive around noon. Another hour to go, and the time stretched like a desert in front of her.

She tried to think of other things, like her wedding dress. She'd picked a white satin fabric from one of Maxine's catalogues. They'd ordered the material, and they'd had to back order it. The satin, along with the lace to trim the gown and for her veil, had finally arrived, last week.

There were three weeks left until Christmas. She and her mother had a lot of sewing to do in a short time, if she wanted to have her dress ready. Her mother had started to plan a Christmas feast to follow their wedding, as a double celebration. They'd wanted to ask a few friends from the fort and town, along with Davie's parents.

But when she'd invited Commander Gregor and Peggy, he'd scotched the idea of a small celebration, wanting them to take the place of honor at the annual fort's Christmas feast. It was very kind of the commander, and she felt honored.

Like the Fourth of July, the woman's auxiliary would decorate the mess hall, provide food, and gather the orchestra. There would be lots of holiday treats and dancing. But no fireworks. At some point, she and her new husband would slip away to spend the night in the Sergeant Hotel.

Crissy had no doubt, once they were alone in the hotel, she and Davie would make their own fireworks.

She gazed out the window, trying to see if horsemen were coming. So much to do and so little time. Besides sewing and planning her ceremony, there was the church decorating she wanted to share with Davie.

Desperate to keep busy, she'd used the time she had to obtain candles from Maxine, who'd given them, albeit grudgingly, saying she was a Protestant, not a Catholic, and didn't hold with idolatrous practices.

Thinking about how tight-fisted her former, gossipy landlady was, she almost giggled.

Her mother had bought some red velvet from Maxine, though the cost was dear, and made several large bows for the wreaths and greenery. Crissy had located a *piñon* tree, down by the pond, which was the perfect shape and height, and she'd experimented with various ever-green trees, deciding cedar boughs would work best for the greenery.

At the same time, she'd found several of the strangely-named Possumhaw Holly trees. They'd lost their leaves, as Davie had said, but the branches were thick with bright, red berries.

She'd discovered some wild ivy, which kept its leaves during winter, to add to the greenery. And the live oaks were full of mistletoe. Of course, mistletoe was a heathen plant, and she couldn't hang it in the church. But her mother was going to decorate the doctor's quarters. She'd promised Crissy to make a kissing ball for their parlor.

And she couldn't wait to kiss Davie under the mistletoe.

Gathering brightly-colored rags to make garlands for the tree had been easy enough. Isabel's laundry, where worn-out clothes often disintegrated when washed, had turned out to be a treasure trove. She and her mother had already fashioned the multi-colored garland to drape around the tree.

The decorations were another story. She'd attempted to make her own from paper and oil paints, but she was no artist and they'd looked poor and flat. Davie could probably do better, considering how talented he was. She hoped so.

She'd canvassed the town, asking people if they'd ever owned a Christmas tree or seen one. And if they had, she asked what kind of ornaments had decorated the tree. She'd gotten a variety of answers: more bows, candy canes, pine cones, popcorn strung on thread, and apples. Jubilee Jackson had said she'd seen a Christmas tree decorated with children's old toys, especially brightly painted ones.

From the families with children, she'd collected a box of broken toys. She'd made some smaller bows and bought candy canes from Maxine. There weren't any pine trees near Brackettville, but she'd gathered some purple-colored buds from the prickly pear cactus and carefully scrapped off the thorns.

One thing everyone had agreed upon and what she remembered, was you needed a star for the top of the tree. She hoped, along with the candle holders, Davie could get the blacksmith to make them a star from some shiny metal to top off the tree.

She looked at the clock and found it had been only ten minutes since the last time she'd checked. She sighed.

Peggy, who she'd set to doing her multiplication tables, appeared at the door to the parlor, saying, "Miss Crissy, I think I'm done, though, you might want to check some of the bigger numbers, like fourteen by fourteen. I hope I carried the number right."

Crissy smiled and put her arm around Peggy. She'd miss the young girl, but there was no help for it. The commander was being transferred, and for the next eighteen months, she and Davie would stay at Fort Clark or go where the Army sent them.

Peggy sat at the kitchen table, where they did her lessons on weekdays. The fort had a school but being the commander's daughter, could have its drawbacks. Brackettville had a one-room school house, but some of the places the commander was sent were frontier outposts, lacking a town. Fort Davis was one of them.

Martha Gregor had decided the best thing was to school her child at home. It had solved some of the problems a commander's child faced, but it had left the little girl isolated, too.

Peggy did have two girlfriends, Mrs. MacTavish's daughter, Mavis, and Mrs. Bullis' daughter, Cathy. But they had chores and homework, and Peggy didn't see them more than once or twice a week.

Crissy understood what it meant to not have many friends. Though her Mama had given up her life as a 'lady of the night' and lived with Renzo as husband and wife, her unsavory past had been well known in San Antonio. Only a handful of Crissy's fellow students, like Aggie, and a couple of the neighborhood children had been friendly.

She hated to leave the little girl, realizing Peggy clung to her, in place of her mother. Since she'd moved to the commander's house, the child's nightmares had tapered off, and Peggy was comfortable to sleep in the dark again.

Crissy was touched by the child's love, and she loved Peggy back. She hoped their parting wouldn't be too wrenching.

During her mother's illness, Peggy's schooling had been neglected. Nurse Phillips had made a few tentative attempts, but she'd had her hands full, especially toward the end. How well Crissy knew.

Peggy was behind her grade, due to the break in her education, and Crissy, when she became housekeeper, wanted to help Peggy catch up. She had a solid grammar school education from the Ursuline nuns, and the fort's schoolmaster was kind enough to share his lesson plans and textbooks.

The commander's daughter was smart and quick to learn. All in all, she was a joy to teach. Crissy sat beside her and scanned the multiplication tables. Peggy had gotten most of the exercise correct, except for fourteen by fourteen and nineteen by nineteen.

The grandfather clock chimed the half hour, and Crissy jumped.

Peggy looked at her and grinned. "It's almost noon. Why don't you go to the parade ground? Maybe they'll come early. You never know."

Crissy patted the child's hand. "Bless you, it's hard for me to sit still, waiting. It's been such a long time."

"I know," Peggy said.

Crissy got up and grabbed her bonnet and cloak. West Texas winters were mostly mild, but it was a bit chilly today.

"Don't you want to come, too?" Crissy asked.

"No." She scrunched up her face. "I think there's going to be a lot of kissing and hugging going on. You won't even miss me."

"Well, I don't like leaving you alone for long..."

"Why not? I'm a big girl, and the fort is safe enough. You made me a sandwich for lunch. And Papa doesn't usually stop for lunch."

Peggy bobbed her head and affected a deeper, almost-grown up voice when she said, "I think we've been neglecting my history lessons. I'm already three chapters behind. I could catch up on reading my chapters."

"But you hate history, and I've been begging you to read those chapters—"

"Got you!" Peggy laughed and made a shooing motion with her hands. "Go! He should be here any minute."

* * *

Crissy watched as the fort's gate swung open and the cavalry troop, vivid in their dress blue uniforms and with the metal harness of their tack shined to a high polish, trotted through the gate.

Davie led the squad. Seeing him, handsome and commanding on his chestnut gelding, made Crissy's heart gallop in her chest. Her hands itched to grab him and never let go. But Army protocol must be observed first.

The commander emerged from the headquarters' building and stood at attention, waiting.

The troop dismounted and stood beside their mounts.

Lieutenant Colonel Gregor called out, "Attention!"

The men brought their heels together and stood up straight, shoulders thrown back. They raised their right hands and saluted. The commander returned their salute.

"Sergeant Donovan," the commander said, "please, report to me at once. The rest of the troop is dismissed. Take your leisure for the remainder of the day." The commander turned smartly and marched back to the headquarters' building.

Crissy saw her chance, though, they'd need to be quick. She flew across the parade ground, not caring what anyone thought, and threw herself into Davie's arms.

Davie laughed and caught her, lifting her off the ground and swinging her around until she was dizzy. He set her down, held her at arm's length and said, "You're still my beautiful Angel."

Crissy could feel the heat rising to her face, and she knew she was turning as red as one of those Possumhaw berries.

Davie leaned down and kissed her… and kissed her… his mouth devouring hers. His hands were tight on her shoulders, holding her close.

One of the corporals, who Crissy didn't know, cleared his throat, and said, "Begging your pardon, Sergeant, but the commander is waiting."

Davie broke their kiss and gazed into her eyes. They were both panting, as if they'd run all the way to the pond. "See you after supper?"

"Yes, uh, but Mama made a special supper for your homecoming. It's a surprise. I don't know what she's cooked. But she'd like for you to join us at six o'clock. I'll make supper for the commander and Peggy and leave them to serve themselves. The commander already knows. There should be no problem."

“I can’t wait.” He caressed her face with his white-gloved hand. But at the same time, she caught him, glancing over her shoulder.

“Well, I’ll see you then.” She turned to see what had caught his attention, but there was nothing to see. All of the troop had dispersed, leading their mounts toward the stables, except for one private.

He stood awkwardly, half-hidden behind a brown mare, peering out and scanning the parade ground, as if he was looking for someone. Did the man have a sweetheart or a wife, who he’d expected to greet him?

If he did, he’d been disappointed. Crissy’s heart went out to him.

Davie turned to the man and said, “Private O’Rourke, you may stable your mount. Then meet me at headquarters.”

O’Rourke swallowed, his Adam’s apple bobbing, and nodded. He saluted.

Crissy thought it was an odd exchange. But she really didn’t care. All she cared was Davie had returned, safe and sound. And he’d kissed her silly, in front of God and everybody. In a little over three weeks, they would be married.

She was so happy, she could cry.

* * *

Crissy licked her lips and swallowed—her throat had gone suddenly dry. Davie had peeled off his shirt—it was one of those unseasonably warm days in December, and he was about to chop down the *piñon* tree she’d chosen.

She’d never seen Davie’s bare chest before, and it was a sight to behold. His chest was washboard flat with the ripple of powerful muscles. Dark hair dusted his chest, and each time he moved, she could see the bunch and slide of his muscles beneath his white skin, contrasting sharply with his deeply tanned face.

He spit on his hands, leaned over, and grabbed the ax handle. He leaned down, gauging the thickness of the tree’s trunk and then he straightened. He pulled back the ax, and she glimpsed the formidable swell of his biceps.

Her heart fluttered in her chest, and her breasts swelled. Between her thighs, she felt warm and sticky, like a pot of heated molasses.

She glanced up. Their everyday shadow, Private O'Rourke, wasn't around, but it didn't mean he wasn't close by. They'd sent him into the cedar breaks to gather more Possumhaw Holly branches.

If she wasn't afraid he'd appear suddenly, like the gremlin he was, she would have thrown herself at Davie and stroked her hands over his naked flesh.

Chop, chop, the metal biting into the hard wood of the *piñon* tree rang out across the pond. It was as if the water amplified the sound.

Davie straightened and glanced at her, grinning. He chopped the tree's trunk one more time and yelled out, "Timber!"

He was such a tease. The tree was about seven feet tall, hardly worthy of a shout-out, but the perfect size to fit in front of the lectern. The thick, evergreen tree toppled to the ground.

Crissy clapped.

Davie looked at her, the heat in his gaze blazing across the yards of meadow separating them. She put one foot forward, wanting to run to him, but as she'd half-expected, a shadow emerged from the tree line, his arms full of red berry branches.

Davie winked at her and grabbed his shirt, shrugging it on. He'd won his stripe back, too, succeeding in setting up the base camp and repelling bandits, trying to cross the border.

He'd wanted to tell her about some of the skirmishes, but she'd demurred, feeling faint when he talked about fighting. Together, they'd decided, once his enlistment was up, he'd work with his father in Galveston. She was blessed he was willing to give up the Army because she feared for his safety.

"O'Rourke, give Crissy the branches. I'll need your help, taking the tree back to the church."

"Yes, sir." The private approached her and handed off the branches.

She cradled them against her chest and followed the men. Davie carried the trunk end with O'Rourke taking the top.

Crissy often wondered why Davie included O'Rourke every day, getting the church ready for Christmas. Was he a kind of chaperone? But it was silly, they would be married in eight days. And Davie had arranged for them to work together, getting ready for Christmas.

He'd obtained a furlough from Commander Gregor until the new year when Lieutenant Colonel Shafter would formally take over the fort. And he'd arranged for Sylvie Pedersen to take over her housekeeper duties.

She met with Peggy during the morning to oversee the child's lessons, but Crissy's afternoons were free. And the days had passed in a whirl of activity, getting the church decorations together. The garlands and wreaths were mostly done. She wanted to add more berries, but then they'd be finished.

The *luminarias* had been set up, and about twenty of the townsfolk had agreed to participate in the Christmas Eve *posada*. Jubilee Jackson, who was a strict Baptist, wanted to join the Catholic tradition, saying it sounded like fun.

The last, but most important part, was getting the tree up and decorating it. And today was the day. She couldn't wait. It was hard to keep from bouncing up and down like a jack-in-the-box; she was more than excited to see how the tree would look.

They'd waited until close to Christmas Day, hoping the tree would remain fresh. Davie had set up a bucket with sand for its stand.

As for the tree's decorations, the bows were made, as was the multi-colored garland. The blacksmith had fashioned twenty, tin candle holders but not a star.

Davie had opposed the star, saying he had something far better, and it was a surprise. Mystified but thrilled Davie was planning a surprise, she'd given in and was crazy with waiting to see what he'd done.

The other decorations, she'd pulled together, based on people's suggestions. It was an interesting array, from fruit and nuts and prickly pear buds to colorful, discarded toys. But she couldn't get the image of those glistening pendants, hanging from the Christmas tree in San Antonio, out of her head.

She'd moved back in with Mama. Isaiah had cleared out a storeroom in his cabin and fixed her a temporary bedroom. It was handy because she and her mother spent most evenings sewing her wedding dress, working until their eyes were scratchy and tearing at the corners.

They'd made progress, but Crissy knew it would be close, getting the dress done in time and fitted.

She trailed after the men to the church and watched as they secured the plump tree in its stand. When it was straight, Davie stood back and dusted his hands, saying, "I didn't know a tree could leak so much sap. I'll need to clean up with soap."

He leaned down and brushed her lips. "You're frowning. What are you worrying about? We're ahead of schedule, and we can start decorating the tree."

"I was worrying about my wedding dress, hoping Mama and I will get it finished in time."

He bumped her with his shoulder, obviously not wanting to touch her with his sticky hands. "Have faith. You'll have the dress ready."

She gazed up at him, wanting him to take her in his arms and kiss her and touch her breasts, as he'd been doing lately. His touch thrilled her, and each night, after supper, they met for a few private moments. It was their time, when Private O'Rourke was at the mess hall.

She'd be resentful, if she didn't believe Davie was being cautious about her reputation, and he needed O'Rourke to help him with some of the heavier tasks. Still, why O'Rourke and no one else? Usually, the privates rotated duties.

It was strange, but she didn't care.

Eight more days... and they'd be alone together... for the rest of their lives.

* * *

Davie unbuttoned his shirt and took it off. He leaned over the water trough and sluiced water over his head, chest and hands. He grabbed the bar of lye soap kept by the pump handle and washed his hands. It was getting on mid-day, and the westbound stage was due.

He'd sent telegraphs, one to the shop owner who'd ordered the ornaments, months ago from Italy, and the other to a jewelry-maker in San Antonio, who he'd had make a very special ornament.

He couldn't wait for Crissy to see his surprises. The jeweler, along with the crafted ornament, was also sending a gold wedding band for her.

And next week, one day before their wedding, his parents would arrive from Galveston. Lieutenant Bullis had an extra room, and he'd been kind enough to host them, so they wouldn't have to stay in town at the hotel.

He leaned forward, gazing at the horizon. How long would Crissy wait for him to come back from washing up?

He saw the stagecoach, coming around the final bend in the road. The horses were puffing and pulling at full speed. The driver, in typical dramatic fashion, whipped them up and made a show of pulling back on the reins, setting the brake, and yelling out, "Whoa, there! Whoaaaa, hosses!"

Davie crossed the street and waited. As soon as the stagecoach slid to a halt, he called out, "Sergeant Donovan here. I believe you have two packages for me."

The stagecoach guard gazed down at him. "Yes, sir. Two packages, Sergeant Donovan." He jumped down, cradling his shotgun in the crook of his arm. "Let me open the boot and get them for you."

Davie expected passengers to come tumbling out, too, but the shades were drawn, and no one emerged. It was odd—no passengers going west. He shrugged and followed the guard to the back.

The guard unlaced the leather boot, reached his hand inside and pulled out two packages: one was small and displayed a jeweler's stamp, the other was large and unwieldy with foreign writing on it and several postmarks.

Grinning, Davie balanced the two packages and said, "Thank you."

"My pleasure, Sergeant."

Davie stopped at the horse trough and tore into the paper and string on the smaller package. When he opened the box and saw what the jeweler had wrought, he gasped. The ornament was beautiful, a work of art!

He found the smaller box, nestled next to the decoration, opened it and glimpsed at the gleaming gold band. Perfect. He pocketed the box and closed the lid of the jeweler's box.

He opened the church door and went inside, pausing for a moment to let his eyes adjust to the semi-darkness.

"You took long enough," Crissy said.

"Maybe, but I was waiting on something special."

"Oh, what?"

"Close your eyes and you'll find out."

"Oh, Davie, you're such a tease! Close my eyes... again."

"Please, Crissy, you won't be disappointed."

She huffed. "All right. My eyes are closed."

"Good."

He noticed O'Rourke had stayed with Crissy, as ordered, but he'd hidden himself behind the lectern and was leaning against the deep ledge of one of the stained-glass windows.

He'd kept O'Rourke with him, not sure why the man had tried to desert. On the Pecos, O'Rourke had acquitted himself with honor and bravery, as Davie had thought he would. It was a puzzle, but after Davie married, he'd let the incident go. Maybe the man had had doubts, leaving for the border wilderness. But he appeared to have gotten hold of himself, and Davie had no intention of watching him for the rest of his enlistment.

Davie put the boxes on the pews next to the tree and opened them. The glass ornaments glistened, even in the half-light. They were packed, row upon row, forty of them, in deep sawdust. One of them was cracked.

He touched the fragile ornament and turned it over. It was only cracked on one side—that was good.

Crissy stamped her foot. "How much longer do I need to keep my eyes closed?"

Davie chuckled. His impatient Angel. He pulled the other box lid off and laid it to one side.

"All right, you can look now."

"Well, it's about time." She opened her eyes.

Davie took her arm with one hand and with the other, he offered the contents of the boxes with a flourish. "My Christmas surprise, I hope you like them."

"Oh, my heavens. Oh, my!" Crissy cradled her face in her hands. "They're beautiful, beautiful." She went to the first big box and caressed one of the glittering ornaments, a pendant-shaped one with twirling red stripes, against a golden background.

She threw herself into his arms, kissing him over and over. "They're wondrous! Like what I saw in San Antonio." She gasped again and pulled away. "Where did you get them?"

"They came all the way from Italy. I'm glad you like them."

"Like them!" She wiped the tears from the corners of her eyes. "Like them? Oh, my gosh, Davie, I love them! But they must have been expensive—"

"Nothing is too good for my Angel. Speaking of..." He took her arm and turned her toward the smaller box. "I had this made, especially for you. It's true the Star of Bethlehem watched over the birth of Jesus, but there were also Angels on high, watching over His birth."

He reached into the box and pulled out the fragile metal angel, forged with gossamer wings and a tiny halo. "I wanted our tree to have an angel on top." He squeezed her hand. "Because you're my Angel."

"Oh, Davie, I'm... I don't know what to say, except thank you, thank you! What a wonderful surprise." She embraced him again and kissed his cheek.

She glanced at the boxes and started to sob. "They're too beautiful, too wonderful. I don't know how to thank you."

He hugged her and heard the front door of the church open and shut. He hoped it was Father Fernández, as he was eager to show the priest the ornaments, too.

But it wasn't the priest. Instead, it was a woman, Betsy McDuff. He hadn't seen her in a while, but he'd been away from the fort. His gaze dropped, and he saw the unmistakable bump beneath her waist.

Betsy was in a family way? He hadn't known she was married... or was she?

She stopped a few feet away and gazed at them. Hate blazed from her eyes. She raised her hand and pointed, "You, Sergeant Donovan, are the father of my baby! Everyone saw us dance at the Fourth of July celebration. You kissed me, too, in front of everybody." She looked down. "You told me we should split up and meet by the pond. I met you there, and..." She paused and caressed her rounded belly. "This is what you gave me."

Crissy gasped and pulled away from him.

"Betsy, that's not right. I never touched you, except to dance. You can't—"

"How could you?" Crissy sobbed. "How could you? You're like all the men who used my mother and..." She ducked her head and ran for the church door.

Betsy stood where she was, smirking.

O'Rourke moved from behind the lectern. He glanced at them and ran for the back door behind the altar.

"You!" Betsy shrieked. "I thought you'd run away and left me."

All the jumbled pieces fell into place, and Davie finally knew why O'Rourke had tried to desert. He hadn't wanted to marry Betsy. But Davie would make certain O'Rourke did his duty.

But first, he had to go after Crissy and explain.

* * *

Crissy ran inside the fort, wondering if her new step-father would shield her from the monster she'd been ready to marry. She opened the door to his surgery. The doctor was tending a private who had a festering wound on his thigh from one of the skirmishes on the Pecos.

Thinking of the Pecos and border bandits reminded her of Davie, and she wanted nothing more to do with him... ever. He was a monster, a lecher. He'd gotten Betsy in the family way but had continued to court and want to marry her.

Burning in hell wasn't good enough for him!

Her mother was making tea on the stove. She looked up and said, "Crissy, I didn't expect you home..." Then her mother must have seen her tears and distress. "What happened?"

Isaiah came into the room and asked, "Crissy, what's wrong. Are you all right."

She didn't want to speak, didn't want to explain how she'd been duped, like her mother. At least, she wasn't married yet. She shook her head and ran to her bedroom, bolting the door.

Then she saw it, draped over her bed—her wedding dress. Her mother had obviously been working on the gown, and it was almost finished. All that was left was to stitch the lace around the neckline and sleeves.

How she hated the dress!

It was the worst possible reminder of how much she'd looked forward to joining her life with Davie's.

Her mother called out, "Crissy, Davie is at the door and wants to talk to you."

"I never want to see his face again, Mama. He betrayed me in the worst way. Please, please, keep him from me."

There was a long pause, and her mother asked, "Are you certain, Crissy?"

She leaned against the door and whispered through the wooden slats. "He got Betsy McDuff in the family way. He needs to marry her."

"Oh, Crissy, are you sure?"

"Yes, Mama, I'm sure."

She turned to her wedding dress and found her sewing scissors, lying beside the measuring tape on her bureau. Tears streamed down her face, but they didn't keep her from stabbing, slicing, and shredding the white satin to tattered rags.

When the gown lay in a sickening mess of strips on the floor, she covered her face with her hands and sobbed, sorrow spilling from her in wrenching howls.

From the corner of her eye, she glimpsed Davie's drawing above her bed. His first gift to her; she'd treasured it for months. Her tears had subsided, but inside, her stomach rolled, and rage roiled through her.

She snatched the picture off the wall and tore it into tiny pieces. They drifted, like confetti, to mingle with her ruined wedding gown.

Her heart, along with all her dreams, was shredded and ruined, like the wedding dress and Davie's picture.

* * *

Davie shouted and begged and pleaded at the doctor's surgery, but the way was barred to him. Crissy's mother and her new step-father were protecting her. He couldn't blame them, especially considering what she'd probably told them.

And besides, he had a very pregnant Betsy in tow. He couldn't let her get away, having maligned him, until he found O'Rourke and made him confess to what he'd done. So far, Betsy had kept her lips sealed, but she hadn't resisted.

He guessed she'd gone away when O'Rourke said he wouldn't marry her and would run instead. But with the approaching birth of her baby, she'd decided to accuse him instead, knowing people would remember them dancing and watching the fireworks together.

He had to give it to Betsy—she'd spent her time, coming up with a way to make someone marry her. And who better than capricious Davie Donovan, a ladies' man, who'd never took anything seriously... until he'd fallen in love with Crissy.

Turning from the doctor's barred door, he said, "This isn't over. O'Rourke is the father of your baby." He stared at her. "You know it as well as I do."

"I know nothing, except I need a father for my baby."

"All right, we'll do it your way. I'm taking you to Captain MacTavish. He'll put you under house arrest."

"Arrest? How can you treat me—"

"Drop it, Betsy. You've accused me of a foul and hideous deed. We both know I didn't lie with you on the Fourth of July. You'll stay put until I can prove my innocence. And I will prove it."

She turned her face away and didn't respond.

He tugged on her arm, taking her to MacTavish's cabin and explaining why they needed to watch her.

He went to the stables and found Private Bates, the hostler. "Did O'Rourke take out his mount?"

Bates drew up and saluted. "Yes, sir. About an hour ago. Said he had an urgent message to deliver for you, sir."

Davie puffed his cheeks out. "Did you notice which way he went?"

"Uh, northeast, I would say, toward San Antonio."

"Figures." Easier to hide in a big town than in the open. He clenched his hands into fists and nodded. "Saddle my horse."

"Yes, sir."

"Who's the best Seminole tracker?"

"Ah, the best tracker is Scout Moses Washington."

"Thank you, Private Bates."

* * *

Davie scratched his bearded face, not believing they'd been out five days, pursuing Private O'Rourke. He and his scout, Moses, had slept in spurts, getting up as early as there was light and stopping when it was too dark to see the tracks.

They'd finished the beef jerky and hard biscuits. Now, there was nothing to eat, and Davie's stomach rumbled, growling with hunger. Washington was looking a bit ashen, despite his dark skin, and Davie didn't know how much longer they could keep going.

O'Rourke was good, he had to admit, doubling back on his tracks, riding through creek beds to disguise his horse's hoofprints, and creeping through underbrush on foot with his horse's hooves clothed in rags.

Horses with cloths on their hooves made no tracks.

But Scout Washington knew all the tricks and then some. The rags wore out after a few miles, and Moses would range far and wide until he picked up the trail again. Slowly, but surely, they closed in on O'Rourke and wore him down.

The hill country loomed in front of them, lying west of San Antonio. It was an easier place to hide than the flat borderlands they'd come from, with its many canyons and valleys. Davie shook his head, realizing his parents would arrive in Brackettville the day after tomorrow, and no one would be there to greet them.

There would be no wedding preparations, no bride, and no marriage. Davie wanted to cry, but he didn't think Washington would appreciate seeing his commanding officer sob like a child.

They plodded along the rocky, terraced paths, leading their mounts, who were limping and spent. Davie wondered how O'Rourke had kept his mare going. He heard rushing water, as if a waterfall wasn't far in the distance.

Scout Washington put one finger to his lips. “Shhh,” he whispered. “I think he’s there.”

“How do you know?”

“See his horse’s dung.”

Davie glanced down at the pile of horse manure in the path. In the early morning, chilly December air, the muck was still smoking.

Davie’s heart lifted for the first time in five days. He took out his Colt and made sure it was loaded.

Moses did the same.

They rounded a bend in the path and saw O’Rourke, bathing his face and chest in the chilly water. His brown mare was slouched beside the pool of water, drinking slowly.

“Hands up, Private O’Rourke.”

The private looked up, his eyes wide with fright. He had no shirt on, obviously having worn it out, to cover his horse’s hooves. His sidearm lay on the ground. He glanced at it and stretched out his hand.

Davie leveled his Colt. “I wouldn’t try it, if I were you.”

O’Rourke flinched and raised his hands into the air.

“You’re going back and marrying Betsy McDuff,” Davie declared. “A child should have a father. Or you can be court martialed. Up to you.”

O’Rourke turned his face away and muttered, “Not much of a choice.”

Epilogue

Fort Clark, Texas—Christmas Day, 1875

Crissy stood in front of the full-length mirror while her mother fussed with her hair. She had on her best dress, other than the silk moiré ball gown, which her mother had dubbed "too revealing" for her wedding.

The dress she'd chosen was actually a suit, with a wool vest and skirt. Underneath the vest she wore a white blouse, ruffled at the neck. Like her ball gown, the suit was blue, Crissy's favorite color.

Actually, the suit was an aqua-blue, much like Davie's eyes, with black cording. It was serviceable and smart, but not what she'd dreamed of wearing on her wedding day.

The tattered remains of her white satin wedding dress were long gone—thrown into the dust bin. She mourned its loss but only had herself to blame. She glanced up at the bare space over her bed—Davie's picture—she'd destroyed it, too, in a fit of rage.

She should have known better, should have trusted Davie. But all the ugly times she'd lived through with her mother, had overcome her common sense.

How sorry she was—but Davie had forgiven her—it was a Christmas miracle.

Her husband-to-be had spent seven days in the wilderness, tracking, apprehending, and bringing back O'Rourke. He'd forced the private to marry Betsy and give his child a name.

Davie had convinced the commander to forgo court martialing O'Rourke for desertion if he would promise to be a faithful husband to Betsy and take care of his child.

Crissy bit back the bitter bile, knowing if the man had run twice from being married, he'd probably run again. If he did, there would be no mercy. She hoped Betsy's relatives would be more accommodating if such a thing happened, not wishing Betsy to know desertion, as her mother had.

Her mother patted her hair in place and said, "There. You look beautiful. Let me fetch your nosegay."

Crissy smoothed her skirts and waited. Her mother returned with a jolly-faced bunch of colorful pansies, tied with a white silk ribbon. Crissy raised them to her nose, wondering how Jubilee Jackson could have grown such cheery flowers in mid-winter.

The pansies were bright, yellow and white and purple, with black centers. But they didn't smell of anything. Still, she was touched by Jubilee's offering.

Mama stood beside her. "Are you ready?"

Was she? She of little faith?

"Yes, Mama."

"Good girl." Her mother laced her arm through hers. The doctor followed them, wearing his best suit.

They walked through the fort and to Ann Street where St. Mary Magdalene's Catholic Church stood. She'd never realized it before, the irony of the name of their church. It was named for the most famous prostitute in the Bible.

Her mother had been a prostitute, and her mother's experiences had poisoned Crissy's thoughts.

She stopped and stared at the church. Today was her favorite holiday, the birth of her Savior. Jesus had forgiven Mary Magdalene and accepted her.

Had she really forgiven Mama?

Was her lack of forgiveness why she'd been ready to believe the worst of Davie? Because she'd never forgiven her mother for the life they'd had to lead?

But she loved her mother—how could she not have forgiven her?

She didn't know anymore. But then, suddenly, she knew... knew the real truth... the reason for all her doubts.

Tears came, streaming down her face. She was ashamed, so ashamed. Her heart opened, and forgiveness poured into her, cleansing her, and removing all the darkness she'd been harboring. She bent her head and mumbled a brief prayer of thanks.

Another Christmas miracle—she was so blessed.

Turning, she threw her arms around her mother and said, "Mama, I forgive you. Truly, I do, from the bottom of my heart."

Her mother hugged her back. "I know you do, Crissy. I know." She reached up and wiped the tears from Crissy's cheeks. "No tears now. It's your wedding day. Be happy."

Crissy's heart lightened, realizing she'd finally banished the shame of her family's past. It was as if a boulder had been weighing her down before. Now the heavy burden was gone. And she was happy! So happy!

She glimpsed the unlit *luminarias* lining the pathway to the door. She'd not seen them lit or taken part in the *Noche Buena Posada* last night. Instead, she'd met Davie's parents and had supper with them. They were a nice couple, kind and generous-hearted, like her husband-to-be.

Her mother opened the church door and handed her off to the doctor to give her away. She lifted her head, tilting her chin up, ready to start her new life. Her heart was singing with joy. She saw her smiling friends and neighbors filling the pews, and her heart expanded.

Peggy turned and waved. She smiled back.

To her right, she glimpsed the Christmas tree of her dreams. The garland had been hung, the candles were lit in their holders, and the marvelous glass ornaments dangled from the tree. And on the top of the tree was an angel, looking like it was made from spun sugar, so light and airy, but bright and shiny, too.

Christmas magic—fairy magic—a wish come true.

She turned her face from the Christmas tree. As beautiful as it was, it was a tree. Her dress was a dress. And Davie's sketch had been a pretty picture. Nothing more. People were important... not things.

She gazed at the altar. Her fiancé, decked out in his best dress uniform, stood straight and tall, waiting for her. He was so handsome with his dark, curly hair, turquoise eyes, and charming dimple. How had she gotten so lucky?

Their gazes caught and snagged. Davie was what was important—not trees or dresses or...

He smiled, and his dimple deepened.

Her heart lifted and took wing, soaring with love and hope and faith for their future. She smiled back and walked, as if treading air, embracing their love, and holding it close. Joining him at the altar, he took her hand, and the doctor stepped away.

His touch made her tremble with love and longing. And as she gazed into his eyes, she knew love had transformed them both.

He leaned close and whispered, “I love you, Crissy, forever and ever.”

“I love you, too, forever and ever. Until the end of time.”

* * *

Mallory: The Mail Order Bride

By Hebby Roman

Historical Western Romance

☆Estrella Publishing☆

Author's Note

Following the Mexican American War, México formally ceded the Trans-Pecos area to the United States. Seeking trails to gold-rich California, Americans pushed west of the Pecos River. The first settlers began to drive their cattle into this rich land in the late nineteenth century at the end of the American Civil War. By the 1870's the violent skirmishes between settlers and the Native Americans (mainly Mescalero Apache and Comanche tribes) warranted intervention by the United States government.

Fort Davis played a major role in the history of the Southwest. Named for Secretary of War Jefferson Davis, who would later become President of the Confederacy, the fort was first garrisoned by Lieutenant Colonel Washington Seawall and six companies of the Eighth U.S. Infantry in 1854. The post was located in a box canyon near *Limpia* Creek ("*limpia*" means clean in Spanish), on the eastern side of the Davis Mountains, where wood, water, and grass were plentiful.

With the outbreak of the Civil War, the federal government evacuated Fort Davis, and the post was occupied by Confederate troops from the spring of 1861 until the summer of 1862, when Union forces took possession. In June 1867, Lieutenant Colonel Wesley Merritt and four companies of the recently-organized Ninth U.S. Cavalry (nicknamed the "Buffalo Soldiers" by Native Americans), reoccupied the fort. They erected new officers' quarters, two enlisted men's barracks, a guardhouse, temporary hospital, and storehouses. Fort Davis became a major installation with more than 100 structures and quarters for 400 soldiers.

Fort Davis' primary role of guarding the West Texas frontier against the Comanches and Apaches continued until 1881, though, the Comanches were defeated in the mid-1870's. In a series of engagements, units from Fort Davis and other posts, under the command of Colonel Benjamin Grierson, forced the Apaches and their leader, Victorio, into México, where the Apache were killed by Mexican soldiers.

With the end of the Indian Wars in West Texas, Fort Davis was ordered abandoned in June 1891, and in 1961 the fort became a national historic site.

This book follows the general outline of the history of Fort Davis, but all the characters herein are fictional, except for the occasional mention of well-known historical persons.

Mallory: The Mail Order Bride

Chapter One

East of Fort Davis, Texas—1877

The stagecoach hit a bump, sprang into the air, and came down with a hard jolt. Mallory Metcalf Reynolds bit her tongue and almost cried out. She grabbed for the strap beside the window and hung on, frowning.

The man across from her drawled, "Riding in a stagecoach ain't civilized-like. Feels like we're what's for dinner, being stirred in a big pot." He combed his fingers through his long, grimy beard, threaded with beads and shiny bits of metal. "I prefer me mules. They mosey along, slow and calm-like."

She nodded and forced her mouth into the semblance of a smile. She'd never seen anything like the man's beard before. She wrinkled her nose, reaching in her skirt pocket for her handkerchief. And she'd never smelled anything like him, either. Rancid possum meat crossed with a liberal dressing of horse dung came to mind.

Since she'd left the relatively civilized environs of Galveston, Texas, her experiences had been almost other-worldly. The land, crossed by the lurching stagecoach, lay spread before her—a huge expanse, thinly dotted with settlements. Except for San Antonio, where they'd stopped for one night, there weren't any large towns. And the stagecoach stops were nothing more than crude log cabins or dirt and timber dugouts, outfitted with a rudimentary kitchen and dirty bunks.

Her fellow passengers, like Mr. Spofford, sitting across from her, were another breed of people than back home. Some men were downright sinister with huge Stetsons pulled low and loaded pistols riding their hips. Others, like her present company, sported greasy, fringed buckskins begrimed with enough dust to start a sizable vegetable garden.

Women were few and far between. One woman in faded calico and a huge poke bonnet hiding her face hadn't spoken a single word for two days. The other woman was of another variety, sporting henna-dyed red hair, too many feathers, and a dress with a neckline that defied gravity.

Mr. Spofford, a muleskinner, was headed to Fort Davis, too. He wasn't so bad, or at least, he didn't seem sinister. He'd freely told her he'd taken a new job, freighting supplies from San Antonio to the fort and taking cow hides and wool back to San Antonio. If the fort was as important as he claimed, she hoped it was larger than the tiny settlements they'd passed. She'd wanted to ask him about the place but felt constrained, not wishing to enter into a protracted conversation.

She sniffed her scented handkerchief and wished he believed in bathing more than twice a year... if that often.

She glanced at the prairie they'd been crossing for the past few days, surprised to find the flat, endless land had begun to fold into low creases, featuring rolling hills. Leaning out the window, she could see the hazy outline of mountain peaks in the distance.

Her heart leapt to her throat—they must be getting close. Mr. E. P. Murphy, her intended, had claimed his ranch was set in the prettiest of country with majestic mountains and verdant valleys. He'd asserted the climate was healthy and restful, warm in the day and cool at night. She hoped he hadn't exaggerated, as her destination was beyond the outer reaches of a land so immense, her poor faculties couldn't encompass it.

But her excitement didn't last long. The harder she stared, the more the mountains seemed to shimmer in the distance, not getting any closer, no matter how she strained to judge how far away they were.

She pulled in her head and folded her hands. Weeks of travel had exhausted her. She wanted nothing more than to sleep in a decent bed. Lulled by the swaying coach, and the heavy contents of the noonday meal, drowsiness threatened to claim her.

The stagecoach stops offered the same food: huge hunks of half-cooked beef, potatoes roasted in the hearth, and stale bread. She'd eaten as little as possible of the mid-day meal, but the food had settled in her stomach like a brick. One stop, between Galveston and San Antonio, had served grits for breakfast. But they'd not tasted like Georgia Lowcountry grits, more like sawdust mixed with dishwater.

She missed the Lowcountry fare she'd been raised on. Just thinking about crab cakes, oyster soup, gumbo, or red rice and beans, made her mouth water.

Returning the handkerchief to her pocket, she absently searched for the silver-framed photograph of her beloved Macon. Then she remembered she'd stowed the picture in a secret compartment of her luggage, not wanting to risk anyone asking questions.

Instead of the photograph she cherished, her fingertips brushed the crackly pages of Mr. Murphy's last letter. Feeling low, she pulled it out and skimmed the contents, picking out key phrases.

"Wealthy gentleman rancher... wanting to start a family... good Christian... medium height and build... forty-six years old... salubrious climate... well-appointed home..."

Like a talisman for luck, she traced her fingers over the writing, praying his words were gospel, and she was going to a better place to start her life over.

And if it wasn't a better place? It didn't matter—she had no options left.

Her eyelids drooped, and her head was heavy. She closed her eyes and let her head sink forward, drifting to sleep.

A loud thump hit the stagecoach. Her eyes opened, but she was groggy. She shook her head and stared at Mr. Spofford, who had his carbine pointed out the coach's window.

Several more thumps hit the stagecoach, and a staccato of gunshots splintered the silence. The stagecoach driver yelled at the horses, and the conveyance lurched forward at a faster pace. Hoofbeats thundered and a howling cascade of yips and barks, sounding like a cage of wounded foxes, made the hair on her neck stand on end.

"What is wrong? What is that horrible noise?" She craned her neck to look out and saw arrows buried into the side of the coach.

She gasped, and the blood ran cold in her veins.

Spofford grabbed her arm. "Don't! Git away from that there window. Git down!" He pushed her to the coach's filthy floor and covered her with his body. "Injuns, Miss. Most likely 'Pache. Stay down if'n you want to keep that purty yellow hair of your'n."

Her stomach somersaulted, threatening to climb into her throat. Her heart pummeled her chest, feeling as if it wanted to escape the confines of her ribcage. Over the blood pounding in her ears, she heard more gunfire and strangled grunts. Something big and hard hit the ground, and the coach veered sharply left, almost turning over.

Horses neighed and the stagecoach bumped and lurched, shuddering as if it was a living thing about to die. She scrabbled on the floor, wanting to get out, to run for her life. Suddenly, the stage stopped, throwing them against the front bench.

Spofford half-rose and slid back the bolt on his carbine, checking the gun and aiming it at the door. He glanced back and said, “Shssh. Keep quiet and make yerself small. I’ll hold ‘em off as long as I can.”

“You mean—?”

“Hah!” The stagecoach door flew open. A dark, squat man stood in the doorway, his face covered in streaks of paint. He spouted guttural words she couldn’t even begin to understand and gestured with a long, deadly-looking rifle.

Spofford pulled the trigger. Too late. The man knocked the barrel of the carbine aside. The bullet went whining, shattering a hole in the stagecoach’s roof.

The dark man put the barrel of his rifle to Spofford’s head and pulled him out of the coach. The attacker wrenched Spofford’s carbine from his hands and tossed it to another paint-streaked native. He pushed Spofford to the ground, and the second native trained his gun on the muleskinner.

Despite cringing and rolling into a ball, the first man must have spied her, huddled on the coach floor. He grunted and loosed another spate of unintelligible gibberish. His hands, like the claws of an animal, clutched her, biting into her skin.

She opened her mouth to scream. The man holding her put a knife to her throat. She clamped her mouth shut.

A taller native, his arms crossed over his chest, approached them. He was bare chested and, like the others, his face was painted. Unlike the other hostiles, he had a wealth of feathers braided in his long, straight black hair.

The man holding her started talking. More gibberish with one word spoken over and over, sounding like "Is-dan, is-dan."

The taller man nodded. He reached out and touched her hair. More babbling with the repeated words of, "Lit-su sha, lit-su sha." Then he jerked his head, indicating a band of natives, bunched in a semi-circle, sitting on barebacked paint ponies.

The tall man half-lifted and half-dragged her toward the mounted men. He drew a knife and held it at her throat, too.

A deep, dark fear, like walking in a cemetery at midnight, suffocated her. She couldn't breathe, couldn't think. Her knees gave way, and she went limp like a ragdoll.

He grunted and applied pressure, cutting into the skin of her throat.

She gasped and felt the sickening, sticky slide of blood. The world spun and tilted. Black dots swarmed from the corners of her vision, blanketing her sight.

And then... nothing.

* * *

Colonel William Gregor rode beside his best scout, Hosea Lincoln. Gregor gazed at the shifting patterns of afternoon sunlight on the mountains. "How much further to Seven Springs?"

Hosea turned to him. "About a mile, sir, in that canyon."

He half-remembered the approach to Seven Springs was through a canyon with high, steep walls. Not an ideal place for a parley.

They were headed toward one of the three outlying camps from Fort Davis. The camps, strategically located on known Apache trails, were stocked with hidden caches of supplies, and served as launching points for scouting parties against raiding hostiles.

Seven Springs was the outpost closest to the San Antonio-El Paso Road; the other two sites, Eagle Springs and Wild Rose Pass, were buried deep in the Davis Mountains and lay athwart ancient native hunting trails.

Glad for the twenty men of Company B who rode behind him, he belatedly wondered if he should have brought fifty. Deer Stalker had claimed the raiding party was no larger than fifteen braves. But fighting in mountainous terrain could be especially challenging, depending upon the situation.

As commander of Fort Davis, he seldom rode on patrol. Though he'd familiarized himself with the three rough outposts when he'd first been assigned to the fort, he hadn't journeyed to the camps since then.

The day before yesterday, one of the regular patrols on the San Antonio-El Paso Road, had stopped an attack on the eastbound stage. The Apache braves had been driven off and were last seen riding toward Seven Springs. His patrol had captured three Apache women and a baby.

Gregor had kept native hostages before, mostly Comanche, when he'd been stationed at Fort Concho. He remembered one squaw, who'd lost her child to a fever, had tried to kill herself.

In just the space of twenty-four hours, he'd found the Apache women were hell-bent on killing themselves. They refused to eat or drink water. The one mother nursed her child but soon her milk would give out. At every turn and the slightest chance, they tried to harm themselves, pulling nails from the walls of the guardhouse and gashing their wrists. They banged their heads against the walls until they passed out and used everyday items to inflict harm on themselves.

Clearly, they would rather die than be hostages. He had to literally keep them tied up for their own good. Deer Stalker, an Apache scout, who acted as a translator and go-between, had ridden into the fort two hours ago. He'd brought news that Caballero, the leader of the raiding band, was waiting at Seven Springs to parley and make an exchange for the hostages.

Gregor wanted to send the women to the New Mexico Apache reservation, but he doubted they would last long enough to reach there. Given the grim realities of their resistance, he'd come to negotiate with the Apache war chief.

He wondered what Caballero had to exchange. Not that it mattered. He'd not have the Apache women's unnecessary deaths on his head. He knew many of his fellow officers and commanders didn't feel that way. Because hostiles killed women and children, most Army officers believed in "an eye for an eye," and they felt justified in murdering women and children.

He lived by a different set of rules, ones that ran bone-deep from his upbringing and early training. If at all possible, he tried to spare native women and children from the ravages of war.

The pathway narrowed into a deep canyon, and Gregor glimpsed the reflection of sun off steel. Most likely, hostiles were on the cliff, sighting down on them with rifles.

The Apache still used their bows and arrows for rapid shooting. But they were also equipped with guns, stolen from raids or purchased from the Comancheros, outlaws who sold firewater and arms to the hostiles. Usually, though, their rifles were older, and single-shot, unlike the Army carbines.

He put up his right hand, halting the column. Deer Stalker, who'd been following the troop, rode up.

"Must stop. Go no more. Wait," the Apache cautioned.

Gregor glanced at Deer Stalker, wondering if he could trust the man. Or was this whole setup an excuse for a well-planned ambush?

When serving at Fort Concho, he'd been at war with the Comanche. They'd murdered settlers and raided stock to survive. Their way of life had disappeared with the slaughter of the buffalo herds. And he'd been duty-bound to retaliate and subdue them to protect the settlers.

Even though the Comanche had been the enemy, they'd earned his begrudging respect. They had their own set of values and sense of honor. They lived their lives as they always had, superb horseman of the plains, surrendering to reservations only when they couldn't fight any longer.

But the Apache were cut from a different cloth. Victorio, the head chief of the Mescalero Apache, had surrendered and retreated to a reservation in New Mexico. But it didn't stop him from sending his war chiefs to raid and murder when he felt aggrieved.

Gregor understood Victorio's motives, especially when some of the Indian agents cheated and stole from the reservations. Victorio had his braves raid in retaliation as a protest against the flawed reservation system, wanting to protect his people from ill treatment.

Unfortunately, killing innocent settlers, including women and children, did nothing to address the chief's grievances with the Indian Agency. If anything, Victorio's raids added kerosene to an already blazing fire, enflaming hostilities and sustaining a cycle of escalating retaliation on both sides.

Two wrongs don't make a right.

His mother, God rest her soul, had been a devout Christian, who'd lived by two principles: "do unto others as you would have them do unto you," and "two wrongs don't make a right." As a boy, she'd taught him her faith and principles. They were inscribed on the bedrock of his soul, and he tried his best to live by them.

He smoothed the reins in his gloved hands. "All right, we wait. But for what?"

"Caballero come. He bring hostages to exchange. And big wagon," Deer Stalker explained.

Big wagon?

He'd surmised Caballero had raided to have something to offer, but he'd expected stolen livestock, not the stagecoach. What about the passengers? He bit back a curse. Not even his strict routine of patrols could stop the raids—there was too much road to cover.

He nodded and waited. But he didn't give his men their ease. No, they needed to be on the alert.

He expected Deer Stalker to enter the canyon and bring Caballero out, but the Apache were all around them, looking down from the canyon walls. The war chief would come when he was ready.

The tell-tale rumbling of the coach over the rocky canyon broke the silence. It was being pulled by six braves. The driver's seat was empty, not a good sign. He clenched his jaw, fearing the worst.

Caballero and his men had already taken the horses. He doubted they intended to return them. They must have better things to trade.

His throat went dry, thinking about the driver, the guard, and any innocent passengers who might have been taken.

As of yet, despite government promises, the telegraph lines didn't extend to Fort Davis. There was no way to know, ahead of time, if the stage carried passengers or not. Sometimes, the coaches were empty except for mail and packages, but the coach would have had a driver and guard.

Caballero and three of his braves came riding up. Though he'd never met the Apache war chief, he recognized him by the numerous feathers he had braided in his hair, making him look like a sharp-beaked hawk, ready to swoop onto his prey.

Caballero was bare-chested and covered in war paint. He jerked his head, and the six braves pulling the coach dropped the wagon's shafts and melted back into the canyon.

Gregor advanced a few yards and stopped, waiting.

Deer Stalker said, "He wants go there. Meet half-way."

Gregor nodded, thinking the Apache was a master at manipulating the situation to make himself appear more important.

He turned and told Sergeant Springer, who was in charge of the patrol, to wait for him. He urged his mount forward... alone, except for Deer Stalker who trailed him. He couldn't do without the translator. He'd learned a few words of Comanche, but the Apache language, guttural and heavily accented, had eluded him.

Caballero raised his right hand in a salute. He followed suit. The chief jerked his head again and said something.

Deer Stalker turned to him, but he didn't meet his eyes. "Caballero wants you dismount."

"He's not going to dismount. Is he?"

"No."

"I see." He let his horse's reins drop, ground-tying him. He threw his right leg over his horse's neck and dropped to the ground. He stood, gazing up at Caballero. He could play the chief's game, if it meant getting innocent people freed. Deer Stalker dismounted, too, and stood beside him.

Caballero swept his arm toward the stagecoach and spit out some words.

Gregor kept his gaze trained on the chief, not daring to blink. "What did he say?"

"He says big wagon, nothing taken. All good."

"I'll bet," he muttered under his breath, knowing the Apache would have stolen what pleased them.

"What about the stagecoach driver and guard?"

More words were exchanged between the Apache men.

Deer Stalker hunkered down and took up a stick, drawing patterns in the sandy ground. "Dead. Killed during attack."

He took several deep breaths and fisted his hands. Guilt and frustration swamped him. He'd done everything he knew to stop the raids and attacks. But it wasn't enough; he either needed more men or to change his tactics.

His first instinct was to attack the Apache, avenging the driver and guard's deaths, but they had the advantage, perched on the canyon walls, able to easily pick off his men.

He'd learned the hard way, after twelve years on the frontier, fighting the hostiles was a war of attrition with small victories and a slow whittling away of their numbers and resources. It took nerves of steel and an unwavering commitment to his men, waiting for the right place and time.

He'd not sacrifice his soldiers to certain slaughter. He'd wait and bide his time, picking his battles when the odds were better.

"Do they have the bodies?" he asked. "I want to give them a decent burial."

As if by magic, two braves leading paint ponies, appeared with the lifeless bodies of the driver and guard draped over their backs. The braves pulled the men off and dumped them on the ground.

Gregor turned around, not caring if the Apache chief took offense. He motioned toward Sergeant Springer and called out, "Strap those men to two of your mounts and have the men ride double. We'll bury them in Fort Davis."

"Yes, sir," Sergeant Springer saluted and picked two men to help him.

Gregor turned back. He narrowed his eyes and scowled. "And the horses pulling the coach?" He already knew the answer, but after seeing the dead men, he wanted to hold Caballero responsible for each of his actions.

"His horses now," Deer Stalker said. "For big wagon."

Gregor pulled off his gloves and slapped them against his thigh.

The chief, his black eyes narrowed, followed his movements, probably wondering if he was insulting him.

"Tell the chief he can keep the big wagon. He's already killed two men." He turned around and walked back to his horse. "I'm done here."

Deer Stalker nodded and spoke.

The chief sputtered something in an angry tone.

"Men dead—they killed three Caballero's braves. Fair fight," Deer Stalker said.

Gregor stopped walking, but he didn't turn around. A fair fight? A band of fifteen Apache warriors had attacked a stagecoach with only two men. "If the men are dead, what does he have to offer?"

"White man and white woman." Deer Stalker had followed him.

Gregor's heart dropped. But he wasn't surprised. The chief hadn't sent for him without having hostages to trade for the Apache women.

Deer Stalker came and stood in front of him. "He wants Apache women. Woman with baby is new wife of chief. Wants wife and son back."

Finally, a bargaining chip.

Gregor turned around. "Have the passengers been harmed?" He hated to think what condition they might be in, especially if they'd struggled or tried to break free. The only hopeful part was that they hadn't been captives of the Apache for long.

Deer Stalker and Caballero exchanged words.

The translator turned to him. "No, no harm. Woman has sunlight hair. Very young. Give you many children."

Gregor snorted. *If only.* He'd wished all of his and Martha's children had lived, but they hadn't. And in his culture, women weren't broodmares, to be bought and sold.

"Let me see them. I need to *see* them before I agree," he demanded. "And Caballero will have to come to the fort to get his women and the baby."

Deer Stalker hung his head, obviously reluctant to translate.

"Tell him!"

The translator didn't look up. He gazed at his feet and mumbled a few words.

Caballero scowled and swelled up before his eyes. He jerked his head again and one of his band dismounted and opened the stage door. A dirty, bearded man spilled out, his hands tied behind his back. He sported a black eye and a red, swollen welt covered his left cheek.

Obviously, the war chief's idea of harm was different from his own. He prayed the woman had fared better.

As soon as the bearded man saw him, he rushed forward and fell at his feet. "I'm purely tickled to see you, Colonel. These savages—"

"Be quiet. We're still parleying. Don't interfere, and I'll get you free. Patience," he cautioned.

But it was too late; the Apache who'd jerked him from the stage, yanked the man to his feet and raised his hand.

Gregor stepped forward and caught the brave's arm. Locked together, they gazed at each other, rancor rolling between them, thick and bitter as week-old coffee.

Caballero half-turned and spoke sharply. Two braves, holding a woman between them, appeared from behind a boulder. The woman sagged in their grasp, and her eyes were rolled back in her head.

Good Lord, what had they done to her?

"*Hat' ii baa nadaa*?" Caballero barked and pointed at him.

Gregor looked to Deer Stalker, but the translator walked away. He let the Apache's arm go. The man grunted and moved beside Caballero's mount.

The two braves came forward and dropped the woman at his feet.

He bent down and cradled the woman's shoulders. She had blond hair, pulled into a bun, though half of her hair had come loose and fell around her face. He looked her over for injuries but only found a few bruises on her arms, and a thin, red line of blood on her throat.

Seeing her blood, worn like a hideous necklace, he wanted to strike Caballero, but he couldn't do that. He must remain calm and collected. Not show any emotions or weakness. And not get his men slaughtered.

A shadow shrouded him. He glanced up.

Caballero had dismounted. The Apache chief stood over him, snarling words he didn't understand.

He glanced back to find his translator and called out, "Deer Stalker, if you want this month's pay, you'll tell me what he's saying."

Deer Stalker shuffled his feet and bobbed his head. "Caballero says take woman and man. He no go fort for women. You bring to road fork."

Gregor glared at Caballero, realizing he didn't want to parley anymore. Not now. He knew which fork the Apache chief meant. One mile east of the fort, a wagon trail branched off, leading to Murphy's spread, the Lazy M Ranch.

He nodded.

The Apache chief glared back and spat out two words.

"Caballero wants white chief's promise," Deer Stalker said.

He shifted the woman's shoulders and raised his right hand. "You have my word. At sunrise tomorrow?"

Deer Stalker explained. Caballero grunted, crossed his arms, and inclined his head.

"We're done," Gregor said.

The translator bowed to Caballero and spoke a few words. The chief turned and walked away stiffly, his back ramrod straight.

"Deer Stalker, as soon as we get back to the fort, let the Apache women know they'll be returned tomorrow morning to their chief." Perhaps if they knew they were going to be freed, they'd quit trying to harm themselves.

The interpreter nodded and returned to his mount.

As gently as he could, Gregor got his arms under the woman and lifted her, cradling her head and torso. She mumbled something and tried to pull away, but she didn't open her eyes. Turning around, he walked back to his patrol. Deer Stalker led their mounts with the rescued passenger, trailing behind.

"Sergeant Springer, hitch up four of our best horses to the stagecoach. Those men can ride their mounts and guide the stage." He turned to the rescued man. "Sir, I don't know your name. I'm Colonel Gregor, commander of Fort Davis."

"Sam Spofford's the name. I'm a mule skinner, workin' fer Oberlin Freight." He grimaced. "Thought we was done in. I can't thank you 'nuf fer saving—"

"Glad to meet you, Mr. Spofford." He inclined his head and said, "Sergeant Springer, Mr. Spofford will be riding with you."

The Sergeant saluted and offered his hand to Mr. Spofford. The muleskinner climbed up behind Springer.

"What about the lady, sir?" Springer asked.

"I'll carry her back." He glanced down. "It's the least I can do, given what she's been through."

His gaze wandered over her, taking in details he'd been too distraught to notice before, like her clothing. Her traveling dress was made of good quality material and looked fashionable. She was corseted and bedecked unlike any woman he'd seen in a long time... probably not since his days at Fort Clark. And she was light in his arms, not weighing above a hundred pounds, if that, despite her long legs.

He wondered how to get her in the saddle without disturbing her. He didn't see any head wounds. He assumed she'd fainted from fright and would awaken soon. On second thought, maybe it would be easier for her, lying down in the stagecoach than being jostled on the back of a horse.

But he hated to let her go... for some reason.

Her eyelids fluttered open, and he stared into her eyes. The irises of her eyes were a rich combination of green and light brown. She had hazel-colored eyes, like his Martha's. And the woman had his Martha's ash-blond hair, too, before illness had turned it white.

He clutched her to him, the feel of her body stirring parts of him he'd thought were dead and buried. He tightened his hold, crushing her against his heart, not wanting to let go.

She reached up and touched his cheek. Then her hand trailed over his uniform. "You're from the fort? The Indians who...?"

He shuddered, feeling the soft brush of her hand. How long since he'd felt a woman's touch? "We've rescued you, Miss. The Apache are gone."

Her smile shimmered, as bright as a new-day dawn. "Take me home, soldier, please."

“Do you want to lie down in the stagecoach? We can—”

“No, please, hold me.” Her voice slid over him, a slow Southern drawl, like honey spread on biscuits. She clutched at his sleeve and closed her eyes, shaking her head.

He couldn’t refuse her, though, it would be a rough way to travel. “Hosea,” he called over his shoulder, “help me get this young lady situated on my horse. I’ll have to hold her. I don’t think she can ride behind me.”

His scout dismounted and saluted, holding out his arms.

She opened her eyes again. “I’m stronger than I look. I can ride behind you and hold on, soldier. Please.”

Chapter Two

Dazed and trembling, Mallory clasped her arms around the soldier who had rescued her. She felt as if she'd been caught in a hurricane, carried on a high wind and flung to the ground. She couldn't stop shaking, and her brains seemed scrambled, not fully comprehending what had happened. When she thought about the savages who'd taken her, she wanted to roll into a ball and disappear. But she had to get hold of herself.

Clinging to her rescuer, she burrowed into his back. His chest was broad and muscled. His longish hair, curling over his collar, was brown with shimmers of red shot through it and a few silver stands. He wasn't a young man, definitely older than thirty, maybe even forty years. But he was strong and capable.

His presence comforted her, though her stomach still sloshed with nausea and she hoped she wouldn't throw up again, as she had when the Indians took her. That had been past humiliating.

He smelled good, too, of soap and bay rum, with the lingering scent of coffee clinging to his clothes. He must like his coffee, as her father had.

An hour before, she'd thought her life was over—that she'd be subjected to the vilest of horrors men could inflict upon a woman.

How well she knew what it felt like to be violated.

Disgust dug at her, turning her thoughts to Hiram. But she wouldn't allow herself to dwell on that dark time—never again. Her tumbling thoughts strayed to Macon, her beloved son.

The stagecoach lurched and rattled behind them. The Indians… the Apache had gone through its contents, scattering some things to the four winds, but mostly, they'd left her trunk alone. If she was lucky, Macon's picture would still be there, hidden in a side pocket.

Thoughts of Hiram usually made her skittish, making her shy away from men. Despite what had happened today, she hoped she could pull herself together and be a dutiful wife for Mr. Murphy. At least, he wouldn't see her like this, as there had been no way to tell him which stage she'd be on.

If she won Mr. Murphy's regard, she could send for her son, and they'd be a family—*if* her husband-to-be was a kind and forgiving man—*if* he was as gentle as she instinctively knew this soldier to be.

For some reason, the soldier reminded her of her childhood sweetheart, Beauregard Jackson, a boy from the neighboring plantation. He'd marched off to the War Between the States and returned, fatally wounded. She'd helped his mother nurse him, but it had been no use. His wounds had been deep and had festered.

She and Beau had been dedicated to each other from childhood, and he was a kind and gentle boy. War hadn't changed him. Even as he lay dying, he'd been more concerned about her future than his death.

And if he'd known her future, he wouldn't have passed peacefully.

Had Beau lived, how different her life would have been. But the past was behind her, and she needed to make a new future in this hostile place.

The horse stumbled, throwing her to one side. She clutched at the soldier and burrowed herself deeper into his strong, muscled back, lacing her fingers across his tight stomach.

"Sorry, Miss. I didn't see the prairie dog hole."

"What's a prairie dog?"

"Hard to explain." He shook his head and glanced back at her. His eyes were a silvery-blue, like storm clouds rolling over the ocean.

"A prairie dog is something like a stout squirrel that lives underground in tunnels. They dot the land with their holes, entrances to their tunnels. We try to keep the main road clear, though, as the holes are dangerous. If a horse steps directly into one, he can break his leg, leaving his rider afoot."

"Oh, I'd like to see a prairie dog. But I guess I'll need to be careful when I'm riding." She couldn't believe she was chatting with him. They hadn't been formally introduced, but he had saved her life.

As if he'd read her thoughts, he said, "I think I should introduce myself." He touched the wide brim of his navy-blue hat. "I'm Colonel William Gregor, the commander of Fort Davis."

She'd known he was a man of substance. To be rescued by the commander of the fort was more than lucky—it was a miracle. She bowed her head and offered a short prayer of thanksgiving to her Savior.

"I'm privileged and honored to make your acquaintance. My name is Mallory Metcalf Reynolds. And I'm beholden to you for saving my life."

"My privilege, Ma'am, to be sure. May I inquire where you were headed?"

"To your fort, Commander. I'm a mail order bride. Mr. E. P. Murphy placed an advertisement in the *Texas Christian Advocate*, a Methodist publication that is widely circulated throughout the south. My good friend, Nancy Arledge, a minister's wife, showed me the advertisement. I answered it, and Mr. Murphy and I exchanged letters."

When she said "the South," she could feel his muscles tense. Like as not, he'd been a Federal soldier during the war, fighting on the other side. But she'd given up her prejudice against Union soldiers, though the war had torn apart the fabric of her life.

"I know Mr. Murphy," he said. "He's a good man and a devout Christian. He built a Methodist church in town and hired a minister from his own funds. And his ranch is one of the largest around." He inclined his head. "There's the fork leading to his spread. Was he expecting you?"

"Yes, though, I couldn't telegraph him when I was due to arrive."

"I understand. We're scheduled to string wire from Barilla Springs, the farthest point west. We're waiting on the telegraph wire to arrive. Eventually, the telegraph will stretch to Fort Bliss and El Paso."

"I'm pleased to hear it. I can't imagine how cut off you must feel without a telegraph."

"Yes, it hinders our efforts to coordinate with other forts to fight the hostiles."

She shuddered and glanced back at the two men who'd died today. This was a wild and untamed land with danger lurking around every corner. Beau hadn't been the only casualty of the war; she'd seen enough death and suffering to last a lifetime.

Hosea, who'd helped her onto the back of the horse, was a Negro, as was all of the men of Commander Gregor's patrol, except for the native translator. She'd heard of such, Negro men serving in the Army, but she'd seldom seen them in uniform.

It was unusual, but the world was changing, and she was determined to change with it. That was what her new life was about, adapting to change. She might have been born in the South on a plantation with numerous slaves, but to her way of thinking, people shouldn't own other people.

When her English-born mother had died of a fever, two months before her father marched off to the war, she'd had no one but Negro servants to take care of her. Her Mammy, Astarte, had been her surrogate mother, and all of the servants had remained, even after Lincoln freed them, to care for her and the house.

"You're more than welcome to stay with me and my daughter, Peggy," the commander broke into her thoughts. "We have an extra room, something of a luxury on a fort where lodgings are in short supply."

He looked over his shoulder again and smiled. "Though, I'll warn you, I keep a bachelor's establishment. My wife passed away, almost two years ago."

"My condolences to you, Commander. This must be a harsh place to live without a proper helpmate."

"Yes," he said, as if considering, "yes, it is. I miss my..." He stopped and cleared his throat. "You're very perceptive, Miss Reynolds. Mr. Murphy is a lucky man."

"I hope he feels as you do, Commander."

"I'm sure he will." He patted her hand, but almost awkwardly, like someone would pet their dog or horse. "Martina, my housekeeper, can draw you a bath, and you can rest and get cleaned up. I'll send one of my men to Mr. Murphy's ranch to tell him you've arrived."

"I'm sure he'll be distressed to find out *how* I arrived." She chewed on her lip and hesitated, not knowing what to think about his offer of a room when he was a widower. “Uh, Commander, I can’t thank you enough for your kind offer of putting me up, but I’m an unmarried woman and as such—”

“No explanation necessary.” He shook his head. “I forgot how it might look. I had an unmarried woman live with me and my daughter at Fort Clark, but she was betrothed to one of my sergeants, and no one thought the worst of her. Out West, we don’t always have the luxury of observing the proprieties. You’re still welcome to my home, and I can sleep at my office. I want you to feel safe and looked after. I’ll post a guard for you and my daughter at my cabin. Will that suit you?”

“Oh, I don’t want to trouble you, Commander. Is there a hotel or boardinghouse in town?”

“Fort Davis doesn’t have a hotel yet. Though, there’s a Mrs. Johnson who rents out rooms but not for a night or two. She prefers boarders on a monthly basis. Besides, a single woman alone in town is more... vulnerable than onc at thc fort. Please, won’t you reconsider?”

She sucked in her breath, realizing what the commander was saying. The Apache were all around them, raiding and making war. And a single woman wasn’t safe in town at a boardinghouse?

When she’d accepted Mr. Murphy’s proposal, she had no idea what she was getting herself into.

“All right, Commander, I will accept your hospitality, though, I hate to put you out.”

“Not to worry, Miss Reynolds. I will be pleased to host you, and I know my daughter will enjoy having you, too.”

“Thank you, Commander. Though, I hope you’ll come home for your meals.”

“I’ll sleep at my office, but I’ll be home for meals. I can’t desert Peggy, my daughter.” His voice sounded gruff, heavy with unspoken emotions. “We’re almost to the fort, and we’ll have you married in no time. I’m assuming you’ll marry in town at the new church?”

“I guess so,” she said.

And then she had an idea, though, she knew there was no turning back. But for some reason, after what had happened today, she didn’t want to be delivered to Mr. Murphy like a wrapped-up package. No, she wanted to ride out and see his ranch first.

Why? She didn't know. And she could ill afford doubts.

Still, the idea stuck in her head, and she could be stubborn. Too stubborn for her own good, her father had often told her.

"Commander, rather than sending a soldier to fetch my intended, would you escort me to his ranch? I'd like to surprise him."

"Uh, Miss Reynolds, are you sure..."

"Very sure."

"Well, I can send one of my officers with you, but I've pressing duties. I don't know if I can find the time to—"

"Please, Commander," she implored. "After all, you're the one who saved me."

"I was just doing my job, Miss Reynolds. I, uh..."

"Please, Commander." She tightened her grip, almost hugging him. "I would consider it a special favor if you would escort me to my husband-to-be."

"All right, Miss Reynolds, if you put it that way. I'll take you the day after tomorrow. That should give you plenty of time to rest and recuperate before you meet Mr. Murphy."

"Thank you. You're such a kind man."

As she said the words, she knew them to be true. He was kind. And since Hiram, she'd not looked upon any man with favor. She hoped it was a good omen of her life to come.

* * *

Gregor sat at the kitchen table, picking at his breakfast. Peggy, who sat to his right, was chattering like a magpie with Miss Reynolds. He lifted his coffee cup and gazed at them over the rim, realizing his daughter was growing up fast.

When she'd celebrated her twelfth birthday last month, he'd given her a pair of tortoise-shell barrettes. Sally Rodgers, one of his captains' wives, had cut her long braids, leaving her with shoulder-length, wavy blonde hair.

Sally had helped her pick out several bolts of fabric, too, and was teaching her to sew. Peggy with her loose, flowing hair and a new pink dress, looked more like a young lady than a girl.

He sipped his coffee and realized the thought of Peggy becoming a young woman was disconcerting. Not that he expected her to remain a child forever, but without his wife to guide her, he worried how he would handle the next stage of his daughter's life. He felt poorly equipped to help his daughter with female concerns.

His daughter laughed at something Miss Reynolds said, and her blue eyes sparkled. He was glad she'd taken a liking to Miss Reynolds, as there weren't many women in Fort Davis, at the fort or in town. Sally was the one lady who Peggy seemed to enjoy being around. Their housekeeper, Martina, spoke only rudimentary English. Peggy, on the other hand, was learning Spanish with ease.

It was a good thing his daughter was learning something. Since they'd moved to Fort Davis, her education had been sorely lacking. There was only a handful of officers' children at the fort, and so far, no regular classroom had been established. Each of the families took charge of their children's education.

He put down his coffee cup, realizing he missed Crissy, his housekeeper from Fort Clark, who'd been well-educated and had served as a governess to Peggy. Crissy and his daughter had been close with Crissy acting as a surrogate mother after he'd lost his wife.

Crissy had written last week to tell him Davie had finished his enlistment, and they were moving to Galveston where her husband would take over his father's carpentry shop.

Crissy, in the first year of their marriage, had given birth to a baby boy, named William, after himself. He wished he could have gotten away for the christening, but the fort's business was too pressing. Now, Crissy was pregnant again.

Not that he was surprised. Davie and Crissy had been in love, and he knew their family would grow quickly. But he missed them, especially Crissy.

At Fort Davis, he'd churned through several of the local women, all Spanish-speaking, hoping to find someone like Crissy, but in the end, he'd settled for a good cook and decent housekeeper. He was in charge of his daughter's lessons, and he knew he wasn't giving Peggy the education she needed.

Miss Reynolds laughed, a tinkling, cultured sound, and reached for Peggy's hand. He hadn't been paying attention, but it was obvious the woman had found something his daughter said amusing.

Raising his eyes, his gaze swept Miss Reynolds. Doc Winslow had examined her and said her wounds were superficial. Bathed and rested and with a cameo on a thick ribbon, hiding the wound on her neck, she'd appeared at the breakfast table, looking like a vision and smelling like a meadow filled with flowers.

She had on another expensively-tailored dress, her waist cinched in, made tinier by corseting. Out West, few women wore corsets, except to church or other special occasions. The climate with its hot days and manual labor made corsets cumbersome.

As enticing as her hour-glass figure was, he couldn't keep from stealing glances at her face. She was so much like his Martha when she was young. Her ash-blond hair and hazel eyes reminded him of his late wife. Her features were regular and handsome, as his Martha's had been. Even her southern drawl was reminiscent of how his late wife had spoken when they'd first met.

They'd met at a barn-raising dance on the Kentucky border. He was from Ohio, and she was from Kentucky. His father was best friends with Mr. Rawlins, the farm where they'd gone to help Martha's people were distant cousins of the Rawlins. They'd fallen in love at first sight. He winced and closed his eyes, fighting back the pain of remembering too much.

"Papa," his daughter's voice broke through his memories, "can I show Miss Reynolds around the fort and town? She says she'd love to explore with me."

Miss Reynolds patted his daughter's shoulder and said, "Please, not Miss Reynolds. I'll call you Peggy, and you must call me Mallory."

"Miss Mallory then." His daughter grinned.

It was good to see his daughter smile. Despite her youth and enthusiasm, he knew she missed her mother and, like him, hadn't stopped grieving. He often heard her sobbing into her pillow, trying to muffle the sound, realizing with her young-old sensibilities that he was hurting, too, and not wanting to add to his misery.

“What about your lessons, young lady? I stayed up late, outlining your lesson plan for this week. You need to work on your division, and you’re several chapters behind in history. I wrote out some sentences for you to diagram, too.”

“Oh, Papa, can’t my lessons wait? Miss Mallory will be leaving tomorrow. You said you’d be taking her—”

“Don’t contradict your father, Peggy. If you’ve lessons to do, I’m more than happy to help. I had an excellent governess when I was young. She was quite a task master, and then I finished my schooling at Miss Prentiss’ in Charleston. My best friend, Nancy, believes I would make a good teacher.” She hesitated, lowering her head and fiddling with her teacup. “Though, I thought it best to choose another destiny.”

He’d been right about Miss Reynolds, she *was* from a life of wealth and privilege. Only the privileged could afford a governess. If that was true, why had she risked her life to come west as a mail order bride? The Civil War was most likely the answer. Many wealthy plantation owners had lost their fortunes and free labor during the war.

“You’re our guest, Miss Reynolds. No need for you to assist Peggy. She knows what she has to do,” he said.

His daughter scowled and set her mouth in what he called her stubborn-as-a-mule look.

“I’d be honored to help, Commander. I may be your guest, but I owe you more than I’ll ever be able to repay.” She reached her hand across the table as if to touch him, must have thought better of it, and drew her hand back. “Please, let me go over Peggy’s lessons and if she finishes what you’ve set out for her, we might have time to explore later.”

“Yes, Papa, please.”

“All right, then. I doubt I’ll be back for the mid-day break.” He fixed his gaze on his daughter. “Make certain you finish what I’ve set you to do and after the mid-day meal, I want you to lie down for an hour. Then, if there’s time, you can show Miss Reynolds around. I’m certain she would be particularly interested in the new church. But don’t go beyond the church.”

Peggy jumped up and threw her arms around his neck. "Thank you, Papa, thank you! I'll apply myself and get my lessons done in no time."

He gazed at his guest. "Thank you, Miss Reynolds, I appreciate your willingness to help." He shook his head. "I'm afraid it's a struggle, making certain my daughter does her lessons while I've pressing matters at headquarters."

Not only had he stayed up late, outlining his daughter's lessons, he'd ridden out, hours before, at sunup, to personally deliver the Apache hostages to Caballero and his braves. Caballero hadn't bothered to show up, sending his medicine man, Cloud Walker, in his stead.

He might not be able to trust the war chief's word, but it appeared Caballero had no such reservations. He sighed. It was a heavy burden, trying to stop the Apache depredations. And most of the time, he failed miserably.

On his ride to Seven Springs he'd had an idea of a better way to deploy his troops. He was optimistic about his new idea, which was a good thing, as he often doubted himself and became frustrated with the slow progress in this remote, mountainous area.

He'd thought increased patrols would thwart the Apache and lessen the raids, but the troops never seemed to be in the right place, at the right time. It was puzzling, and with two stagecoach attacks in one week, he needed a different strategy. First, though, he had to meet with his two cavalry captains, Rodgers and Myerson, to go over the terrain again.

After delivering the hostages, he'd attended the burial of the stagecoach driver and guard. The new Methodist minister had officiated. The fort had a chaplain, but the men were civilians, and he thought it best to engage Reverend Finley, hoping to get the young man accustomed to the demands of his ministry on the frontier.

He pushed back from the table, keen to start strategizing. Martina came from outside with a pail of milk. She set the pail down, bobbed her head, and started clearing the breakfast dishes.

Miss Reynolds, with her arm around Peggy's shoulders, led her to a table in the corner, saying, "Show me your father's lesson plan, and we'll start right away."

Peggy gazed up at Miss Reynolds, naked adoration in her eyes. He winced and gulped. He'd not seen his daughter look like that since they'd lost her mother… and then Crissy.

His almost-empty stomach clenched, and he straightened his back, reaching for the front door latch. Life was hard and, he often thought with his wife gone, if he hadn't been committed to making the frontier safe, he should retire and return to Ohio.

But he'd chosen his path, and now, he must stay the course.

* * *

Mallory held Peggy's hand as the girl led her through the fort, pointing out the various buildings and their purposes. Fort Davis was a bustling place with soldiers drilling, performing everyday tasks, and erecting new buildings.

As she'd noticed the day before, the mounted soldiers were all Negroes, except for the officers. But there was a sprinkling of white soldiers, too, working at various jobs, as carpenters and masons on the half-built structures. It was a singular way of dividing the duties.

"Peggy, why are all the mounted soldiers Negroes, and the other soldiers—"

"Oh, the mounted cavalry, they're our Buffalo Soldiers."

"Buffalo Soldiers, what does that mean?"

Peggy swung their hands and glanced at her. "You're from a long way off, aren't you?"

"Yes, I grew up in Georgia."

"I was born here in Texas," the girl declared proudly. "Papa says the frontier is different from any other place."

"I'm sure it is but Buffalo Soldiers?"

Peggy hitched one shoulder. "That's easy, it's what the Indians call the Negroes, saying their grizzled hair reminds them of buffalo pelts."

"I've never seen a buffalo, except in a book."

"Well, you probably won't see them around here, either. They mainly stay on the plains, not in the mountains. And the Buffalo

Soldiers are our mounted cavalry because they're awesome scouts, tracking Indians better than anyone, except other Indians."

"Well, that makes sense. But what about the other soldiers?"

The young girl wrinkled her freckled nose. "They're our infantry units. Papa says they're not suited to pursuing hostiles, marching on foot. He uses them to keep the fort running and to build the new buildings we need."

"Sounds like your father knows what he's doing."

Peggy dropped her hand and ran forward. "Corporal, can I pet Boots?"

"To be sure, Miss Peggy." The corporal was walking a roan horse that looked familiar. He stopped and held the horse's bridle.

The commander's daughter reached into her pocket and brought out a sugar cube. The horse lipped up the treat, and Peggy giggled. "He tickles!" She patted the horse's gray-speckled neck. "Isn't he a beauty? He's my Papa's favorite mount."

Now Mallory remembered, though to be honest, most of yesterday was something of a blur. The commander's horse had been a roan gelding. Accustomed to being raised around superior horseflesh, she scanned the gelding's confirmation and saw why Peggy was enthralled. He was a stunning horse.

"Papa had to pay for part of Boots. The Army didn't want to buy him because he was too expensive." She stroked the horse's nose. "But I think he's beautiful, and I'm glad Papa got Boots."

"He is handsome," Mallory agreed. "But why do you call him 'Boots?' He doesn't have socks."

Peggy gave the horse a last pat and returned to her side. "For 'boots and saddles.' It's a nickname for the cavalry. Want to see the town?" She wrinkled her nose again. "Not that there's much to see, but the new church is there."

"Yes, please show me."

They joined hands again, and Peggy led her to a dusty road leading away from the canyon, a natural defensive position that made her feel safe.

But how would she feel on a secluded ranch, miles from nowhere?

Despite feeling relatively safe, she was curious, though, about the manner in which the fort had been built. "I thought the fort would be enclosed by a wall or palisade."

"Not in the West. My Papa says western forts rely on their soldiers and guns, not walls, for keeping away the hostiles. Though bad men have sold the Indians guns, and Papa says having guns have made the hostiles more fearless."

"Oh, I didn't know."

She vividly recalled the thud of arrows into the stagecoach, but she also remembered the man who'd captured her was holding a gun, and all of the braves seemed to have some kind of firearm.

"The commander who picked the site for Fort Davis chose it for the natural protection of the canyon walls, along with *Limpia* Creek," Peggy informed her. "*Limpia* means clean in Spanish. Martina has been teaching me Spanish."

"Learning other languages is a good thing. My governess taught me French."

"Really?" Peggy gazed at her. "I've never heard anyone speak French."

"Well, if you were to go east to New Orleans, you'd find many French-speaking people."

"Hmmm, I'd like to go there and see those big riverboats. The ones with the paddlewheels."

"They're wonderful boats. Smooth to ride upon and very luxurious. Maybe someday, you'll go east and travel on one."

"I'd like that." Peggy dropped her hand again and skipped ahead.

The rutted road, leading away from the fort, appeared to be the main street of the town. As Mallory glanced around, she was disappointed to find the town was small and had little to offer beyond a dry goods store, a green grocer's, bakery, butcher's shop, livery, lumberyard, and saloon. Most of the stores were made of wood or limestone, like the fort's buildings.

Behind the main street, there were some scattered houses. A few were wooden, but most were constructed of a smooth, earthen-looking substance.

They were nearing the end of the street, and a small, half-painted building with a cross above the front door stood in solitary splendor.

Peggy stopped in front of the building and pointed. "There it is. Appears Reverend Finley hasn't finished painting the church. Too bad."

She looked the squat church over; it was like no other church Mallory had ever seen. The structure was rectangular with clear glass windows along the sides. In place of a steeple, there was another box-like structure placed at the front of the roof line. And the building was made from that peculiar earthen-looking substance, too.

"What is the church built from? I've never seen anything like it."

"Oh, that's called adobe, and it's how the Mexicans build. It's a kind of sunbaked mud, either bricks or filler between a wooden frame. If the walls are thick enough, the buildings are cooler in the summer and warmer in the winter.

"Papa says the Mexicans learned how to use adobe from the more settled Indians, like the Navajo and Hopi." Peggy bobbed her head. "He told me about Indian towns in New Mexico, built out of adobe, which are one huge building, divided up into many homes for the families. I'd like to see that."

"Yes," Mallory agreed, "though, it's hard to picture." In Charleston, after the war, some builders had erected three-and-four story buildings with shops below and apartments for tenants above. She wondered if the strange adobe structures in New Mexico looked anything like them.

Standing still, she could feel the sun, beating down on her head. She shaded her eyes and glanced up, taking in the blue sky, stretching for miles with a few puffs of white clouds. "Being cooler in the summer and warmer in the winter is quite an advantage," she said.

They'd napped for the prescribed hour, and though it was only April, Mallory could feel the sting of the sun on her skin. Not that it was as hot as the Lowcountry in summer, but the sun here seemed stronger. She must remember not to go out-of-doors without her parasol for fear of ruining her complexion.

"I hadn't thought it would be this warm during the day," she remarked.

"That's because the air is thin up here."

"Pardon me?"

"Papa's reasoning. When he can get them in the mail, he reads what he calls 'scientific journals', and there's a theory the higher up you go in the mountains, the thinner the air is, making the sun feel hotter."

"How fascinating. I would have never taken your father for a reader of scientific journals."

"Why not?"

"I don't know." She shrugged. "Something about him reminds me of my friend's husband who's a minister."

Peggy leaned closer, a mischievous gleam in her eye. "If you can keep a secret, I'll tell you something."

Mallory had to smile. Children and secrets, like iron and magnets, couldn't resist each other. Shc touched the young girl's shoulder and said, "I'm very good with secrets." She crossed her heart and kissed the palm of her hand. "I promise."

"Papa wanted to be a preacher. Then he met Mama, and they married."

"But preachers marry; why did he give up on being a preacher?"

Peggy shrugged. "I'm not sure. Grown-up stuff, something about having a decent home."

"Oh, I see." But Mallory didn't understand why his being a preacher would preclude him from having a nice home. Most preachers lived in parsonages, free of charge, built for them by their congregations.

Peggy's secret did answer one question—now she knew why the commander struck her as a kind and an upright man.

"Too bad the preacher hasn't finished painting," Peggy said again. "Once it's white-washed, the church will look a whole lot better."

Mallory nodded. She couldn't help but agree. The original adobe color was a muddy brown. The parts of the church that had been painted at least looked clean and inviting.

"I guess Reverend Finley won't have time to finish, not before your wedding anyway."

"Most likely." Mallory pursed her lips, trying to envision her wedding day, taking place within the next week. She had brought an appropriate dress, nothing too showy but probably far more elegant than most folks had seen in this tiny, far-flung town. She hoped her husband-to-be approved.

Despite their stilted, formal letters to each other, it struck Mallory she'd be marrying a veritable stranger, a man she knew very little about. Thinking of it, her heart fluttered in her chest like a dove, beating its wings against the bars of its cage.

"How many people live in town? Do you know?" she asked.

"At last count, Papa said about five hundred, but there's new people moving here every day, especially because Fort Davis is the county seat."

"So, the town is called Fort Davis, too?"

"Used to be called Presidio, but now that's the name of the county instead." Peggy grabbed her hand again and tugged. "Want to see the inside of the church?"

The way she was feeling, as if this squat, half-painted structure would be her sacrificial altar, she'd rather not see inside, but she couldn't tell Peggy such a thing. Instead, she said, "Of course."

They entered the building, which smelled strongly of fresh paint, and found an austere interior, composed of simple wooden pews, a communion rail, and a pulpit.

From the shadows, a raw-boned, young man appeared. "Welcome, I'm Reverend Finley, and it does my heart good to see your interest in our new church."

Peggy pushed her forward. "She's getting married here in the next few days, so you better be ready."

Mallory put out her hand and said, "I'm pleased to meet you, Reverend Finley. My name is Mallory Metcalf Reynolds, and my intended is E. P. Murphy."

He took her hand. "Ah, the mail order bride of our benefactor. I'm pleased to make your acquaintance, and I look forward to joining you in holy matrimony."

Peggy gazed at her, her mouth hanging open. "You're a mail order bride? Papa didn't tell me. And you're to marry that old man Murphy?"

At the young girl's innocent words, a shudder slithered down her spine. She knew Mr. Murphy was forty-six years old from his letters, but it didn't mean he was an old man. Or, not exactly.

Still, the proprieties must be observed, and she protested, "Peggy, that's not kind."

"Awww," Peggy huffed.

Mallory glanced up to see the reverend, running a finger between his neck and clerical collar. She could understand his anxiety, as it mirrored her own. She'd often wondered what her husband-to-be looked like. Unlike other mail order catalogues, *The Texas Christian Advocate* frowned on the exchange of pictures, believing a marriage shouldn't rely on outward appearances.

"Mr. Murphy is not old, Miss Reynolds, though his face might be creased from spending time out of doors." The reverend defended his benefactor. "I can assure you he's in the prime of life and a distinguished man."

"I'm sure he is." She stuck a smile on her face. "Thank you, Reverend, but it's getting late, and we should return to the fort for supper."

"I understand." He coughed. "Would you like to visit the men's graves before you leave?"

"What graves?" She couldn't keep the note of alarm from her voice.

"The men we buried this morning, the stagecoach driver and his guard." He peered at her through his thick glasses. "You *are* the young lady who was rescued after the coach was attacked. Am I correct?"

News traveled fast in this small outpost, but it was the same back home. People loved to talk and gossip.

She gulped. "Yes, I am. And you're right, I would like to pay my respects."

He inclined his head and gestured with his arm. "This way."

They followed the reverend out the back door and down a short staircase to what was a desolate and dry-looking plot of ground, ringed by split cedar logs. Two new mounds of earth with crude wooden crosses caught her attention. Compared to the lush, tree-lined cemeteries back home, this place was barren and forbidding. She trembled inside.

The reverend stood for a moment with his head bowed and then glanced up. He ran his finger around his collar again, and perspiration beaded his upper lip. "Such a terrible thing. I've only been here two weeks, and I've already buried six people murdered by the Apache. I hope the commander can bring them to heel soon."

She opened her mouth to defend Commander Gregory, but when she saw Peggy's scowl, she decided not to put her two cents in. The reverend struck her as a particularly nervous young man, and she doubted he would last long on the frontier, even though he kept to the relative safety of the town.

"Not to mention three men killed in a gunfight in town," he added.

For a minister, he really was a kill-joy.

She put her arm around Peggy and said, "I think we should go." She glanced at the men's graves again and bowed her head. "God rest their souls."

"Good day to you," the reverend said, tipping his hat.

"And to you." She raised her head and took Peggy's hand again.

The reverend returned to his church, and they stepped outside the split-rail fence. Off to the right-hand side, she glimpsed another huddle of adobe buildings. But instead of being white-washed, the dumpy buildings sported a bright array of pastel colors, as if, with false gaiety, they could compensate for their stubby structures. The cluster of adobe buildings were separated by a ravine from the other part of town.

"Is that part of Fort Davis?" she asked. "Funny, how it's off there by itself. Do we have time to explore?"

Peggy shook her head. "I'm not allowed to go there. It's a dangerous part of town, called Chihuahua. Papa says his soldiers go there to do bad things, even though they're forbidden."

"Oh, I see."

Mallory could guess what kind of establishments Peggy was talking about. If it hadn't been for her friend Nancy, she might have...

"All the people who live there are Spanish-speaking. They were there before the fort, Papa says. México owned this land until we won it in the Mexican-American War. Most of the people in Fort Davis are Mexican."

"Well, then it's a good thing you're learning Spanish. If you stay here, you'll need to speak the language."

The young girl shrugged. "Papa never gets to stay in one place for long. Makes it hard to have friends," she added wistfully.

"I'm sure it does. But you're sweet and smart; you must make friends easily."

Peggy looked down and drew an arc in the dust with the toe of her lace-up boot. "Maybe. I suppose."

Poor girl, she was at that awkward age, and with her mother gone and her father's vocation, she didn't have it easy. Mallory's heart went out to her. She took Peggy's hand and squeezed it.

Mallory looked over her shoulder at the sprawl of adobe buildings in the forbidden part of town. She wasn't in a much better place than Peggy, only a little older.

She'd come west for a fresh start and almost been ravished and killed by the Apache. Most servants, like Martina, were probably vanquished Mexicans who'd had their land taken from them. And if men like Mr. Spofford was an example of the other inhabitants of this place, though he was a brave man, she'd need to learn their rough ways. Not to mention the reverend's broad hints about even more violent types, dying in gunfights.

And Peggy had called her intended an old man.

What was she doing here? Could she learn to make this dangerous and forbidding land her home? Could she lay with a stranger, an older man, and not recoil when he touched her?

Chapter Three

Colonel Gregor unfurled the map and laid it on his desk, securing the four corners, so it wouldn't curl up. He rose and stretched out his arms on either side of the map, supporting himself and studying it.

Captains Rodgers and Myerson stood on the other side of his desk at attention. He should give them their ease, but he wasn't feeling generous today. Too little sleep, too much to worry about.

He'd reviewed the map, over and over, until he knew every road, trail, ranch, and the few landmarks sketched on it. For some reason, he was drawn to the map, believing it held the key to overcoming the hostiles. Perhaps that was why he never got tired of looking at it. The crude map drew him, like an alluring woman... like Miss Reynolds.

Enough of that. She was espoused to Mr. Murphy, a fine man.

But he couldn't forget the way her arms had embraced him, the simple touch of her, holding onto him in the saddle. It had been a long time since he'd felt a woman's touch. His Martha had been ailing for at least two years before the good Lord had taken her, and he'd buried her at Fort Clark almost two years ago.

Glancing at the sketchy outlines of the mountains on the map, he had a revelation. Standing up straight, he said, "Captain Rodgers, fetch Sergeant Hotchkiss. On the double."

Rodgers looked startled and then saluted. He turned and marched out of the headquarters' office.

"Captain Myerson, I need for you to bring me Captain French."

"Yes, sir, but I thought we were going to talk about containing the hostiles. It's well known the infantry has failed—"

"Yes, yes, of course." He waved his hand. "But I've had a thought, and I'll need Captain French's counsel and coordination."

Captain Myerson drew himself up and saluted. "Right away, sir."

Gregor sat down and fiddled with his coffee cup. His orderly had brought it when he'd arrived, but the coffee was already cold.

He downed a gulp and grimaced. Might as well do something useful while he waited.

He pulled a stack of papers toward him—the latest dispatches from Fort Bliss and Fort Stockton, his nearest neighboring forts.

Fishing in his jacket pocket, he retrieved his spectacles. He hated wearing spectacles. They made him feel like an old man. But for close-up reading, he needed them.

Reading the dispatches, especially from Fort Stockton, was like going over his own dispatches. Same problems, same slippery Apaches who confounded the cavalry, melting into the mountains or returning to their reservation in New Mexico when they were hotly pursued. Only to reappear when least expected.

The door opened and Captain Myerson, along with Captain French, stepped into the room. He rose and greeted the infantry captain, who had a puzzled look on his face.

A few minutes later, Captain Rodgers returned with Sergeant Hotchkiss. He sat down and offered thc men their ease, urging them to take seats across from him, except for the sergeant, who he motioned to his side.

"Hotchkiss, you're fair at sketching. Right? And you've been stationed how long at Fort Davis?"

The sergeant joined him on the other side of the desk and pursed his lips. "I can draw simple things, sir. And I've been at Fort Davis for six years."

"Good man." He clasped the sergeant's shoulder and pointed at the map. "See this rendering of the mountains? It's just a bunch of squiggles with no focal point, no canyons, or gullies, or watering holes." He shook his head. "We need a terrain map, Hotchkiss." He glanced at the man, standing beside him. "If you've been here six years, you must have been on about a hundred patrols."

Hotchkiss swallowed, his Adam's apple bobbing. "Yes, sir, I guess I have been on a lot of patrols."

"Then you must know the terrain. Can you draw me a more detailed map? From your experience. With the trails but also the topography of the mountains, where's there a pass, stand of forest, canyon, or watering hole?"

"Uh, yes, sir, I think I can do it. Would you want me to cover the same area as this map? If so, I will need a much larger—"

"Let's concentrate on a thirty-mile circumference, Hotchkiss, with the fort as the central point." He squeezed the man's shoulder. "Can you do that for me?"

"Yes, sir. No problem, sir." The sergeant glanced at Myerson.

"You're relieved of your other duties, Sergeant Hotchkiss," Myerson said. "Get to working on the commander's map. I'll assign your duties elsewhere."

"How long do you think it will take?" Gregor asked. He walked to a cabinet and pulled out several long sheets of paper, handing them to Hotchkiss.

"I'll get right to it. Shouldn't take me more than a day or two."

"But you've got to make this detailed, Hotchkiss, marking all the relevant topography. You understand?"

"Yes, sir. I'll do my very best, sir. It might not be pretty—"

"Just make it accurate. And as soon as you're done, bring the map directly to me. We'll go over it together."

Hotchkiss straightened, took the sheets of paper and saluted. "Yes, sir."

"Dismissed."

Hotchkiss turned in a tight square and quit the room.

Captain French watched him go and then he faced Gregor. "Sir, if this is about containing the hostiles, we've known for years that infantry men, on foot, are no match. The savages gallop off in a cloud of dust, laughing at my men."

Gregor sighed. What French said was true. The Indian wars would probably have been over by now if the Army had possessed a bit more foresight. But after the Civil War, it had been easy to dispatch infantry troops to the West, thinking they could overcome the native tribes. The poor men had marched for days, back and forth, around most forts, being led on a wild goose chase by the natives, who were always on horseback.

It had been one of the more embarrassing chapters for the Army.

"I'm well aware of your men's limitations in dealing with the hostiles," Gregor replied. "That's why I've put them to building structures and patrolling the fort." He scratched his chin. "And if we had the wire, I'd put them to stringing the telegraph from Brilla Springs, but I'm still waiting on supplies." He shook his head. "The Regional Commander in Fort Sam Houston says the wire is on its way, but for now, I don't know when we'll get it."

"I understand, sir."

French should understand, being a lifer like him. Supplies of any kind usually took three times as long as the Army promised. But that was part of guarding the frontier, and he'd learned to adjust to it.

"What are your men working on, Captain French?"

"Storehouses, sir. We're building storehouses."

"Well, we can do without a few more storehouses for now. If we run out of room, we'll use the quartermaster's storage or the stables."

"We're to stop building and do what, sir?"

"Have you been drilling your men?" Gregor tossed back.

"Yes, sir, a forced march every other day after reveille."

"How fast can your men cover five miles?"

"Depends, sir, on the terrain and the pace."

"Double-time and mountainous terrain."

French puffed his cheeks and blew out his breath. "Double-time in the mountains is... challenging."

"I know. Give me an idea."

French shook his head. "Two to three hours, maybe half a day, sir."

"Good enough. That gives me something to work with."

"But, sir," Captain Myerson interjected, "as Captain French has pointed out, infantry can't—"

"Captain Myerson, I'm well aware of your objections." He rubbed the back of his neck. Myerson was always quick to voice his opinion, mostly of the negative variety. But the course they'd been following wasn't working. Time to try something new.

"I have a plan. You might think it's worthless, but we need to give it a try. I want to station a company of infantry at each of our outposts. The men can be rotated out, every few weeks." He paused and glanced at French.

"And once Hotchkiss has drawn up his map, we'll probably station more companies, at likely sites, based on the terrain. The infantry's mission will be to reconnoiter the area around their stations for five miles, every other day." He held up one hand. "They will be accompanied by two scouts, one from the Ninth Cavalry and the other from the Tenth. If there is any sign of hostiles, one of the scouts will ride, with all due haste, to the fort. Then we'll dispatch a cavalry patrol to intercept the hostiles *before* they can carry out their raid."

He leaned forward and stabbed the map with his index finger. "That way, instead of being on the defensive, we'll take the offensive, driving them off before they can strike. The cavalry will still patrol the road and surrounding ranches, too." He straightened and looked each one of his captains in the eye. "Do I make myself clear?"

"Yes, sir, my men will be eager to see action," French said.

"Perfectly, sir, I believe it's a good plan," Rodgers said.

"I understand, sir," Myerson said, and then he couldn't help but add, "it will be a challenge, getting the cavalry there in time."

"But we're all agreed to give it a try," Gregor demanded.

French and Rodgers nodded.

"Yes, sir. Of course, sir," Myerson said the right words, but the tone of his voice was begrudging.

Gregor grunted. "Good. Prepare your men, French. Pick the scouts for this next month, Myerson and Rodgers. As soon as Hotchkiss finishes the map, we'll talk again about deployment."

He raised his hand and saluted them. "Dismissed."

* * *

Mallory turned in her saddle and waved goodbye to Peggy. The young girl, her eyes suspiciously bright, waved back. Though she'd only known the child for two days, she was loath to leave her, realizing Peggy needed a mother in the worst of ways.

She chewed her lip and turned around, resolutely letting her mount carry her away from Fort Davis. Though, it was past hard, and her heart ached. Peggy reminded her of how lost she'd felt when her mother had died, and shortly thereafter, her father had marched off to the war. Children needed their parents.

She shut her eyes, willing the tears away. Macon was in good hands and with a bit of luck, she'd be sending for him soon. She must remember this was only temporary, leaving her child behind.

After about an hour of trailing behind Major Gregor on a black mare, her thighs chaffed from rubbing against the saddle. She'd never ridden astride before, only side-saddle, as a proper southern lady would do. But when they'd given her the mare, fitted with an Army saddle, she'd not protested, realizing, on the frontier, there probably wasn't a sidesaddle within a thousand miles.

Four soldiers flanked her and two more rode behind. Her trunk was strapped to a mule, which one of the soldiers led. Macon's picture was tucked safely inside it.

She hoped the commander knew what he was doing, riding out with so few men. She was as nervous as a long-tailed cat in a room full of rockers. The vast land spooked her, and she couldn't help but wonder if there was an Apache hiding behind every boulder.

She gazed at the commander's broad back and wished she was *his* mail order bride. Not that she wanted him as a woman should, because her experience had taken that away from her. But the commander was a good man, a fellow Christian, and though, she knew everyone spoke highly of her intended, she couldn't help but worry he wouldn't find her suitable.

Her wedding night loomed ahead, filling her with terror. What if she couldn't abide her new husband's touch? What if he realized she wasn't a virgin? All the disturbing thoughts she'd pushed to the back of her mind came to the forefront, leaving her ashamed and worried.

How on earth would she beguile an unknown man to be a doting husband and get him to agree to send for her son?

Why had she wanted to ride out to Mr. Murphy's ranch? Because, after her near escape from the hostiles, she'd felt fragile and frightened. Somehow, it had seemed the right thing to do. Now, she wasn't sure. If she'd been observing the customary proprieties, she would have sent for Mr. Murphy. She shook her head, feeling like she'd already ruined herself again.

They turned down the fork in the road and after another mile, a huge weathered wood arch stretched above them. On the top of the arch, the letter M scrolled out, lying almost vertical against the wood, as if it was resting or... lazy.

An interesting choice for the name of a ranch. She could understand the letter "M" for Murphy, but nothing about this harsh land made her feel lazy.

Her horse shied and side-stepped. She glanced down to find several of the holes the commander's horse had almost stepped in the first day. Tightening her hold on the reins, she gazed out over the rolling grasslands, hoping to catch a glimpse of the strange, rodent-like creature the commander had tried to describe.

The tall, wheaten-colored prairie grass, dotted with rainbow-colored wildflowers, waved in the wind, but there wasn't a prairie dog in sight.

The commander stopped his roan and glanced over his shoulder. "Better take care, Miss Reynolds. There's quite a few prairie dog holes. I would have thought Mr. Murphy would have..." He stopped himself and pursed his lips. "There's a lot of work to do on a ranch of five thousand acres. I'm certain it's an oversight." He dipped his head. "The mare is sure-footed, but you might want to watch out, too."

At the mention of five thousand acres, she covered her mouth with her hand, suppressing a gasp. Very few plantation owners, even before the war, owned that much land. Her husband-to-be hadn't lied when he'd claimed to be wealthy. Not that his financial position helped allay her fears. If anything, she feared he'd be even more exacting.

"Of course," she said, looking at the ground. "I'll watch for holes."

They rode in silence for another half of a mile, avoiding holes in the winding trail. Then they topped a rise in the track, and a long, low building came into view. Surrounding it were other, smaller buildings and a series of wooden corrals. The main building, which must be the ranch house, was made of the strange earthen material Peggy had called adobe. The roof and green-painted shutters were wooden, though, and helped to "dress" the outside of the plain house.

They approached the ranch house, which had a deep front porch, supported by cedar posts. Several men from the nearby corrals must have seen them because they came drifting over and stood in the shade of a side porch.

The men wore their wide-brimmed Stetsons pulled low, half-covering their eyes. Mallory had the distinct impression she was being reviewed, measured, and appraised. Not that she could blame them. There were few enough women on the frontier, and here she was, set on being mistress of this sprawling spread.

A tall, thin man opened the front door of the ranch house and stepped onto the porch. He was clad in a blue cotton shirt with a red bandana at his throat and rough denim trousers. A holstered gun rode on his right hip.

His face was creased and lined, but his hair and the smudge of mustache above his narrow mouth was ginger-colored without a speck of gray in it. If this was her soon-to-be husband, he looked younger than his forty-six years.

He wasn't a bad looking man, but he wasn't handsome. Somehow, though, he wasn't what she'd expected. There was something about his demeanor that belied his character, especially given everyone's praise of Mr. Murphy as a distinguished Christian. This man struck her as almost sinister, a far cry from how she'd pictured him.

She swallowed and composed her features. Needing something to do, she drew the reins through her gloved hands, stroking them as if they would lend her a kind of solace.

The commander dipped his head and touched the brim of his hat. "Ben, good to see you. You've not been to town for a while. Hope you're doing well."

The man the commander had called Ben, smiled. But for her, his smile was more of a grimace, not even reaching half-way to his eyes. "Been well enough, Colonel." He spat a wad of tobacco on the ground and wiped his mouth with his shirtsleeve.

Startled, she didn't know what to think. She despised men who chewed tobacco, but then again, the commander had called this man by the name of "Ben," not "Edward." Secretly relieved, she stayed quiet and waited for her to-be-husband to appear.

"What brings ya out here, Colonel? Didn't know ya left the fort much."

"No, you're right, I don't, but this lady..." He turned around and extended his hand toward her. "Needed a special escort. She's your brother's mail order bride, and E. P. should thank his lucky stars she made it here. Her stagecoach was attacked, and she was taken by Caballero and held captive until we rescued her."

"Well, don't that jist beat all," Ben said, chortling. He glanced at her and narrowed his eyes. "What a plumb sad fact that, her being taken by Caballero and all... fer nothing."

"What do you mean, Ben?" The commander asked.

Ben half-turned and hitched his thumb toward a huge pecan tree in the yard. Beneath the tree was a wooden cross at the head of a freshly-turned grave. "Cause poor ole Ed done met his Maker. We buried him yonder, three days ago." He squinted. "'Twere an accident. He was herding some stray cows in Painted Rock canyon, and his horse must have mis-stepped." He reached inside his pocket and pulled out a fresh plug of tobacco. "We found 'em both at the bottom of that there ravine."

He took a bite of tobacco and turned his gaze on her. "Missus, yer husband-to-be, my dear brother, is dead."

This time, she couldn't suppress her gasp. She felt as if someone had punched her in the stomach. She swallowed, feeling discomforted and suddenly nauseous. But she was determined not to be sick, especially in front of the ranch hands.

The commander glanced over his shoulder at the grave. "I'm sorry to hear that, Ben." He swung his head back to face the reedy man on the porch. "I'm surprised you didn't send for Reverend Finley. E.P. would have wanted a Christian burial."

Ben worked his jaw muscles, pushing the wad of tobacco around in his mouth. "Tweren't no time. He'd been dead for three days afore we found him." He smiled, a mocking smile. "Poor ole Ed was a mite ripe when he finally turned up. No time to send fer that fancy-pants Reverend."

"I thought you said E.P. died three days ago," the commander pointed out. "Was it three or six days?"

"Did I? Well, ya know how it is out here. Time, 'cept fer the day's chores and the seasons, don't mean much." He chewed vigorously, and a thin trickle of nut-brown saliva slithered down his chin.

Watching him, Mallory shuddered. If the older brother had been anything like his younger sibling, she would have been hard-pressed to marry him. No matter how rich he was or how faithful a Christian.

Suddenly, she realized she was free. A wave of relief rolled over her, leaving her almost giddy and light-headed. She didn't have to get married or have a stranger touch her. It was as if someone had been holding her underwater, and she'd finally broken loose and risen to the surface, able to drag air into her lungs.

She took several deep breaths. Then she glanced at the mound of earth again and felt ashamed. Ashamed and guilty that a good man had died, and all she felt was a sense of liberation. But with freedom came responsibility. What would she do now?

The commander must have been thinking along those same lines because he asked, "Are you prepared, Ben, to honor your brother's agreement?" He gestured toward her. "This lady has traveled hundreds of miles, braved an Apache attack, and—"

"Hold yer horses right there." Ben put out his right hand, palm out. "I don't know what yer thinking, Colonel, but I've not got any responsibility here. It was all ole Ed's doing, wanting a wife so he could birth a passel of young'uns to follow in his footsteps."

Was the commander suggesting Ben take over her marriage contract?

The thought of marrying such a man made her heart stop in her chest. When the gaunt rancher vehemently refused, she breathed again, deeply.

Besides, she was not a side of beef to be bartered back and forth. Her marriage arrangements had been made with Mr. Edward P. Murphy, not his younger brother.

"I see," the commander said. He glanced at her and then gazed at the men, gathered around the porch, following their conversation with avid stares. "Could we go inside and discuss the situation in private."

"Ain't nothing to discuss, Colonel." Ben waved his hand and spat again. "She's free to go right back whar she came from. Simple 'nuff."

The commander held up his hand. "All right, I won't force you to have us inside, Mr. Murphy. But I do need one minute."

"Take all the time ya need, just don't be staying after sundown. My housekeeper left, sudden-like, a couple of weeks ago." He hitched his thumb over his shoulder. "Inside's no place fer a lady."

"I see," the commander repeated. And then he turned his roan around and rode beside her, leaning in close. He cleared his throat. "Miss Reynolds, do you have the... uh, the financial means to return to your former home? I believe you said you hail from Georgia?"

Then it struck her. She covered her mouth with her hand. She was as poor as a church mouse, having given most of what remained from her inheritance to Nancy for Macon's upkeep. The journey had been long and expensive, and she hadn't brought much pocket money. She doubted she had enough to buy a stagecoach ticket to San Antonio, if that far.

Now, she was ashamed and humiliated. Impoverished and unwanted, ever since the war, she'd fought an uphill battle, clinging to her previous status and making "do" with her father's straitened circumstances.

She shut her eyes, remembering all the sacrifices she'd made, the pandering to her rich aunt in Charleston, only to lose her head and ruin herself. Her aunt had turned her out, and polite society had shunned her. Then her father died, leaving mounds of debt that gobbled up her inheritance.

Mr. E.P. Murphy, the man who laid dead beneath that tree, had been kind enough to send her the funds for the journey. Everything else, except a little pocket money, she'd left with Nancy.

Tears trolled down her cheeks, remembering her past struggles, and believing they were over. But here she was again, penniless and without options, and far from home.

She shook her head, and her words were barely a whisper. "No, Commander, I haven't the means to return to Georgia." She fingered the intricately-carved, ivory cameo she wore at her throat. It had been her mother's, and it was the last remaining piece of jewelry she hadn't pawned. "I have this cameo. If there's a pawnbroker in Fort Davis, I might be able to sell—"

"You'll not be selling your cameo, Miss. Let me handle this."

She nodded.

Gregor turned his roan around and faced Ben again. He'd surmised she might be without funds. A proper lady, handsome, too, wouldn't have come this far, facing such a long and dangerous journey if she had the means to stay safely at home.

He clenched his jaw, determined to do right by her. "Mr. Murphy, the lady will need funds to return home. I know you have the money. You must assume the responsibility to see Miss Reynolds home."

"Now why would I want to do that? She ain't nothing to me. It was ole Ed's idea. Wanting young'uns, and he didn't make no provision for her, neither. He didn't even bother changing his will, saying he wanted to see if'n she'd give him a son first." He beat his scrawny chest. "He had me as his rightful heir, didn't need to be getting no 'lady' from back East to breed on."

Gregor stared at him, his eyes narrowed. He couldn't believe the meanness of the man. But he shouldn't be surprised. If ever two brothers were unalike, it was E.P. and Ben. There was a large gap in their ages, and if local rumors had it right, they were only half brothers, having different mothers.

And there was the strange coincidence in timing of E.P.'s unfortunate accident. When he'd first been stationed at Fort Davis, E.P. had shown him around, familiarizing him with a huge swath of the territory. The older rancher knew all five thousand of his acres like the back of his hand, and he was an excellent rider. This was a dangerous, rough terrain, but somehow, he didn't believe E.P. had let his mount fall into a ravine.

He decided to try a different tack. "Miss Reynolds was officially betrothed to your brother. She has numerous letters, stating his intent. The circuit judge will be back in a week or two. If you won't give her the money to return, I can ask for his legal opinion as to what claim she might—"

"Ya can ask," Ben sneered, "until the cows come home. Won't do ya no good. I ain't gonna give her one red cent." He put his hand on the butt-end of his holstered Colt. "We're done here,

Colonel. I'd be mighty happy to see ya off our land." He jerked his head toward a bunch of men, standing beneath the porch overhang. "If'n you can't see yer way clear, my men will show ya the way out."

Again, he wasn't surprised by Ben's animosity and hint of violence. Presidio County was too poor to have a Sheriff, and as the commander of the fort, he was responsible for keeping the local peace. Every time Ben came to town, there was a violent episode, ranging from tearing up a saloon, to beating up one of the "soiled doves" in Chihuahua, along with brutal fistfights. He'd had to intervene several times and throw Ben and his men in the fort's guardhouse until they sobered up and paid fines.

Once there had been a gunfight, and Ben had survived. The miner, who was a rough fellow, but no killer, had been shot dead. Everyone in town, especially Ben's men, had sworn the fight had been fair and Ben had acted in self-defense. But Doc Winslow had thought differently, based on the trajectory of the bullets in the miner's belly, though there had been no way to prove it.

He'd worried about Ben when Miss Reynolds had declared she was betrothed to E.P, but he'd pushed his doubts aside, certain E.P. would keep his younger brother in line, especially at home.

Now, he wouldn't put anything past the man—up to and including murdering his own brother, so he wouldn't have to share the ranch if E.P. had children.

He sat up straighter in the saddle and stared at Ben. "My men and I represent the United States Army. You cannot order us off your land."

Ben descended the two porch steps and stood in front of his horse. His beady, black eyes were fixed on him. "Oh, I can't, can I? This here is private property, and if'n you and yer men ain't pursuing no hostiles, ya have no right to be here." He swung his head from side to side, exaggerating the movement. "I don't see no hostiles anywhere near here. How about you, men?"

A low murmur erupted from the ranch hands, and then shouts of: "No, Boss, no Injuns here."

Ben nodded and touched his Colt again.

The staccato sound of pistols being cocked and carbine bolts rammed home lent an added layer of menace to their stand-off.

Ben angled his head. "You're outnumbered, Colonel, at least five to one. Why don't ya call it a day and git on back to yer fort? Where ya belong."

"Are you threatening me, Murphy?"

"Maybe, maybe not, Colonel, but see'n as how there's a whole lot more of us than there is of yer'n, wouldn't be no witnesses left to say—"

"And how would you explain our deaths." He glanced at Miss Reynolds. "Not to mention there's a lady here."

Ben guffawed. "I don't see no lady here. If'n she had to travel this far to find a husband, she must be soiled goods. I told E.P. so meself, 'course, he wouldn't listen."

Gregor heard her gasp again and start to sob. But he couldn't turn away from Ben; he had to stand him down. "How would you explain our deaths, Mr. Murphy?"

The skinny rancher hitched his thumbs in his gun belt. "There are ways to make it look like the Injuns got ya."

"You mean you allow the Apache to camp on your ranch? You give shelter to our country's enemies?"

Ben unhitched one thumb and wagged his finger. "Don't be putting no words into mah mouth, Colonel."

He felt a tug on his sleeve. He turned his head to find himself gazing into the smoky-green depths of Miss Reynolds' eyes. "Please, Commander, let's go. I don't want his money."

"Now that's one right-smart lady," Ben said. "Why don't ya run along home like the 'skirt' wants ya to, Colonel?"

Slowly but surely, his anger had been building. Ben Murphy wasn't good enough to lick Miss Reynolds' high-top boots, and he itched to prove it, too. He'd never had a head for killing, had only distinguished himself in the Civil War because he'd wanted to survive.

Now, suddenly, he understood what other soldiers meant when they said they'd seen red and the urge to destroy had overtaken them, blotting out their common sense and humanity, turning them into ravaging animals.

He slid off his horse and got into Ben's face. More pistols cocked in the background, but he didn't care. He poked Ben's scrawny chest with his index finger, warning, "This isn't the end of it, Murphy. No one gets away with threatening me, especially you. I'm sending a dispatch to the Regional Commander in San Antonio, and I'll be talking with the judge, too." He towered over the red-head. "And I don't want to see your filthy hide in Fort Davis, neither. Every time you come to town, you break the law. I have proof of that, too."

He turned around, purposely exposing his back. He faced his men and raised his voice, "Attention! Wheel!" His six men turned their mounts around, facing back the way they'd come. Miss Reynolds followed suit, too. "Forward." His men spurred their mounts, and they trotted down the track.

He put his foot in the stirrup, glaring at Murphy across his roan's neck. "And I don't believe your brother's death was an accident. If enough reward is offered for the details of his death, you might be surprised how loyal some of your men are... or aren't."

Chapter Four

Mallory held the battered book close to the kerosene lamp, reading out loud, "The Prince came and took Cinderella to his castle, and they were married that very day." She glanced at Peggy and saw that the girl's eyelids had closed. Leaning over, she kissed Peggy's forehead and tucked the covers around her.

Then she closed the volume of "*Household Stories*" by the Brothers Grimm and put the book on the bedside table. Folding her hands, she watched as Peggy slept, thinking of her son and wondering if Nancy was reading to him and tucking him in.

She stayed seated, going over what had happened at the Murphy ranch. She was back to where she'd started—not knowing how to go forward, or how to take care of her son with the limited funds she'd inherited. Only now, she'd made things worse, putting over sixteen hundred miles between them and with no way to return home. She'd left enough funds with Nancy to send for her child, but there would be precious little money remaining. How would they live, if she had no husband?

She'd been such an innocent, not even considering what could happen, traveling countless miles to marry a stranger. She should have asked Mr. Murphy for sufficient funds to make the round trip. But it hadn't occurred to her, and Mr. Murphy might have viewed her request with suspicion, thinking she'd go back on their arrangement and return if they didn't suit.

By not planning ahead, the worst possible thing had happened. Her intended had died and now she was stuck in this frontier outpost with few prospects.

Nancy had wanted her to move to northern Georgia, where the details of her shame weren't common knowledge, and apply for the position of a school teacher. She had the necessary education, and Nancy's husband would have given her a reference.

But moving away with her son and posing as a war widow had seemed daunting. And even if she'd found a position, she worried the school board would want a reference from Miss Prentiss. She shuddered, imagining what Miss Prentiss would say about her in a letter.

The commander was worried his daughter, without a local school, was falling behind in her lessons. And he'd mentioned there wasn't a school at the fort. She wondered about the town, but Peggy hadn't mentioned a school when she'd shown her around. Perhaps she could start a school here, and then send for her son.

She bit the inside of her cheek, realizing she had no idea what starting a school would entail. She'd need a building of some sort, desks or tables, a chalkboard, books, and...

Her thoughts tumbled, ranging over the details and the cost. The children's parents might be willing to help with the initial expenses, but she couldn't know for certain. On top of starting a school, could they afford to pay her? What was a fair salary? What would she need to live on?

She was in over her head, and she knew it. There was only one person she could count on and having moved from fort to fort, he should be able to advise her.

As if her thoughts had conjured him, the commander pushed the door open and stuck his head inside. He glanced at his sleeping daughter and whispered, "Is she asleep?"

Mallory nodded.

He inclined his head. "I've made us tea. Would you care to come to the kitchen where we can talk?"

Rising, she nodded again. She'd been expecting this conversation, as soon as Peggy was asleep. She was dependent on his charity. When she thought about how he'd championed her at the Murphy Ranch, a warm feeling enveloped her, and she got teary-eyed.

Dashing the sentimental tears away, she knew they had to come up with a plan. The commander couldn't keep sleeping behind his office, and they couldn't live together openly, notwithstanding his declaration about frontier morals being less rigid than back East. If it was the last thing she did, she'd observe the proprieties.

She'd ruined herself once and that was more than enough.

The commander stood at the table, holding out a chair for her. He was such a gentleman.

She smiled and took her seat. "Thank you."

He placed the creamer and sugar bowl in front of her and took his seat across from her.

She busied herself with pouring cream and dropping two lumps of sugar into her teacup, dreading the conversation to come. Her circumstances were more than humiliating, and she had no ready answers.

He cleared his throat. "First off, I'd like to say what I told Ben Murphy today, weren't idle threats. I will try and raise reward money to see if we can obtain more details about your intended's death. And if you'd be kind enough to give me a few of your letters, where you and E.P. discussed arrangements, I'll present them to the circuit judge, Judge Beadle. I'd like to see if we can obtain a judgment for your return fare."

She opened her mouth to contradict him, not wanting anything to do with Ben Murphy again. The man frightened her out of her wits. But upon further consideration, she decided to let the commander handle the legal aspects of her situation.

Nodding again, she stirred her tea and took a sip.

He lifted his teacup. She noticed he had slender, elegant fingers.

He tipped the cup and swallowed. "In the meantime—"

"I will need somewhere to live..."

They had spoken on top of each other. She stopped and deferred to him.

He smiled, a smile of reassurance. "I think we were headed in the same direction. Investigating E.P.'s murder and getting funds from Ben might take a while. In the meantime, you'll need a place to live and an income." He rubbed the back of his neck. "As I mentioned before, I need help with Peggy's lessons—"

"I know you worry about Peggy and her lessons, and I was thinking of starting a school here in Fort Davis."

"A school?" He took another taste of his tea. "I hadn't gotten that far yet. I was going to offer you a job as my child's governess." He dropped his head and cleared his throat again. "I don't suppose you'd want to be a housekeeper, too." He pursed his lips. "We'd have to come up with some kind of alternate living arrangements."

"Commander, I'm ashamed to say it, but I've not been trained in the domestic arts. I know very little about cooking and probably even less about keeping a house in order." She fiddled with her teacup, feeling the spurt of shame heating her neck, her ears, and then her face. "Being raised on a plantation with household slaves, er, servants, I never learned."

She raised her head and stiffened her back. "Nancy, my good friend, was trying to teach me some rudimentary skills while I was corresponding with Mr. Murphy; though, Mr. Murphy assured me he had plenty of help on the ranch, a cook and housekeeper." She drained her teacup and folded her hands. "So, you see, I couldn't give you good service as a housekeeper."

"I understand."

"Though, I'm willing to learn."

She surprised herself with her declaration. She'd thought to marry a wealthy man, similar to what she'd been bred to wed, but now that dream was shattered. She needed to fend for herself.

He nodded and said, "That's admirable, your willingness. But I don't believe it solves your present situation."

"No, of course, you're right." She turned her teacup in the saucer.

"Would you care for another cup of tea?"

"Yes, I would. Thank you." Not that she was thirsty but having the teacup to fiddle with gave her something to do.

He poured her another cup from the teapot. She noticed the china was quality tableware, a pristine white enamel, adorned with curling pink roses. The tea set must have belonged to his late wife.

"I think, if I can be so bold as to venture, you'll find your boarding expenses to be the major rub," he said. "That is, given what I could pay you as a governess."

"What can you pay me?" As she said the words, she cringed. Never had she thought to be haggling for her upkeep.

"I paid Crissy, my former housekeeper and Peggy's governess, five dollars a week. Right now, I'm paying Martina three dollars a week for cooking and keeping house."

"That leaves only two dollars, Commander." She shook her head. "I don't know how much a boardinghouse costs but—"

"I've had a promotion since then, Miss Reynolds. I could afford to give you three dollars a week and your meals. You might get a discount at Mrs. Johnson's if you don't eat there. Peggy and I would enjoy having you here for mealtime."

"That's a kind offer, but still..."

"I know. I know." He shook his head. "We could ask at Mrs. Johnson's, but it would still be tight." He frowned. and his forehead furrowed. "I have another thought. Captain Rodgers and his wife live two houses over, and they have the next largest cabin on the fort with an extra bedroom. They lost their only child, a son, last summer. I believe they'd welcome you."

A tremor shook her. She lowered her head and squeezed her eyes shut, fighting back the tears that came too readily. Hearing about someone losing their only child was devastating.

She'd nursed Macon through what had seemed like countless childhood illnesses, only too aware the next fever could take him... forever. It was the scourge of parents, childhood ailments like measles, chicken pox, consumption, and scarlet fever, just to name a few.

He reached his hand across the table, palm up. "I see you've a kind heart and are fond of children. I didn't mean to upset you, but I thought I should explain. Though, his wife is young and they're trying to have another child, it could take some time before..."

She didn't take his hand, though, she was unexpectedly drawn to him. But she couldn't afford any gesture that might seem the least bit improper.

He looked down and withdrew his hand, cradling his teacup instead. "Living with the Rodgers might give you some breathing space, until—"

"I couldn't live on their charity. I would have to pay them something, but I will need to put money aside, too, for my fare back."

"Yes, I understand. I think you could come to a reasonable accommodation with the Rodgers. His wife, Sally, is a nice lady, and I believe you would get along. As for saving money, I don't know about a school because there are so few children at the fort.

Only officers are allowed to have families. Enlisted men may marry, but they need to have their commanding officer's consent."

"Oh, I didn't know."

"As for the town, most of the children speak only Spanish."

"Peggy mentioned that when she showed me around."

"There are a couple of families, though, who might be happy to avail themselves of your services. If you took on a few students from the fort and town, along with what I can pay you, I believe you could make enough to save something back."

She raised her head again and forced her mouth into the semblance of a wan smile. Not since her father, had a man been so understanding and willing to help.

"You've given this a lot of thought, haven't you?" she asked.

"Well, yes and no. I'd like to be of help, and I wish I could give my child a better education."

"I think you're very, very kind, Commander." This time, she wanted to reach out to him, but she didn't dare to appear forward.

It would be easy to allow her emotions to rule her, as they had when she was young and foolish. He was kind and considerate, kinder to her than any man had been, even her own father.

He spread his hands on the table and gazed at her. "Thank you for the compliment, but I've a vested interest in keeping you around for a while."

"Oh, and what is that?"

He had the finest blue-gray eyes, like the hazy horizon over the mountains. Her heart fluttered in her chest. Was he going to express a tenderness toward her? Did she want that? Perhaps. But perhaps, unknowingly, he was inciting her vulnerability, making her wish for more than he was willing to offer.

She shook herself, feeling in uncharted territory. Since Hiram had wooed her, she'd been afraid to trust her instincts about men. That's why she'd opted for an arranged marriage with an older gentleman. At least, she knew what to expect... or so she'd thought.

He inclined his head toward his daughter's room. "Peggy, she's very taken with you. Haven't seen her like this since Crissy..." He hesitated and poured himself another cup of tea. "I know you could be a big help with her studies. At least, until you had to go back home."

She nodded, both relieved and disappointed, a strange mixture of emotions. She stirred her tea and took a sip. "Have you thought of sending Peggy away to school?"

"Yes, I've thought of it, but I can't... I can't bring myself to do it." He caught her gaze and held it. "You see, I'm not such a paragon of virtue as you would believe." He shook his head. "No, I'm selfish, thinking of myself, rather than her education and future."

"You mean you don't want to be without her."

"Yes, exactly." He stirred his tea. "Martha and I tried to have children, but Peggy is the only one who survived. A few years ago, we had a little boy, Luke, at Fort Concho, and we were hopeful." He shook his head again. "He only lived a week. Then my wife took sick, and we lost her at Fort Clark."

She gasped, covering her mouth, and biting down on her fist. So many sad stories, so much death and loss. Even though the conception and birth of her son had ruined her, he'd been worth it. She'd give the world for Macon.

"I'm sorry... so sorry," she said. Such feeble words of comfort. "But I don't think you're selfish at all, Commander. I think you've done the right thing, keeping Peggy with you."

He looked up from his teacup and managed the ghost of a smile. "I'm happy to hear you say that." He shrugged and looked sheepish. "Makes me feel a little bit better, not so selfish."

He lifted his teacup and held it out. Not understanding what he was doing but wanting to comfort him, she lifted her teacup and touched it to his.

"To keeping you with us, Miss Reynolds, for a little while, at least." He grinned. "We'll start tomorrow. I'll introduce you to Sally Rodgers, and we'll see about rounding up some youngsters for you to teach. Will that suit you?"

* * *

Gregor stretched and yawned. He pulled the full coffeepot off the pot belly stove and filled his cup, placing it on the corner of his desk. He glanced out the window, wondering where Hotchkiss was.

It had felt good to sleep in his own bed again last night. He'd spent yesterday taking Miss Reynolds around the fort. First, he'd introduced her to Sally Rodgers and her husband. They'd agreed to let Miss Reynolds stay in their extra room for a fraction of what a room at the boardinghouse would have cost.

And he'd prevailed upon his new governess to take her mid-day meal and supper with him and Peggy, on the pretext of refining his daughter's manners, at the table and elsewhere.

Then he and Sally Rodgers had taken her around to the other wives of the fort who had children. Unfortunately, all his captains, who could have afforded her services more readily, didn't have children. French was a bachelor, Myerson's children were grown, and the Rodgers were young but still trying...

That had left several of the lieutenants who had children, and most of their wives had expressed interest, depending on the cost. Their fees for her teaching had been a touchy subject, as they could ill afford to pay what he was paying. But along with holding class in the morning for all the children, he'd managed to convince Miss Reynolds to "double-up" on Peggy's lessons, instructing her in the afternoons, too, until she reached her grade level.

Sally and Miss Reynolds had appeared to get along well enough, and they'd moved her things into the Rodgers' cabin in the afternoon. Today, Sally would take the new school teacher to some likely families in town. And Miss Reynolds, armed with a chalkboard and a few school primers they'd found in the quartermaster's storage, would set up a classroom in his parlor.

He took a swallow of coffee and looked out the window again. He couldn't afford to waste any more time. He sat down and picked up a pile of dispatch papers. Flipping through the official notifications from Fort Bliss, he put on his spectacles and concentrated.

There was a knock on his door, and his orderly, Corporal Walsh, stuck his head in the door. Corporal Walsh looked like he hadn't wiped his mouth after breakfast, but Gregor knew that wasn't the case. The young man was trying to grow a mustache. So far, his sandy-colored facial hair wasn't much better than a light dusting along his upper lip.

"Yes, Corporal?"

"Sergeant Hotchkiss, sir, to see you."

"Show him in. I've been waiting for him."

Walsh stood at attention and saluted. He opened the door wider and Sergeant Hotchkiss stepped inside with a roll of paper under his arm. The corporal closed the door and returned to his post on the front porch.

"Finally, Hotchkiss, I was beginning to wonder when you'd show up."

Hotchkiss stood at attention and saluted. "My apologies for keeping you waiting, sir, but I hadn't reckoned on the relative scale of things." He shifted the roll of paper to his other arm. "I had to redraw it several times to get the scale correct."

He returned Hotchkiss' salute and rubbed his chin. "The scale. I hadn't thought about making the map to scale, Sergeant. If you've managed to introduce the scale of things, along with the topography, I can't wait to see your map."

"Yes, sir." Hotchkiss unrolled the paper.

Gregor cleared off his desk and rose, putting his coffee cup on the shelf next to the stove. He turned around to find Hotchkiss pinning down the four corners of the map with some agates Peggy had found around the fort. He used the multi-colored, concentric-banded stones as paperweights. And he especially prized the two that had broken open to reveal sparkling crystalline cores.

He joined Hotchkiss behind his desk and gazed at the map. He could easily see the sergeant had spent long hours getting the details of the land around the fort correctly portrayed and as close to scale as the length of paper would allow. Looking over Hotchkiss' work, he was reminded of Davie from Fort Clark, Crissy's husband, and what a fine artist he was.

He clapped the sergeant on the shoulder. "Well done, lad. Well done." He traced his finger over the Davis mountain range, taking in canyons and trails, patches of forests and natural springs. All three of the forts' outlying camps were depicted, along with other important landmarks.

Skimming his fingers over the San Antonio-El Paso Road, he hesitated when he got to the rough outline of the Lazy M Ranch. Most ranches around the fort had yet to fence in their land. Cattle from neighboring ranches often wandered between other spreads, mingling with their neighbors' cattle.

Each year, all the cattle ranchers from the surrounding area organized a spring roundup. At the roundup, which had taken place a few weeks ago, the ranchers brought the herds of cattle together, sorted the older cattle by brand, branded the new-born calves, and divvied up any strays, based on the relative size of their herds. It was a good system, keeping the mountains open and fence free, neighbor relying upon neighbor, and trusting in each other's honorable intentions.

He gazed at Hotchkiss' outline of the western side of the Murphy spread and then he drummed his fingers on the map, considering.

Most years, the Apache turned up during the roundup, hoping to pick off stray cattle for their own use. Victorio was like a spider, sitting at the center of his web, ostensibly "civilized," and living on the New Mexico reservation.

But it was common knowledge, when the supplies didn't come from the Indian agents or were lacking or late, Victorio sent out his war chiefs to raid and fill in the breach. Then there were those times when some ill-advised settler impugned an Apache's honor. Victorio made certain his braves exacted their own kind of revenge, upon the first white men they could find.

This year, there hadn't been any Apache sightings during the roundup. He'd been mildly surprised, but he hadn't given it much thought at the time, believing Victorio and his followers had received adequate supplies and were content on their reservation.

But after the roundup was over, the Apache had come swarming back like fleas, attacking the smaller ranches in the vicinity, along with the stagecoach line and any wagon trains, despite his increased patrols.

Thinking about Ben's hostile attitude, along with E.P.'s untimely death, a half-baked idea formed in his mind.

He lifted his head and raised his voice, calling out, "Corporal Walsh!"

The corporal opened the door and entered, coming to attention and saluting. "Yes, sir?"

"Fetch Captains Rodgers, Myerson, and French, on the double."

"Yes, sir." He saluted again and exited.

Gregor crossed to his cabinet and pulled out another sheaf of papers, handing them to the sergeant. "I need you to make me another map, starting from where this one leaves off, at the western perimeter of the Murphy Ranch. I want you to draw me a topographical map of the Lazy M, to scale, if possible."

Hotchkiss raised his eyebrows. "Yes, sir, I'll do my best, but I don't know how accurately I can render the features inside the ranch." He waved his hand. "You see, sir, we don't patrol the Lazy M as much as the smaller ranches."

He noted Hotchkiss' tentativeness. It was true, what the sergeant said, and like his predecessor before him, he'd focused his attention on the smaller ranches in the area—those who didn't have the men to hold off an Apache attack. E.P. had always kept fifty or more cowhands on his ranch, all of them capable with firearms, enough men to tend his large acreage, as well as intimidate the hostiles.

"I understand, Hotchkiss. Do your best from what you remember with the important landmarks, and in particular, the best access points to the ranch, ones near water holes." He glanced at the sergeant. "Can you give it a try?"

"Yes, sir, I'll do my best." He gathered the blank papers under his arm and stood at attention.

Gregor thought to dismiss him, but then he changed his mind. For Hotchkiss to do his best work, now that his attention had been drawn to the Lazy M, he wanted the sergeant to hear the discussion and understand the importance of accuracy.

"At ease, Sergeant. Have a seat. Would you care for a cup of coffee?"

"Yes, if it's not too much trouble, sir."

He fetched his tin cup from the shelf and another one for Hotchkiss. He filled the two cups, using the last of the coffee. If the captains wanted coffee, the corporal would need to make more.

The door opened and Captain Myerson, followed by Captain Rodgers, entered his office. They stood at attention and saluted, chorusing, "Reporting as ordered, sir."

He returned their salute. "At ease, Captains. Come around to this side and see what the sergeant has drawn. Do you want coffee?"

They shook their heads to his offer and joined him on the other side of his desk. He sipped his coffee, allowing them time to review the map.

"Fine work," Rodgers said.

"Very detailed and to scale," Myerson added.

The door opened again and French entered. "Reporting, sir." He saluted.

"Come over here and take a look at what Hotchkiss has done," Gregor offered. "Would you care for some coffee?"

"Yes, sir, I'd be obliged. I missed mess hall this morning."

"Oh." Gregor straightened and caught his eye. "Problems?"

"Some of the temporary braces in one of the storehouses didn't hold. They fell in overnight."

"Anyone hurt?" Gregor asked.

"No, sir, but I needed to get them braced as soon as possible."

He inclined his head. "Get Corporal Walsh in here. He can make some more coffee."

French did as he asked, and the five men surveyed the map while Walsh puttered around, brewing another pot of coffee.

Gregor pointed at the three outposts, his finger hop-scotching across the map. "French, you remember what I said at our last meeting? Deploy your infantry accordingly." He glanced up at the other captains. "You'll need to give him scouts who are good riders. Understood?"

They both said, "Yes, sir," in unison.

Then he pointed to several more places, natural access points, with plenty of water and cover for a raiding band. "Here, too, French. You'll need to bring in supplies, as well. Let me know what you need. I'll make sure the quartermaster gets you the necessary rations—say for the next five or six months. At least through the summer and into September."

"Yes, sir," French said.

"All right. I've got some new information. But nothing is set in stone," Gregor admitted. "Let's say it's a strong hunch." He paused, wanting to be discreet about Miss Reynolds' situation, but needing to give his captains enough to understand his suspicions.

The coffee pot sputtered and rattled. Walsh refilled his and Hotchkiss' cup, along with another cup for French. Then he returned to his post outside.

"I took Miss Reynolds to meet her intended husband, E.P. Murphy, and learned he'd died several days back."

All four of the men looked up and nodded.

The fort grapevine was working well, Gregor noted. He cleared his throat and gave his direct reports an abbreviated version of how Ben Murphy had treated him, along with the threats and Murphy's slip-up when he mentioned the Apaches.

He ended with, "I don't know why Ben Murphy would give succor to the Apache. I'm still trying to figure out what he's after. But no raids during the roundup is coincidental, too, as if one of the ranchers is already supplying the Apache with cattle.

"Hotchkiss is going to draw up a map of the Lazy M with the important landmarks and best access points." He looked up and snagged French's gaze. "When he's done, Captain, we'll decide the other places to deploy your infantrymen." He turned to the other two captains. "And I'll need scouts for those encampments, too."

French nodded and said, "Yes, sir." He swiped his face with his hand, as if considering. Rodgers saluted but didn't say anything.

"Yes, sir, but..." Myerson started.

"Speak your mind, Captain," he said.

"Well..." The captain rubbed his chin. "It's an awful lot of coincidences, isn't it? I mean, sir, I know Ben's reputation, especially after all the times we've had to arrest him. But to murder his brother and aid the Apache..." He shook his head. "I don't know."

"Yes, I agree, Myerson, it's hard to understand. And I'm not certain of Ben's motives, either." Gregor waved his hand over the map. "You have your orders, Captains. Any questions, let me know. I'll get back with you when Hotchkiss finishes his map of the Lazy M, and we'll deploy more troops. Maybe we'll know more by then, maybe not."

He put his hand on the sergeant's arm. "Hotchkiss, how long?"

"Another day or two, sir?"

"Good enough. Dismissed." He saluted and turned back to his captains.

* * *

Mallory squeezed Sally Rodgers' hands. "I'll be fine. I just need to post a letter to my good friend in Georgia." They were standing in front of the post office, a small wooden building. "You go on ahead."

"Well, I wouldn't leave you, but it's late, and I need to get Frank's... er, Captain Rodgers' supper. He doesn't like to eat in the mess hall. Says the food is, er... not very good."

"You've done more than enough." She released the other woman's hands. "Please, Sally, I appreciate all your help and hospitality. I don't want to keep you."

"If you're certain?" Sally scanned the dusty main street.

Mallory followed her gaze. The tiny town was quiet and almost deserted. She watched as a housewife entered the green grocer's, a cowboy with his distinctive headgear pulled over his face, snoozed in front of the saloon, and the butcher was sweeping the wooden walkway in front of his store.

"I think it's safe enough, and I'll only be a minute," she said.

"All right," Sally gave in. "I'll expect you after supper then?"

"Of course."

Sally turned and walked a few steps. Then she turned back and waved.

Mallory waved, too, and smiled. She liked Sally. The woman had welcomed her into her home without a moment's hesitation, and her husband, Captain Rodgers, seemed nice, too.

Sally had introduced her to several families in the town of Fort Davis, who might be interested in the school she was starting. They didn't have much money, though, it was plain to see and, like the lieutenants of the fort, could only afford a fraction of what the commander was paying her.

She chewed her lip. The familiar gnaw of guilt made her uneasy. She owed the commander a great deal and, if she hadn't needed his money to return to her son, she'd turn down his offer of three dollars a week. In some strange way, she didn't like being beholden to him, though, with due regard to the sleeping arrangements, they were observing the proprieties. Still, his offer was so generous.

But if she was honest with herself, she knew the commander wanted her as a substitute mother for Peggy. Not that he would come out and say it, but that was why he was willing to pay her. And Peggy needed a mother in the worst of ways.

Still, some small part of her felt as if she was taking advantage of his goodness. She chewed on her lip again. More reason to exceed his expectations with regard to teaching and mothering his daughter. She'd make sure he didn't regret paying her extra.

She entered the post office and pulled the letter to Nancy out of her pocket. Glancing at the address on the front, she wondered how it would be received. With her best friend, she'd left nothing out, from her abduction by the savages, to the unexpected death of her intended husband, and her new circumstances. She'd written Nancy, telling her everything. Her best friend was one of the few people she could trust.

She'd considered buying a round-trip stagecoach ticket to San Antonio, wiring Nancy to send Macon, and returning to the fort. But that would have taken most of the funds she had left. Then what? She and Macon would be together, but she'd need to earn enough money for them to have a proper place to live. And the thought of bringing her child to this dangerous place, without the protection of a husband, was disconcerting.

A gray-haired lady stood behind the desk. She approached her and held out her hand. "I'm new in town, staying at the fort. My name is Miss Reynolds. Are you the Postmistress?"

The woman gave her the once over, and the back of her neck heated. She'd seen how Sally and the lieutenants' wives, not to mention the townspeople, were dressed. She stuck out like a sore thumb, swathed in a lavender-colored day dress with lace at her neckline and cuffs.

"Yes, Ma'am, glad to meet you." The Postmistress bobbed her head, her gray curls wreathing her face. "I'm Mrs. Burnside. Do you have a letter to post?"

"Yes." Mallory put it on the desk and paid the postage. She thanked the Postmistress and turned to go.

"Oh, Miss, seems you have a letter from the same lady you're writing to." Mrs. Burnside held up an envelope. "Here it is."

Seeing the familiar handwriting of her friend, her heart galloped, wanting to burst from her chest. She grabbed the letter. "Thank you, thank you so much, Mrs. Burnside."

"My pleasure, Ma'am, hope to see you again."

Giddy with happiness, she skipped out of the post office and stopped at a half-rotten bench, a few yards away. She sat down and smoothed the envelope. She couldn't wait to read about her son and how he was doing.

But first, she slipped her hand into her skirt pocket and brought out her picture of Macon. She had taken his picture out of its silver frame, wanting to have his image with her all the time.

She hadn't told anyone about her son. If she did, she'd need to lie and say she was a war widow or admit her shame. Neither option appealed.

She traced her index finger over his eyebrows and then his cheekbones. A tear trickled down her cheek, and she brushed it away.

She tore into the envelope and skimmed the contents.

"Macon misses you but he is well... he likes first grade and is a good student... his teacher says he excels in math... Was she married yet...? What was her new husband like...? She'd try to write every week... she hoped Mallory would write as often... she would read her letters to Macon."

Mallory chewed the inside of her mouth until she tasted blood. She could go and ask for her letter back, but it would be embarrassing. Surely, Nancy would read through her letters before she read them out loud to her son. Wouldn't she? Especially her first letter, filled with all kinds of ugliness. Of all she'd suffered and endured. She didn't want her son to know any of it.

She couldn't wait to return to her son. With what the commander paid her and what the others could afford, even with the pittance she was paying the Rodgers, she'd be hard-pressed to save enough money to return. It would take months, and she'd need to keep her expenses to a minimum. Except for one thing…

She needed some simple day dresses. She was tired of people, like the Postmistress, looking at her as if she was a fish out of water. She wasn't much at housekeeping, but she could sew a fine seam. With Sally's help, she hoped to buy some inexpensive fabric and make a few everyday dresses.

Other than day dresses, she wouldn't spend a penny she didn't need to. And the sooner she saved her money—the sooner she could get home to Macon.

She tucked the letter inside her pocket beside Macon's picture and rose. She'd read her friend's letter again before retiring. But now, she needed to get back to the fort as promised.

Her glance fell on the cowboy snoozing on the saloon's front porch. He looked up, and she could have sworn the cowboy was Ben Murphy. Her heart clenched in her chest, and her palms started to sweat.

The cowboy lowered his head, and she looked away. Surely, she was seeing things? The commander had been adamant about Ben not coming to town. But considering how arrogant and hostile the man had been, would he have listened?

She didn't know, and the cowboy, whoever he was, gave her the shivers. She picked up her pace, hurrying along to the fort.

Chapter Five

Mallory leaned over Peggy's shoulder. "Yes, you've got the subject and the verb correct." She pointed at the sentence Peggy was diagraming. "Now, what's the direct object?"

Peggy pointed at the word "street" and glanced up. The sentence read: "Jill threw the ball into the street."

"You're close, but it's the word 'ball' that's the direct object. 'Street' is part of a prepositional phrase. The direct object is a noun or pronoun that receives the action of a verb or shows the result of the action. The direct object is not always the noun at the end of a sentence. Many times, it is, but not always."

Peggy's bottom lip jutted out. She lowered her head and finished diagraming the sentence.

"All right. Very good. Let's take a look at this next sentence," Mallory pointed to the primer.

She moved back, took a handkerchief from her pocket and wiped her face. The weeks had rolled into June, and most days, even though the sun was strong, the air was cool. But today was different—it was the heat of the day—just after their nap. She was perspiring in her new lightweight cotton dress worn without a corset.

She'd settled into the life of the fort. In the mornings, she taught three children from the fort and two from town, along with Peggy. They ranged in ages from a fifteen-year-old boy, Jeb Houghton, from town, and a fourteen-year-old girl, Annie, who was Lieutenant Richter's daughter, to a six-year old girl from town, Becky Lovell, who was the same age as her son. The other two children, a boy and girl who were non-identical twins, were about Peggy's age, and were the children of Lieutenant O'Sullivan.

Because of the school, Peggy had struck up a friendship with Tammy O'Sullivan. Before they'd known each other in the schoolroom, Tammy and her twin, Thomas, had been inseparable. Now, Peggy had a new "best" friend, and Mallory liked to think she'd helped the girls to get to know each other.

So far, she'd been able to save a few dollars, after she'd sewn a few appropriate dresses, but it would be months before she had the funds to return home.

Nancy was keeping her word, writing every week, telling her details about her son that made her heart glad. Though, the letters didn't always come once a week. Sometimes, a couple of weeks would pass, and then she'd get three letters, all at once.

She wrote Nancy each week, too, letters that were full of small, newsy details, suitable for reading out loud. She'd learned, if she needed to write Nancy about "adult things," to include a separate note. That way, Nancy didn't have to be concerned about reading her letters to Macon.

Nancy had been suitably appalled at what had happened to her when she'd first arrived, but her life had become routine now.

She glanced to see if Peggy had made progress. The young girl chewed on her pencil. She scrunched up her eyes and wrinkled her freckled nose. Then she threw her hands in the air.

"I don't know, Miss Mallory." She shook her head and tears formed at the corners of her eyes. "I can figure out the subject, the verb, the adjectives, and adverbs... but the direct object... I just don't understand."

She pushed back from the desk. "And I'm tired of diagraming sentences, Miss." She turned her woebegone eyes up and fanned her face with her tablet. "It's so hot today, Miss, like a furnace in this doggone parlor. Can't we go outside and sit on the porch where there's a breeze?"

Gazing at the pleading look in Peggy's eyes, she put her arms around the girl, something she'd wanted to do for a long time. She'd been concerned about forming an attachment and then leaving after only a few months. But now, she knew she wouldn't be heading home anytime soon. And she'd grown fond of Peggy. Giving in to her feelings, she embraced Peggy and stroked her long blond hair.

"It is hot in here, you're right." She kneeled beside the girl. "Don't you worry, you'll get it eventually... the direct object, I mean. One day, with practice, it will seem easy." She patted the girl's shoulder. "You'll see. You're a very smart girl."

"I wish my Papa thought so."

She straightened and rose, keeping her hands on the girl's shoulders. "Oh, he does, Peggy. I know he thinks you're smart. He just feels concerned that—"

"Guilty, you mean." Peggy shook her head.

She pursed her lips, wondering how she should answer. "Guilty because your studies have been neglected?"

"No, guilty... guilty that... my Mama died."

"Oh, Peggy." She leaned down and embraced the girl again. "You shouldn't think like that! Your father is a good and kind man. I'm sure he loved your mother very much, and I doubt he feels responsible for her getting sick. It was the will of God, nothing your father did."

"He meant to take her to the hospital sooner, but he couldn't get away from Fort Concho." Peggy turned her face up again. "I was littler then, but I remember. He was upset and angry when the hospital said it was too late." She lowered her head and buried her face in Mallory's skirts, sobbing. "I wish he would forgive himself. I know I have. It was the district commander who was to blame, not giving him permission in time. Not my Papa."

Mallory held the girl tightly, letting her get the grieving out of her system. She'd sensed something had been bothering the girl, but Peggy must have felt as constrained as she did. Afraid to open up. Afraid to let her see her darkest worries and grief. Mallory understood how it made life simpler to hide one's feelings.

She patted Peggy's back and lifted her chin. With her handkerchief, she wiped the girl's eyes dry and said softly, "Let's forget about lessons for today. We can sit on the porch and enjoy the breeze, like you said. Maybe do some sewing or..." Then she glimpsed the crude drawing of a paddle boat on the corner of Peggy's tablet.

The young girl was fascinated by paddlewheel steamships. They'd been reading history this morning with the other children, about La Salle, the French explorer who'd discovered the Mississippi River. Seeing the rough sketch, gave her an idea.

"Peggy, have you ever seen a stage play?"

"A stage play, Miss? Like on a big wooden platform with people talking?"

"Yes, just that."

The girl wrinkled her nose. "Uh, maybe one about Jesus being born. One Christmas, when I was little, we were staying in San Antonio before Papa was posted to Fort Concho. I remember there was a play at the church where we went. It was about Jesus being born."

"Did you enjoy it?"

"Oh, yes. I wish I could see another one, now I'm older."

"What about being in a play... acting a part?"

Peggy's blue eyes, so like her father's eyes, lit up. "Oh, Miss, what fun that would be! I would love to be in a play! What would it be about, something from the Bible?"

"No, not the Bible. I have a portfolio of plays my father gave me the Christmas before... I lost him." She hesitated and then smiled, trying to lighten her tone. "There's a play I know you'll like. It's about life on the Mississippi, and part of the play takes place on a paddle boat, too. It's called '*Kit, The Arkansas Traveler*.'"

"Oh, Miss, can I see it? Is there really a part for me?"

"Well, there's a little girl in the first act, and then she grows up—"

"Where is it? Can we read it right now?"

Mallory laughed, glad she'd hit upon something to brighten Peggy's day. "Of course, *right* now. Tell you what, have Martina make us some sweet iced tea, and you clean up your desk. I'll step out and get the portfolio of plays from my trunk at the Rodgers' cabin. Can you do that?"

"Yes, Miss! Oh, I can't wait to read it."

"Then meet me on the front porch in about ten minutes."

"You're wonderful, Miss Mallory. You know?" Peggy rose and embraced her, putting her arms around her and hugging her.

Mallory hugged her back, enjoying the smell of the young girl, a mixture of rose-scented soap and starch. She wished she hadn't waited to embrace Peggy. Besides being fond of each other, they both needed comforting. Peggy missed her mother. And she missed her son. They made a perfect pair.

* * *

Gregor stepped through his front door and heard raised voices coming from the parlor. He smiled to himself and shook his head.

Who would have thought a play would capture his daughter's imagination? Miss Reynolds was a godsend, helping Peggy with her lessons, fostering friendships, and... mothering her. Thinking about them together and their animated chatter, his heart warmed.

At the same time, he was amazed at how much work went into staging a play. Knowing what he did now, gave him pause, remembering the times he'd dismissed play actors, feeling they were charlatans or worse, earning a living by spouting a few words on a stage.

Now, he knew better. There appeared to be lots to do to stage a play properly. Miss Reynolds had appropriated his best carpenter, Sergeant Campbell, to build them several sets. One of the sets, Peggy had painted by herself.

It was a two-dimensional painting of a riverboat, complete with an oversized paddlewheel tacked on. Who knew his daughter was as captivated by paddle boats as most girls were of castles and princesses? The riverboats were an endless source of fascination for her. Someday, he hoped to travel east and take her for a ride on one of those luxurious, floating palaces.

Again, it was Miss Reynolds who'd noticed his daughter's interest, and the discovery had given her the idea of putting on a particular play, "*Kit, The Arkansas Traveler.*"

Of course, Peggy couldn't play the lead role, that part had gone to the fifteen- year-old boy from town, Jeb. Annie Richter would be Jeb's wife, and Thomas O'Sullivan had been cajoled into playing the villain. No one wanted to play the villain, least of all Thomas. His sister, Tammy, Peggy's new friend, was excited to portray all the female walk-on parts with enough costume changes to gladden any girl's heart.

There had been a heated discussion as to who would act the part of the young child in the first act. Miss Reynolds had wanted Peggy to portray the child, but Peggy had begged to play the part of the grown-up daughter. Miss Reynolds had said Peggy would need to wear face paint for the part of an older girl, which had sent his daughter flying to him, asking permission to wear rouge, lip paint, and face powder.

He didn't hold with such things, but to make his daughter happy, he'd agreed. He'd been surprised Miss Reynolds had the necessary cosmetics. Not that he'd seen any hint of make-up on her clear, flawless complexion.

She'd sewn herself new dresses, more appropriate to the West Texas frontier. He approved and hoped she was becoming accustomed to life at the fort.

These days, he found himself thinking about Miss Reynolds at the oddest times. He'd remember a gesture of hers, the way she drawled certain words, and even the way she walked. She charmed him without trying.

He hadn't stopped thinking about Martha, too. Small things reminded him of her, like her rose-painted china set or the way Peggy furrowed her brow. Even the faint floral scent that clung to Miss Reynolds reminded him of his Martha.

He ducked his head, considering. He'd never expected to be attracted to another woman after he lost his wife. He still grieved for her, missing her sorely, especially at the day's end when they would sit together, drink tea, and talk about the latest news.

But as much as he'd believed his heart had petrified, he couldn't deny the almost-painful pull of Miss Reynolds and her tinkling laugh.

He wished he knew more about her, but she, unlike his Martha, was aloof and seldom spoke about herself. He needed to draw her out. But when their conversations turned to her home in Georgia, she'd always managed to bring the conversation back to Peggy, the fort, or the other children in her school.

He rubbed his chin, considering.

Hanging back from the doorway into the parlor, he didn't want to attract attention. As usual, Miss Reynolds was going over Peggy's lines. He shook his head, surprised by the amount of rehearsing that went into a play. He doubted the other students rehearsed so much. But his daughter loved doing it.

He watched as Peggy crossed dramatically to the hearth, placing one hand over her heart and declaiming, "You villain, you!" She pointed her finger at an imaginary character. "I know you. You can't fool me! You're Sydney Snodgrass, the man who..."

She glanced up. "Oh, Papa!" Peggy ran to him. "I didn't see you."

"Hey, don't mind me. You better get back to rehearsing. Martina should have supper soon. Let me watch you."

"But you make me nervous, Papa, and then I forget my lines." His daughter gazed at Miss Reynolds with a beseeching look.

"Peggy, you're going to be performing in front of lots of people, not just your father. You need to get used to—"

"I know, Miss, I know. I just want to memorize all my lines first." She twisted her hands together.

Martina came to stand behind him. "*Señor* Colonel, supper, she is ready."

Gregor turned to Martina and said, "*Gracias*, Martina, we'll be right there." He turned back and clapped his hands. "Time for supper."

"Maybe we can practice after supper," Peggy said.

"Nope, not tonight." He decided to put his foot down. "You've been practicing every night all week. Tonight, is Saturday. Church tomorrow. I think you need to give Miss Reynolds some time off to see to her, uh, her..." He rubbed the back of his neck. "I'm sure she has some chores or sewing or—"

"Thank you, Commander, for championing me." She laughed. "Your daughter is quite the task master."

"Yes, she is, at least, about this play." He glanced at Peggy, enjoying it when she smiled, her face lighting up. He turned to Miss Reynolds. "Have you decided when you'll be putting on the play? How's Campbell coming with the sets?"

"Sergeant Campbell is an excellent carpenter. He's so clever with making a few sheets of plywood come alive. Our sets will be beautiful." She cocked her head to one side, as if considering. "As to when we'll stage the play, I wanted your opinion. Sally and I have been discussing the upcoming Fourth of July celebration. As I understand it, the Fourth of July, as a holiday, is only second to Christmas."

"You're right. Everyone enjoys the Fourth, especially the fireworks."

"Oh!" Miss Reynolds exclaimed and clapped her hands. "Are we going to have fireworks?"

"That's the usual big finale for the Fourth." He remembered the final celebration at Fort Clark; it had been right after he'd lost Martha. "That's if the fireworks arrive in time. According to the last dispatch, something got mixed up with our order, and they haven't left San Antonio." He shook his head. "It will be a somber holiday without the usual fireworks."

"Oh, Papa, you can't let that happen. Couldn't you shoot off some cannons or something?"

He grinned. "Cannons might make a big boom, but they don't light up the sky with sparkling colors."

"You're right, Commander," Miss Reynolds said. Then she went on tiptoe and peered around him, adding, "I think Martina is worried our supper will get cold."

"We can talk more over supper." Something, maybe it was the twinkle in her green-flecked eyes, made him hold out his arm. "I'll escort you in."

"Why, Commander," she took his arm and said, "how gracious of you."

He smiled at her, liking the touch of her small hand on his arm. Maybe that was why he'd offered to escort her a few feet to the kitchen table. He held out her chair, and she seated herself.

He took his own seat and said, "Let's bow our heads in prayer."

After their prayer, supper passed in a round of animated conversation and laughter. They talked about the play, and he was brought up to date on their progress. Originally, Miss Reynolds had envisioned Becky Davidson, the six-year-old girl from town, as being included as a walk on. But since Peggy didn't want to play the childish part, little Becky would need to play a pivotal role in the first act.

At first, Miss Reynolds had been concerned such a young child would be hard-pressed to memorize her lines. Along with Becky's mother, the two women had come up with a solution. Becky would deliver her part from the side of the stage with her mother repeating her lines from offstage.

Several sergeants, along with Campbell, had been enlisted to help move the sets and open and close the homemade curtains, along with filling in for the male walk-on parts. Sally and Miss Reynolds had already begun to sew the necessary costumes for the actors. And they'd decided on using the raised dais in the mess hall to stage the play.

Again, he was fascinated with all the preparations that went into it. But he had to admit the children's play was a welcome relief from the everyday problems he faced.

He relaxed, stretching his long legs beneath the table, happy his daughter was enthusiastic and lively. It had been too long since Peggy had acted like the child she was. He was fortunate Miss Reynolds had come west in more ways than one.

When they'd finished dessert, demolishing the berry cobbler Martina had made, Miss Reynolds wiped her mouth, folded her napkin, and put it beside her plate.

She rose and turned her gaze on him. "I think I'll take care of my chores, as you mentioned, Commander."

"Aww, no bedtime story?" Peggy piped up.

He turned to his daughter. "Not tonight, Peggy. Let's give Miss Reynolds an early night. She's been working awfully hard, putting this play together." He lowered his voice to a soft growl, "And I think it's time you got ready for bed, young lady. Don't you?"

"Fine." Peggy got up and started to flounce out of the room. She stopped and turned. "But you could read me a bedtime story, Papa."

Both he and Miss Reynolds burst out laughing at the same time. They exchanged glances over the girl's head.

"Not tonight. I need to attend to some paperwork in my office." It was a small white lie, and he didn't like fibbing, but his daughter needed to rely on her own resources at times.

Now that Miss Reynolds had given Peggy the attention and affection she'd been sorely missing, and his daughter had a new friend, he felt better about her. But he wanted her to learn self-reliance, too. The last thing he wanted was to spoil her because she'd lost her mother.

"You can read yourself a story. How's that?" he said. "Though, when I get back, your lamp better be out. Church tomorrow," he repeated.

Peggy's bottom lip poked out. "All right, Papa. I'll read for a little while. You'll check on me when you get back?"

"Of course. I'll make certain you're tucked in and asleep. And Martina is still cleaning up. She can fetch me when she's done. Good enough?"

"Yes, Papa."

"Well, you're going back to headquarters," Miss Reynolds remarked. "I'll say 'good night' to both of you."

He rose and took her arm. "Let me see you out."

She glanced at him. "Certainly."

When they reached the porch steps, she pulled her arm free. "Well, good night again. I'll see you at church."

Sunday was her day off. Usually, she spent it at church and then returned to the Rodgers' cabin. Some Sundays she joined him and Peggy for Sunday dinner. Other times, she stayed away.

Tonight, he had no intention of letting her leave quickly. For some reason, he wanted to spend time alone with her. And he wanted to get to know more about her, too.

"Miss Reynolds." He took her arm again. "My apologies, I told a white lie. I don't have anything critical waiting at headquarters." He ducked his head and swallowed. "I know I said you should have some time off... but tomorrow's Sunday and—"

"You wanted to speak with me?" He noticed the slight tremor in her voice.

"If you can spare a few minutes?"

"Of course."

He smiled and steered her to the other side of the porch, the farthest part away from Peggy's room. They settled into the two rockers there.

Gregor stared out at the starry night; a thousand pinpricks of light dotted the inky sky. It was a beautiful country but treacherous, too. And he was keeping her waiting, not knowing how to start.

He cleared his throat. "We talked a lot about the play at supper, but didn't you mention something about wondering when we should stage it?"

It was as good a beginning as he could think of, though, they were back to talking about events at the fort. But he was nervous about blurting out what had been uppermost in his mind for weeks: 'What's a beautiful, educated, and cultured woman doing in a frontier backwater as a mail order bride?'

"Oh, yes, I quite forgot." She folded her hands in her lap. "Sally and I've been discussing the Fourth of July celebration. She said there's usually plenty of food, dancing, and then the fireworks. But she mentioned last year's dance as being sort of a..."

"Dud?" he finished for her.

She smiled. "Well, that's not exactly the word Sally used, but close enough. Seems there aren't many ladies who attend, and most of the men, without partners, just hang around the dance floor, drinking."

"Yes, what Sally says is true." He shook his head. "Heaven knows, we don't have many women at the fort or in town for that matter. At my other posts, the neighboring ranchers came to our celebration and brought their families, including wives and daughters, which helped make up for the lack." He lowered his head and clasped his hands between his knees.

"Problem is, most ranchers around here, like E.P., aren't married. They have no families to bring, just their cowhands, which makes the disparity between the men and women even greater. There are a few of the ranchers who have families, but it takes a strong woman to live on a remote ranch, tucked into the mountains, seldom seeing anyone but her husband and their hands."

"That's what Sally said, which gave me an idea, but I wanted to ask you first." She turned her gaze on him. "What if the fort doesn't hold a dance this year? Instead, after supper is served, we could put on our play and then top off the evening with the fireworks." She reached across and touched his arm, smiling. "What do you think of that?"

He shook his head slowly. The woman was a wonder! What a marvelous idea! Staging a play would be a treat for everyone. Better than a mismatched dance with the men grumbling and drinking too much, and then the inevitable squabbling over the too few women.

Obviously, Sally hadn't been specific about what had happened last year. His first Fourth of July celebration at Fort Davis had turned into a free-for-all. He'd had to break up a nasty brawl toward the end of the evening. Blackened eyes and loose teeth had put a damper on the fireworks finale.

This way, the children would be the center of attention, staging their play. It might even lessen the amount of drinking and make the evening go smoother, especially if the fireworks didn't arrive in time.

He grabbed her hands and said, "That's an excellent idea!"

He could feel her soft hands trembling in his. She started to pull free, stopped herself, and licked her lips. He couldn't help but notice her mouth. Her lips were wet and glistening.

Then a thought struck him, as if someone had smacked him upside the head. Why hadn't he asked her to marry him when they'd found E.P. had died? If she'd been willing to marry a stranger, why not him? He wasn't a spring chicken, but then again, he was a few years younger than E. P. had been. He wasn't a wealthy man, either. But most of E.P.'s wealth had been tied up in land and cattle.

He couldn't offer her riches, but he could afford a housekeeper and as the commander of the fort, he had the nicest home on the post. She and Peggy had grown fond of each other, too. He dreaded the day when she had enough money to return to Georgia, knowing how attached his daughter was, like she'd been to Crissy.

How many times did his Peggy's heart have to be broken, finding a woman to care for, and then losing her again? Wouldn't their marriage solve both her problem and his? Even if it was, at first, a marriage of convenience?

Originally, he'd considered offering her the funds to return to Georgia as a loan. He had the savings put back, and he knew Miss

Reynolds to be well-bred and honorable. She would have returned his funds, over time.

But something had held him back. For one thing, he had serious doubts she'd take the money, looking upon it as charity. She was an independent woman. Or perhaps, even from the beginning, he'd hoped, despite all that had happened, she'd decide to stay.

It had been selfish of him, he knew, but he wanted his daughter to have an adequate education and, for that, Miss Reynolds had been a godsend. Or was that an excuse? He had to admit, even though he'd expected to remain single, grieving for his Martha, he was attracted to Miss Reynolds.

Gripping her warm hands, his mind was spinning with the thought of making her his wife. Her hands were so fine and smooth. Just touching her heated his blood and turned his thoughts to the bedroom.

But was he ready to take a wife, especially in the Biblical sense? He hadn't stopped missing Martha or grieving for her. And if he still had those feelings, would it be right to re-marry? Though, he had to admit, lately, the grief and sorrow dragging at him had receded. Even so, was he ready to be a husband in all ways?

And he couldn't help but notice Miss Reynolds was skittish about contact of any kind. Except the day when he'd rescued her. Then she'd clung to him, wrapping her arms around his waist. Unfortunately, that day she hadn't been herself; she'd been in shock. He wondered how she would have fared if E.P. had lived, they'd married, and her new husband had wanted to start a family immediately.

Miss Reynolds was a very attractive woman. At this moment, her mouth sorely tempted him to take a taste. He leaned in closer.

She shifted in the rocker and pulled her hands free. "I'm glad you approve of my idea, Commander. I think your soldiers and the townspeople will like seeing a play. It's something everyone can enjoy."

She'd retreated again, but this time, he didn't want to let her go. "I think, Miss Reynolds, it's high time we dispensed with the formalities. May I be allowed to call you by your given name, Mallory?"

Looking at her lap, she twisted her hands together. "Of course, Commander—"

"None of that. If I'm to call you by your given name, you must call me by mine. It's William."

"All right." She looked up and smiled. "But I prefer Will, if that's all right with you?"

"Actually, that's what my folks used to call me. My father's name was William."

"Oh, I see." She hesitated and wet her lips again with her tongue. "You don't think it will give Peggy the wrong idea, do you?"

His gaze was riveted on her mouth. He hadn't felt like kissing a woman since... since...

"No, I don't think so. We're more informal on the frontier. You must have noticed I call Mrs. Rodgers by her given name, Sally."

"Yes, I noticed."

"Mallory is an unusual name. I've often wondered—"

"It was my mother's maiden name." She lifted one shoulder in a half shrug. "A southern custom, I believe, using surnames as given names."

"What about Metcalf?"

"Ah." She chuckled. "My grandmother's maiden name. I think it's a way of keeping the women's names in the family."

"What if your mother's maiden name had been Hotchkiss or O'Sullivan or..."

She gazed at him, her eyes twinkling. "Well, there are limits to certain customs. Though, I had a distant cousin who went by the name of Tarleton."

"A young lady, not a man?"

"No, Tarleton was a girl, and she hated her name."

"I can see why." He chuckled, too.

Now he was getting somewhere. He'd managed to steer the conversation to her past and the South. Perhaps, he'd learn something about her—if he didn't haul off and kiss her first.

"Tell me more about your home, Miss... er, Mallory." He grinned. "I'd enjoy learning about where you come from."

"Oh, there's not much to tell. Really." She snagged his gaze. "You didn't fight in the South during the war?"

"My battalion unit never got further than western Virginia. I was with the First Ohio Volunteers."

"So, you volunteered for the war?"

"Yes, I hadn't planned on being a soldier. I was in seminary school. I was committed to being a traveling preacher, going to frontier settlements to preach the gospel. Then the war started, and I didn't want to see the Union dissolved, so I volunteered."

"Were you already married? I mean, when the war started?"

"Heavens, no. I didn't expect to marry, thinking an itinerant preacher had no right to a wife." He shook his head. "Wouldn't have been fair to a woman."

"But then how did you marry?"

"I was on furlough. I'd taken a musket ball in my calf." He grimaced and stretched out his right leg. "Still gets stiff and achy when the weather's cold." He lowered his head and leaned forward. He took her hands again and, this time, she didn't recoil.

"We met at a barn raising. Not that I did much raising with a bum leg, but afterwards, there was a dance. Martha was there.

"We talked and talked." He grinned. "I couldn't do much dancing. Before the night was out, we'd promised to write. She waited for me. I didn't finish seminary, decided soldiering would be my profession, knowing it would give me more security to raise a family."

"Do you regret it sometimes? Giving up the seminary?"

He lifted his head and looked into her sparkling eyes. How had she done it? They were supposed to be talking about her—not him. She'd turned the tables on him once more, diverting the conversation from herself. She was clever, very clever.

If he couldn't best her at conversation, maybe he could get to know her in another way. He leaned in and pulled her closer. His lips brushed hers.

She started and her eyes widened.

"Colonel Gregor, Colonel Gregor," a man's voice interrupted them.

He looked up to see Corporal Walsh running toward them. The corporal skidded to a halt at the edge of the porch, panting. "Colonel Gregor, Doc Winslow sent me for you. Reverend Finley took an arrow in his leg. The doctor said to fetch you, as he knew you wanted to be informed of any Injun attack."

He let Mallory's hands go and rose, wondering how much the corporal had seen. From the corner of his eye, he glanced at Mallory and could read the concerned look on her face, knowing she was wondering the same thing.

"You did the right thing, Walsh, coming for me. Let me see Miss Reynolds home and ask Martina to stay with my daughter. Then I'll be right there." He'd reverted to using her proper name, hoping it had been too dark for Walsh to have seen anything, hoping there would be no gossip.

She got to her feet, too, and touched his sleeve. "Let me stay with Peggy. It's late, and I'm sure Martina wants to go home." She shivered a little in the warm air, probably remembering her abduction by the Apache. "After, will you come and tell me what happened?"

"Of course, and it's kind of you to stay with Peggy."

"I want to."

"But don't tell her about the reverend yet. Let me break it to her." He shook his head. "Sometimes, she has nightmares. Besides, she'll learn soon enough, tomorrow in church."

"Yes," she said, "and I understand about having nightmares. Sometimes, I have them, too."

Chapter Six

Gregor watched as Doc Winslow expertly cut the arrowhead from Reverend Finley's leg, leaving a flap of skin to stich over the puncture wound. Finley, who'd refused whiskey to deaden the pain, writhed on the Doc's operating table and arched his back. He was held down by four soldiers, including Corporal Walsh.

The doctor had given Finley a stick to bite on, and the man was crunching it between his jaws. His eyes rolled back in his head, and he sank onto the table.

Doc Winslow grunted. "Better that way." He glanced over his shoulder at his assistant, Corporal Richardson, and said, "Bring me more gauze, the needle I had you boil, and thread. I'll have him patched up in no time. Just a flesh wound, doesn't look like any arteries or muscles were hit."

The doctor patted Finley's shoulder. "He's a lucky man." Then he held up the shaft of the arrow he'd broken off, looking it over. "Appears to be Apache."

"Not too surprising," Gregor said. "That's why I wanted to speak with the reverend, but with him passed out, I won't be able to question him."

The doctor held the needle up to the lantern light and threaded it. "You can question him, Colonel. No worries. My stitching him up will probably bring him around. If not, I've smelling salts."

Gregor nodded and folded his hands behind his back. "I'll stay then. I need the details of what happened."

The doctor's movements were quick and deliberate, closing up the wound swiftly. He motioned to his assistant and, after saturating the gauze in whiskey, he applied it to the raw looking wound.

Reverend Finley's eyes flew open, his back bowed as if he wanted to lift himself off the table. He spit the stick out, roaring, "Aaargh! Save me, Lord! It feels like hell's demons are..." He stopped and sank back onto the table, digging his fingers into the wood.

"All done, now." Doc Winslow patted the reverend's shoulder again. "You're a brave young man."

"No, I'm not. Truth be known, I'm a lily-livered coward." The reverend rolled his head from side to side. "It's why I asked for a transfer. I lay awake nights, thinking about Indian attacks and, before my replacement could get here, this happened." He groaned and bit his lip.

That was news to Gregor; he hadn't known the reverend was leaving them. He stepped forward. "Where did you take the arrow, Reverend? I need to try and find who shot you. Where did it happen?"

"I was at the Bolton's ranch, Colonel, saying prayers over a cowhand who was gored by their bull. We were standing at the grave, praying. Phineas Bolton leaned down and stepped forward to throw a handful of dirt on the cowboy's coffin. That's when the arrow hit me."

"How many hostiles?"

"I only saw the one. He was waiting in ambush behind a large boulder about twenty yards away. After he hit me, he jumped on his pony and rode off."

"What about the Bolton family?" Gregor knew Phineas had a wife and two daughters. "Are they all right?"

"They're fine. Phineas tried to shoot the Apache, but he missed. They brought me to town, after securing their ranch. Their cowhands are standing watch, taking shifts. The family is spending the night with the Lovells, but they'll be heading home tomorrow morning."

"I'll send troops with them. They'll reconnoiter the area and make sure everything is clear." He shook his head. "Speaking of which, Reverend Finley, if you're concerned about Apache attacks, why didn't you ask for an escort to the Bolton's spread?"

"It didn't occur to me, their place being so close to town. I guess I thought I was safe, but I should have known better." He closed his eyes and sighed. "It's good of you, Colonel, to send troops with the Bolton family. I'm sure they'll appreciate all the help you can give them. Phineas is one of my best parishioners, but I don't know how he manages to raise enough cattle to keep his family fed. His spread is so small, he can barely afford to pay his hands. He's been thinking of selling to Mr. Murphy."

Hearing the reverend mention Murphy, suspicions that had been churning in the back of his mind surfaced, and pieces of the puzzle started to fall into place.

"Do you think the Apache meant to shoot you, Reverend? They don't usually take aim at holy men. It goes against their superstitions."

"No, I don't think so. I think he meant to shoot Phineas, but then Mr. Bolton leaned down to get a handful of dirt and step closer to the grave. I think the Indian hit me by mistake."

He groaned again and reached for his thigh. "I'm more than glad to take an arrow for Phineas." He managed a weak smile. "I think."

Doc Winslow pushed the reverend's hand aside. "Don't touch the wound, unless you've sluiced your hands in whiskey, man. You don't want it to fester, do you?"

"No, of course not, Dr. Winslow."

"Good then. Do you have someone who can take care of you until you get on your feet?" The doctor asked.

"Mrs. Johnson, where I board, will be happy to help me."

"All right, that's fine," the doctor said. "I'll check on you every day for the first week or so, until I'm sure the wound is healing. After that, we'll see about getting you some crutches made, so you can start moving around. But not until I tell you to."

"Yes, I understand."

"Good." The doctor turned to Gregor and said, "I'm going to give him a dose of laudanum, so's he can rest. He can stay with me tonight. Tomorrow, I'll need a pair of orderlies and a litter to move him to the boarding house."

"I'll be sure you get what you need. Just send for Corporal Walsh, and he'll see to it." He glanced at the corporal.

"Have you finished questioning him?" Dr. Winslow asked.

"Yes, I have." He looked at his orderly again. "Walsh, if the doctor doesn't need you, I want you to go to the Lovell's home, and tell Phineas I'd like to talk to him after church tomorrow."

"Yes, sir. Right away, sir."

"And have Captain Rodgers come here, I need to speak with him about the patrol I'm sending with the Bolton family."

"Very good, sir."

The doctor put his hands on his hips and gazed at his patient. "Speaking of church, who's going to hold services tomorrow?"

"Bob Lovell can hold the services. He's my head deacon." The reverend glanced at him and asked, "Can Walsh tell Mr. Lovell when he takes your message?"

"Of course," he said and looked up at Walsh. "Be sure Mr. Lovell is informed." He inclined his head. "Bring the captain first before you go to town, Corporal. I'll be waiting for him on the front porch." He saluted. "Dismissed."

Walsh saluted and exited the room.

Gregor stepped forward and put his hand on Finley's arm. "Take care of yourself, Reverend. Be sure to do what the doc tells you. He knows his stuff."

The reverend nodded, his eyes drifting shut. "No worries there, Colonel. I'll be a model patient."

He squeezed the reverend's arm. "Good man." He turned to the doctor. "I'll wait on your front porch, if you don't mind."

He nodded his head at the three remaining orderlies. "Help the doctor get the reverend settled for the night. Then you're dismissed. I appreciate your helping out."

The three privates saluted, and he returned their salute.

"Good night, Doc, and thank you for all you've done."

"Good night, Colonel."

He exited the doctor's office and pulled the door shut behind him. He looked up and saw a small crowd had gathered, mostly soldiers from the fort with a sprinkling of townspeople.

Word traveled fast in these parts.

He held up one hand and raised his voice, "You can all go home now. The reverend took an arrow in the fleshy part of his thigh, but Doc Winslow says he should be fine."

Then he noticed a man in the back of the crowd—a stranger. The man had his Stetson pulled low. He wore a red-checkered bandana at his throat, a white shirt, and a sturdy-looking pair of denims. On his hips, slung low, were two holstered Colts.

He wanted to know who the man was. The last two stagecoaches, one headed west and the other east, hadn't brought any newcomers to town. He stepped off the porch and called out, "You, there! I'm the commander of Fort Davis. Would you care to introduce yourself?"

The man whirled around and leapt onto the back of a brown mare. He didn't look back, just dug his spurs into the mare's sides and took off toward town.

Gregor looked around for someone to go after the man, but everyone was afoot.

Captain Rodgers pushed through the remnants of the crowd, most of whom were drifting away, returning to their homes.

Rodgers came to attention and saluted. "You sent for me, sir?"

He watched as the stranger melted away, swallowed by the darkness. Then he turned to Rodgers. "Yes, I did. I need for you to pull together a patrol of twenty men to escort the Bolton family to their ranch tomorrow after church services. They're staying with the Lovells in town. When you get to the ranch, have your patrol search around the ranch house in a five-mile-wide perimeter. See if there are any Apache nearby."

"Yes, sir, I'll get the men together tomorrow. If we encounter Apache, what do you want us to do?"

He rubbed the back of his neck. "Well, it will be too late to conclusively tie any hostiles you find to the attack on the reverend." He shook his head. "Talk to them, see why they're on the Boltons' ranch. And then warn them off. It's all we can do for now.

"Who's on guard duty?" he asked, changing his focus.

"Corporal Jenkins of Company H, sir."

"All right." He gazed at the captain. "Have you seen a stranger, wearing two Colts and with a red-checkered bandana? He's riding a brown mare."

"No, sir, I haven't."

"Hmmm, odd timing for a stranger to turn up. See if Corporal Jenkins saw which way the man rode. He was waiting outside with the crowd, wanting to hear about the reverend, but when I spoke to the man, he high-tailed it."

"Not a good sign."

"No. Rouse some of your men and go look for the man in town, after Jenkins tells you which way he's headed."

"Yes, sir."

"Oh, and another thing," he added, remembering the Apache might be watching the Bolton ranch. "If you encounter Apache on the Bolton spread, you'll need an interpreter. Take Deer Stalker with..." He stopped himself and considered. "Come to think of it, I haven't seen him around for a while."

"I thought you knew, sir. He got paid last month and then he disappeared."

"No, I didn't know. I've been busy deploying the infantry troops and rotating them." He stared at the captain. "Why didn't you tell me?"

The captain lowered his head. "Uh, I thought Myerson told you. Deer Stalker was attached to his unit. Not mine."

"Yes, you're right, Captain. I forgot which unit he was officially with. The translators go where they're needed." He rubbed his chin. His skin was bristly; he hadn't shaved since this morning. And he'd kissed Mallory.

He shook himself. She crept into his thoughts, no matter how hard he concentrated on the matters at hand.

"He left after the last payroll, you say?" he asked.

"Yes, sir."

"That would have been a couple of weeks after he helped me with Caballero and the hostage situation?"

"That's correct, sir."

"Odd timing, all of this." He glanced at the captain. "You have an interpreter assigned to your outfit?"

"Yes, sir, Pale Hawk."

"Well," he said and puffed out his breath. "He's not as adept as Deer Stalker, but until we can replace him, take Pale Hawk with you."

"Yes, sir."

"And tell Myerson to report to me after church tomorrow. I want to know..." He stopped himself. Myerson and Rodgers had enough of a rivalry going without him stoking the fire. "Just tell him to report."

Rodgers straightened and saluted.

"You've got your orders. If your men find the stranger tonight, I want to be wakened and told. You can question him, but if he didn't break any laws, you can't take him into custody. Understood? And if you don't find the man, report tomorrow before you take the Bolton family to their home."

"Yes, sir."

"Dismissed."

* * *

Mallory leaned over the front porch railing, staring at the blazing lights coming from Doc Winslow's surgery, across the parade ground. The commander had been gone for a long time, and she was worried about the reverend.

She hoped the Methodist minister wasn't badly hurt. He was such a nervous young man. And she'd thought the commander's new strategy had been working. The Apache raids had lessened, based on the conversations she'd had with Sally. But now Reverend Finley had been shot.

She took out Macon's picture and gazed at it in the half-light from the kitchen. She couldn't wait to get home to her son and away from the dangers of the frontier.

Jittery from the anxiety gnawing at her, she put Macon's picture away and paced back and forth on the porch. Perhaps, she should check on Peggy. But she'd just checked on the girl a few minutes ago, and Peggy had been fast asleep. Earlier, she'd hurried over to Sally's to tell her about the reverend and explain she was going to stay with Peggy until her father returned.

Then she'd come back and helped Martina clean up. After that, she'd returned to the porch and to wait for Will.

She put her fingertips against her lips. He'd kissed her. Never in a thousand years had she expected him to kiss her. Funny, when she thought of the commander as Will, just his name sparked something deep inside her. Some long dormant yearning... to belong, to be desirable to a man.

It was something she thought had withered away, washed away by betrayal and disillusionment.

The more she thought about Will, the more her thoughts tumbled, like dice in a cup, clattering around. What were his intentions? They must be honorable, knowing he'd trained as a preacher.

And the more she knew about him, the more she'd grown to admire him. He was kind and fair-handed with his men. He expected his soldiers to perform to the best of their ability, but he gave them every opportunity to meet his expectations. He was the same way with his daughter, tough but caring. The perfect mix in a man, to her way of thinking.

Knowing him as she did, after her initial instinctive reaction, she hadn't minded them holding hands and him kissing her. Not nearly so much as she would have thought.

Was she attracted to the commander... to Will? It was hard not to be. He was tall and well-built, his rangy frame belying the muscular body that lay beneath his uniform. His features weren't parlor-style handsome. Instead, his wide-set, blue-gray eyes, blade-thin nose, and chiseled mouth combined to make him ruggedly good looking. Even the spray of gray hair at his temples added to his appeal.

As much as she might be attracted and secretly admire him, she couldn't help but remember how trusting and naïve she'd been about men before. Hiram had been exceptionally handsome and charming. And she'd thought she'd known his character, too, but she'd been a fool. A simple and silly fool.

She never wanted to be that kind of foolish again.

The summer night was turning cooler, and she wished she had her shawl. She shivered, wrapping her arms around her waist and hugging herself.

She returned to the front porch rail and gazed across the parade ground again. Shadows shifted and milled in front of Doc Winslow's window. Straining forward, she hoped Will was coming soon.

After what seemed like hours, the lights in the doctor's office dimmed. Will should be coming back. She heard the crunch of his boots on the gravel before she glimpsed his form, silhouetted against the dark night.

He strode toward her, his back ramrod straight and his head thrust forward. She wanted to run to him, to nestle in the comforting circle of his arms. But she knew better than to show her emotions too blatantly.

She waited and then he was beside her, joining her without a word. Standing alongside her and leaning against the rail, he gazed out at the dark night.

As strange and silent as his approach had been, she wasn't frightened or anxious. Not now. Not now that he was here. A kind of peace settled between them—as if being together was enough—offering each other comfort without words. She'd never felt this way about a man, not even her sweet Beau.

Finally, he shifted and extended one leg, standing with his boot over the edge of the porch. "How's Peggy?"

"She's fine. I checked. Sleeping."

"Good." He nodded. "Thank you again for staying."

"My pleasure. You know I care for Peggy."

"Yes, I do, and it gladdens my heart."

Hearing him say such a thing, so open and easy—her own heart leapt in her chest, beating faster. She sucked in her breath. "How's the reverend?"

"He took an Apache arrow in the fleshy part of his thigh. Doc Winslow got the arrowhead out and sewed him up. Barring an infection, he should be fine." He turned toward her. "Did you know the good reverend asked to be transferred?"

She was surprised, but not shocked. She'd never thought the man was suited to the frontier. "No, I didn't. Though, I could have guessed."

"How so?"

"It was obvious from the first day Peggy took me to the church; he wasn't happy here."

He puffed out his cheeks and nodded. Facing her, he leaned his back against the porch rail and rested his elbows on the wooden bar. "The arrow wasn't meant for the reverend."

"What do you mean?"

"Looks like the Apache wanted to kill Phineas Bolton, a rancher. He owns a small spread between town and the Lazy M. The reverend was officiating at a funeral, one of Bolton's cowhands. Reverend Finley thinks when Mr. Bolton leaned down, the Apache shot him by mistake."

"Oh, no, that's terrible." She shook her head. "But why would the Apache want to kill Mr. Bolton? Were they raiding his cattle?"

"No, I don't think so. As far as the reverend knows, it was a lone hostile. I plan on talking to Phineas tomorrow, though, to be certain of my facts."

"Sally mentioned since you've deployed the infantry, the raids have dwindled."

"That's true, but I think this was more planned, more purposeful."

"How so?"

"You remember the way Ben Murphy treated us?"

She shuddered. "How could I forget?"

"He seemed set on inheriting his brother's ranch, and he mentioned something that made me think he shelters the Apache for his own ends."

"But why would he do that? Isn't he afraid of them?"

"I doubt he's afraid of them. He has a small army at his command. No, I think he's using them to run off or kill neighboring ranchers. Then, he can take over their land."

She gasped. "What a terrible thing to do."

"Yes, but not as terrible as killing your own brother so he can't marry."

"You still believe that. Don't you?"

"Everything points to it." He sighed. "Though, I have no way of proving it." He shook his head. "I tried to raise a reward, but people around these parts are hard-put to make a living. They've given a few dollars, and the reverend gave me a donation, but it's not enough money to get one of Ben's men to come forward. Without someone on the Lazy M to verify my suspicions, there's nothing I can do.

"I didn't tell you before because I was disappointed." He shook his head. "When Judge Beadle, the circuit judge, came to town, I asked him about Ben's financial responsibility to you." He shrugged one shoulder. "The judge didn't think there was anything he could do, no law on the books—"

"I don't want Mr. Murphy's money." And as much as she wanted to return to her son, what she said was true. She wanted nothing to do with Ben Murphy.

"I understand, and I can't say as I blame you." He lowered his head and scuffed his boots on the wooden planks.

Then he looked up. "Have you or Sally noticed a stranger in town? I know you go most days to town for fabric, needles, and such."

"Yes, we do, but we haven't noticed anyone new."

"There was a stranger, waiting outside Doc Winslow's. I tried to introduce myself, but he took off. He was of medium height and build, wearing a Stetson, and a red-checkered bandana, knotted at his throat. He rode a brown mare."

She shook her head. "No, I can't remember anyone who..." Then she suddenly remembered that far-off day when she'd received Nancy's first letter. She'd thought, for a split second, the man lounging in front of the saloon had been Ben Murphy.

She'd pushed the disturbing image to the back of her mind, but listening to Will's suspicions about Ben and his concern over a stranger, she wondered if she should have said something sooner.

"I... I, uh, now that you mention it..."

His head came up, and he gazed into her eyes. "Did you see the man?"

"No, not the stranger you saw tonight. Not him. But I thought I saw Ben in town one day, after you warned him off."

"Why didn't you...?" He stopped himself and held up one hand. "Forget I said that. You were scared and not certain it was Ben. Am I right?"

She gulped. "Yes, I was frightened." She clasped her hands and twisted them together. "Thinking about Ben Murphy upsets me. And that day, I'd gotten my first letter from home. Sally was with me, but she had to get back to cook supper for her husband. We'd been in town, talking to families about the school. Sally didn't want to leave me, but I thought I would be fine.

"We both looked around and didn't see anyone threatening. But there was a man, sitting on the bench in front of the saloon. He had his Stetson pulled over his face, as if he was sleeping."

"Why did you think it was Ben? What was he wearing?"

Her knuckles popped and she untangled her fingers, pushing her hands into her apron's pockets. "I didn't notice what he was wearing. I was too excited to hear from home, so I sat on a bench outside the post office and looked over my letter."

She reached up and patted the bun at the back of her head. "Then I got this creepy feeling, and I glanced up from my letter. The man in front of the saloon was staring at me. I thought I recognized him as Ben, but before I got a good look, he lowered his head again and pulled his hat down." She grimaced. "I hurried back to the fort."

"You did the right thing." He rubbed the back of his neck. "Do you remember when this happened?"

"Only a couple of days after we got back from the Lazy M."

"That would have been when the payroll for the fort was due in."

"Do you think Mr. Murphy was in town to steal the payroll?"

"No, it arrived intact. But it might explain why my best translator took his pay and quit without a word."

"Oh," she said, though, she didn't quite understand. What did one of the fort's translators have to do with seeing Ben Murphy where he wasn't supposed to be in town?

As if reading her confused thoughts, he said, "If Ben is using the Apache to drive his neighbors from their land, he needs a translator. Some Apaches speak English but only a few. And the few who do, seldom admit it.

"Most Apache speak Spanish, though. They've been fighting the Mexicans for at least two hundred years and have learned their language. Their chiefs usually adopt Spanish names, too, like Victorio and Caballero, but they hate the Mexicans worse than they hate us. Ben's shrewd enough to not use a Mexican to translate for fear of insulting them. That's why I think he needs Deer Stalker."

"I see. It seems everyone has enemies on the frontier. And Mr. Murphy stirring up trouble, makes things more difficult."

He sighed and admitted, "It's just a hunch of mine... about Ben. I need more facts to prove it." He turned toward her and smiled. "I think that's enough for a Saturday night. You must be tired. Can I escort you to Sally's?" He put his arm around her shoulders.

Instinctively, she shied away from him.

He let her go and gazed into her eyes.

She stared at his mouth, wishing he would kiss her again. But she'd pulled away. Now, he'd never kiss her. And she didn't want to drive him away. She wanted him near. His strength kept her going in this alien land.

She was flattered he'd explained his suspicions about the Apache who'd shot the reverend and his missing interpreter. Most men didn't confide their business to women, thinking the female sex was too flighty or dim-witted to comprehend men's undertakings.

Even her father had been unwilling to teach her how to oversee the plantation, and when she'd asked how the Cotton Exchange would work, he'd told her women didn't have a head for business.

Will's consideration of her as a person warmed and pleased her. Wanting to make amends for pushing him away, she took his arm and draped it over her shoulder, glancing up at him.

His lips quirked into a smile. "I'll take you home… or would you care for a cup of tea before you go? It's been an exhausting evening. I know I could use something."

She giggled, a nervous laugh bubbling forth. "I agree. It's been very upsetting, especially about the reverend, and your suspicions." She shook her head. "I don't know if I can go straight to sleep. A cup of tea might be nice."

"Come on. Let's see how Peggy is. Then I'll brew some tea."

"Would you happen to have something stronger on hand?"

"Why, Miss Reynolds, I never took you for a tippler."

She half-smiled. "I'm not, only on occasion. You don't know much about me, do you?"

"No, I don't. But I wish I did. Would you care to enlighten me, over some brandy, perhaps? I keep a very smooth French brandy, brought in from Galveston."

She giggled again and, this time, it wasn't her nerves. "I'm surprised, Will. I wouldn't have taken a former seminary student for a drinker, either."

He laughed. "*Touché*. I don't partake often, but sometimes, as you so elegantly put it, the occasion calls for a tot of strong drink."

He caressed her arm. "I think tonight might be one of those times. Don't you?"

"Yes, I do, and I'd be delighted to join you."

"Only if you promise to talk about yourself. I'd like to know more about you, Mallory." He lowered his arm and squeezed her waist. She leaned into him.

She was tall for a woman, but he towered over her. Curving her body into his long, rangy frame felt so right, as if they belonged together.

"How about it?" he asked.

She blinked. What was he asking? He wanted to hear more about her? She could do that... to a point.

She turned her head up and smiled. "All right, Will, we have a deal."

Chapter Seven

Mallory watched as Will reached into the topmost cabinet and fetched a bottle of expensive-looking brandy. He turned and grinned, putting his index finger to his lips. "I keep it hidden. Don't want Peggy and Martina to know about my bad habits."

"Oh, you have other bad habits? What would those be?"

He fetched two glasses and wagged his finger. "You're doing it again."

"Doing what?"

"Steering the conversation toward me. I want to hear about you, Mallory. I thought we had a deal."

"You're right, we do."

He poured the brandy and handed her a glass. He raised his glass and touched it to hers. "To hearing more about the very cultured and refined Mallory Metcalf Reynolds."

She saluted him with her brandy and took a sip. The brandy burned a pathway to her stomach. She hadn't tasted good brandy in a long time, not since she'd lived in Charleston.

The grandfather clock in the parlor chimed, ten times; she counted the strokes. It was later than she'd thought, but as she'd told Will, she would have been hard-pressed to fall asleep after the distressing events of tonight.

"Well?" he asked.

She smiled. "All right, then. Let me think." She tapped the side of her glass with her finger. "As you know, I'm from Georgia. I grew up on a plantation near Savannah. We called it Riverbend, as our home was in the bend of the Chattooga River. We grew rice in the lowlands, but our primary crop was cotton. We had a townhome in Savannah, too. I guess you could say we were wealthy. My father had inherited the plantation; my father's family were some of the original settlers."

"I thought so, everything about you told me you grew up privileged."

"Is it so obvious?"

"Yes, but not in a bad way, Mallory." He shook his head. "That's not what I meant. No one could call you snobbish. But you're cultured, well-spoken, and educated. The mark of a true lady."

She took another sip of brandy, savoring the nutty taste. And savoring his kind words. It had been a long time since she'd heard such compliments, and then those had been a foil and a trap.

But not with Will. The man was as open and expansive as this wild frontier he inhabited. Her skin prickled and heated. "That's kind of you."

"Kind, perhaps, but my honest opinion, as well."

His compliments warmed her, better than the expensive brandy. She was transported back in time to when she was a debutante in Charleston. Then, she'd felt beautiful and special, like a spanking-new gift, tied up with a big bow.

She hadn't felt that way in a long, long time.

Her neck and face heated, and the tips of her ears burned. She knew she must be blushing.

She lowered her head. "It's true, I was well-tutored from an early age. I'm an only child and my father wanted me to have the best education, even though I was female. My mother was English. My father met her when he toured Europe as a young man after university. But she was like a hothouse orchid and very frail.

"When I was eight, we lost her to yellow fever. I was so filled with sorrow, like a misplaced lamb. She was gentle and kind." She paused, thinking it odd the same qualities her mother had possessed, she valued in this strong, brave man.

Her father had been different, brash and ambitious. And she'd thought she wanted a man like her father.

Sighing, she continued, "I didn't think I'd survive the loss. All I wanted was to go to my sweet mother and join her in heaven."

He inclined his head and cleared his throat. "It's no wonder you and Peggy have formed a bond. She lost her mother at about the same age."

"Yes, I've often thought of that."

He reached across the table and touched her hand. "I'm so sorry. So very sorry."

"Yes." She nodded and tried to smile but failed. "I knew you'd understand what a blow it was."

He lowered his voice and spoke softly, "And after your mother passed?"

"Oh, it was a bad time." She lifted her glass and took a swallow. "The War Between the States had started, and my father marched off to the war at the head of a cavalry unit of Georgia volunteers. Mostly men of importance like himself, banding together."

This time, she managed to smile, remembering. "My Mammy, Astarte, used to say there were too many chiefs and not enough soldiers."

He took her hand and squeezed it. Then he released her and sat back. "We often say that in the Army." He finished his brandy and poured himself another. He held up the bottle, offering.

She shook her head.

"So, you were alone on the plantation with your Mammy?"

"Yes, and the other house servants and my governess. Papa left an overseer to run the place, too, but I was lonely." She sipped her brandy, almost finishing the glass.

"Now I know why you're so strong. You've had to rely on yourself from a young age."

Oh, my, another compliment.

Her head was swimming, and she didn't know if it was from the brandy or his obvious admiration. But she didn't dare tell him the whole story. If she did, would his admiration turn to disgust?

The next part was tricky—should she tell him about Beauregard and how she'd nursed him when he returned from the war? But to what use? Yes, she'd cared for Beau, but he was gone, and his passing might have changed the course of her life, but to talk about her childhood sweetheart seemed unnecessary.

"After the war, my father came home, unharmed. In that, we were blessed. And Sherman didn't destroy Savannah, either, not like Atlanta. The Union general was taken with the town's beauty and "gifted" the city to Lincoln for Christmas. Sherman was satisfied with destroying the Charleston-Savannah railroad, which cut us off from the rest of the South.

"Despite our blessings, my family was financially ruined. Most of our slaves had remained on the plantation, as my father was a kind master. They became sharecroppers. But he still couldn't find enough laborers." She shook her head. "Then the carpetbaggers descended."

She fiddled with her brandy glass. "They were like locusts, those men from the North who..." She glanced up. "My apologies, I didn't mean to speak ill of—"

"No apologies necessary. I may have fought for the Union, but there were good and honorable men on both sides. And there are always men who take advantage of people's misfortunes."

"Thank you for your understanding. The carpetbaggers took over the local government, assessing enormous taxes on the plantations. Bankrupting many of the planters." She chewed on her lip. "My father sold off some of our land and our townhouse. He managed to pay the taxes, but then he took out a loan to start the Savannah Cotton Exchange with his friends. They felt commerce, rather than agriculture, would be the South's future and restore their fortunes."

"Clever man. What went wrong?" He finished his brandy.

This time, he refilled both their glasses without asking.

"Let me backtrack a bit," she said. Now, she was on shaky ground, and she'd need to be careful not to tell him everything without lying.

"While my father was trying to restore our finances, my aunt, my father's sister, invited me to join her in Charleston. My aunt, Sephora Claiborne, paid the tuition to Miss Prentiss' Finishing School. She wanted me to finish my education and be introduced into society."

"I gather your aunt wasn't lacking in money."

"Oh, no, her husband owned a middling-sized plantation, but most of his money came from shipping. And despite the blockade during the war, enough of his ships had gotten through to make him very wealthy, indeed. With the war over, his fortune grew.

"As soon as the Charleston-Savannah railroad was restored, I was sent to my aunt Sephora. I finished school and was presented to Charleston society through my uncle's membership at the St. Cecilia Society. My aunt paid for all my gowns and accessories, as my father was struggling to start the Cotton Exchange."

She stopped and sipped her brandy. The clock chimed eleven times. She hadn't been up this late since those heady days of her debut.

"Did you enjoy your debutante season?"

"Yes, of course, but I did something very foolish." She hesitated.

He filled her glass for the third time, and she knew she must refuse more. But right now, the world was a comforting, vague place, hazy but pleasant.

"What could you have possibly done?" His question drew her back.

"I quarreled with my aunt. It was a silly thing."

"Over a gentleman?"

He was perceptive. How had he almost guessed her secret?

"Yes, in a way. He was unsuitable for me." A stretch of the truth, but not too far from wrong. If ever a man had been unsuitable, it was Hiram.

"What happened?" he asked.

"My aunt's feelings were hurt because of all she'd done for me. She asked me to leave Charleston and go home." She lifted the glass to her lips. "I did as she asked and settled on our plantation again, helping out as much as I could.

"A few years later, my father died of apoplexy. It was very sudden, completely unexpected. He was a vigorous man to the end."

"My condolences again." He reached for her hand once more, and this time, he stroked the inside of her wrist, making her pulse race and her body feel liquid and light, as if she might float away.

"Why didn't you stay on your plantation and run it?"

"Because my father had mortgaged our plantation to start up the Exchange. I had to sell our place to pay off my father's debts. I still have my shares in the Exchange, and in a few years, they might be worth something. Once I sold Riverbend and paid the debts, there wasn't much cash left."

She hunched her shoulders, drawing into herself, wanting to banish the past. "My good friend Nancy, whose husband is a minister, welcomed me into her home. But I couldn't remain living off their charity. I was considering teaching school when her husband showed me Mr. Murphy's ad in the *Texas Christian Advocate*. His ad resonated with me." She laughed at her idealistic dreams. "I thought I could start my life over."

She put her free hand on the table, palm up. "Now, you know why I came west. What do you think? Did I make a mistake, coming to this wild place?" She lowered her head. "I think I did make a mistake, as nothing has turned out as it should have." She chewed on her lip again. "Nothing."

He rose and came to her, kneeling beside her chair, holding her hands in his. "Don't say that, Mallory. If you've made a mistake, then I'm the most blessed man in the world to have known you." He held her hands to his chest, letting her feel his galloping heart.

"Mallory, the more I've come to know you, the more I admire you." He dipped his head and cleared his throat again. "I know this might be unexpected... But you came west looking for a husband. I'm not as wealthy as E.P. was, but..."

He hesitated and then lifted his head, gazing into her eyes. "Would you do me the honor of being my wife?"

His unexpected proposal shook her, spiraling through her with the swiftness of a speeding arrow. His intentions were honorable, and she'd be a fool not to accept.

But still, she hesitated, wondering if she should marry him. She'd told him that he knew everything, but it wasn't true. And like a scaly, scary monster, her past haunted her.

"I know you're virginal and innocent. I've felt how you react when I touch you... And I understand." He squeezed her hands. "Uh, we don't have to be... that is... at first, our marriage could be for convenience's sake. We'd make a family for Peggy, and you wouldn't have to worry about returning to Georgia."

He pressed her hands between his. "If we grow to love each other, then later, we might have a real marriage. Even a family, if you want."

At his kind, kind words, and the affection he was offering, her throat burned. Unable to stop them, her tears flowed over, streaking her cheeks. She'd never heard such a lovely proposal before. Not that she'd heard many, but he'd given his heart into her safekeeping... a brave step for a man still grieving.

That was why he'd been adamant to know more about her. Now, it all made sense. But of course, she hadn't told him the most important thing. How could she? He'd trained as a minister, was an upright man. He'd even called her a virgin. How appalled would he be to learn she had a son?

Even more, if theirs was a marriage of convenience, and they didn't share a bed, how could she expect him to take in her son?

No, she couldn't marry him unless she told him the truth, and he accepted Macon. With her head full of brandy-induced cotton, and her fears newly aroused by the happenings around the fort, was she capable of making a rational decision?

Probably not.

She leaned forward and kissed him, a light kiss, barely touching her lips to his. She needed to express herself, to let him know how moved she was by his proposal.

He kissed her back and tried to deepen their kiss, lingering. His mouth was warm and tender, their lips fitting together like two well-crafted couplets of a poem.

As much as she wanted him to kiss her and hold her close, she couldn't.

Not now. Not yet. She had to think, to consider what to do.

She splayed her hands on his muscular chest and leaned back. "Will, you honor me with your proposal. But this has been rather sudden. Can you give me time to think it over?"

* * *

Mallory watched as four sergeants lifted the scenery backdrop, which featured a steam paddle wheeler. They nudged the set into place. The plywood scene showed the river steamer in all its glory with its wedding cake-like, white steamship, sporting a huge, many-spoked paddlewheel at the rear, and with wispy curls of smoke spouting from two tall stacks.

It was hard to believe Peggy, with only minimum help from the other students, had painted the steamer with such loving care, as to make the ship look lifelike. The two final scenes of "*Kit, The Arkansas Traveler*" took place on the river steamer, and it was one of the reasons Mallory had chosen the play.

She hoped someday Peggy would have the joy of traveling on a real riverboat. And as if her thoughts had conjured her, Peggy ran up and tugged on her sleeve, saying, "Miss, can you fix my bonnet."

"Of course." She leaned down and adjusted the girl's bonnet, making certain her face was properly framed, and then tied the ribbon into a big bow. "There you go. It's perfect."

"Thank you, Miss." She scurried away to stand by the curtain.

Jeb Hawkins, the lead character, who was playing Kit, motioned to her. They were trying to stay organized and quiet behind the makeshift curtain, but with six children in the play, along with Sally, Becky's mother, and the sergeants who'd been pressed into helping backstage and doing the walk-on parts, she had her hands full.

So far, the play had gone better than could be expected, especially after Becky had limped through her child's part in the first act. They were getting ready for the next-to-last act, where Peggy was featured and the villain is unmasked. The final act would be a rousing fight scene between the villain, played by Thomas, and Jeb, who would finally dispatch the dastardly villain, fulfilling justice. Peggy would have a few more lines with her father, Jeb, as they were reunited.

But first, Mallory had to be certain everyone was ready to go for the third act. She hurried over to Jeb and helped him pull on a fresh shirt and vest. Then she took him by the shoulders and said, "You've done a great job, Jeb. Chin up! You can do this, go out there and break a leg."

His eyebrows shot up.

She chuckled and squeezed his shoulders. "Theater talk. It means get out there and knock them over! You've got them in the palm of your hand."

His mouth quirked into a smile. "Thank you, Miss Mallory."

She shoved him toward the curtain and held up one hand, counting noses to be certain all the actors were in place. Then she nodded to Sergeant Campbell, who hauled on the rope, drawing back the curtain.

The audience exploded into applause, cat-calling, whistling and stomping their feet. All the fort, except for a small force, guarding the perimeter, had been given the holiday off, and the soldiers had come to see the play. Most of the townsfolk were here, too, along with a sprinkling of ranchers. Thankfully, no one from the Lazy M had shown up.

She scanned the crowd. Off to one side, not sitting, but leaning against the wall was a stranger, someone she hadn't seen before. He wore a red-checkered bandana, knotted at his throat, and had two Colts riding on his hips. Remembering what Will had said about the man running from him, an odd chill touched her.

Shaking it off, she looked for Will. He was seated in the front row, but there was no way she could alert him. It would ruin the play, and the children had worked so hard. Instead, she caught his gaze and nodded, letting him know Peggy was ready for her big scene.

He grinned and lifted the bouquet of wildflowers they'd picked that afternoon for Peggy. For a moment, the controlled mayhem of backstage receded, and she let her mind wander to a few hours ago.

Will had taken the afternoon off, and he'd shown her the canyon where *Limpia* Creek came from. In this cooler mountain climate, the wildflowers from spring bloomed all summer long, a veritable rainbow of colors. Together, they'd picked burgundy-colored winecups, red and yellow firewheels, pink primroses, crimson-colored Mexican hats, and white day lilies—a cornucopia of vibrant color.

She couldn't wait for Will to present the bouquet to his daughter, who was playing the female lead. She wished she could have been with Will to watch the play, but it wasn't possible, as she was in charge of her students and everything else.

It was a good thing when she'd decided to distract Peggy with something fun, that when she was a student at Miss Prentiss' finishing school, she'd taken part in a play.

Not being one of the "smart set" at the school, she'd only had a walk-on part, but the theatre had intrigued her and she'd helped backstage, learning everything she could.

And tonight, she'd had plenty of help. Sally had lent her hand to everything from managing the children to mending broken seams or sagging hems. Becky's mother, the butcher's wife in town, had proved to be a no-nonsense, level-headed woman, eager to help her daughter play her part. With a firm hand and lots of love, she'd managed to coax her daughter through the first act.

Now, it was Peggy's turn. As close as she and Will's daughter had become, the young girl was like her own child. She bowed her head, said a brief prayer, and held her breath.

At her nod, Peggy flounced onto the stage and stopped short when she glimpsed Thomas, rigged as the villain, with a tall, black stovetop hat and a horsehair mustache that stuck out three inches from either side of his face.

"You villain, you!" The audience hushed as Peggy pointed an accusing finger at Thomas and declaimed, "You villain! I know who you are." She tossed her head. "You can't fool me! You're Sydney Snodgrass, the man who abducted me and my mother. Because of you, my sweet mother..."

Mallory nodded, following Peggy's speech from the script, amazed at her ringing recital of the lines. She exhaled and closed her eyes. All that practicing after supper had paid off. Peggy's voice carried throughout the packed mess hall, her words clear and sharp.

As quick as the flick of a horse's tail, the third act was over. A riotous roll of applause greeted the drawing of the curtain.

Peggy rushed to her, her eyes bright and a huge smile sweetening her face. She threw herself into Mallory's arms. "I did it, Miss. I did it! I didn't miss one line." Peggy pointed at the script. "Did I?"

Mallory swallowed the lump lodged in her throat and hugged the girl. "You were perfect, Peggy, picture perfect! I couldn't have done half as good as you." She leaned down and looked into Peggy's eyes. "I'm so proud of you, so very proud."

Peggy lowered her head and blushed. "Aww, Miss, I couldn't have done it without your help." She lifted her face, her eyes suspiciously bright. "You know that, I hope. I can't thank you enough—"

"Let's get some powder on your shiny nose. All right?" She released Peggy and rushed to the makeup stand in the corner, grabbing the powder puff. "You've still got the finale with Jeb, and we don't want your nose to be shiny."

She knew she'd cut off Peggy, but when the girl clung to her like that, saying how she couldn't have performed without her, Mallory understood how deep their relationship had become.

It was another reminder of their closeness and the new life she'd found. Time was passing and with every day, she became more attached to Will and his daughter. But she'd yet to give Will an answer to his proposal.

As much as she loved Peggy and cared for Will, she hadn't told him her awful secret. Each time she thought she'd worked up her courage, she backed off. Will was an upright Christian man, a former seminary student. Would he... could he forgive her?

And if he didn't? Would it be so terrible?

She'd need to leave the fort, of course, return to San Antonio and wire Nancy for her money. It wasn't ideal, but it wasn't the end of the world. In some ways, the thought of putting the dangerous frontier behind her was appealing.

At least, Reverend Finley was doing better, hobbling around on crutches. He was seated in the front row with Will and eagerly awaiting word of his replacement.

Could she turn her back on Will and Peggy? Would they be so easy to give up? They'd both earned a place in her heart and with Will as her husband, her life stretched before her, full of bright and shining days, filled with wildflowers and rainbows and...

"Miss Mallory, Miss." Someone tugged on her arm. "I can't get this trick knife to work. I don't want to stab Thomas for real." Jeb chuckled.

"Oh, no, I'm sorry. I was getting the powder puff for..." She turned and faced him. "Never mind. Let me see the knife." She fumbled with the sliding mechanism, which pushed the wooden blade into its sheath, making it appear as if the knife had buried itself into the victim's body.

"You're right, Jeb. It doesn't seem to be working." She handed him the knife and turned him around, giving him a gentle push. "Tell Sergeant Campbell. He made the prop knives. I'm sure he can show you how to fix it. And please, hurry, we haven't much time."

"Yes, Miss." He sprinted across the stage to where Campbell stood by the curtain rope.

She clutched the powder puff and returned to Peggy. "Let's powder your nose." She fluffed the powder over the girl's freckled nose. Peggy loved wearing makeup, and she lifted her face up, smiling.

"Do you know all your lines for the last act?"

"Sure, Miss. The finale is a cinch. Now the hard part is over with."

She leaned down and hugged Peggy, thinking, there really wasn't any going back. And she didn't want to go back. She wanted to make a family with Will, Peggy, and... her son. She needed to quit dithering, tell Will the truth, and see how he reacted.

"Good. I'm glad." She released Peggy and dabbed at her eyes with a handkerchief.

"Are you crying, Miss? Why? The play's going good and—"

"Oh, no, no." She shook her head. "Just something in my eye." She sniffed. "Probably some of the loose powder."

"You want me to look in your eye for you?"

"No, I want you to take your place for the next scene."

"Yes, Miss. Wish me luck."

She half-grinned. "Break a leg."

Peggy smiled and rushed off.

Across the stage, she saw Jeb, working with his knife, making certain Sergeant Campbell had fixed it. He clicked it and the wooden blade slid out, then in, out and in, out and in... Mesmerizing.

Across from him, armed with the same kind of prop knife, Thomas practiced his moves, too, thrusting and circling with the knife drawn.

They were all having a wonderful time and here she was, sniffling and feeling sorry for herself. That wouldn't do. She needed to face Will and tell him. Sooner rather than later. He'd been patient, very patient, but she couldn't put him off forever.

* * *

Mallory put her hand in Will's, and they edged away from the crowd, stepping into the shadow of the mess hall. As soon as the play was done, she'd scanned the crowd for the stranger, but he'd melted away. She'd peeked out between each act, and she'd only seen him the one time. It was as if she'd seen a phantom.

Or was he only in her imagination?

Will pulled her away from the crowd. They backed up a few more steps and crossed behind the mess hall.

"I need to tell you something, Will."

"Yes."

"I think I saw that man—the stranger you mentioned. But only briefly, he was standing off to one side of the mess hall. I didn't recognize him, but he wore a red-checkered bandana and had two Colt pistols."

He stopped and turned to her. "Why didn't you tell me?"

"I thought about it, but I saw him right before Peggy's big scene. I didn't want to ruin it for her, especially if you went after him and missed..."

He squeezed her hand. "I understand. But you saw him?"

"Yes. I was checking the audience between each act to see how the play was being received. I only noticed him the one time. He wasn't seated, just leaning against the wall. And after the play, I looked for him, but I didn't see him." She let go of his hand. "I'm sorry."

He put one finger under her chin and raised her head. "Don't be. You did what you had to do. I wouldn't have wanted to miss Peggy's scene or cause a distraction. I know how much tonight meant to my daughter." He nodded, as if to confirm. "We'll find him." Then he stroked her face, his fingers feathering along her jawline.

His tender touch brought on a rash of gooseflesh and left her trembling inside.

"Besides, I don't know if he's done anything, except purposely avoid me." He shook his head. "Maybe he doesn't like soldiers."

"Perhaps."

He grabbed her hand again and said, "We need to hurry up. We can't be gone long."

"Where are you taking me?"

"Back to *Limpia* Creek Canyon."

"Why? At this time of night, won't there be rattlesnakes and—"

"You worry too much." He chuckled. "All the snakes will have curled up under rocks. We'll keep to the path. You wanted to see the waterfall, but we didn't have time this afternoon."

"But it's dark out."

"Don't worry, the water reflects in the moonlight."

A cannon boomed behind them, shattering the air and leaving wisps of gunpowder floating on the breeze.

They hurried along, leaving the fort and heading into the foothills behind the row of buildings. As they reached the mouth of the canyon, the cannon grew silent. A few moments later, what she knew was going to be a twenty-one-gun salute reverberated through the night. Under her breath, she counted each rifle shot.

He tugged on her hand, pulling her along the rocky pathway. They crossed the canyon floor, a multi-colored carpet during the day. But tonight, the wildflowers were just another part of the dark, swaying grasses surrounding them.

The canyon got narrower and rockier. They hadn't had the time to go there this afternoon. She'd barely had time to get away from last minute preparations for the play to pick wildflowers for Peggy's bouquet. As it was, it had been a close thing.

"We're lucky, full moon tonight." He pointed up.

The sky overhead was a cloudless canopy with a huge, white moon shining on them. Fanning out from the moon's incandescent glow was a million, billion stars shimmering in the vast void.

He couldn't have planned his timing better—she knew he wanted to creep off and steal a few kisses. As he'd liked to do, these past few weeks, after he'd proposed to her.

She enjoyed his kisses, more than she'd ever dreamed possible. But the closer they became, the more her heart wrenched, thinking how she needed to tell him about her secret shame. For a few moments more, though, she wanted to enjoy their stolen time together.

"I hope no one was too disappointed, since the fireworks didn't get here in time," she said.

He squeezed her hand again. "Thanks to you and the children, everyone loved tonight. Your play was the best entertainment anyone has seen in Fort Davis... ever. If you hadn't thought of having your students stage a play, tonight might have been a disaster."

Stopping, he made a flourish with his hand and bowed. "I was entranced, as was the audience. Your students acquitted themselves very well, indeed."

"Have you ever seen a play before?"

"Of course, once in Cincinnati when I was a boy, and another time in St. Louis, when Martha and I were traveling to my first frontier posting."

"Then you have a fair comparison."

"Never better. I didn't think too much of those two plays, bunch of over-the-hill geezers, spouting windy speeches. But you chose an action-packed play and the children were troopers."

She laughed, releasing her pent-up anxiety. "Oh, I'm glad. I knew it would be fun, but then the fireworks didn't come..."

"We'll have them another time."

Perhaps, but would she be here to see them?

"Well, at least we saved dessert for after the play," she said. "Sally's idea, and it helped. And then you gave them a cannon fusillade, along with a twenty-one-gun salute and the band. It's a fitting finale."

"The cannons were my daughter's idea. Remember?" He chuckled. "Seems like the women of this fort know how to keep us entertained."

She laughed again. "I guess you're right." She took his hand. "Though, I'm glad Peggy will be sleeping over with Tammy. I don't know if I could have gotten her to go to bed..."

She hesitated, considering how she sounded, as if she was already Peggy's mother. "Uh, or you, Will. I don't think it would have been easy to get her in bed, she was so excited and keyed up. Not that I can blame her. She was over the moon when you gave her the bouquet and honored her in front of the fort." She gazed at him. "And giving Jeb the penknife, to honor his performance, too, was a stroke of genius."

"I shouldn't be seen as showing favoritism, you know."

"How true. And I've never seen Peggy so animated and excited." She shook her head. "Like as not, if I remember my younger days, she will spend most of the night, under the covers, whispering with Tammy."

"And she's welcome to staying up all night. If not, we wouldn't be able to see the waterfall."

"Yes, that's true." She chewed on her lip.

He glanced down at her, and she could feel the warmth of his body, radiating from him. It was a clear, cool night and getting cooler by the minute. She pulled up her shawl, draping it over shoulders.

"Cold?" he asked, his voice rough. He pulled her closer and put his arm around her. She froze in his embrace but didn't flinch, like before.

With the way he'd looked at her and from the tone of his voice, she knew he desired her. But if he thought to sneak off and anticipate their wedding night, he'd be unpleasantly surprised.

She'd never allow herself to be compromised that way again, not even with… Will. And she had to tell him everything. Tonight, before the kissing and hugging. Before anything.

From far off, she thought she heard the fort's band swing into "The Star-Spangled Banner." The song signaled the official end of the July Fourth celebration.

She knew he was counting on most of the soldiers to stay up, drinking. For her sake, she hoped Sally didn't miss her. If she did, she'd say she was in the back of the mess hall, gathering together the props from the play.

She didn't like lying, but they shouldn't be going off like this, either. She should have said "no." Was she still that weak-willed girl of eighteen? Hadn't she learned her lesson?

Then she felt a vibration in the air, even before she heard the sound of rushing water. They rounded a barrier of tumbled boulders, and the waterfall came into view.

Gallons and gallons of sparkling water, cascading down the mountainside, leaping and feinting, from rock to rock, ledge to ledge. Spilling in a shimmering curtain-like shower and spewing a soft, misty spray into the air.

Magic, pure magic.

She gasped and covered her mouth with her hand.

"Beautiful, isn't it?" he asked.

She nodded. She'd never seen anything like it. The water-misted air was chillier. Despite the chill, she pulled free from his grasp, clutching her shawl tighter around her shoulders. She was drawn to the sparkling stream of water like a baby to a bright new toy.

For some reason, she wanted to touch the water, let its miraculous coolness slip through her fingertips. Before she could reach into the waterfall, her foot slid from beneath her, and she stumbled on the stony ground.

"Hey." He grabbed her and pulled her into his arms. "Don't get too close. You can't see it at night, but all the stones are slippery. Moss, lichens, water, and..." He hesitated, gazing down at her.

He lowered his head and nuzzled her neck. "You always smell so sweet, like all the flowers in this valley."

She melted against him, like a pat of butter on a steaming bowl of Lowcountry grits. Leaning into his arms, she shuddered, as his lips trailed over her neck, the tender lobe of her ear, and along her jaw.

Then his mouth covered hers, gently at first, as he always kissed her, with infinite tenderness and finesse. This time, though, something was different. She could feel it, as sure as she felt his arms around her. Maybe it was the night, the privacy, the shimmering waterfall, or all of those things.

He deepened his kiss, opening his mouth and sliding his tongue over her lips, testing the seam of her mouth with the tip of his tongue. He slanted his head first one way and then the other, ravishing her mouth and making her forget her earlier resolutions.

Her body ached as if she'd ridden horseback for miles. Her nipples hardened, brushing against the rough wool of his uniform. She opened her mouth, and he thrust his tongue inside.

As if the shimmering waterfall had lodged inside of her, she lit up, burning within. She relaxed into his embrace, opening herself to him. Lifting her arms, her shawl fell to the ground. She didn't care. He warmed her like nothing else could.

She cradled the back of his head, pulling him closer. Needing him, craving the feel of his muscular body and warm lips.

Kissing Will, she'd found, was a new experience. With Beau, she'd exchanged a few chaste pecks. With Hiram, when they'd been courting, he'd kissed her long and deep and with a great deal of passion. But her body hadn't responded to his embraces.

She'd *allowed* Hiram to kiss her, knowing she must submit. The other girls at Miss Prentiss' school had gossiped, saying a woman was expected to allow her intended kisses, but nothing more. She didn't have to enjoy a man's kisses or passion—just submit.

And looking back on her time with Hiram, that's what she'd done... submitted... until that terrible night when he'd violated her. But his kisses and caresses hadn't touched her and set her afire, not like the way Will's touch did.

With Will his passion struck a spark of desire within her, driving her crazy with wanting him. *Was this how it should be—how it felt to be in love with a man?*

A loud boom sounded overhead, ricocheting in her head. With his mouth on hers, it was as if the sound was far away. Another boom and then several sharp staccato sounds split the stillness of the night.

Will broke off their kiss and stood stock-still, his head cocked. Then another boom sounded, and he gazed to the east.

She followed his gaze, and from far away, she saw what was making the strange sounds. Fireworks! The Fourth of July fireworks! Blossoms of bright lights splashed across the night, raining down in a thousand spiraling streamers, glowing against the black velvet sky.

Had Will planned a surprise and then...? No, that couldn't be right. The fireworks weren't going off over the fort, somewhere further away.

"Will, where did those come from?" she asked. "Looks too far away to be the fort, and I thought you said—"

"Hell, and damnation! Those sons of bit..." He stopped himself, clamping his mouth shut and scowling. Even in the half-light of the moon, she could see the dark stain creeping over his face.

"I'm sorry, Mallory. I don't usually hold with cussing."

"You're forgiven." She tried to smile. "But why are you so angry?"

"The fireworks are coming from the Lazy M," he said through gritted teeth.

"You mean Mr. Murphy stole the fort's fireworks?"

He frowned and shook his head. She could sense the tenseness in his body, the raw rage reverberating from him.

"Worse than that. A freight wagon was due in yesterday. It didn't come, and then I knew we wouldn't have fireworks for the Fourth. But empty or filled with something else, that wagon should have stopped at the fort."

He fisted his hands. "No wagon, but more important, no sign of the driver or his guard. And I bet we won't see them, either. Not alive, anyway."

She gasped. "Oh, my heavens, no! But why would Mr. Murphy do such a thing?"

"Pure mean cussedness." He rubbed the back of his neck. "And maybe to test the Apache, keep them occupied, or as a diversion."

"You mean, Mr. Murphy had the Apache slaughter the freight master and his guard to prove..."

"That's what I'm worried about." He leaned down and retrieved her shawl, draping it across her shoulders. Then he took her hand. "We've got to get back to the fort."

Chapter Eight

Will steered Mallory along the rocky path, hurrying as fast as he dared. And silently cursing himself, three ways to Sunday, for pulling in most of his troops to enjoy the holiday. He should have known. Should have guessed what would happen. Ben was nothing, if not cunning.

The freight wagon had been late but only a day late. Unlike the stage line, which ran on a strict schedule, the mule skinners were an independent bunch. They brought freight to and from the fort on a pre-arranged schedule but, depending upon a variety of factors, they could be a day or two late or arrive a day early.

He'd known Murphy was up to something with the Apache—he hadn't counted on him having the hostiles attack the freight wagon. And like as not, the driver and guard were dead. But what Murphy really wanted were the smaller ranches, ringing his Lazy M spread.

The Apache attacks had dwindled in the past few weeks. He'd thought it would be safe to pull in most of his men and let them celebrate. It didn't absolve him, but he would bet the freight wagon attack had been a diversion. Thinking about it, a sick feeling twisted his guts.

It was a diversion that had cost two innocent men their lives. Their blood was on his hands.

A figure loomed in the darkness, coming toward them. He unbuttoned his vest and reached inside his coat, pulling out his Colt. With his other hand, he clutched Mallory's elbow and tucked her behind him.

"Stop! Who goes there?" He barked.

The shadowy form raised his hands over his head. "Corporal Walsh, sir. You're needed back at the fort. There's been another attack."

"Who told you where to find me?"

"Uh." The corporal advanced slowly, coming into view. "Uh, that is, sir, it was Captain Myerson."

So much for thinking they'd slipped away without anyone seeing them. Fort life was like living in a fishbowl, everyone knew everyone else's business. Now he'd compromised her. More reason to proceed with getting married.

Despite agreeing to honor her wishes and be patient, he didn't see how they could wait. And if he was any judge of character, he thought she'd started to trust him. At the same time, he knew how frontier life frightened her. He needed to put a stop to the raiding, the Apache, and Ben Murphy.

They needed to marry as soon as possible. Otherwise, Mallory would be shunned at the fort and in town. And despite the success of her play, few, if any, of the parents would consider keeping her as their child's teacher. Not now.

He turned around and pulled her beside him. No use in hiding any more.

Corporal Walsh approached and stopped. He threw back his shoulders and stood at attention.

He inclined his head toward Mallory and said, "Corporal, you know Miss Reynolds."

The corporal stood straighter, if that was possible, and nodded. But he didn't meet his eyes. *Found out, judged, and deemed guilty.*

"Yes, sir, good evening to you, Miss Reynolds. I enjoyed the show you put on with the school children. It was one of the best Fourth of July celebrations I can remember. Even without the fireworks." He glanced over his shoulder.

"Why, thank you, Corporal Walsh." She smiled. "That's very kind of you."

"You saw the fireworks, too, Walsh?"

"Yes, sir. Didn't know what to think about it. Never have known ranchers to spend their hard-earned money on such things."

"I doubt they spent a cent, and I have a pretty good idea what's waiting for me at the fort. But you can tell me while we walk back."

"Company H, who was patrolling the perimeter, found the freight wagon."

"And?"

"The mules and contents were gone. The driver and guard are dead, riddled with Apache arrows."

Mallory gasped and shuddered. With their arms linked together, he could feel her trembling.

He sucked in his breath. "Think the Apache were setting off those fireworks?" He inclined his head toward the east. Now, the night sky was undisturbed, spangled with stars and brightened by the full moon.

"I hadn't thought of that, sir, but it does seem strange."

"Yes, more than strange." He shook his head. "Corporal Walsh, you've done your duty, fetching me. You can go back to the fort and alert Captain..." He hesitated. He'd prefer Rodgers riding with him, but Sally and Mallory would both feel safer with Rodgers at the fort.

Besides, if Myerson was so interested in his whereabouts, he should be the one to go without sleep after a night of celebration.

"Have Captain Myerson gather his men, Company A and G. Tell him to have his men ready to ride before daylight."

The corporal saluted. "Right away, sir."

"And don't let any of the men touch the wagon or the..." He cleared his throat. "Or the bodies. I want to personally look them over first, before we make the proper arrangements. Understood?"

"Yes, sir."

"And have Captain French wait for me in my office." He hesitated. "Send Rodgers, too, I need to have him follow up something for me."

Rodgers' men hadn't found the stranger in the days leading up to the play. Now that Mallory had seen the man again, Rodgers would need to redouble his efforts.

"Yes, sir," the corporal said.

He returned the corporal's salute. "Dismissed."

The corporal trotted off, braving the steep, rocky path without hesitation.

He wanted to sprint after him, but he needed to get Mallory back safely to the Rodgers' cabin. For a few moments, they walked in silence. He was planning what to do, and she must be considering what had happened tonight.

Then she asked, "What are you going to do?"

"Well, first, I want to look over the victims and the wagon. See if there's anything odd or amiss or—"

"Something that might tie the attack to Mr. Murphy?"

"Yes."

"But you're going out to his ranch, whether you find anything or not?"

"Yes, but this time, I'll have plenty of men. Ben won't try anything if he's evenly matched. He's a coward, and cowards sneak around and..." He shook his head.

"Are you expecting him to confess?"

"No, just putting him on notice, hoping he will stop before anyone else gets hurt."

"And if he doesn't?"

"There's more than one way to skin a cat."

"What do you mean?"

"Let me worry about that." He stopped and gazed down at her. "I'm sorry this happened, and I know it frightens you. But we'll get to the bottom of it and stop the raiding. One way or the other."

"I hope so." She pursed her lips. "You sent the corporal for Captain Rodgers, too. Is he going with you?"

"No," he said, pulling her closer. "He will be at the fort with you and Sally. Please, try not to worry." He leaned down and brushed a kiss across her forehead. "Captain Rodgers had a detail of men, searching for the stranger you saw. They didn't find him, so I'd released the men. I need to tell Rodgers what you saw and have his men start looking again."

"I hope I'm right. I wouldn't want to lead your men on a wild goose chase."

He touched her cheek, caressing it. "Quit worrying, Mallory. Some extra caution is never wasted effort."

She turned her face into his hand and kissed his fingertips. "If you say so, Will."

"I do say so." His voice was gruff, even to his own ears. He wanted to kiss her but now wasn't the time or place. Instead, he took her arm and steered her along the path.

"While I'm taking care of Murphy and the Apaches, I believe you have a wedding to plan, and the sooner the better."

"But, I, uh, I haven't accepted your proposal, Will. You told me you would be patient. I don't know if I'm cut out to be an Army wife."

"Well, you grew up on a plantation. How about a farmer's wife?"

"What do you mean?"

"I've only five years to retirement. Then, I'm going home to Ohio and my family's farm. It's a nice-sized farm, lying fallow. With my only brother killed in the Civil War and my sisters married, I'm the only one left to care for it. Both my parents are dead."

She inhaled sharply. "You never told me that."

"Why should I? To stir up old feelings of sorrow and regret?"

She held his elbow tighter. "I guess farming would be fine, especially away from the frontier."

The fort loomed ahead. He walked faster, and she kept stride with him. They crossed the parade ground and came to a stop in front of the Rodgers' cabin.

"I'm glad you approve." He cleared his throat. "How long for you and Sally to pull the wedding together?"

"Uh, I don't know. Two weeks, maybe three."

He shook his head. "I'm sure you brought a wedding dress with you, since you were going to marry E.P. And the reverend has his crutches and can stand up long enough to bless our union. All you and Sally have to do is decide how many people to invite to the reception and prepare for that."

"I still haven't said yes to your proposal, Will."

"I'd like you to want this marriage, Mallory, but it can't be put off any longer." He took her hand and laced her fingers with his. "You've been raised to be a proper lady. You, more than anyone, should know you've been compromised."

She recoiled and pulled away. He let her go.

He stared at the ground. "Both Myerson and Walsh know." He pulled his hand through his hair. "By this time, the whole damned fort knows."

She shook her head. "I shouldn't have gone off with you to see the waterfall. Today, we went out and picked wildflowers together."

"Yes, and even that could have started tongues wagging. But it's not the same as being out at night together."

"All right." She shrugged. "I guess I haven't any choice."

His heart dropped to the soles of his feet and the old, sick feeling he'd had, watching Martha being taken from him, returned. Dark disappointment dropped over him, like a shroud.

If he'd thought he was marrying Mallory for their mutual convenience, tonight had taught him otherwise. He wanted her, desired her like a young man would. Thinking of his life without her, even though he had his daughter, was like crossing a desert, bleak and desolate.

Was he falling in love with her?

He'd thought she cared for him. Perhaps, but perhaps not. Evidently, the idea of marrying him, wasn't particularly appealing. But if he loved her, wouldn't she, in time, come to care for him?

Did he want her that way?

What if she hated frontier life so much that five more years was like a life sentence? What if her fears and homesickness kept her from caring for him?

The last thing he wanted, no matter how much he might care for her, was an unwilling wife.

"Look, Mallory, no one is forcing you to marry me. But if you don't, you can't stay at Fort Davis. It will be terrible for you." He gazed at her and dropped her hand.

She bit the inside of her cheek and sniffed.

Was she about to cry? Because of what he'd done or what he'd said? Now, he felt horrible. Blood on his hands, and he'd compromised a refined young lady, all in one night. Why on earth had he thought she might want him?

"Mallory, I can loan you the money to return to Georgia. You can pay me back, a little at a time. You do have a choice. I don't want you to feel forced because of my thoughtlessness..." He cleared his throat again. "You're welcome to the money to get back home."

She pulled out a handkerchief and blew her nose. "No, no, Will, it's not that. It's not that I don't want to marry you. It's that I need to tell you something."

His heart lifted, hope sprouting again.

"All right. Fine, then. Tell me."

"Remember when I said my aunt and I quarreled over a young man?"

"Yes. That's when she asked you to leave."

She shook her head and looked down. "It wasn't as simple as the man not being acceptable, Will. He—"

"Colonel Gregor, Colonel Gregor, sir. We need you over here." Corporal Walsh came running up again.

He grabbed her hands. "Tell me. Whatever it is, they can wait. I want to hear why you can't marry me."

She glanced over his shoulder at the corporal hovering nearby. Lowering her head, she murmured, "Not now, Will. Not now. When you get back." She rose on tiptoe and kissed his cheek. "Please, take care of yourself. Come home safely."

* * *

Mallory heard a tap-tapping on her door. Only half asleep, she threw back the covers and reached for her wrap. "Come in."

Sally opened the door and clucked her tongue. "What a sleepy head you are. You missed breakfast."

"I wasn't hungry." She put her wrap on and tied the belt.

"I saved you some biscuits and bacon."

"That's kind of you, but I don't think I could eat anything."

Sally stepped into the room and perched herself on the ladder-back chair. "Want to talk about it? The captain is gone, and I know you were out late and—"

"Yes, I was out with the commander." And as she said the words, she knew how she sounded—sarcastic and self-indulgent. "I'm sure the whole fort knows and is waiting with bated breath to find out the next chapter and verse."

Sally rose and hugged her. "The rest of the fort and town can think what they want. But I know you and the colonel, and neither of you have a dishonorable bone in your body." Sally pulled apart and held her shoulders, gazing into her eyes. "You'll always be my friend, and you must know I will defend you to the end."

Mallory sighed. Sally only thought she knew her. She wasn't the least bit honorable. No, she was the epitome of dishonorable. First, Hiram, and now, William.

But that wasn't fair, at least not to William. He was more than ready to do the honorable thing. She was the dishonorable one, dithering over what to do with her life. Too afraid of the consequences to make a decision.

It was on the tip of her tongue to tell Sally everything and see what she thought. But then she'd be back to living her life beholden to someone, like she had been with Nancy, a charity case. The very thing she'd come west to overcome.

Sally released her. "If you're not hungry, want to come to town with me? The eastbound stagecoach is in, and their mailbags are full." She smiled. "You've probably got letters from back home."

At the thought of hearing about her son, her heart lifted. He was still the one bright, shining star in her life.

"Yes, I'd love to come to town. It's been a while since I got letters from my friend." She plastered a smile on her face. "Let me get washed up and dressed. I'll be right there."

"Good. I'll start the mid-day meal while you get ready." Sally closed the bedroom door behind her.

Was it that late? Mallory peeked out her window to see the sun riding high in the sky. Good thing she'd given her students the day off after the celebration. Today, of all days, she would have been worthless as a teacher.

Last night, she'd barely slept, on and off, a few minutes at a time. She'd paced the floor and considered what to do. How to tell Will her shameful secret? How to be prepared when he didn't want her and packed her off to Georgia? He'd lauded her for being a refined and proper lady. Now, he would learn the sordid truth.

But it wasn't her shame she was afraid of… not now. No, she'd been awake when Will and Captain Myerson had led out the two companies this morning. And seeing Will astride Boots, her heart had stopped.

For her, he was the most handsome man she'd ever seen, looking confident and commanding in his blue uniform. He sat his roan as if the horse was a part of him, while issuing orders with the decisiveness of a man who hated injustice—a man who wanted to stop the bloody murders, single-handed, if possible.

She'd long admired Will, since that first day he'd rescued her. But when had her admiration and respect turned into love? With her heart in her throat and clutching the windowsill, she'd had to restrain herself from rushing to him, begging him not to go into danger. Pleading with him to hear her out, to forgive her, and to love her.

Summoning all her self-control, she'd stopped herself from running to him. More public displays weren't what was needed. What was needed was the strength and courage to tell him and then live with the consequences.

Knowing what she knew now—that Will was probably the first and only man she'd loved as a woman, how could she risk losing him? First, she'd lost Beau to the war, but she'd been little more than a child. She and Beau had grown up together and, at the time, she'd thought their friendship was love. More like puppy love.

Then there had been the suave and debonair Hiram. Wealthy when most southerners didn't have two dimes to rub together, he'd swept her off her feet with worthless promises. And she'd fallen for him. Pure infatuation, nothing more.

This time, if she lost Will, she didn't know if she wanted to go on living.

Except for her son.

Clinging to the hope of hearing about her son from Nancy, she washed quickly and got dressed, pulling her hair in the severe bun she usually wore.

When she and Sally stepped outside, Sally linked their arms together. "Don't worry if you get some strange looks."

"I won't. Will and I didn't do anything wrong." She lifted her head and jutted out her chin. She knew the drill. She'd lived with the shame after Hiram deserted her.

"Good. I've got several stops to make," Sally said. "Here's a letter I need posting. Can you do that for me?" She handed Mallory an envelope. "I know you'll want to go to the post office first, but I need to go to the butcher's and the general store. You can read your letters and wait for me."

"Thank you." She smiled and squeezed Sally's arm. She put the letter in her apron pocket, along with two letters she'd been meaning to send to Nancy. Sally was kind, thinking ahead, knowing she'd want to go straight to the post office.

They parted ways in the middle of the street. Mrs. Lovell was there, talking to another lady. Mallory nodded but Becky's mother looked past her… as if she didn't exist and as if Mrs. Lovell hadn't helped with the play last night.

It had already begun.

She entered the tiny building and held out the letters to Mrs. Burnside. "Good morning."

Mrs. Burnside looked up and pursed her lips, appearing as if she'd been sucking on a lemon. She had a desperate glint in her eye, as if she couldn't make up her mind to go with her natural inclinations or to give into professional courtesy.

Finally, she took the three letters and bobbed her head. "Morning."

"Do you have—"

"Yes, Miss Reynolds, three letters for you today."

She took the letters. "Thank you."

Mrs. Burnside stared at a spot over her head and nodded.

She didn't care. It had been almost a month since she'd heard from Nancy, and she couldn't wait to read the letters. She settled on the wooden bench outside and glanced at the postmarks. As was her custom, she'd read the oldest one first.

She shuffled the envelopes into order but when she touched the last letter, posted over a month ago, a frisson of something swept her, as if she'd walked over someone's grave.

Looking right and then left, she found the street was deserted. There wasn't even a stray lounger on the saloon's front porch. Pushing the odd feeling aside, she tore open Nancy's first letter and skimmed the contents:

"Macon sends his love… misses his Mommy… still doing well in school… but can't wait for summer vacation…"

She lifted her head. Back East, summer vacation was a time-honored tradition, but in the West, where no one knew if there would be an instructor from one year to the next, children were granted fewer holidays. Here, she was expected to hold school all year.

She lowered her head and continued to read:

"… was shocked to learn Hiram's wife, Sybil Rutledge Calhoun died in child birth… Hiram inconsolable…"

Shaking her head, she didn't want to hear about Hiram. What did Nancy think she should do, rush back to Charleston and demand that Hiram marry her and recognize his son?

In a pig's eye!

The letter went on:

"... surprised to learn Reverend Finley doesn't like Fort Davis... asked to be transferred... Texas Methodist Conference couldn't find a replacement... he asked my husband... proud to say... found a family man here in Georgia... willing to move to Fort Davis... Mr. Whitehead and his wife, Katherine... must make them feel at home..."

Mallory finished the letter, not knowing what to think about Nancy's tasteless inclusion of Hiram and his wife's death.

But despite her mixed feelings, she bowed her head and said, "God rest her soul."

She opened the flap of the second letter, a note, really, just a few terse words scribbled across one piece of paper. The words literally leapt off the page:

"...Hiram out of his mind with grief and wanting his son... must have known about Macon... has been to our house... we hid the boy... Hiram will be back... his money can buy him... the authorities will... the reverend and I are trying to find a way... keep Macon safe."

Her heart clenched in her chest and a fine sheen of perspiration coated her. Her stomach knotted, and her hands trembled as she ripped open the third and final letter:

Dearest Mallory,

If you got my last note, you will know the reverend and I had to find a safe place for Macon. After much discussion and prayer, we decided to send Macon to you with the new pastor and his family, a Reverend Whitehead, who will be taking over for Reverend Finley. The Whiteheads have a boy who is Macon's age and a little girl who's four years old. His wife, Katherine, is very good with children and Macon likes the family. He's so excited to be joining his mother in the West.

Not knowing what else to do, we bought his steamer ticket with the funds you left us and entrusted Reverend Whitehead with some pocket money for the boy. The Whiteheads, good Christians that they are, didn't want to take anything, but with two of their own to feed, we convinced them. If you need the remainder of your funds, we will gladly wire them to you if you can travel to the nearest telegraph office.

Like you, they will travel from Charleston to Galveston via steamship. Then the good reverend intends to purchase a buckboard and a team of mules to transport his family and their belongings to Fort Davis.

They should be leaving within the week. The Reverend expects, if all goes well, to reach Fort Davis in six to eight weeks, sometime in August.

I pray, my good friend, we did what you would have wanted. I know you miss your son, and you've found a profession there, teaching school, so, I hope there will be no hardship. Please know we pray daily for Macon and the Reverend Whitehead family's safe arrival. If we hadn't taken action, I feel certain Hiram would have taken the boy from us, and I know you wouldn't want that.

Please reply as soon as you can to let us know you received this letter. My blessings.

Your Fellow Sister in Christ,

Nancy Arledge

Mallory folded the letter and tucked it into her apron pocket, too stunned to think straight. She pulled out Macon's photograph and traced her fingers over his beloved face, noticing the way his eyes crinkled at the corners when he smiled for perhaps the thousandth time.

Her son was on his way to her and for that blessing, she felt a glow inside, lighting her up. But at the same time, her chin trembled and her heart raced in her chest, knowing the dangers he and the Whitehead family would face, crossing this vast frontier.

Given the third letter's postmark and how fast steamship travel was, her son was already here, somewhere in the wide expanse of Texas, riding a buckboard across the prairie.

She bowed her head, closed her eyes, and prayed. She prayed as hard as she knew how, with all her heart and soul, begging God to keep her son safe.

Someone tapped her on the shoulder. She muttered a hasty, "Amen," and glanced up. Sally stood there with her eyebrows drawn together and her forehead creased.

"Are you all right?" Sally asked. "I hope it's not bad news from home? But you said you don't have any family left, except an aunt and cousins."

Despite her neck feeling like a piece of wood, she nodded. At the same time, she wanted to scream, 'but I have a son, who is traveling across the frontier in a buckboard!' Instead, she bobbed her head like an idiot.

She tried to smile, failed, and turned her head away. She had to tell Will. She wanted to tell Sally, but she couldn't blurt the news out to her now. It wouldn't be right.

She dusted off her skirts and got to her feet. "I'm fine."

"Who's the little boy?" Sally asked.

In her distress, she'd forgotten to put away Macon's photograph. She stuffed it, along with the other two letters, into her apron pocket.

"Uh, he's the son of one of my many cousins. They sent me a photograph."

Sally whistled under her breath. "They must have a lot of money to afford sending a photograph to a distant cousin."

"Yes, they do." She grimaced. "They're show-offs like that."

"Hmmm." Sally put her arm through hers. "How was Mrs. Burnside?"

Her mind was still racing, wondering how far away her son might be, and if there was a way she could intercept him. It was hard to pay attention to what Sally was saying.

"Oh, uh, Mrs. Burnside was... not nice. Barely spoke."

Sally nodded. "Do you and the colonel have an understanding? I could get the word out if you'd prefer...?"

She pulled loose from Sally's grip, and she knew the look on her face was this side of stricken. "The commander has offered to... to... marry me, but..."

The thunder of a hundred horses' hooves shook the ground, and the bright, brassy sound of fifty mounted soldiers' harnesses jangled. She looked to the east and saw Will, riding at the head of his two companies of soldiers. Captain Myerson rode beside him.

Will and the captain drew abreast with them. Will smiled and touched one finger to the brim of his hat.

Now was the time to tell him.

She patted Sally's shoulder. "I need to speak with the commander. Please, excuse me." She hurried off in the wake of the dust cloud thrown up by the cavalry.

Sally called after her, "Will you be taking your mid-day meal with us?"

Turning, she said, "Probably not. Don't make extra for me. Thank you for all your kindness."

Ten minutes later, she was waiting in the headquarters' office, biding her time until Will dismissed his troops and joined her. She'd asked Corporal Walsh to tell the commander she was there.

He opened the door and stood on the threshold, gazing at her. "I didn't expect you to meet me in my office." He stepped inside and shut the door. "I hope you didn't worry. Nothing to worry about. The only thing Ben Murphy respects is a show of force."

She wanted to ask him if he'd learned anything, how Ben had reacted, and why Corporal Walsh had called him away last night. But she didn't dare. Then she'd never tell him.

He looked like he wanted to take her in his arms and kiss her, but something, perhaps the look on her face, stopped him. "I can see you have something important to tell me." He waved his hand at the row of chairs in front of his desk. "Please, take a seat."

"I'd rather stand."

"All right." He leaned against the front of his desk and crossed his arms over his chest. "What's so important—?"

"I have a son. His name is Macon. He's six years old. He's on his way to Fort Davis with the new reverend and his family." She dug the letter out of her pocket and held it up. “I just found out. He should be here sometime next month.” She lowered her head. “If something doesn’t happen to him.”

“We’ll double the patrols on the San Antonio-El Paso Road,” he said and then he stared at her. “Did you say you have a son?”

“Yes.”

“Then you were married before. Why didn’t you tell me?”

“Because I was never married.” She lifted her head and looked him directly in the eye. “That’s the shame of it.”

“Oh.” He circled his desk and sat down. His face was a study of bewilderment and disappointment. “You weren’t married, but you have a son. Did E.P. know about your son? Why didn’t you bring the boy with you?”

“Shame. Fear.” She shook her head. “I don’t know. I needed to start over. I thought in time, when E.P. knew me better, I would tell him and he’d accept my son. Then I would send for him.”

“You didn’t tell E.P. either?” His voice was a harsh rasp.

“No. I didn’t.”

“And now you say the boy is coming here. Is that why you told me?”

“No, no, Will.” She clasped her hands together and twisted them. “I would have told *you* before we married. Remember, last night, I tried to tell you—”

“But Corporal Walsh interrupted us.” He nodded. “I remember. Seems a second freight wagon came in last night with our long-awaited telegraph wire. That’s why the corporal needed me.”

“That’s a good thing, the wire coming.”

“Yes.” He cleared his throat. “But Mallory, I gave you ample opportunity to tell me about yourself. You know I did, but I practically had to drag the details of your life from you.” He rubbed the back of his neck. “Were you afraid to tell me?”

“I don’t know.” She hesitated and looked at the floor. “Yes, I was afraid. That’s why I’ve put off accepting your proposal.”

“You were in town. How was it?”

“As you said, I’m a marked woman. Becky’s mother wouldn’t speak to me, and Mrs. Burnside was barely civil.”

He stroked his chin. "So, we have a situation on our hands." He pointed his finger at her. "One of your making, Miss Reynolds. You should have told me from the first you had a son or, at least, had the decency to tell me when I proposed to you."

"Yes, of course, you're right."

"Now, your son is coming to a place where his mother cannot stay because she's ruined herself again—"

"Will, it was your idea to slip off to see the waterfall last night. I've tried my hardest to observe all the proprieties, but..."

He nodded again. "You're right. I let my emotions get the better of me. But it's a dilemma for sure. You have to stay until your son arrives, but after that, you will need to turn around and go back—"

"I can't go back. That's why my friend sent my son. His father is searching for him. He's an immoral and horrible man, but he's also very wealthy and has all the right connections. If we return to Georgia, he will take my boy from me."

He leaned forward and put his elbows on the desk. "What you're telling me, Miss Reynolds..." He hesitated and closed his eyes, as if he was praying. "Is that we *must* marry because you have nowhere else to go. Is that right?"

There was a knock on the door and Corporal Walsh stuck his head in. "Both Captains Rodgers and French need to see you, sir."

He held up one hand. "Not now, corporal. Tell them to go about their duties. When I'm ready, I'll send for them."

"Yes, sir." The corporal saluted and pulled the door closed.

She exhaled. She hadn't known she'd been holding her breath. She could hear her heart pounding in her ears, and her empty stomach churned.

He gazed at her. The look in his blue-gray eyes was as sharp as a shard of flint. "Am I correct, Miss Reynolds?"

He'd stopped calling her Mallory. He hated her. Despised her for what she'd done or hadn't done.

She approached him. "I thought you cared for me, Will. I thought you wanted to marry and not just for convenience's sake, either."

"You're right, I *did* want to marry you. Very much. I've admired you since the first day." He rubbed the back of his neck. "But now... now... when your son arrives, what do I tell Peggy?"

"You could tell her I was widowed—"

"You want us to live a lie?"

She twisted her hands until her knuckles popped. "We could be a family, you and I, and my son and your daughter. I would be a good wife to you, Will."

He shook his head. "I don't know. I just don't know... now."

"Guilty until proven innocent?" She couldn't help the note of sarcasm in her voice. "Isn't that the way all women are judged if they have a child out of wedlock? It's because I'm a fallen woman."

"No, it's because you didn't tell me until you had to. Because I won't know if I can trust you."

"I don't believe you."

Somehow, she'd thought Will would be different. Stupid of her; shc should have known better. She sighed and felt as if her heart had shriveled in her chest, turning into stone.

"I expected the truth from you, Will. Not an excuse about you not being able to trust me."

He frowned and started to speak.

She held up her hand, wanting to stop him. "No, no more excuses. You don't have to say anything. I can see your feelings on your face. You despise me because I bore a child out of wedlock."

Chapter Nine

Will stared at the beautiful woman standing before him. Even in a plain calico dress, with her hair pulled into a tight bun, and her eyes red and swollen from too much crying or not enough sleep or both, she was still a beautiful woman. Desirable, too, with or without a corset. Intelligent and charming and...

He had fallen in love with her.

And he wanted nothing more than to take her in his arms and kiss her until they both couldn't see straight. He searched his heart. Had he expected a fresh, young virgin for his bride, and she'd disappointed him by bearing a child out of wedlock?

He hoped that wasn't why he was disappointed and distraught. If so, he wasn't much of a Christian. Jesus had told the woman at the well to go and sin no more, forgiving her.

He could forgive Mallory for her fall from grace; few people were perfect. But she had kept her secret from him until the last possible moment. Perhaps she would have told him the truth last night, before she knew her son was coming. Perhaps not.

He'd never know for certain.

What he was having trouble finding was the ability to forgive her for lying. Or if not lying outright, she'd misled both E.P. and himself. She shouldn't have come west under false pretenses, expecting to start a new life and then sending for her son.

It wasn't right—and he didn't know if he could trust her. He'd told her the truth of it. But that didn't make him stop wanting her.

"I haven't told anyone but my father, my aunt, and my friend, Nancy, the story of what happened." She broke into his thoughts. "How I bore a child out of wedlock. Would it help if I told you what happened?"

He didn't like seeing her like this, almost begging. Surely, if they didn't marry, he could find another place for her when her son arrived. But for now, he knew she wanted to tell him what had happened, to absolve herself. He understood why she wanted him to hear her story. What he didn't know was if it would change his feelings.

He nodded.

"I told you most of it before. About the finishing school and my debut." She took a deep breath and sank into one of the chairs. "It was at one of the debutante balls that I met Hiram Calhoun. He—"

"His last name is Calhoun?" He whistled under his breath. "As in John C. Calhoun, the former Vice President?"

"Yes, Hiram is a distant cousin. He's also a distant cousin of my uncle's family, the Claiborne's."

"I see."

But he really didn't. He was a simple farmer from Ohio, and he'd lived his adult life, serving his country. He wouldn't have known what a debutante ball looked like if he'd fallen face-forward into one.

She twisted her hands again. "There's a standing joke in the South."

"Yes."

"All the original planters are cousins, one way or another."

"Sounds like it could be true."

"Yes, most of the planter families intermarried over the years." She paused, as if considering, and shook her head. "Hiram was appealing, especially to an eighteen-year-old girl with no dowry and fewer prospects."

"But wasn't Hiram cash-strapped, like your father, if he was a planter?"

"No, his family had some plantations, but most of his money came from shipping. Remember, I told you about my aunt's husband who was in shipping?"

He nodded.

"My uncle had the largest fleet of ships in the South when the war started."

"And you said your uncle's firm was successful at running the blockade."

"Yes, they were. The blockade cut down on the number of ships getting through, but the few who did, made profits a hundred times over. The entire South depended upon those few ships."

He lowered his head and steepled his fingers. “Quite a lucrative but dangerous undertaking. That was your uncle’s business. What did it have to do with Mr. Calhoun?”

“Hiram owned a part of my uncle’s shipping firm, and he was the most successful blockade runner. He became fabulously wealthy from the war.”

“I see. Quite a catch.” He ran his finger along the collar of his shirt. “I’m sure he was easy on the eyes, too.”

“Oh, Will, don’t, please.”

“You said it yourself, Miss Reynolds, you were an impressionable eighteen-year-old. Used to wealth and privilege, brought down to living on your aunt’s charity. He must have been irresistible.”

She stared at the toes of her shoes. “I’m not proud of it, but I did believe I loved him. And he told me he loved me, too.”

He snorted. And then he felt small.

She raised her head. “He offered to marry me, but he said his family was against our wedding. They wanted him to marry Sybil Rutledge, to tie their fortunes with the Rutledge family. They own the only functioning iron works in the South.”

“Sounds like a marriage made in heaven.” He heard the note of sarcasm in his voice, and his neck heated with embarrassment.

“Yes, on the face of it, but Hiram said he didn’t love Sybil. He claimed to love me.”

“What happened?”

“Hiram said we should elope. Once we were married, his family couldn’t pressure him to marry Sybil. He asked if I was willing to slip away from my aunt’s home and meet him at his lodgings at midnight. He said he’d obtained a special license and that he’d have a reverend there, waiting to marry us. I agreed.”

He sucked in his breath and shook his head. It was difficult, hearing how naïve she’d been.

“I know I was stupid, Will, but I believed him. He was a hero, a southern war hero. I thought a man like that couldn’t be dishonorable.”

“He was clever—having you leave your aunt’s home at midnight to meet him. That fact alone, compromised you.”

"Yes, I realize that." She gazed directly into his eyes. "There was no reverend at his lodgings. He said the reverend was late. He offered me champagne, but I panicked and tried to leave. I wanted to return to my aunt's home before I was discovered."

She licked her lips. "He wouldn't let me go. Said he knew I desired him, or I wouldn't have come. It wasn't true. I thought we were getting married. I knew nothing of desire until..."

She looked down again. "He took me by force, Will. I struggled and tried to cry out, but he was prepared. He overpowered me and stuffed a rag in my mouth and..."

She turned away, but not before he could see the tears rolling down her cheeks. She sobbed and gulped. "Now you know everything. I won't bother you any longer."

Hearing what had happened, his heart wrenched, and his eyes burned. If ever there was a woman who didn't deserve such a terrible fate, it was Mallory. Now, he understood why she'd pulled away when he first touched her. Thinking about it, his gut clenched, and he'd like nothing better than to break Mr. Calhoun in two.

He got up and came around the desk, pulling her into his arms. "You can't go, Mallory, we'll figure something out." He smoothed the feathery tendrils of hair around her face, while wishing he could see her hair spilling over her shoulders.

She lifted her red-splotched face and asked, "Have you forgiven me?"

"I forgave you before you told me Calhoun forced you."

"Then you... you...?"

"It's not so simple. Your son is coming. We'll have to explain. You saw what happened today. Perhaps, your idea of a war widow isn't such a bad notion. And we'll need to let everyone know we're getting married."

"More lies then?"

He sighed. "I don't like it, either, but..."

"It's kind of you, Will, but I think your initial reaction was the right one. How will you know if you can trust me? And later, after the first flush of desire, all that might be left is pity." She licked her lips again.

He wanted to lick her dusky-rose lips and then taste her fully, as he had last night.

"I don't want to live with a sword hanging over my head, wondering if you… if you…" She stepped back and turned toward the door. "I'll suspend school, and as soon as my son arrives, we'll go. Find someplace new to settle and—"

"Give it some time, will you? Are you sure? Think it over, Mallory."

"All right." She nodded. "I have plenty of time to think. I have to wait for my son." She took out a handkerchief and blew her nose. "Would you like to see a photograph of him?"

"Yes, I would."

She pulled a dog-eared photograph from her apron pocket and handed it to him.

He gazed at the photograph for a long time, searching for Mallory's features. He handed it back. "He's a handsome lad. He has your chin and the shape of your mouth."

She blushed and took the photograph, returning it to her pocket. "Yes, he is handsome and a sweet boy."

"And now Mr. Calhoun wants the boy? Didn't your father try to get him to do the right thing when he learned you were pregnant?"

"Oh, yes." She bobbed her head. "At first, my father was furious with me, thought it was my fault. Over time, he came to believe me. He would have fought a duel for my honor had I begged him not to."

She took a deep breath. "After my aunt turned me away, everyone knew the sordid details. I went home to stay on the plantation. That's when my father learned Hiram had ruined other young girls in the same way, and he'd killed the men who'd tried to avenge them. He was a dead shot with a pistol and an accomplished swordsman.

"My father took care of me, and we tried to keep Macon's birth a secret." She pursed her lips. "My father always wanted a son. I think I was something of a disappointment."

He reached out and touched her cheek. "You hold yourself in too light esteem."

"No, I think not."

She flinched this time, like she used to do. “When I had a boy, my father was delighted. It gave him the incentive to risk everything and start the cotton exchange. He wanted to leave Macon a legacy, to give him a chance, since the boy wouldn’t have a father.” She glanced at him. “You know the rest.”

“Except for one thing—why does Calhoun want your boy now, when he didn’t want anything to do with you or your son before?”

“My friend’s letter said Sybil died in childbirth. She was carrying a boy, but he died, too. It seems Hiram has come unhinged, losing both of them. It didn’t matter that I stayed hidden in the country. Hiram found out about Macon, but as long as he was married to Sybil, he couldn’t acknowledge him.”

She lifted one shoulder. “Now, he can. Like my father, he wants a son to leave his legacy. He can take Macon and raise him as his own. He has the influence and the money. No one would stop him.”

“I’d like to put him and Ben Murphy into a pit together, armed with Bowie knives, and see who came out on top.”

Her eyes widened. “Why, Commander, I wouldn’t have believed you to be a vindictive man.”

“Usually, I’m not. But what Calhoun did to you is beyond evil.” He shook his head. “And now he wants to take your son from you.”

“Thank you for your understanding. I appreciate it.” She turned toward the door again. “But I know you have pressing business.”

He reached out and caressed her cheek again. “What will you do Mallory? Let me take care of you.”

She shook her head. “I don’t know. I wanted to tell you what happened, so you wouldn’t think ill of me. Now, I’m not sure if I did the right thing. I should have let you think the worst, then you couldn’t pity me.”

“Mallory, marry me. Yes, I feel sympathy for you, but it doesn’t change my other feelings.” He gazed at her, and their gazes caught and held. “I never thought I’d want another woman, after I lost my Martha, but I want you. At least, let me tell everyone we’re to be married. When your son comes, we can make a final decision.”

"No, I don't want to live a lie any longer. You've made me realize it."

"But..."

"I'll tell Sally. She'll understand. I can live with her until Macon arrives."

"What about Peggy?"

She sucked in her breath. "I can keep tutoring her if you want, but we can't give her the false hope we'll marry. It wouldn't be fair."

He puffed out his cheeks and rubbed the back of his neck. "What are you going to tell Peggy when the other children don't come to school?"

"The truth, their parents don't want them to attend school anymore."

"She will hear the rumors."

"I know. I'll deal with them as best I can, but I won't lie to her."

"Please, think about what you're doing."

"I will." She nodded. "I probably won't be able to think of anything else."

* * *

Mallory straightened up the corner of the Rodgers' sitting room where she gave Peggy her lessons. The Rodgers' cabin was smaller than the commander's house and after she sent Peggy home, she liked to stack the school books and put away the paper and pencils.

For three weeks, she'd seldom ventured outside. Considering all the gossip swirling around her and the commander, along with the other children withdrawing from her school, she had decided to tutor Peggy at the Rodgers' home.

She'd told Sally everything, except for her intimate moments with Will... the commander. Sally had begged her to reconsider and marry him, seeing it as a neat solution to all her problems.

She'd sworn Sally to secrecy, but the woman must have said something to her husband because Captain Rodgers still treated her with respect. Perhaps, the commander had spoken with him, too. Though, she couldn't know for certain, since she hadn't talked to him since the day after the Fourth of July.

Sally kept her abreast of the news. The commander had abandoned most of his infantry outposts to ring the Lazy M with a cordon of soldiers, hidden in the mountains, putting the ranch under surveillance to watch for the Apache.

As he'd promised, he'd doubled the cavalry troops, patrolling the San Antonio-El Paso Road. For that she was thankful.

Now, all she had to do was wait. Her days bled into one another, each one much like the other, except for Sundays. On the Lord's Day, for the first time in her life, she didn't attend church, not wanting to encourage more gossip. Reverend Finley, who could hobble around with the help of a walking cane, visited her on Sunday evenings and prayed with her.

For the remainder of the week, she tutored Peggy, helped Sally, prayed, and laid awake nights, wondering where she'd gone wrong.

Peggy had withdrawn from her—their old closeness erased like chalk wiped off a blackboard. And the young girl missed having the other children. Though she didn't say anything, she must have heard some of the gossip, too.

Mallory had tried to explain, telling Peggy her father had shown her *Limpia* Creek's waterfall, the night of the Fourth of July celebration. For some people, it meant they had done a "bad" thing, but they hadn't.

Peggy had asked why they didn't marry. The young girl had heard if they married, the gossip would go away, and the other children would return to school. When Peggy asked her about marrying her father, she'd almost cried, realizing the girl still wanted her as part of their family.

She'd didn't have an answer for Peggy because she didn't have an answer herself. As much as she thought about marrying Will, as many sleepless nights as she pondered it, she didn't feel right about it now.

Will, the commander, had opened her eyes. She'd come west to find a well-to-do man to take care of her and her son, as her father had. But she'd been a sham and a fake to do so. Will was right, she should have told E.P. that she already had a son, a son without a father. Or she should have learned to take care of herself and her son, by herself.

It was a hard lesson to learn—it went against all of her upbringing to be responsible for herself as well as her son.

Where did that leave her feelings for Will? Yes, she loved him, but she'd ruined it. Again, he'd been right. It was bad enough she'd set out to dupe a stranger, but far worse she hadn't possessed the courage to tell the commander the truth from the start.

Even if she had told him the truth, they would have been forced to tell lies about her past. She hadn't counted on that part, not thinking that far.

In the beginning, she'd thought she would marry E. P., a man who lived on an isolated ranch in the mountains. There would have been precious few neighbors to ask where her son had come from. But Will was another story. He was the commander of the fort, as well as the stand-in sheriff and mayor for the town.

Married to the commander, she couldn't fade into obscurity and, feeling the way she did now, she didn't want to spin a web of lies.

She dusted her hands and shook out her skirts. Sally was banging pots around in the kitchen. She could probably use some help getting supper together.

Someone knocked on the front door, but she hesitated. Sally probably hadn't heard the knocking in the kitchen. Mallory smoothed her hair and decided to open the front door. Peggy stood on the porch.

She smiled. "Hello, did you forget something? I tidied up our space, and I didn't see anything."

"No, Miss, I came to ask if you or Mrs. Rodgers needs anything from the general store." She held up a nickel. "Papa read your latest report last night. He was pleased by my progress, especially with Algebra. He said I could go to town for some candy after school. I'm going now. I asked Tammy, but she couldn't come. Her mother said she has chores to do."

"Why, how generous of your father. If I'd known, I would have sent more notes home."

Peggy looked up at her, her eyes glowing. "Thank you, Miss. I'd like that."

Seeing Peggy brighten at her words, her heart turned over. How she wished she could hug the child, as she used to. But that wouldn't do.

"I don't need anything, Peggy, but let me ask if Sally does. It was kind of you to stop by."

Peggy looked down and scuffed her high-top boot on the porch. "I forgot." She pulled a note from her apron pocket. "Papa said for me to give you this when I came for my lessons. But I forgot," she repeated, sticking out her bottom lip. "I'm sorry, but I couldn't lie to you, Miss. It's why I came back, not because I was thoughtful."

She sucked in her breath—there it was again. The commander lived what he said, teaching his daughter that being truthful was not something to take lightly. She cringed inside, remembering how she'd lied to him.

That was behind her now. She'd changed or so she hoped.

She took the note from Peggy, wondering what Will... the commander had written. She wanted to read it in private. "Thank you, Peggy. Come inside but wipe your boots first. Let me ask Sally."

She entered the kitchen and found Sally pouring cornbread batter into an iron skillet. "Peggy came back. She's going to town. Do you need anything?"

Sally pulled open the oven and popped the skillet inside. Then she wiped her floury hands on her apron. "I could use a spool of navy thread and a packet of needles. Frank is always tearing his uniform, and sometimes, the laundresses stitch up the rips. Other times, they miss the places or..." She hunched one shoulder and reached into her skirt pocket. "Here's a quarter. Tell Peggy if there's any change, she can keep it."

"Kind of you."

Sally smiled and turned back to the oven.

Mallory joined Peggy at the front door. "Here you go." She handed the girl the quarter. "Sally needs a spool of navy thread and a packet of needles. And she said you can keep the change, too."

"Whoopee!" Sally yelled. "Maybe I'll have enough to get something for Tammy."

"That would be nice."

"See you in a little while, Miss." Peggy opened the front door and let herself out.

Mallory turned and crossed to her bedroom. She didn't want Sally to know about the note from the commander. Sitting on the edge of the bed, she opened the folded note and scanned the contents:

"...our scouts have discovered a band of Comancheros on Lazy M... what Ben has promised the Apache... a safe haven for purchasing munitions and... could be a desperate fight... have made provision for Peggy... my sister Deborah Olson... would be beholden if you could escort her to Ohio... County of Jackson... Oak Hill... necessary funds with the quartermaster... with my love, Will."

She gasped and tears sprang to her eyes, seeing his declaration of love on paper. Then a chill crawled down her spine. When had he ridden out? Why hadn't Peggy said anything? Or Sally... Sally! What about Frank, had he gone, too?

With the crumpled note in her clammy hand, she rushed into the kitchen. "Sally, is Captain Rodgers with the commander? Did you know about them riding to the Lazy M?"

Sally didn't turn. Instead, she leaned against the pump sink, sobbing.

"Oh, no, Sally, Sally!" Mallory grabbed her friend's shoulders and turned her around. "Why didn't you tell me?"

Sally sniffled. "I thought you knew. They rode out before sunrise. My husband, Colonel Gregor, Captain Myerson, and even Captain French, along with four companies of cavalry."

No, she hadn't seen or heard the men ride out. After two nights of pacing the floor, she'd succumbed last night, taking a packet of sleeping powders Dr. Winslow had given her. She'd slept like a baby until Sally had shaken her awake.

And now she knew why Sally had been quiet and withdrawn today.

Sally pulled a handkerchief from her pocket and blew her nose. "The infantry took their 'mountain guns' with them, the howitzers, mounted on wagons. They'll need all the firepower they can muster, going up against the Comancheros, the Apache, and possibly Murphy's men."

"Who are these Comancheros?"

Sally gazed at her. "I forget you're not acquainted with the frontier. They're desperate men, outlaws and murderers and such. They sell the hostiles firearms, bullets, knives, even whiskey. They've been doing it for years, started out supplying the Comanches. It's how they got their name. They're desperados, ready to fight to the death, knowing if they're taken, they'll most likely be hanged without the bother of a trial."

"Oh, my heavens. No!"

"Yes, and I'd hoped the men would be back by now." Sally shook her head and twisted her handkerchief in her hands. "But they're not. The longer they're gone..."

"Oh, Sally." She pulled the woman into her arms. "I'm sorry. I didn't know. Peggy forgot to give me the note from the commander this morning." She held up the crumpled sheet of paper. "I just found out."

"I wondered. Thought it was strange Peggy didn't say anything or..."

"I doubt Peggy knows. The commander wouldn't want her to know." She gulped and swallowed, but she couldn't contain the tears spilling down her cheeks. "He left me a note, wanting me to take Peggy to his sister in Ohio if something should happen."

"Yes, I knew that. He told Frank, too." Sally pulled apart and gazed into her eyes. "He loves you, Mallory. He's a good man. Whatever you've done or he's done... Can't you find it in your heart to marry him?"

"Ssssh." She pulled Sally close again and tried to soothe her, stroking her long, brown hair. "I know he loves me, but I'm not... I'm..."

She let go of Sally and sat down at the kitchen table. "Please, would you mind putting on some water for tea?" She looked down at her clenched hands. "I think it's time you knew everything."

Sally nodded and grabbed the teakettle. She operated the hand pump, filling the kettle and then fetching the tea leaves and teapot.

It was time she told Sally the truth to see what she thought. With Will facing what sounded like the battle of his life, she needed to tell her friend everything to see if there was a way forward.

Knowing Will might be facing death at this moment or already lying wounded or worse, she realized how deeply she loved him. She wanted him, more than anything. And from his note, he still wanted her.

Couldn't they overcome the past and find a way forward--if Will returned?

* * *

Hosea Lincoln crept forward, dodging between boulders and keeping as low to the ground as possible. Gregor watched him, straining his eyes against the rising sun, just beginning to rim the tops of the Davis Mountains to the east. Below them, a sheer cliff dropped into Painted Rock Canyon.

He could understand why Ben had picked this particular place to have the Apache rendezvous with the Comancheros. It was a deep box canyon with rough-hewn walls on three sides and only one entrance to the canyon floor. Ironic, too, that it had been the place of E.P.'s demise, most likely at the hands of his brother.

Gregor knew the entrance to the canyon would be closely guarded by Comanchero sentinels, hidden in the cliffs. Hosea had ridden to the fort, late last night, and given him the layout. Finally, after two weeks of redeploying his troops to ring the Lazy M, he'd hit pay dirt.

Ben's plan was simple but effective. Use the Apache to drive his neighbors off their land; then he could gobble up their ranches at bargain prices. To reciprocate, he allowed the Apache to rendezvous with the Comancheros, restocking their firearms and ammunition, along with other trade goods, alcohol, and even slaves or hostages.

Knowing how deadly the Comanchero crossfire would be at the entrance to the canyon, Gregor had brought along Company C of the Twenty-Fifth Infantry, his gunners, who knew how to operate the unwieldly guns.

Usually, the heavy howitzers sat silent at the fort. They were called “mountain guns” because they could be taken apart and transported on pack horses. But they weren’t suitable for the kind of hit-and-run skirmishes fought in the mountains.

Today, he’d brought two of the big guns on sturdy buckboards, assembled and ready to fire. For this particular situation, he’d decided to utilize the howitzers against the Comancheros in the cliffs, providing cover for his cavalry troops.

He held up his hand, wanting the men to wait and keep as silent as possible. He’d brought plenty of troops, but the Comancheros, as well as the Apaches, were fearsome fighters, ready to fight to the death if they were cornered.

He said a prayer under his breath and waited. Hosea turned toward him and nodded. He backed up Boots slowly and carefully. He turned and nodded at Captain French. The captain returned his nod and silently directed his gunners. They clambered from the wagons and bcgan packing the cannons with gunpowder and stacking the cannonballs.

Hosea came back and stood straight, saluting. “Reporting, sir.”

“Yes, Corporal Lincoln?”

“Looks like about twenty sentinels hidden in the cliffs along the canyon mouth. Forty or so hostiles and maybe twenty-five more Comancheros, trading goods on the canyon floor.”

“Any sign of Murphy or his men?”

“Not that I could tell, sir. Most of the Comancheros wear Stetsons like the ranchers.” Hosea untied the bandana at his throat, tipped back his hat, and mopped his brow. “Too far away to be certain, sir.”

“Understood, Corporal. Mount up.”

“Yes, sir.”

He rode over to Captain French and said, “Fire when ready, Captain.” He pointed at the rocky ledges, overhanging the canyon mouth. Then he returned to Captain Rodgers and Myerson, each heading a double column of men.

He raised his hand again and called, “Wheel! Forward!”

The captains and their men turned quickly and scrabbled back down the rocky slope to the canyon entryway. He touched his spurs to Boots' flanks and rode to the front of the two columns. Myerson and Rodgers followed him to the front of their men.

Boom! Crack! Pop!

The cannons roared and cannonballs whistled through the air, striking the mountainside and exploding. Pieces of the mountains, rocks, and splintered fragments of brush, along with human bodies, went flying through the air.

Gregor grimaced. Despite twenty years as a soldier, he despised killing other human beings. His use of cannons on the Comanchero sentinels wasn't the most honorable way to kill an enemy. But given the kind of men the Comancheros were, he owed his soldiers a deadly diversion to keep them from being slaughtered in the narrow canyon mouth.

Screams and shouts, mixed with loud curses, rang around him. He paused at the canyon mouth, hoping none of his men would be hit by the debris pouring down, but knowing there might be casualties from the bombardment overhead.

He raised his hand again. "Fix bayonets!" He attached his own bayonet at the end of his Springfield carbine and cradled the rifle in his left arm.

"Bugler!" He hesitated for a moment until the bugler's brassy notes cleaved the air. "Draw sidearms! Fire at will!" He let his hand drop. "Charge!"

He urged Boots forward, holding the gelding's reins loosely in his left hand, while keeping his Colt cocked and ready in his right hand. His men followed suit.

They surged into the canyon, firing their Colts, which had six shots, as opposed to their single-shot, breech-loading Springfield carbines.

Taking aim at a group of Apache and Comancheros who'd hidden behind a jumble of boulders, he emptied his Colt. He holstered it and took up his carbine with the bayonet fixed and plunged forward.

He was almost on top of the boulders when Caballero stepped out and took aim with a Winchester rifle. He felt a burn in his shoulder, but Boots' momentum drove him on top of the Apache. He ran the hostile through with his bayonet. The Apache dropped to the floor of the canyon.

Wrenching his bayonet free, he glanced up to see Ben Murphy's sneering face. The man leveled his Colt and fired. Boots sidestepped, not wanting to step on the downed Apache, and the bullet whistled overhead.

He raised his carbine, took careful aim, and fired. Ben Murphy's sneer turned to a grimace, and his eyes widened. He clutched his chest and crumpled.

Pivoting Boots around, Gregor looked for cover where he could reload. But all the gunfire was coming from his troops, mopping up the Comancheros and Apache. The cannon had stopped booming, but his head was still ringing. And the canyon floor appeared to tilt.

He replaced his carbine in its scabbard and with his empty Colt in his right hand, he reached up and touched his left shoulder. He brought his wet hand away, seeing the bright blotch of blood. His vision clouded, and he shook his head.

Dizzy and shaking, he turned Boots toward the canyon mouth, but before he could reach it, black dots swarmed before his eyes like a nasty cloud of gnats. Then he was falling...

The ground rushed up and everything turned black.

* * *

Mallory watched Sally absorb what she'd told her. Sally took a sip of her tea. She put down her teacup and reached across the table, taking Mallory's hands in hers.

"You made some mistakes, but the colonel has obviously forgiven you," Sally said. "Why can't you forgive yourself?"

"I like to think I *have* forgiven myself."

"Not if you're going away. You say you love the colonel. He returns your love. Why throw it away?"

"Because the colonel has a position of authority here, and I would have to tell more lies when my son comes. Make up something about a dead husband. I don't want to tell any more lies, Sally."

"Psssh! The frontier is a forgiving place. If you and the colonel marry, you won't need to lie about your son. You were *forced*, Mallory, violated by an unscrupulous man. People will understand." Sally released her hands and touched her chest. "I understand. And I'll make certain the other women do, too."

Mallory lowered her head and her voice, "But it's so humiliating to let the truth out—so shameful." She shuddered. "I can imagine the look of pity." She covered her face with her hands. "I don't know if I can face it." She shook her head. "And what about the ones who don't believe I was—"

"Pish!" Sally grabbed her hands again and squeezed them. "You can do this, Mallory. You're stronger than you think. And if some of the folks don't believe or understand, then you don't need them. Think what you have to gain. It's more than worth it. Don't let people's petty prejudices rule your life. It's time you took control."

Despite the shame swamping her, for the first time in weeks, a tiny bud of hope burned in her chest. Could she marry the colonel and face down people? It was a bold plan, and she wanted to believe it was possible.

"What about Peggy?" she asked.

"She's probably already heard more ugly gossip than any truth you might tell her," Sally said. "You're strong," she repeated. "Stronger than you think. Look at what you've done, coming west, being taken by the hostiles, starting a school, staging a play. I know you can do this."

Then a thought struck Mallory… Peggy. Where was the girl? She gazed out the window, noting the angle of the sun. "Speaking of Peggy, she's been gone an awfully long time. I had better go and look for her."

"Do you want me to go?"

"No, if I'm going to face people down, I should start now. And you need to finish supper."

A knock sounded on the front door.

Mallory sighed with relief and rose. "That's probably Peggy. I'll get it."

"I guess I'll see to supper, but I wish the men were back."

"Me, too."

Mallory crossed to the door and pulled it open, expecting to see Peggy's freckled face. Instead, a dark-skinned youth stood on the porch. He looked her over and said, "*Señorita* Reynolds?"

"Yes."

He thrust a piece of paper at her. "For you. Tell no one if you not want Peggy hurt." He spoke in a heavily accented voice.

She took the paper. Her heart dropped, and her stomach clenched. Someone had Peggy and they wanted to hurt her. Why?

She opened her mouth to call after the youth, but he'd sprinted away, cutting behind the cabins ringing the parade ground.

With her heart in her mouth, she opened the unsigned note and read:

> *Mallory,*
>
> *I want my son, the boy you named Macon. I've had a Pinkerton man watching you and the fort. I know you must have him hidden. The Aldredges were searched and watched. My son is no longer there.*
>
> *Tell no one. My men and I have Peggy Gregor, your pupil and the daughter of your lover. If you bring my son, I will return Peggy to you, unharmed. If you don't come or you try to rescue Peggy, I will kill the girl.*
>
> *I have men watching you. You have one hour.Come with my son to the yellow house at the foot of the main street of Chihuahua. Enter through the backdoor. I will be waiting.*

Chapter Ten

Sally stood on the threshold of the sitting room, wiping her hands on her apron. “Was it Peggy? Where are my needles and thread?”

The contents of the note stunned Mallory. She felt as if she was gasping for air, being dragged down a deep well with the water closing over her head. Her stomach twisted into knots and threatened to crawl up the back of her throat. Her heart pounded in her ears, and she was dizzy.

Despite the raw terror tearing at her, she had a fleeting thought. Now she knew who the elusive stranger was—likely as not he was the Pinkerton man Hiram had hired.

How could Hiram take Peggy and threaten to murder her? She shook her head—knowing the answer in her heart. Hiram was capable of anything to have his way. Wasn’t he? She should know.

But her son Macon hadn’t arrived, and she had nothing to exchange for Peggy. Exchange for Peggy. She stifled a sob. It reminded her of being taken hostage by the Apache. Flesh and blood exchanged like so many trading beads.

She’d never trade her son, nor endanger Peggy. But Peggy was in danger now because of her past. There would be no trading. No! Hiram’s evil had to be stopped here and now. Once and for all.

But how could she get Peggy released when Will and the captains were out fighting? What could she do? Where could she turn?

Sally crossed her arms. “Well, was that Peggy? What about my sewing things?”

She put one finger to her lips and handed Sally the note. She shook her head, afraid to speak—not knowing what to say. Sally was an Army wife. Perhaps, she would know what to do, how to get help and rescue Peggy.

“I must go,” she said, “to buy some time. I’ll try and reason with him. Tell him I’m not hiding his son, that Macon is on the way here but hasn’t arrived.”

Sally scanned the note. She lifted her head and raised her eyebrows, widening her eyes. "Then he'll have you both, Mallory. I don't think you should—"

"I can't leave Peggy there. He's only given me an hour. We don't know when the colonel and captains will come back."

She didn't want to add there was no way to know in what condition their men would be. "I have to go for Peggy. It's the least I can do. I brought this on myself by not bringing my son in the first place." She chewed her lip. "I can't wait. Don't you see?"

"I guess you're right. But I'll see what I can do." Sally reached out her hand and then let it drop. "Take care of yourself. Shouldn't you have a weapon? My husband gave me a derringer. It's small and easy to use."

Frightened to death and wondering if there was any way someone could overhear them, she gazed at the open front window and pointed.

Sally crossed the room and closed the window. Then she hurried into her bedroom and brought out a short-nosed, small pistol.

Mallory gazed at the derringer. "Won't they search me?"

"Not if you put it down the front of your corset. They won't find it there. You've taken to wearing your corset again, haven't you?"

"Yes. My pitiful response to redeem my respectability, I guess." She took the small gun with the rounded stock and unbuttoned the top button of her dress. She pushed the derringer inside her corset, snugging it against the whalebone stays.

"Be careful. It's loaded and primed. One shot only."

"I will. I must go."

* * *

Gregor slumped over in the saddle. Corporal Walsh had Boots' reins, leading him. A necessary precaution, since he'd passed out, after taking a bullet. But Walsh had taken care of him. He'd staunched the blood from the wound in his shoulder, splashed water in his face to bring him around, and fashioned a makeshift sling. He and Walsh were headed back to Doc Winslow to get the bullet dug out.

He'd left Rodgers in charge of rounding up the few survivors, a couple of Comancheros hiding in the cliffs, and four Apaches who'd surrendered. Rodgers would see to the two soldiers who'd been wounded. They'd lost one man, a Private Wilson.

The wounded men, hostiles, Comancheros, and his soldiers would have their wounds field dressed, and then they'd be brought back to the doctor. He'd send the Comancheros to the local authorities in El Paso, and the Apache back to their reservation, under guard, as soon as they could travel.

He'd put Myerson in charge of cleaning up the canyon, burying the dead, and carrying Ben's body back to the Lazy M headquarters. Gus Pedersen, Ben's foreman, could take over from there.

He hated killing, though it was his profession. Despite his regrets, he believed their pre-emptive action had put a stop to the raids on neighboring ranches and the San Antonio-El Paso Road.

He shook his head, trying to clear his vision, feeling weak and light-headed. They trotted down the main street of town, and the fort's buildings came into view. They stopped at Doc Winslow's. He dismounted and Walsh opened the door.

He stepped into the doctor's surgery and the first thing he noticed was Sally Rodgers' talking to both the doctor and the soldier he'd left in charge, Lieutenant Richter. They were all looking at a piece of paper on the doctor's table.

The three of them glanced up, the minute he came inside.

Sally let out a squeal of surprise, mixed with a sigh of relief, and rushed toward him, waving the piece of paper. "They've got Peggy and now Mallory. She went to try and reason with Hiram."

She handed him the note. "Mallory explained everything about her past. Peggy came by and left your note. She'd forgotten to bring it earlier. But then she went to town by herself and didn't come back. By the time we started worrying, someone brought this note to Mallory. I was in the kitchen. She went to the door, thinking it was your daughter."

He mopped his brow and sank into one of the doctor's chairs. "Now I know who the stranger was, a Pinkerton man, watching the fort and Mallory." He shook his head, trying to clear it. "Richter, get ten men together, pull them off guard duty."

The lieutenant saluted. "Yes, sir."

Getting up, he gazed out the window at the setting sun. It would be dark soon, which would help, since he knew the lay of the land. The Pinkerton man probably knew it, too, but maybe not as well as he and his men did. It was a slim hope, but better than none.

They'd have to be especially careful. He didn't know if, as according to the note, they were being watched. Or it could be a bluff, Calhoun saying he had additional men. No one had mentioned new strangers in town.

Sally touched his arm. "I know you're overwhelmed and upset… not to mention wounded, Colonel, but I have to ask, is my Frank—"

"Captain Rodgers is fine." He patted her shoulder. "We killed most of the Comancheros and Apache, along with Ben Murphy, who was the ringleader, bringing the Apache and Comancheros together. We lost one man, a Private Wilson." He shook his head. "I'll need to write his family."

"Oh, thank you, Colonel, thank you. I'm so glad Frank is…" She gulped back tears and swallowed.

"They should be along soon, but he's bringing the wounded. They can't move as fast with the buckboards." He raised his head and gazed at the doctor. "Doc, you'll need to be ready for the wounded men."

"I will. But shouldn't I take a look at your shoulder first?"

"No, I've got to go with Richter to get my daughter and fiancée back." There, he'd said it.

He and Mallory would be married, if they all survived. He'd stop her from wallowing in self-pity and putting him off. When you stared in the abyss and realized you might lose the two people in the world whom you loved the most, everything else paled in comparison.

As the Good Book said: "*Man is like a breath; his days are like a fleeting shadow.*" He didn't want to waste any more time, living without Mallory.

"Lieutenant, have the ten men drift, one at a time, over the next hour to the saloon and then gather at the back entrance. You know the arroyo there, the one that splits Fort Davis from Chihuahua?"

"Yes, sir. I know the terrain."

"Good. Have the men climb down into the ravine. I'll meet you there after the doc does what he can."

Richter came to attention and saluted. "Yes, sir."

He nodded.

"Sally, I know you're concerned, but I don't want to worry about you, too. Can you go home and wait for Frank?"

"Of course."

He patted her shoulder again. "Good. Thank you for all you've done. And for being Mallory's friend, too."

She flushed pink. "My pleasure, Colonel. I'm glad you're going to marry."

"Okay, Doc, change the bandage, give me a belt of whiskey, and some smelling salts in case I need them."

"That bullet should come out, the sooner the better."

"Nope, not now. After you finish digging on me, I'll be in no fit state to get Mallory and Peggy back."

"Can't you trust Richter—?"

"What would you do if it was your daughter and intended bride?"

"All right. I'll do as you ask. But if you keel over from the loss of blood, don't say I didn't tell you so."

* * *

Mallory knocked on the back door of the yellow house. After a few moments, the door opened a crack and the stranger grabbed her arm and pulled her in. The one-room adobe house was dark with the windows shuttered. But she could sense others in the room and hear their breathing.

Someone struck a match, and the light flared. She glimpsed a man who looked like Hiram, but his face was covered in a heavy beard. He lit a kerosene lamp, and the light picked out his features.

What she saw was disturbing. Along with the heavy beard, Hiram's eyes were blood-shot, and his skin was covered in patchy red blotches. And he stank. He was as different from the well-dressed, debonair gentleman she'd known in Charleston, as a mule was from a Thoroughbred. She wouldn't have recognized him in a crowd.

She heard a whimper and saw Peggy, bound and gagged, lying on the floor in a corner of the room. Her heart went out to the girl, and seeing her trussed-up like an animal, struck a spark of smoldering rage within her.

The room was almost empty, containing only a narrow cot, a table, two chairs, a dry sink, and a shelf with some tin mugs and plates. Why hadn't they laid Peggy on the cot? Why had they left her huddled on the hard dirt floor?

Behind her, she was aware of the stranger with a rifle cradled in his arms. His red-checkered bandana had seen better days—now its red-and-white checks had bled into one dusty color.

"Where is the boy?" Hiram demanded in a raspy voice. Then he turned and coughed, spitting up a glob of mucous.

Seeing the man who had ruined her life and sensing his menacing attitude, she wanted to bolt through the door, to run back to safety. But she couldn't leave Peggy.

She gazed at the girl, trying to send her a look of reassurance. But Peggy's eyes were wide and bulging, and her cheeks were streaked with tears.

"Macon isn't here yet, Hiram. He was at the Arledge's home, but when they realized you were looking for him, they sent him west with the new Methodist reverend and his family. They're coming overland from Galveston, so—"

"Shut your lying mouth, slut! I know he must be here."

She put out her hand, to push back or plead with him, she wasn't sure which. Perhaps just to appease him, like one tried to calm a ravaging beast.

"I'm not lying. You've had me watched for weeks." She inclined her head toward the Pinkerton agent. "If Macon was here, don't you think your spy would have caught a glimpse of him?"

"Lying slut, filthy, lying whore!" He lunged at her, his hands raised and forming two pincers, wanting to throttle her. She took a step back.

The Pinkerton man moved between them. “I don’t hold with harming women or breaking the law. I told you that when I hired on.”

Hiram dropped his hands and turned. He slumped down into one of the chairs at the table. He cradled his head in hands.

She snorted and glanced at Peggy. “Doesn’t look like you mind harming children.”

The man gazed at her. “I’m a private citizen, doing a job. But we Pinkerton agents uphold the letter of the law. The girl might not be comfortable, but she’s not been harmed.”

“What about the note your employer sent me, threatening to...” She stopped herself. Peggy was listening, and the poor girl looked as frightened as a rabbit caught in a snare. She didn’t dare say the word “kill.”

She wished she’d brought the note with her, so she could show the Pinkerton man, as he appeared to be more reasonable than Hiram. Perhaps she could make him understand and let them go.

“I don’t know nothing about what was in that note, Miss. And my employer has a right to his son.” He shrugged. “Sometimes threats can be effective. But threatening don’t harm no one, neither.”

She folded her hands and lowered her head. It appeared the Pinkerton man didn’t condone physical harm, but everything else was on the table.

Hiram pulled a flask from inside his vest, fetched one of the cups, and pulled a small bottle, half-filled with a reddish-brown liquid from his pocket. He filled the tin cup from the flask and poured a shot of the reddish-brown liquid into the cup. He tipped up the mug and drank deeply, wiping his mouth with the back of his hand.

She noticed his hands were trembling.

When they’d been courting, she’d realized Hiram drank heavily. Many men, especially in the defeated South, found succor in hard liquor. At the time, she’d been so besotted, she’d made excuses for him.

Heavy drinking was bad enough, but wasn’t the reddish-brown liquid laudanum? If so, and he was mixing it with liquor, it would account for his appearance and erratic behavior. Not to mention the tremor in his hands.

For now, the liquor and laudanum mixture appeared to have calmed him. She decided to try again. "Hiram, your son, Macon, will be arriving in the next few weeks with Reverend Whitehead. If you can be patient—"

"No!" He brought his fist down on the table so hard it jumped. "I'm through with being patient, and besides, I don't believe you. You're a Jezebel, woman!" He pointed his index finger at her. "I came to see you when I learned you were in the family way, offering to set you up as my mistress in a fine townhouse in Charleston." He thumped the table again. "You turned me down flat, you whore."

She had tried to forget the time he'd come to her father's plantation. It was the one detail she hadn't told Will or Sally because the encounter had been humiliating and pointless. Hiram had come when she'd been laboring to birth Macon, and at the time, she'd wondered if his presence had been a delusion brought on by her labor pains.

As it was, she'd been lucky her father had been in town, and Astarte was helping her to birth the baby. She remembered screaming at Hiram, telling him to go home to his rich wife and to leave her alone. It had been fortunate her father hadn't been there. Otherwise, the two men might have dueled.

Now, she needed to try and reason with a drunken madman who'd forced himself on her, deserted her when she became pregnant, and nursed a grudge because she'd refused to become his "kept" woman.

Evil, pure evil.

She looked the Pinkerton man squarely in the eye. "If I can't produce my son to satisfy your employer's whim, what do you propose doing—keeping Peggy and I as hostages for several weeks?"

Hiram rose and tottered toward her, his fisted hand raised in the air. "No need for that, I'll beat it out of you! And if that don't work, I'll cut the kid's face so no man will want her."

She gasped and gazed at the Pinkerton agent.

He raised his rifle and sited it at Hiram's shoulder. "No beating of women on my watch, sir."

Hiram pushed the rifle barrel aside and roared, "Then git out, git out! I don't need your lousy help."

The door behind her burst open.

Will towered over her, pointing his Colt at the Pinkerton agent. "Colonel Gregor, United States Army, Commander of Fort Davis. Drop your gun!"

The Pinkerton agent let the rifle slide from his hands. It clattered on the floor. He raised his hands. "I'm not here to break any laws or go against the United States Army."

"Good." Will pushed him to one side. "Then you can unbuckle your holster and drop it, too." He glanced at her, and then stepped around her, kicking the rifle out of the way. He was focused on his terrified daughter.

From the corner of her eye, she saw Hiram reach inside his coat. She'd already drawn the derringer. Corporal Walsh and Lieutenant Richter stepped inside, backing up Will.

She noticed Will's left arm was in a sling. He was hurt!

He put his Colt into its holster. Intent on his daughter, he rushed to Peggy's side, thinking his men would cover him.

But like the snake he was, Hiram had dropped to the floor with his revolver in hand, pointing the barrel at Will's back.

She'd never fired a handgun before, only a rifle when shooting quail. She raised the tiny gun and took aim at his outstretched arm. No recoil and barely a sound, the tiny gun went off with a poof of powder. Had it misfired?

Hiram's eyes widened and he screamed. Blood poured from his forehead. She'd missed! He grimaced and managed to lift his revolver, struggling to pull the trigger with blood streaming in his eyes.

Will whirled around and went for his Colt.

She wished she had a second shot. Desperate, she ran forward and kicked the revolver out of Hiram's hand.

Corporal Walsh grabbed the Pinkerton's discarded guns. Lieutenant Richter rushed over and picked up Hiram's revolver. Then he searched him for other weapons, pulling a wicked-looking Bowie knife from his boot.

Hiram tried to roll away, cradling his head in his hands and writhing on the floor. He looked up at her and screamed, "You, filthy slut, you! You shot me!"

Will kneeled beside his daughter, ungagging her and untying her hands and feet. Peggy was sobbing and gasping for air. Will gathered her into his arms and lifted her. She clung to his neck as if she was drowning and her father was a lifeboat.

"Corporal Walsh, get two of the men and take that piece of vermin to the doctor. If he lives long enough."

The Pinkerton agent stepped forward. "I have two good men with our horses in a mesquite thicket out back. If I may, sir, I'd like to join them and head for El Paso." He glanced at his erstwhile employer, thrashing on the floor. "I believe our business here is concluded."

Will glanced at the Pinkerton agent, spearing him with a steely gaze. "My soldiers have your men under guard." He looked the man up and down. "You say you haven't broken the law? Like hell, you say! You abducted a child. I don't know what law you go by in Chicago, but out here, that's a serious offense, mister."

He swung around and commanded, "Lieutenant Richter, escort this man and his friends to the guardhouse." He nodded at the Pinkerton agent. "You want to go to El Paso? I'll see you get to El Paso and, as a bonus, you'll pay a visit to Judge DuVal, of the Western District Federal Court. Let's see what he thinks about you helping to abduct an innocent child."

The Pinkerton man muttered and cursed under his breath, but when Lieutenant Richter came forward to tie his hands, he didn't resist.

Watching Will in action, with his daughter in his arms and blood staining the bandage on his shoulder, her heart swelled with pride. He was like an avenging angel, putting everything right.

This was the man who loved her, honest and brave as the day was long. And she loved him more than life itself.

Tripping over her skirts, she rushed to join Will and his daughter, kissing Peggy's cheek and promising, "I won't let anybody hurt you again. You have my word."

Peggy threw one arm around her neck and kissed her back.

Will enfolded both of them in his embrace. "Nothing is ever going to harm either one of my girls, not while I've breath left in my body." He looked Mallory directly in the eyes. "And you're going to be my wife and the mother of my daughter. No more hiding and shame. All right?"

She nodded and swallowed back her tears, kissing his cheek.

He kissed her back and then he kissed Peggy, hugging them tighter.

She bowed her head and offered a silent prayer of thanksgiving. Home… she'd finally come home.

* * *

Mallory urged her mare forward. Will, his shoulder still in a sling, touched his spurs to Boots' flanks. They'd received notice from the stagecoach driver, earlier this morning, that a buckboard with Reverend Whitehead and his family were only a few miles outside Fort Davis.

When she'd gotten word, she knew she couldn't wait to see her son. She'd begged Will to let her have a mount and escort to meet Macon. He'd obliged her but refused to let her go unless he went along. Peggy was waiting at home with a lop-sided cake she'd baked, all by herself, for her "new" brother.

They passed the fork in the road that led to the Lazy M. She allowed herself a small shudder, realizing what they'd all been through, since that long-off day she'd come west as a mail order bride.

Will's shoulder was healing. The bullet had buried itself in his muscle, missing the joint by a fraction of an inch. Doc Winslow had dug it out, but he'd cautioned Will his shoulder might be sore and stiff for a long time.

Hiram's wound had proven superficial, grazing the top of his head. He'd bled a lot, but the doctor had patched him up. Locked in the guardhouse with his Pinkerton men and the surviving Comancheros, he'd suffered, getting free of his addiction to the laudanum.

Two days ago, Will had sent the prisoners with a military escort to El Paso to await trial for their crimes.

She'd shot a man. Her son's father. And she'd vowed to herself never to lie again. She was stunned by her audacity. But she'd shoot Hiram all over again, if it would save Will's life.

Besides, there wouldn't be any more lies, not really. When Macon had been five years old, he'd asked why he didn't have a father, like his friends. She'd lied to her son then—telling him that his father was dead. To her, the man who'd ruined her and caused such pain and sorrow, was dead.

Macon's father would go to prison and when her son was older, she would tell him the truth. Then Macon could make his own decision, whether to meet his father or not. For now, she hoped Will and Macon would form a strong bond, and her son would learn to care for his "new" father.

She topped a rise and glimpsed a cloud of dust. She dug her heels into the mare, and a few hundred yards away, she saw a lumbering buckboard, being pulled by a team of four mis-matched mules.

Raising her hand, she called out, "Macon, son! Reverend Whitehead!" She raced toward the wagon.

Will rode beside her and grinned. She smiled back at him.

The driver of the wagon, a man in a clerical collar, pulled back on the reins, calling out, "Whoa there, whoa mules!"

Before the wagon could halt, her son clambered over the side and dropped to the ground. She reined her mare in, and she jumped down, running to her son with her arms outstretched.

Macon rushed into her arms and hugged her. With joy overflowing her heart and tears welling in her eyes, she hugged her son back. "Macon, oh, Macon, I've missed you so much! I'm so glad to see you!"

She kissed his cheek and held him at arm's length. "Let me look at you, son." And with those words, she gazed at her child, thinking he'd grown almost a foot since she'd left him in Georgia.

Wiping her eyes with the back of her hand, she hugged him again, cooing, "Oh, Macon, my son. I can't tell you how happy I am."

Reverend Whitehead got down from the wagon and greeted her. They shook hands and he introduced her to his wife, Katherine, and their two children, George and Emily.

Someone cleared their throat, and she glanced up.

Will dismounted from Boots' and offered his hand to the Reverend and then his wife, introducing himself, "I'm Colonel Gregor, Commander of Fort Davis. And this is a blessed day, you bringing my fiancée her son." He put his arm around her.

The Reverend glanced at her. "I hadn't heard about your engagement. I hope you'll allow me to officiate at your wedding. Glad to make your acquaintance, Colonel."

Then Will bent down and looked Macon in the eye. "I'm the Commander of the fort, Macon. It's a pleasure to make your acquaintance, too."

Her son gazed at Will's navy-blue uniform with the brassy buttons and shiny epaulets. He looked at Will's sling. His hazel eyes widened. "You're a real commander of a fort and all. The kind that shoots down Injuns?" He pointed at Will's bandaged shoulder and asked, "Did an Injun hurt you, sir?"

He glanced at her and grinned. Then he turned his attention back to Macon. "As a matter of fact, it was an Apache war chief who shot me."

"Why Mister Commander, I'm right glad to meet you." Macon thrust out his hand. "Can I meet a real-life Injun, too?"

Will shook his hand and solemnly said, "I can introduce you to Pale Hawk, one of our Apache interpreters."

Macon let out a whoop. He looked at her and said, "Mama, it's just like the books and all. Ain't it?"

"Isn't it?" she corrected.

Will put his hand on her son's shoulder. "What would you say, Macon, if I told you that me and your Mama are going to be married?"

Macon looked down and scuffed his high-top boot in the dirt, a shock of his ash-blond hair falling over his forehead.

"Well, since my Pa's already gone..." He glanced at her.

She nodded and smiled.

"And since you're an Injun fighter and the commander of a fort, I'd say I'm honored, sir."

"Good." Will patted Macon's shoulder. "What if I told you that I have a daughter who's twelve years old? You'll be getting a big sister in the bargain."

Macon gazed up at him and wrinkled his nose. "A sister! Do I have to?"

She looked at Will. He caught her gaze and smiled. Then they both broke out laughing and hugged Macon.

* * *

Will stood at attention by the altar rail. Dr. Winslow had removed his sling the day before, and he was decked out in his dress uniform. He'd appointed Macon as his best man. Peggy would be Mallory's maid of honor.

Doc Winslow had offered to give the bride away, and Reverend Whitehead was officiating. Reverend Finley, sporting a slight limp, had left Fort Davis, traveling east, as soon as the new preacher had shown up. The young man had been singularly relieved to put the wild frontier behind him.

The small church E.P. had built was packed to overflowing, along with a crowd outside. Inside were the fort's officers and families, along with many of his soldiers and a nice turnout from the town.

Sally, true to her word to his bride-to-be, had done her job well, spreading word about Mallory's troubled past and her son. After his daughter's abduction and rescue, most of the folk, in both the fort and the town, had rallied around Mallory.

Captains Rodgers, Myerson, and French were missing from the crowded church, as were Lieutenants Richter and O'Sullivan, along with Sergeants Hotchkiss and Campbell, and Corporal Walsh. He smiled to himself, guessing where they were.

His fiddlers from the fort's band tuned up their instruments for a few moments before breaking into his favorite classical song, "*The Four Seasons—Spring*" by composer A. Vivaldi. The strains of the beautiful music washed over him and filled the church.

The front doors of the church burst open, and he gasped.

Mallory, on Doc Winslow's arm, stood there, looking like a vision from heaven. He didn't know much about women's fripperies, despite being married for almost twenty years to Martha. All he knew, as she floated down the aisle, was his intended was a sight to behold in a fitted, white satin dress, complimenting her full bosom and tiny waist. The collar and the hem of the skirt were trimmed in white lace.

At her throat, she wore her mother's cameo, and she carried a bouquet of white day lilies. But it was her hair and veil that took his breath away. For the first time, she wore her hair down, shimmering golden waves reaching mid-way down her back. Her golden locks were framed by a gossamer veil of a lace so fine and sheer, it looked as if it had been spun by fairies.

She joined him at the altar, and he took her hand, gazing into her eyes. His chest was tight and it hurt to breathe. He was overcome by his good luck, finding it hard to believe such a beautiful woman loved him and wanted to join her life with his.

The doctor stepped away, and Reverend Whitehead began the ceremony with a prayer.

Their wedding vows passed in a blur, and he was slipping a gold band on her finger before he knew it, listening to the reverend's admonition to: "love, comfort, honor, and keep her for better or worse, for richer or poorer, in sickness and health, and forsaking all others, be faithful only to her, for as long as you both shall live."

He looked into Mallory's eyes, his heart brimming with love and said, "I do."

Mallory promised the same, gazing at him and saying, "I do."

"I pronounce you husband and wife." Reverend Whitehead finished with, "You may kiss the bride."

He dipped his head and kissed Mallory long and deep, besotted by the sweetness of her mouth.

They turned and marched down the aisle and stood on the front porch of the chapel. Lined up before them were the missing captains, along with Lieutenant Richter. Across from them were Lieutenant O'Sullivan, along with Sergeants Hotchkiss and Campbell, and Corporal Walsh.

All eight men had their swords drawn and touching the man's sword across from him. It was a time-honored military tradition, known in the Army as the Arch of Sabers, welcoming his bride into military life.

Mallory glanced up at him with a questioning look in her eye.

"It's to honor you, my bride, Mallory Gregor."

She nodded and they walked between his men. The crowd outside started throwing rice at them. At the last two men, Walsh and Richter, they lowered their swords, blocking the way.

Mallory looked up again.

He bent his head and whispered, "They're demanding I kiss you before we can pass. More tradition." He leaned in and kissed her cheek. "But first, I have a surprise for you. I'm taking a two-month furlough, and we're going on a honeymoon."

"What about the children?"

"They're coming with us. This is a special treat. We're boarding a riverboat in New Orleans and traveling upriver to Cincinnati. I want to show my new wife the farm we'll be retiring to."

"Oh, a paddle ship, Peggy will be in heaven." She gazed at him from the corner of her eye and grinned slyly. "But children on a honeymoon?" She fingered the lapels of his dress jacket. "How will we have any privacy?"

"Don't worry," his voice was almost a growl, husky with desire. "I've engaged a suite for us. There will be plenty of privacy."

"My handsome and resourceful husband."

"My beautiful and cultured wife."

And then he kissed her lips.

Epilogue

On the Mississippi River, south of Memphis—October, 1877

Mallory twirled her lacy parasol, blocking out the worst of the sun. She pulled a handkerchief from her skirt pocket and wiped her face. She'd forgotten how hot and humid the South could be, even at this time of autumn. Back home... in Fort Davis, the air would be crisp and the nights cool.

She never thought she'd miss the frontier, but at this moment, she yearned for the beautiful West Texas mountains and their mild climate. She hoped she liked Will's farm. Then she shook her head. The climate and terrain of their home didn't matter. As long as she was in Will's arms, she was home.

"Home was where the heart was." Now, she understood what the old saying meant.

Peggy, pulling Macon along, came running up, breathless. "Miss Mallory, Captain O'Malley says we can help steer the ship! He's going to show us around, how they shovel in the coal to keep the paddle wheel turning and everything!" Peggy jumped up and down. "Can we? Can we go? We'll be careful and I'll watch that Macon doesn't fall overboard."

Macon frowned, and Mallory laughed. She tousled her son's wavy hair. "What do you say, Macon?"

He glanced at his new sister and lifted one shoulder. "I'd like to see how the boat runs, but I'm big enough to take care of myself."

She leaned down and hugged him. "Of course, you are, son." She gave Peggy a sideways look and declared, "Maybe it's you who should be looking after Peggy, since you've grown so big and turned seven."

Peggy smiled at her and nodded. She let go of Macon's hand and offered her arm, "If you'd be so kind as to escort me, Mr. Macon."

Macon, warming to his part, bowed at the waist. "I'd be delighted, Miss Peggy." He took her arm. Luckily, he was tall for his age, like she'd been, and despite a difference of almost six years, they were almost the same height.

Arm-in-arm, her new family traipsed off, looking like a proper lady and gentleman.

Mallory smiled and shook her head.

She felt someone behind her and whirled around. It was Will. He'd been below, drawing some cash from the purser.

He put his arms around her. "What are you smiling about?"

"Everything! Our children and you." She fingered the tailored edges of his civilian dress coat. "I've never been so happy in all my life." She hugged him. "All because of you."

He nuzzled her neck. "Is that so? Sounds like an invitation to me." He nipped her ear lobe and then laved it with his tongue tip.

She pulled away and shook her finger at him. "Colonel Gregor, what are you doing?" She glanced around the open deck. A few couples, arm-in-arm, promenaded up and down the deck. "You must behave yourself. We're in public view here."

He straightened and smiled. "I know. I'll try and restrain myself." He inclined his head toward the dwindling forms of Macon and Peggy. "Where are they going?"

She put her arms around his neck and pulled his head down. "The captain is going to show them the bridge of the boat, the engine room, and how to steer the paddler."

"Hmmm, that's kind of Captain O'Malley. Sounds like a lot of territory to cover. Might take them all afternoon."

"That's what I was thinking, Colonel Gregor. What do you want to do? We could get some deck chairs and read or go to the game room and see if there was a game of whist or..."

He grabbed her hand, pulling her toward their suite. "I think I have a better idea, Mrs. Gregor."

She grinned and ran ahead of him, taking the lead and tugging on his hand. "I thought you'd never ask."

* * *

Thank you for reading A West Texas Frontier Trilogy by Amazon Best-selling author Hebby Roman! Your opinion would be appreciated if you could please post a review at Amazon. If you'd like to read more of Hebby's books or post other reviews, you can find them on her Amazon Author Page.

Copyright

This is a work of fiction. Names, characters, places, and incidents are either the product of the author's imagination or are used fictitiously, and any resemblance to actual persons living or dead, business establishments, events, or locales, is entirely coincidental.

Published by Estrella Publishing
Cover designed by Earthly Charms
ISBN978-1-7293-4722-5

About the Author

Hebby Roman is a New York traditionally published, small-press published, and Indie published #1 Amazon best-selling author of both historical and contemporary romances.

Her WEST TEXAS CHRISTMAS TRILOGY is an Amazon Bestselling and Award-Winning series. Her first contemporary romance, SUMMER DREAMS, was the launch title for Kensington's Encanto line. And her re-published e-book, SUMMER DREAMS, was #1 in Amazon fiction and romance. Her medieval historical romance, THE PRINCESS AND THE TEMPLAR, was selected for the Amazon Encore program and was #1 in medieval fiction. She won a national Harlequin contest. Her book, BORDER HEAT, was a Los Angeles Times Book Festival selection. She has been a RONE Finalist three times and in three different categories.

She is blessed to have all her family living close by in north Texas, including her two granddaughters, Mackenzie Reese and Presley Davis. Hebby lives in Arlington, Texas with her husband, Luis, and maltipoo, Maximillian.

Made in the USA
Middletown, DE
04 September 2021

47601543R00265